D1003930

POLAR BEAR DAWN

LYLE NICHOLSON

RED CUILLIN PUBLISHING

POLAR BEAR DAWN by Lyle Nicholson

Copyright© 2013 by Lyle Nicholson

All rights reserved

No part of this document may be reproduced or transmitted in any form or by any means, electronic, mechanical, photocopying, recording, or otherwise, without prior written permission of the author.

This book is a work of fiction. Any reference to real people or real locales are used fictitiously. Other names, characters, places, and incidents are the product of the authors imagination and any resemblance to actual events or locales or persons living or dead, is entirely coincidental.

www.lylenicholson.com

Edited by Rachel Small
www.faultlessfinishediting.com

Front cover designed by Charles Winslow
www.charleswinslowphotography.com

Interior and back cover formatted and designed by Ellie Searl, Publishista®
www.publishista.com

ISBN-13: 978-0988154810
ISBN-10: 0988154811

Library and Archives Canada Cataloguing in Publication

Nicholson, Lyle, 1952-, author
    Polar bear dawn / Lyle Nicholson.
 ISBN 978-0-9881548-1-0 (pbk.)

    I. Title.
PS8627.I2395P64 2013   C813'.6   C2013-907252-7

RED CUILLIN PUBLISHING
Kelowna, BC
Canada

Other books by Lyle Nicholson

Dolphin Dreams, A Novella (2013)

A series of events collide when dolphins keep Niklas awake at night and enter his dreams. The request they make of him will change his life—if he agrees.

Dolphin Dreams asks the question we might ask ourselves when we see dolphins in captivity, "What are the dolphins thinking?"

Pipeline Killers, A Novel (2014)

This is the second book in the Detective Bernadette Callahan Mystery Series.

RCMP Detective Callahan is called to an industrial accident beside a pipeline in Canada's Western Province of Alberta. Something is strange about the death.

There are no outward injuries to the body, yet the body has been consumed by something—from what looks like a foreign object. The pipeline is perforated, bleeding oil.

Detective Callahan soon finds that this accident has worldwide implications—someone has developed a new weapon that could bring all of the world's pipelines under attack.

This book is dedicated to my lovely wife Tessa.

Every Friday night for a year, Tessa would sit there and read the pages of this book while I made us dinner. She would painstakingly correct punctuation, and make comments where she thought things weren't flowing. What a lucky man I am.

CHAPTER ONE

*T*HE POLAR BEAR HAD WALKED *miles from the shores of the Beaufort Sea to the Arctic Oil Camp. The sea ice had thinned, the seals were scarce. The bear was hungry. After marching across the windswept January snow, he arrived at the camp on the second day.*

The lights of the camp shone like a beacon in the winter's darkness. Large flood lamps made pools of light around the massive camp that was stacked on pylons ten feet above the frozen earth.

The bear moved easily underneath the living quarters of the camp. The structures were stacked three high and radiated out from the main buildings. Humans were active inside. The bear's keen sense of smell picked up food, lots of food.

He could pick up the smell of a seal three miles away, even under the ice. The camp was a sensory overload. Bacon, grits, potatoes, beef, and the smell of frying eggs assaulted his senses. His stomach ached. He had not eaten in many days.

Large machines hummed from the generating plants, and trucks moved constantly to and from the camp. The smell of food was mixed with that of diesel and gas that powered the large camp. A twenty-four-hour commercial laundry shot off clouds of steam.

His last meal had been a tub of lard. He had scared a cook away as he was about to drop the lard in a rubbish bin. The lard had been licked down to its last bit of goodness before it froze. His large tongue had made short work of the meal.

Now he moved cautiously below the living quarters of the camp. Metal stairways led away from emergency exits every twenty feet. He moved between them, using them as cover, always aware of the humans and the threat they posed. They were a source of food and a source of danger. His massive paws walked the fine line.

He had been shot twice with rubber bullets from a shotgun and frightened with an air horn by the humans. The bear had not liked the experience. He tried to keep away from them but close enough to their food. If he waited by the stairs, they would drop things when he rushed at them.

He was waiting patiently now, under a set of stairs. The fierce wind ruffled his fur. He put his nose down between his paws. He did not sleep. His stomach growled as his hunger increased.

A noise from above startled the bear—a crash of metal and a loud thud that pierced the Arctic night. A large, dark object bounced twice down the metal stairs and landed in a heap at the base.

Startled at first, the bear backed away from the noise and the object, but curiosity and survival eventually moved him forward. The object was a human. It lay in the swirling snow. There was no movement.

The bear approached slowly—his first instinct was always to protect himself from injury, the second was to survive. He nudged the body. There was blood on the forehead, the eyes stared. The bear looked only briefly around before accepting this offering of warm meat.

What should have been a feast for the hungry bear was rudely interrupted. Oil workers getting ready for their 7:00 a.m. shift had looked out the windows of their rooms. It didn't matter that the grey Arctic dawn would not appear for another four hours—the habit of looking outside in the morning is ingrained in humans.

What workers saw at first looked like a National Geographic moment: a large polar bear outlined by halogen lights from the building feasting on something. Then, as one, the workers realized the something was a human. They jammed the camp switchboard with calls.

Security guards rushed to the door, grabbing their Arctic survival gear and shotguns loaded with rubber bullets. In minutes they stood outside the door, the large bear below them. One crouched on the second uppermost rung, the other stood.

The first rubber bullet hit the bear in the hindquarters. He spun around, still on all fours, his mass covering the body, his coveted prize of food. Another shot rang out. It echoed amongst the two buildings. This one hit the bear in his shoulder.

He stood. He could now see his attackers on the stairs. Ten feet of white polar bear rose up, his massive paws raised in defense of his meal. The third shot was directed in his chest. The oil workers who watched from their rooms above could hear the woof of air that escaped the bear.

The bear had had enough. The humans with their rubber bullets had knocked the wind out of him. He dropped down to all fours, and with one longing sideways glance at the body, he ambled away. A short distance away, he stopped under the buildings, in the shadows, and watched to see if the humans would give him back his dinner.

The security guards cautiously made their way down to the body and began radioing for backup. There were no signs of life left in the body, and the Arctic cold was already turning it to ice.

CHAPTER TWO

SENIOR SECURITY OFFICER TROY MERCURY was in the Arctic Oil Camp gym running wind sprints and intervals on the treadmill; he was working out hard and enjoying it. His shift had finished at 0600 hours, and he had wanted to have a workout before breakfast.

The TV, turned to CNN, was blasting the latest reports of Politicians behaving badly in the lower forty-eight states. Both his pager and cell phone were vibrating in the recesses of the treadmill. He couldn't hear them over the noise of the television.

A few minutes later, Troy slowed the machine down, seeing Junior Security Officer Chuck Lindgren come into the room. He turned the TV down with the remote on the treadmill. His cell phone and pager were still vibrating.

"We have a dead body outside of the D wing, and Security Chief Braddock has requested your presence ASAP, Sir," Chuck said as he approached Troy, looking stressed out. Chuck was an ex-marine straight from Iraq and Afghanistan, but dead bodies anywhere still unnerved him.

Troy grabbed the towel off the machine and began to dry himself off. "What's the situation Chuck? How'd they find him? Does anyone know how he died?

"Well, they claim he was attacked by a polar bear. Caucasian male, about twenty-seven year's old, contractor." Chuck rattled off the stats as if he were standing to attention in front of his former army commander. Everyone liked Chuck—he was a little too formal and military sometimes, but he meant well. Chuck was still very military in appearance, his crew cut, and pressed coveralls and shiny boots stood out.

Troy stepped down off the treadmill. They were the same height, tall, but Troy was lean, dark skinned, and dark haired. Troy was born in Alaska to a Dene Native mother, and a Caucasian father. On the reservation he'd been called a "baked potato and fake native," by the reservation kids, in Anchorage the white street kids had called him worse names. He'd used his fists to explain to them the errors of their ways. His attitude now tempered, still showed.

"No shit, a polar bear. Well that figures, a white guy getting eaten by a polar bear. The Indians are too smart to get eaten by bears." Troy broke into a smile and gave Chuck a pat on the shoulder. "Tell Braddock I'll be right there."

"Thanks for the information, Sir. I'll try to have you with me when I meet a bear. And I'll let Braddock know." Chuck smiled, threw an unnecessary salute, whirled around, and hurried out of the gym.

Troy headed for his room, which was close to the gym. He pushed through the heavy fire door that separated the main quad from the sleeping quarters. A large sign said "DAY SLEEPERS. PLEASE BE QUIET." Troy was supposed to be one of them.

He'd been flippant about the bear attack with Chuck, partly because it was his nature and to relax Chuck, but a bear attack at the Arctic Oil Camp was not a funny thing. The security team tracked polar bears from one camp to another and sent out alerts when they were near. Now, one had gotten through the entire network of camps and had somehow killed a man. This was not how his security team was supposed to roll.

In his room, he stripped off his workout gear and hit the shower, glad that the guy in the next room was not using the shared shower. After toweling off, he put on his security coveralls, attached his Glock .40 sidearm, and grabbed his gear: survival parka, bib overalls, felt pack boots, and leather mitts with woolen inner liners. The weather forecast for that day was minus forty degrees Fahrenheit. *A shitty day to be outside, living or dead,* he thought.

He jogged down to the security office at the front entrance of the camp, picked up his two-way radio, and ran down to the D wing. He put on his survival gear when he reached the exit door, where a security officer was putting yellow tape over a red stain. Troy was going ten feet down the stairs. Ten feet in minus forty—a cold that causes frostbite in less than a minute to exposed skin. Today, the weather would leave teeth marks.

As Troy came out the door, he could see a group of men, all encased in Arctic gear, and standing around the body. Two men were kneeling with shotguns pointed to something—something under the camp pylons. The thought only briefly entered Troy's head, "looks like Custer's last freaking stand."

The group gave off clouds of steam as breath escaped out of hoods. The lights from the camp buildings gave the group an eerie glow. No clouds of air escaped from the body on the ground.

The men's faces were covered by the hoods, and Troy could only identify them from name badges. He came up beside Security Chief Braddock. Braddock had to turn his hood towards Troy and move within inches of him so they could hear each other in the wind.

"Chief, what have we got here? Some guy out for a smoke and the bear gets him?" Troy asked.

Braddock yelled above the wind. "Troy, we got blood spatter on that door up there. I think this guy got a helping hand out the door. I've called in police and forensics. They'll be here by noon."

"Shit," Troy said. He looked at the scene. The name Marc Lafontaine was on the parka of the body, and the company contractor name read CLEARWATER TECHNOLOGIES. He could see where the bear had been clawing—getting down to business. He had seen men killed by animals before. Never pretty.

Troy thought about how they had never had a murder in their camp before. Fights, sure, lots of those as men and women in too-close quarters and in the too-long darkness could develop short fuses. The security team would break it up and send the offending parties home, back to the lower forty-eight or Anchorage. They'd cool off, get some sun, and come back happy. But murder, no, not until this.

Troy's thoughts were interrupted as his radio came to life at his shoulder. *"Security assistance needed. We have a 10-52 reported in E wing, room 330. Over."* It was the camp dispatch operator. A 10-52 was an accident or personnel injury.

Troy yelled to Braddock that he'd take it and ran back up the stairs. Once inside, he stripped off his survival gear and saw Chuck, and told him to follow him. They had to run back down the corridor to the central building to connect to the E wing and then up three flights of stairs to get to the room.

When they got there, they saw a crowd of workers outside the room. Troy and Chuck motioned them aside and walked in. A young female oil worker was weeping beside the bed. On the bed lay a young woman. Her eyes bulged, her face was blue.

Troy calmly moved the weeping oil worker away, and Chuck guided her from the room. The woman on the bed was dead. She had headphones in her ears—as if she had been quietly listening to music just before her death.

Troy heard the worker who found her tell Chuck that the bathroom door on her side had been locked. "It had been locked for over an hour and I needed to get ready for my shift," she explained. "I heard nothing in the bathroom, so I decided to go in her room to find out what was up." She'd found her dead.

Troy walked to the door and looked at the doorframe. The names of all room occupants were listed on the doors. The label read, CONSTANCE LAFONTAINE—CLEARWATER TECHNOLOGIES.

CHAPTER THREE

MATTHEW CORDELE WALKED INTO THE Captains' Club Lounge on the top floor of the Captain Cook Hotel to have breakfast and read his *Wall Street Journal*. Cordele was in his mid-thirties, had well-groomed blond hair, blue eyes, a clear complexion, and movie-star looks. People always seemed to smile at him as he went by, wondering if they knew him, or why he looked familiar. He would smile back, a wide, perfectly aligned flash of quick brilliance that meant nothing to him and everything to those he smiled at, as they wondered again who he might be.

Cordele had been born with natural good looks, a love for fine things, and a knack for getting what he wanted for nothing. He was a great con man—he had done a stint in the US Army in Logistics and had been forced out over unproven accusations of supplies being diverted to his own uses. Cordele could have fought his release, but he knew there were too many other things that could have come up in his trail.

Matthew Cordele was in Anchorage, Alaska, using his cover as a logistics consultant to oversee a mission in the Arctic—a mission that was to make him a lot of money. His main concern was that the people hired to do the mission, hired for their expertise, were not getting along. He'd been sent to Anchorage to sort things out before anything got out of hand. They were supposed to meet him tomorrow on their flight back from the high Arctic.

His cell phone vibrated, and Cordele looked down at the message. He realized he was too late: his main contact reported that he had been required to "eliminate" the two technicians, as they were about to blow the mission. He dropped his *Wall Street Journal*, patted his lips with a napkin, and went back to his room, where he dialed the number of his boss in Seattle. He had never seen his boss—had been hired by him over the phone and was given missions by him over the phone—and his voice always unnerved him. This voice ordered Cordele to places like Singapore, Hong Kong, or Dubai to ensure clients secured favorable contracts for their companies, and if things stood in their way, then Cordele hired the necessary forces to remove obstacles. "Remove" could mean blackmail or death. And Cordele's bank account grew.

The call was answered on the second ring. "Go ahead," said the voice on the other end of the line. Cordele was never sure of the age of the voice; it was male, deep, self-assured, never a sign of excitement.

"We've hit a snag at the Arctic Oil Camp," Cordele said. He hurried to explain. "Our contact sent me a text stating the two technicians were about to blow the mission and reveal the intent to Arctic Oil. It seems they wanted to expose our operation for a million dollars. He took them both out." Cordele noticed he was sweating. His upper lip was moist; he wiped it with his cotton handkerchief as he awaited a reply.

"Did they put the devices in place?" the voice asked with no inflection.

"Yes, everything is in place, and my operative has the controls." Cordele sat down on the couch in his room. He could sense where the conversation would go.

"Good, what about our other target, the one on the Beach?" the voice asked.

"I have a report it's ready as well."

"The other two technicians will have to be removed as well. Do this immediately, before the news reaches them—and before the news reaches McAllen." The voice in Seattle hung up.

It's that simple, Cordele thought. Two more people would have to die for him and his boss to make the massive amount of money they were about to make on this mission. The Beach was the code name for Fort McMurray, Alberta, home of the largest deposit of oil, sitting in something called tar sands, in North America. Their devices were meant to sabotage the flow of oil from the tar sands and from Alaska.

Two people had died that morning, and two more were about to die somewhere in Canada as well. To Cordele, death and money were commerce. Sometimes one just had to be traded for the other, especially when it benefited him.

His next phone call was to his counterpart in Fort McMurray, John Parsons, a man similar in age to himself but a large, strapping Newfoundlander with red hair, freckles, and smile that spoke of bad dentistry and too much rum and coke.

"What's up?" Parsons asked.

Cordele quickly filled Parsons in on the situation in Alaska and the command from their boss. They shared the same sense of unease about the boss. Failure was never an option.

Parsons spoke quickly. "Look, they let me know they installed the last device, and our man has the controls. They're out near the tar ponds now. He could do them there . . . hide the bodies . . . know what I mean?"

"You Canadians, always the efficient ones... let me know when it's done," Cordele said. He put away his phone and headed back to the Captains' Lounge to have breakfast. The morning's work had made him hungry.

CHAPTER FOUR

THE NEXT CALL PARSONS MADE was to Emmanuel Fuentes. Fuentes's main credential: he got things done. He was the handler and driver for the two technicians from Clearwater—Kevin Buckner and Alicia Sylvester, two doe-eyed environmental activists that Fuentes hated the moment he met them.

They had clashed immediately and hardly spoke to one another except to accomplish their mission. Kevin and Alicia had signed on to destabilize the oil sands. They had been given the technology to do it, and that was what they cared about. Fuentes had signed on for the money, only for the money. He hated the cold he was subjected to in northern Canada.

When Fuentes's cell phone rang, he had to take it out of his inner parka jacket. He had found out over the past two months that any cell phone left in an outer pocket would freeze. He hated Canada. He swore at it all the time. "Fucking frio, fucking cold Canada," was his favorite expression.

"Yes," he answered, irritated that his hands were out of his gloves to take the call. "What is it?" His breath rose in clouds of steam in the extreme cold.

Parsons was to the point. "Fuentes, there's been a major cluster fuckup in Alaska. You have to eliminate and dispose of our two technicians."

Fuentes's dark features broke into a smile for the first time in two months. "This would be my, greatest pleasure." He smiled into the phone. "We are at the perfect place to get this done. I will call you back when my job is finished. Thank you, muchas gracias."

Fuentes looked over at Alicia and Kevin. They had wondered off to a tar pond. The last device had been installed, and they wanted to take one last look at the devastation of the landscape caused by the oil sands operations.

Fuentes trudged through the deep snow and came up behind them. They were looking at some wolf tracks by the pond and commenting on how man was destroying the wildlife.

Kevin was very tall and slim. At six foot seven, he towered over the five foot eight Fuentes, but size never mattered to Fuentes's knife. He pulled out his large-blade hunting knife, and in one swift motion, he grabbed the back of Kevin's parka hood, pulled him back towards him, and plunged the knife into Kevin's throat.

Kevin's blood shot out in a hot stream in the frigid air. Steam rose from the snow where it dropped. Alicia screamed his name and knelt by his body.

Fuentes stood over Alicia. He waited for her, to see her next actions. She rose up. She was very small, a petite young lady who was now in the shadow of her killer.

Her eyes flashed defiance, and "asshole" was all she said before he cut her throat.

He carefully pulled out his cell phone and called Parsons. "It is finished."

"Where are they?" asked Parsons.

"A tailings pond, with lovely wolf tracks all around. I don't think too many workers come here."

"Excellent, get back here to Fort Mac and we can finish our operations."

"Mucho fantastico. I cannot wait to leave your wonderful country."

"You are a lying little Spanish prick."

"You wound me when you call me a little prick. Please use the term 'El Grande' when you call me a prick," Fuentes protested.

Parsons finished his call with Fuentes and then placed a call to Cordele in Alaska.

When Cordele answered, he simply said, "It's cleaned up."

"Fine, good job."

Just off of downtown Fort McMurray, and about a two-hour drive from many of the oil sands mining operations, Royal Canadian Mounted Police Detective Bernadette Callahan was sitting in her Jeep. The engine was running, her two-way radio was on, and she was scanning her cell phone for recent YouTube videos.

Bernadette was bored. She had been parked outside the house with yellow police tape since 9:00 a.m., and it was now past 11:00 a.m. She was waiting for the coroner and the crime scene investigator to show up, and both were late, as they had been detained by another crime scene on the other side of town.

She was at the scene of a double homicide—a shotgun blast with some knife stabbing thrown in. A party gone wrong with some drug dealers, and no one had heard a thing through the loud music. When dawn's first light came, the ravens started to circle the house.

Ravens will always lead you to fresh meat, she thought. Bernadette had been raised on a Dene reservation in northern Alberta, the daughter of a Native mother and an Irish Catholic father who had wandered off. Bernadette had always walked a line between her native and Irish roots.

Bernadette had joined the RCMP at the age of twenty-two, when politicians were clamoring to bring about an equalization of minorities and gender in the force. Bernadette had made it on both counts and had to work harder than anyone else to get respect.

She had worked her way from one detachment to the next, always staying below the radar but proving skilled enough at solving crimes to become indispensable. It also helped that she took no crap from the male RCMP officers. Her last tangle with a senior officer had left him with bruised balls. She had proven hers were bigger, and she was shipped off to the detective squad—probably because they wanted to get rid of her, but she didn't care.

Bernadette was thirty-five, with medium-length reddish brown hair, light brown skin, and green eyes. She was of average height with a muscular frame that showed off her dedication to the gym. She needed to be able to defend herself, against bad guys, but mostly, she needed to keep her weight down. She loved doughnuts and junk food.

She balanced a double cream, double sugar large Tim Horton's coffee on her knee. A maple-glazed doughnut was standing by. She would hate herself for this later, but this was now.

As Bernadette scrolled down the YouTube site, she came across the video of the polar bear making a meal of a man. The description below stated: "Polar bear in Prudhoe Bay, Alaska, eating an oil worker." Thousands of hits cheered on the polar bear.

Bernadette shifted in her seat, took a swig of her coffee, and sighed. *What is the world coming to?* she thought. She had no idea how much this particular incident would involve her in the very near future.

CHAPTER FIVE

TROY HAD SPENT THE LAST two hours securing the crime scene around the dead bodies. The security team and camp authorities finally realized that at minus forty-five degrees with a wind chill, and an active polar bear, securing the dead body in place outside the camp would be impossible. They placed the body of Marc Lafontaine on a stretcher and found a place for him in the medical room.

Troy was glad they had finally decided to move the body, as he imagined the warm body freezing to the ground and someone with a blow torch having to extract him later. The thought of the arms and legs frozen into their wild contortions was not appealing either. Troy had had to remove frozen bodies in the Arctic on several occasions after accidents—never a memorable time.

He walked back to the security guard office located at the main entrance of the camp. Braddock was in his office, going over reports. The chief had been in meetings with the Arctic Oil Company, the base manager (the one who ran the show), the operations manager, and the safety manager and had placed the camp on lockdown: no one could leave, no one who wasn't already a resident of the camp could come in.

A security guard had been placed at the front door, and oil workers milled around the main entrance, the ones who were supposed to fly home that day. Their shift of two weeks on with twelve-hour days and no breaks was over—they wanted to go home, murder or no murder.

"So how bad is it?" Troy asked as he slumped down in one of the two chairs in front of Braddock's desk.

Braddock lifted his head, finally noticing Troy. "Well, I don't remember having my ass chewed out this bad since I was a young beat cop in Detroit." He smiled at Troy as he spoke. Not too much fazed Braddock. He was mid-fifties and had retired from the Detroit police force when the economy had cut the police budget. Guys like him, too young and too broke to retire, had gone looking for work. Braddock had found Arctic Oil Company in Alaska: great pay, long hours, and lots of paperwork.

Troy shifted in his chair and sipped the coffee he'd brought in. "What's the story with the Arctic Oil brass? They think this is murder? That somehow Marc killed his sister then ran headfirst out the exit door to get eaten by a bear?"

Braddock laughed and ran his hand through his hair. "Actually you're not far wrong. They want to call this a murder–suicide and are damned if they'll let it be known we have an unknown killer in the camp."

"Yep, the shit doesn't change, it just gets deeper," Troy said. "So, what do the closed circuit television tapes show?"

"Well, we had another fuckup." Braddock dropped his hands to his desk. "We've got blank tape for about one hour last night."

"Not possible," Troy said. "Our CCTV has double backups. The only way that could've happened is if someone flipped a switch right here in the control room."

"Yeah, I know that. Cummings and Stewart were on last night. Both deny any knowledge of the CCTV not working, and Cummings was at the console most of the evening. He said he didn't see anything."

"And of course the CCTV wasn't recording, even if he didn't see anything. Interesting . . ." Troy looked out of Braddock's office window. Cummings was at the console again, making busy. Troy had never liked Jason Cummings, a twenty-something-year-old from Southern California. His dad, an ex-cop, had pulled some strings in Anchorage to get him into Arctic Oil. Somehow the young man had managed to cling to his job, in spite of his many screw-ups. Everyone knew he had some pull with the Anchorage head office—no one liked that.

Troy stood, stretched, and finished the last of his coffee. "Look, you know I don't think much of Cummings. I think we get him in a room and sweat him a little, see if he pops. Meanwhile, I'll get the personnel files of our deceased for the police when they get here."

"Oh yeah, I need you to pick up a Detective Mueller and a CSI Franklin on this morning's flight. You'll be their escort while they're here," Braddock said.

Troy stopped in his tracks. "Detective Mueller? Really? Man, we go way back."

"You two have some history?"

"Yeah." Troy smiled. "He busted my ass big time when I was a punk on the streets of Anchorage."

"Well, he's all yours."

"Thanks, Chief." Troy threw a fake salute and walked out of Braddock's office, staring at Cummings as he left. He thought Cummings cringed as he walked by, but he couldn't be sure.

The personnel offices were in the administration area at the center of the camp. As Troy walked by the base camp manager's office, he could hear a heated discussion going on as to the reports the base manager would make. The media would be calling—the camp would need to have a statement. Houston would be calling—the dreaded head-office boys—the camp would need to have answers.

Troy carried on down the hall to personnel and found Della Charles. Della knew about everything and everybody in the camp. They said if a mouse farted in a hay stack in Oklahoma, Della would know about it in her hometown of Baton Rouge.

He knocked on her door and walked in. "Hey, Della, what's up sweetheart? You're looking fine as ever."

"Oh Troy, you talk such shit," Della purred. Her voice a pure southern drawl, the word shit sounded like it had a least 5 i's in it. She wouldn't take any such talk from anyone but Troy. She always held out hope that he would drop by her room one night. He never had, but she hadn't given up hope.

"I betcha want files on the latest deceased—poor things." She reached over to the copies she had on her desk. Della was a big girl. She was a former Louisiana beauty queen, formerly petite, but that was behind her now. So was her girth. She had allowed herself to grow: no pageants, no runways, so she now allowed herself the luxury of food. Her new size could not hide her beauty—green eyes, fair, flawless skin and cascading blonde hair. She was any man's dream in a size twenty-four.

"Sure do, Della. You're always way ahead of me." Troy took a seat in front of her desk and leaned forward.

Della handed him the files with a flicker of lust in her eyes that he found hard to avoid. He took the files, opened them, and began scanning the pages. "Not much here," he finally said, looking up at Della.

"Well, that's all I got from Arctic Oil Contract Central. They negotiate the contracts and send in the contractors once they're cleared," Della said, pained that she'd been unable to help Troy.

Troy noted that the two deceased siblings were Canadians who had traveled to and from Arctic Oil Camp together, and they always flew home to Vancouver, Canada, on their shift change. The files always included flight information.

"Della," Troy said, looking softly into her eyes, "I need to get copies of the files of all the personnel who flew in here at the same time as the deceased. Could you get me that?" He threw in one of his best smiles with the eyes.

"Oh, Troy, only because it's you, honey." Della went back to her computer. Her silver wrist bangles clattered on the keyboard. "This search may take a while. How about I drop it by your sleeping quarters later . . .?" She dropped the last words like a sugar lump, sweet and large.

Troy smiled. "Sorry darling, I'll be with Anchorage PD and crime scene people all day. My office will be fine." He winked at her and headed out the door. He couldn't help feeling that her eyes were attached to his ass like a laser. Probably because they were.

Troy headed back to the security office. The time was 0915 hours, and the Shared Services flight, carrying the detective and crime scene investigator, was to arrive at 1025 hours. He needed to get moving. The wind would be blowing snow on the roads, making the trip to the airport slow.

Troy walked past the oil workers hanging out in the cafeteria—they had nowhere to go. Instead, they drank coffee and speculated about the deaths. Troy knew that somewhere in the camp was a killer—probably looking back at him.

Cordele had just received troubling information from his contact at Arctic Oil Camp. The Anchorage police were on their way to the camp, and his contact needed to be extracted as soon as possible. The situation up there was messy. His man had bribed a security guard to cut the CCTV feed while he committed the murders. The guard needed to be taken care of. *More mess*, Cordele thought.

The worst part was that his man at Arctic Oil camp thought he was being shadowed. He sensed it, and if he did, he was probably right. His man was an ex-spook himself, deep cover from military intelligence.

Cordele wondered who else would be up there. Had McAllen or those crazy bastards from Ironstone Investments hired someone to watch over the mission? He sent the information in a secure text to his boss in Seattle.

The weather in Anchorage was brutally cold at minus twenty-five degrees Fahrenheit, but he needed to get out. He looked out his Hotel window. Ice fog billowed from the cars exhaust in the street below. The hotel window was latticed with fingers of ice. He would go for a walk downtown, find a restaurant with some good food and wine, and wait for his boss's reply.

CHAPTER SIX

IF RANDALL FRANCIS FELT REMORSE over the killings of the four technicians from Clearwater Technologies, he didn't show it to his boss. His boss, Duncan Stewart, was sitting across from him in their New York office just off Wall Street.

Their company was called Ironstone Investments, and it was a front for stock manipulations that twelve stock traders at multiple computers in a glass wall behind them worked at daily, as they went about their business of fraud in the markets. New Yorkers always thought they should be wary of crime in the streets. The crimes in these offices were much greater and did more harm than pickpockets and muggers.

Both Randall and Duncan were listening intently to the caller on speaker as he filled them in on the deaths in Alaska and Fort McMurray.

Duncan threw several menacing looks at Randall throughout the briefing. Duncan was a little man in his late thirties, balding, with a thick red beard and a big voice. He thought of himself as a reincarnation of a pirate and enjoyed the pillaging of markets as they manipulated oil and other commodities by either blackmail or bribery. A riot at a gold mine or an oil tanker running aground in a shipping lane while his traders made millions made him believe he was a maker of his own destiny.

The latest venture, to control oil prices with sabotage in the Alaska and Fort McMurray oil sands, was looking bad. Randall had brought him this "absolute fucking genius idea," and it was looking more and more to be of the fucked-up variety.

Randall only squirmed slightly as he felt Duncan's gaze. Randall was slightly smaller than Duncan, mid-thirties, and had a flat, featureless face that would make him a ghost in a crowd. His voice was one octave below falsetto, and it rose above that when he spoke too fast. He dressed well in expensive dark suits to make up for his pasty complexion.

The speaker on the phone, a male, assured voice, was giving them the final rundown on the venture. The devices that would affect the flow of oil were in place, and their people, the ones the speaker had hired, were now in control. The technicians from Clearwater, who had been hired against the voice's advice, were now dead.

"There is one more item we need to discuss," the voice on the speaker said.

"What is that?" Duncan hated the voice. His face turned beet red, as it often did when he got angry, and he threw another nasty look at Randall. Randall had brought in this voice, the black ops guy, whoever he was, to run this venture, and now it was coming to haunt him.

"Professor McAllen will have to be eliminated in the next twenty-four hours, as we just eliminated his people, and we are sure there will be recriminations for you. We suggest it be done at once."

Duncan switched the speaker phone to mute and stared across the desk at Randall. "And there you have it you fucking idiot. We've got to kill someone else to get this done. In the five years I've run this operation, I've never had to kill anyone to make my profits . . . and now this."

Randall looked across the table. His hands were dripping with sweat; he dared not brush his brow, as he was sure a cascade of sweat would flow. He needed to show calmness in the face of Duncan's wrath, or he would be lost. "Look, for big profits, there are sometimes some great sacrifices, and unfortunately, these four were expendable. And as our contractor just said, the couple in Alaska were about to go to Arctic Oil for more money. So, fair turnaround, don't you think?" Randall managed a weak smile with his last remark, hoping to ease the tension.

Duncan unmuted the speaker phone. "Yes, we do agree with your assessment. Professor McAllen needs to be dealt with." He could not bring himself to say killed.

"Very well then, we will add this to your bill. We have the coordinates of the professor, and we will let you know when this is done. Thank you, gentlemen, have a pleasant day." The speaker ended the call.

Duncan's face turned even more shades of angry red to match his fiery red beard. Randall took his opportunity to leave.

CHAPTER SEVEN

R ANDALL SAT IN HIS OFFICE, watching the three monitors on his desk. The commodities of oil, copper, gold, and silver no longer interested him. He had just agreed to kill Professor Alistair McAllen, the one he had recruited, and whose technology they would use to sabotage the oil fields in Alaska and Canada.

He had found the professor in a science magazine article. Randall read everything and did constant research for Ironstone Investments, which was why he was a major asset to Duncan. Randall could find out who owned what gold or silver mine and the union situation, the oil tanker traffic that could be stopped by a tanker going aground, and which tanker captain had bad gambling debts.

He had been focusing his latest research and reading on looking for the big score, something more than a strike at a silver mine or a tanker running aground. Randall wanted to move world markets. He had found his first ally in the black ops voice on the phone. Actually, the black ops had found him, called him up. The voice had known his name and everything about Ironstone, and asked if he wanted assistance on any "larger projects." The message was implied: greater risks, larger profits.

Soon after the conversation with the disembodied voice on the phone, which would not give a name but promised great assistance, Randall had come across the article on Professor Alistair McAllen and polywater.

Randall had thought the article was a hoax, perhaps a joke from the scientific community. He should have known better, as the scientific community laughs at very little but loves to poke holes in others' research for its own sport. The article discussed how Professor Alistair McAllen had redeveloped polywater.

The term "polywater" was not new, Randall had discovered. A Soviet physicist, Nikolai Fedyakin, claimed he invented it in the late 1960s. It was supposedly a new form of water with a higher boiling, lower freezing point and a much higher viscosity than ordinary water, about that of syrup.

When English and American scientists finally did studies on the Soviet's research, they could not repeat the results. They finally determined that the Soviet had not cleaned his instruments properly and that the residues in the beakers were giving him his results. Case closed, except for several science fiction writers who used the scenario to scare the wits out of readers.

Professor McAllen, head of the chemistry department at the University of Victoria, on Vancouver Island, British Columbia, Canada, was adamant in the article that his invention was not a hoax. He had invited several researchers to verify his findings, and they had in fact stated that he used clean equipment and changed the nature of water each time; although they claimed his water was closer to Jell-O in substance than syrup. The stuff actually "wiggled," they said.

In the article, after listing all the merits of the new and improved polywater, such as its ability to slow floods and act as ballast for ships, the professor went on to remark that oil companies might not like it. He said, "If this were injected into an oil well, the oil would no longer rise to the top. You see, oil needs water for pressure. This would make the water heavier than the oil. No pressure."

It was then that Randall had had his "fucking genius moment," and it was not oil wells—it was oil fields. Two places in the world needed a central source of water. The first was Alaska's North Slope. The high Arctic oil field drew its water from the Arctic Ocean, purified it, and injected it into the oil field to bring the oil to the surface. The other was the Athabasca oil sands near Fort McMurray, Alberta. Each large oil sands mine used a large amount of water drawn from the Athabasca River to generate steam to separate the tarlike substance from the sand. Each of these mines had a central pumping station.

Randall had known the professor would probably not be willing to sell his invention, but wondered if he had a weakness, if he could be recruited. His search of the professor's history had turned up the results he was looking for. The good professor had worked for a large oil company in the alternate energy division in Corpus Christi, Texas. He had been married with two children and had raised his children in sight of some of the largest refineries in the world.

What Randall had found was much better leverage than he could have imagined. Both of McAllen's children had died of leukemia, and the professor and his wife had been listed in a class-action suit against the refineries. The professor had been fired from the oil company, his wife had filed for divorce, and he had moved north. Revenge, Randall Francis found, was often one of the best motivators in the world.

Randall had taken his idea to Duncan, simply announcing that they were going to "grab world oil by the balls!" Duncan liked having anything by the balls—his pirate persona demanded it. He had given Randall his blessing to pursue the project and called him a "fucking genius."

The professor did not agree to a meeting for several months, but Randall kept pressuring. Finally sometime in August, the professor agreed to meet with him but in his home on Galiano Island, near

Vancouver. The trip would take an entire day, but Randall was up to the challenge. He flew from New York to Toronto, and then to Vancouver. The island, a mere seventeen miles long by four miles wide, was accessible from Vancouver by boat, ferry, or float plane—Randall chose the latter, although the thought of landing on water on purpose scared the hell out of him.

Professor McAllen was hard to miss. He towered over the other people on the dock. He was extra-tall, extra-lean with long gray hair that topped an unshaven face with angular features. He wore a ragged T-shirt stuffed into faded jeans and tennis shoes that had not seen tennis but miles of rugged beach. He sported a brand new Seattle Mariners hat, his favorite baseball team. He replaced the hat every year.

The professor walked right up to Randall and introduced himself. Randall wondered how he'd picked him out of the crowd, as he had worn his Armani jeans and calf-skin loafers to "blend in."

The professor smiled. "Son, you would look like a New Yorker anywhere you landed in those rags." He slapped Randall on the back and ushered him to his rusted-out pickup truck. The accumulation of dirt seemed to hold it together.

They drove the short distance to the professor's home, and the old truck weaved across the highway as the professor noted points of interest. Other drivers got out of his way with a friendly wave. There were only two thousand permanent residents on the island, and they all seemed to know him.

His home was a two-story log house with a large deck that jutted out on three sides. The view from the deck was impressive, high above a rocky beach overlooking sea, sky, and boats in the channel. The professor made appetizers of mussels, shrimp, oysters, and scallop ceviche with homemade sourdough bread, and served a few beers to wash it down.

When Randall could not take the small talk anymore, he finally broached the subject of the polywater. The professor just smiled and replied, "Of course. I knew you came for the show."

Next to the wine in the kitchen cupboard sat two vials. The professor grabbed them and led Randall downhill on a switchback trail to the beach. The sun was getting low. The professor chose a tidal pool, scooped out any small fish, and put them in another pool.

Randall remembered standing there breathless; the professor looked like a magician. He reached into his jeans, and with a flourish of his wrist, emptied the contents of the vial into the pool. In just a few seconds, the water began to shimmer. Randall touched the surface and it bounced back—it wiggled.

The professor dumped the second vial into the pool, and the shimmering stopped. The process had been reversed. To Randall, the parting of the Red Sea would not have been more of a miracle than this. He stood there, the setting sun bouncing light across the water, and felt as if he could now control the flow of North American oil—he had never felt such power.

Back in the professor's house, over a dinner of bouillabaisse filled with fresh West Coast crab and fish, Randall laid out his plan to the professor. He was sure to mention several times how Ironstone Investments could use this to sabotage oil fields and hurt the very companies that the professor had sued over the deaths of his children.

Randall saw the light go on in the professor's eyes; saw that he was willing to become an accomplice. He had already thought of devices that would implement his polywater and just how the installation could be done. He had just needed someone like Randall to get his devices there.

A price was attached. The professor was not about to let his polywater invention go for cheap. He wanted five million up front, five million on implementation, and four of his own people—people he trusted, who had been students of his—to be part of the implementation team. He was adamant on this, and Randall could not budge him off either point.

Randall had great respect for the professor and his bargaining skills. McAllen was no pushover. He was eccentric—he repeated himself and lost his train of thought often, as if one thought crowded another too quickly in his head—but he knew the power of the polywater. Over the course of the evening, Randall had become fond of the professor; there was a charisma behind the eccentricity, something you wanted to believe in.

Randall and the professor toasted their newfound partnership, and after several bottles of wine and some fine Cognac, Randall was shuffled off to a bedroom sometime late in the night or early morning. The next morning, the professor handed him his cell phone, which he had left somewhere, and took him back to the dock to catch his series of flights back to New York. Two small vials of polywater were stuffed safely in his bag for a demonstration when he returned home.

On Randall's return to New York, he had gotten Duncan to agree to the professor's terms only when Duncan had realized how much they could profit on the price of oil, if two of North America's largest fields were compromised. Randall had also gotten the cooperation of the black ops, just another ten million, and they were in business. The profits would be in the billions, so ten million to McAllen and the same to the black ops "contractor," as they called him, had seemed small in comparison.

They had started the project in late November with one team going to Alaska and the other going to the oil sands in Canada. The plan had seemed perfect; the devices McAllen had manufactured looked like small thermostats and housed four large vials each: two to start the process and two to reverse it. The professor had claimed that these small vials were all that would be needed, as once the vials were injected, a chain reaction would occur. The effect would be dramatic, Randall and Duncan had been told: two large oil fields would stop pumping oil and oil prices would rise, and Ironstone Investments would know exactly when.

Now, as Randall sat in his office, he realized his dream of riches had killed four people, and he had directly commanded the killing of a fifth. The charismatic and eccentric professor would be dead in the next twenty-four hours. Randall cleared his desk and looked at his watch; it was approaching 7:30 p.m. He was hungry. He decided to hit the street for some sushi.

CHAPTER EIGHT

DETECTIVE FRANK MUELLER OF THE Anchorage Crime Unit kicked his duffel bag in front of him as the line of oil workers moved slowly towards the airport check-in counter. Frank had been called at 6:30 a.m. and told to be on the 8:00 a.m. flight to Prudhoe Bay to investigate a murder-suicide at an oil camp. The flight would not be with a regular commercial airline. This flight was with Shared Services, and the aircraft was owned by the major oil companies in the Alaskan Arctic. To get on the aircraft, you had to be cleared by the oil companies. Detective Mueller had been cleared quickly.

Frank was a tall, sixty-two-year-old veteran of three failed marriages and two attempts at rehab. He was just coming back from his third. He thought maybe three was his lucky number. The last marriage had ended well; he had nothing left to offer for alimony, so the last wife had wished him well and left for California. He hoped his third time in rehab would prove just as lucky.

Frank was lean and muscular, and you could see he had once been a very handsome man. The hair had gone. What was once a long mane of dashing brown waves had started to leave far too early and had been combed over, then trimmed, and then finally "taken down to the deck." Now, his head was smooth-shaven and, he thought, attractive.

"You have a firearm?" the gate agent asked when Frank reached the gate. She was a pretty forty-something brunette, and Frank could easily see her as his fourth wife.

"Why, yes I do." Frank beamed his best smile. He had great teeth that had never seen an orthodontist—just naturally smooth, purely aligned beacons of come-hither-my-darlings that, he thought, worked the very moment he turned them on.

"Then please put it in your checked luggage." She smiled back, but it was a quick, enough-of-you-mister smile. No warmth, just down to business.

"Why, yes, yes of course," Frank answered, a little flustered. He was not usually turned down this quickly and this early in the morning, especially after flashing his badge. He put his Glock .40 firearm with holster into his duffel bag and handed it to the unsmiling gate agent.

The agent put an official tag on the bag, allowing it to go through screening with a firearm, and handed Frank a small piece of paper with a gate number, time, and seat number. No boarding pass.

"Thank you," the agent said, and with a crisp "next please," Frank was dismissed.

He wandered off to look for his gate, a newspaper, a coffee, and perhaps a mirror to see if he had lost his charm entirely. Perhaps he was in fact getting too old to attract the ladies, or his charm was waning, or, most obviously, the gate agent was a lesbian. He smiled as that last thought crossed his mind.

Frank headed through security, picked up his paper, and scanned the *Anchorage Daily Mirror*. There was no news on the incident in Prudhoe Bay—it was still too fresh for the paper's numerous newshounds. Several other investigations into murders in Anchorage and Fairbanks had taken place in the past few days. There was always one month every year when

Alaskans shot the asses off each other. This year it was January. Last year they had waited until March.

There seemed to be a time when the darkness and cold, combined with hard liquor and access to firearms and ammunition, provided the right mix for killing a fellow human being. The police and detectives in both Anchorage and Fairbanks were stretched thin. Frank's captain had said the reason he was on his own for the investigation was that they were tight for personnel, and the Arctic Oil Company had a good squad of security personnel in place to assist him. He never mentioned the real reason he had put him on the case, which Frank knew. It was the elephant in the room: the Arctic Oil Camp was dry. No liquor, no drugs. Frank was on rehab and probation, and a dry destination could not hurt.

The flight was called, and Frank headed for the gate to board. He moved slowly amongst the sea of workers in navy blue parkas adorned with yellow and silver reflective stripping. It was a small herd of men and women heading for the cold depths of the Arctic.

Frank had a window seat, on the left side just ahead of the wing. The plane filled quickly—these were not tourists. The passengers stowed their carry-on items, sat down, and buckled in. They were heading to work.

As the plane lifted off, Frank watched the lights of Anchorage below, lights that made shadows on the snow. The plane banked and turned north over Cook Inlet. The black, icy water mixed with the ice flows, and the ice flows shone back in the moonlight.

Sunrise would be at 9:34 a.m. this morning in Anchorage, but in Prudhoe Bay, light would not come until 11:19 a.m. The sun would set around 3:00 p.m. He was traveling from darkness to darkness.

He settled back in his seat as the plane leveled off. An eerie quiet surrounded the passengers. Some slept, some talked quietly. They were headed for two to three weeks of twelve-hour days, seven days a week. In between, they would fit in eight hours of sleep and four hours of meals and personal time. They had left behind family, friends, and recreation rooms with big-screen TVs for the desolate Arctic.

The acrid stench of oil filled the air. Frank turned on the air above his head. The smell came from the clothes of the oil workers. It was ground into their clothes—they breathed it and they lived in it. It was their cologne, the smell of money. Frank drifted off to sleep and woke up when they landed in Fairbanks fifty-five minutes later.

The aisle seat beside Frank was empty. He watched more passengers enter and immediately recognized the crime scene investigator that was to join him on his trip. She was small and square—she had a square face that sat on square shoulders that framed a square body and hips. She could have been turned out by a high school woodworking class. She was thirtyish, brunette, and wore dark glasses that hid blue-green eyes. What gave her away as a CSI was her shoulder bag, which read: FAIRBANKS CSI. Frank wondered where low-key had gotten to. Obviously it had not reached this lady. She threw her bag in the overhead, dropped into her seat, and buckled up while glancing at her watch. She was an efficient and concise package of energy.

Frank quietly said, "I believe you're Joanne Franklin, my CSI."

She snapped her head in Frank's direction, a bit of surprise registering on her broad face. "Yes, I am, and you must be my detective." She had slightly emphasized "my" to show Frank that he had already pissed her off.

Frank decided to be less asshole, more polite. "Well, I am delighted to be working with you, Joanne." He smiled.

"Likewise." She smiled the same I-do-not-mean-it smile and picked up a magazine.

"So, have you been to Prudhoe before?" he asked. He was not going to let his charm record be tarnished by this square peg of a woman.

"Yep, Prudhoe, Barrow, Nome, and every other place in between—when they die, I fly." With that, she put in her iPod headphones, threw him one last smile, and buried her head in her magazine.

Frank was left with a frozen smile on his face. He had been categorically shut down, and he had to let his smile shine for just a few seconds more to alleviate the humiliation he felt. *Ten, Nine, Eight, Seven, Six . . . yes, that's good enough.* He moved his gaze back to the window. They had lifted off from Fairbanks and turned straight north.

CHAPTER NINE

SECURITY OFFICER JASON CUMMINGS WAS in trouble. Troy wanted to meet with him—he was booked for 1500 hours. "Just a little sit-down to discuss this morning's events," Troy had said. Jason had felt Troy's dark brown eyes—they had accused him. His stomach would not hold down food.

His nausea had started right around the time he had received a simple offer: he was to flip the recording switch on the CCTV cameras for about sixty minutes. A man had explained he wanted a little late-night magic, his words, with a certain tall French Canadian girl and did not want to be seen entering her room on camera.

These extracurricular affairs happened in the camp, but as long as they were kept quiet, they were tolerated. Marriages broke up, new link-ups happened; it was the way of life in the Arctic. Close quarters, far away from home, shit happens.

Jason had been offered a quick grand for the service, had thought, *a grand, sixty minutes? That's some good French stuff this guy is after, but what the hell, a grand is a grand,* and flipped the switch.

When the murders happened, he knew it was the same guy who had asked him to flip the switch who had committed them. The one thousand dollars made him an accessory. If Jason told his superiors, he implicated himself. He would get more than fired, he would get a record, and he couldn't let that happen.

Jason knew he was a failure in the eyes of his father, a twenty-five-year veteran of the Bakersfield, California, police force. He had been decorated and honored, and now he was retired and waiting for grandchildren and feats of glory from his son. Jason was twenty-five years old, tall, and overweight. His face was a mass of pimples, his hair a brush-cut brown. He was a nondescript person who could fill a large space, but when he did, you weren't sure if he was there.

He had failed at college and had been cut from the football team for being too timid. The quarterback got tired of being run over by the offense when Jason was on the line. He only excelled at video games. A true basement kid who, if left alone with his beloved *Halo*, *Star Craft*, *Vanquish*, or *Dragon Quest* video games, would never deal with the real world.

His father, the decorated policeman, had had a different idea. He had gotten him a job with a security firm, pulled some strings, and then got him this plum position in security on the North Slope of Alaska. There was sixty-five to eighty-five thousand a year to be made. His father had told him to keep his head down and his nose clean, and in a few years, he could come back to California, where they would set up a security firm together. He would no longer be a basement kid and instead, someone who might stand out in a crowd. But he had blown it. His stomach gurgled its disappointment.

His cell phone buzzed. It was the man who had bribed him. "Sweeten the offer," the text message said.

Jason texted back, "better b extra swt."

"100K."

Jason was stunned. If it was true, with money like that, he could get out of security for good. To hell with his father's security business. *But this has to be a trap*, he thought. *The killer is trying to lure me into this even deeper. But if he has the 100K on him?* His stomach was churning even more. He swigged a coke, but it would not settle down.

"Let's meet," was the next text Jason received.

Alarm bells pounded in Jason's head, his heart was pounding, and he had to think things through. He needed a way out.

"Sure, where?"

"Men's room, Cor C, 10 min."

Jason flipped the switch on the CCTV monitor for corridor C. He could see the men's washroom clearly. The killer was nowhere in sight. He formulated a plan: he would race to the washroom, get ahead of him, and shoot him the moment he entered. He would tell everyone he had figured out this guy was the killer. He would get the killer, get the credit for the takedown, and make his father proud.

He had seconds to make his plans. He called another security guard to take his place in the monitoring room, saying he needed a bathroom break. Then he checked his weapon and strode out of the room.

There was no one around as he turned into corridor C. Most of the workers had returned to their rooms or had gone to the gym or TV room. No one knew how long the lockdown would be.

Jason could see the washroom as he entered the corridor. It was halfway down the hall, between the lounge and the library. He flipped the safety off his sidearm and slowly opened the door inward and to his right. The bathroom had five stalls, a bank of urinals, and five washbasins. He peered under the stalls and saw no feet. *I made it here first*, he thought.

That was the last thought he had. The killer had been waiting for him behind the door, perfectly positioned out of Jason's view.

Jason only saw a blur. In an instant, the killer hit him hard with two blunt instruments, and then snapped his neck. The killer dragged Jason's body into a stall, and sat him on the toilet and pulled his coveralls down. He wanted others to think the toilet was in use, which would give him more time—time was always of the essence in killing. The farther away from a kill you could get, the better. He took Jason's cell phone as his last few texts would be in there, and then he locked the door and climbed over the stall. He had hid a parka and hard hat in the washroom trash can. He put these on and was careful to avoid the CCTV cameras as he walked down the hallway.

Jason Cummings, now dead, had failed for the last time. There would be no further disappointments for his father in California to deal with.

CHAPTER TEN

C ORDELE WALKED BACK INTO HIS room at the Captain Cook Hotel and began to slowly take off his down parka, unwind his scarf, and pull off his lamb's-wool-lined boots. He had walked only five blocks back from the restaurant where he had eaten lunch back to the hotel, but his face was frozen from the bitter cold. It began to thaw, and his flesh felt like it had just been taken out of the freezer, the skin tingling as blood vessels surfaced in the warmth. Cordele still could not get over the cold. His last mission had been in Singapore, and he had stationed himself at the luxurious Raffles Hotel and watched on his laptop as an operative took out an objective in Thailand. He missed his silk shirts, linen trousers, and loafers without socks. This cold was ridiculous in Anchorage—but he had to admit they had good restaurants, and good wine.

His head was pounding from the extra glass he had consumed. He hadn't wanted to leave the cozy little restaurant with its wood fire and warm ambience, partly because the last text message from the Arctic Oil Camp had informed him that the security guard had been eliminated. Things were getting very messy.

The other text he had received over lunch was from his boss in Seattle, telling him to check his computer for the coordinates of a job they had to do. "Job" usually meant "kill." Cordele suspected who it would be. He ordered coffee from room service and went to his computer. Exactly as he suspected—Professor Alistair McAllen was the job. The message gave him the coordinates of the island some forty miles off of Vancouver and informed him that it was necessary to have the job done by 0700 hours the next day.

Cordele knew the reason for the urgency. The professor would be looking for progress reports from his two people in Alaska and the two in Canada. They were all dead. What the professor could do to screw up the mission obviously no one knew, but neither Cordele's boss nor the Wall Street guys wanted to find out—they just wanted him dead.

When room service brought him his coffee, Cordele was looking over the Google Earth maps of Galiano Island and lining up what assets he would need. He poured a cup, sat back, and looked over the logistics, his specialty. He knew he could call upon Parsons and Fuentes in Fort McMurray for the job. Parsons was an ex–Canadian Army soldier, two years out of Afghanistan, and Fuentes, well, he was some muscle they'd picked up somewhere out of Juarez, Mexico, who would kill anyone for money.

He sipped his coffee. It was good and strong, and his headache from the wine was dissipating. He reminded himself to go back to his one glass of wine with lunch rule and picked up the phone. He looked at his watch: it was 3:15 p.m. in Fort McMurray. Parsons picked up on the third ring.

"Did I catch you at a bad time?" Cordele asked.

"No, no, just some afternoon hockey on the tube is all. What's up, my son?" Parsons answered.

Cordele did not care for the "my son" crap, a term of endearment among east coasters, but he took it from Parsons because he was genuine. He actually liked the guy. "So, we have some more cleanups to do down there in Canada. Are you at your computer?"

"Yep, right here looking at it." Parsons poured himself a coke, took a swig, and gazed back at the screen.

"This needs immediate attention. We need to take out the professor. I'm sending you the coordinates. How soon is Fuentes back?"

"I expect him in the door any minute. He phoned about an hour ago to say he was on his way back from the Synthetic Oil site." Parsons let out a soft belch with his answer.

"Good, you'll be catching a flight to Vancouver followed by a boat across Georgia Straight to a little beach landing on Galiano Island. I'll have some local talent pick you up at the airport, and I'll be sending you all the logistics for the mission and a picture of our target."

"What kind of talent?"

"Asians."

"Ah, Christ, trigger-happy mothers!"

"I take it you don't like Asians?"

"No, love 'em. Love Asian women, Asian food, even Asian beer, but Asian boys like to spray their weapons all over the place. They make a mess. Now, if you could get me some nice Native boys, they like to creep up all nice and quiet like. One shot, one kill, nice boys."

"I don't have contacts with Natives. I got Asians. That's what you're getting, and you're in charge of them. Make sure they know that."

This time, Parsons belched loudly after his swig of Coke. "Sure, sure, Asian kids, I'm in charge, got it."

"And send me a list of what weapons you'll need, as well as body armor."

"Armor? I thought we were dealing with a professor? Did he just develop a set of teeth we don't know about?"

"No, I just like to provide anything you think you'll need."

"Well, for a beach landing, I don't want seven pounds of body armor strapped to my chest, especially if I have to do any swimming. I'll tell you stories of my previous beach landings over a beer sometime, and how much I never liked any of them," Parsons said as he typed in the airline's website address to book his flight.

"Okay, we can communicate about everything else you need by text in your travels. Let me know your status as you board your flights. I'll be in touch." Cordele hung up and got back to the real problem at hand: boats, guns, and his Asian team—it was going to be a long day. He thought he might need more coffee.

As Parsons was hanging up, Fuentes walked in. He was removing his many layers of clothing and smiling. "Hello my friend, what's up? Let's go get some beers and celebrate. This shit caper is done."

Parsons looked up from his computer. "Cordele just called. You need to get a small bag packed. We have a little road trip down south."

"Si, finally we get some warmth." Fuentes was beaming.

"Not that far south, my friend. We're going to Vancouver. Take your rain coat and a vest. We leave in an hour for the airport."

Fuentes face collapsed in a serious frown. "Man, it's so hard to catch a break in this fucking cold country."

"Hey, you get to kill someone while we're down there. Don't be so sad."

Fuentes's face went back to a smile. "Okay that is what I live for. Why didn't you say so in the first place?" He left the room to pack.

Parsons went back to his computer and booked them on flights to Calgary, then on connecting flights to Vancouver. There was a direct flight to Vancouver but they wouldn't make it in time. He booked separate seats so they would not be seen together. Fuentes would drive his truck to the airport, and Parsons would take a cab. They planned to be back by the next flight.

He would leave "Do Not Disturb" signs on their doors—the controls for the devices were in Fuentes's room.

In his room in Anchorage, Cordele had lined up his Asian connections in Vancouver—three gang members who were in between a drug run. They had fast boats and access to weapons. The best approach to the island looked like a boat ride from a place called Steveston Harbour. The drive to the harbor from the airport was about a half hour, and with a half hour to get across the channel, they would have plenty of time to get the job done and be back in time for breakfast.

Cordele disliked unnecessary deaths on a mission. He had been against bringing on the personnel the professor had chosen. As the deal would not have gone through without them, and the money was huge, his boss, and Ironstone had gone along with the professor's wishes. Now, the young contractors were dead, and they were about to eliminate the professor. *This was a sad case of greed over good sense*, Cordele thought.

He closed his laptop and looked at his watch: 3:30 p.m. Alaska time. He had sent all of his information to Parsons, and he was tired. He decided on a trip down to the hotel pool for a quick swim, shower, and steam. Then he would head back to his room to monitor events. It would be long night, and an even longer morning, he hoped everything worked out well for his team of killers.

Cordele's boss sent an email with final instructions to kill professor McAllen, and then entered the estimates for the costs of the proposed execution on an Excel spreadsheet. Flights, guns, and the Asian gang members would all be added to the client's bill at Ironstone Investments.

Cordele's boss was very exact and very precise in determining costs of missions. Cordele's boss was, in fact, a woman. She was Margaret Ashley, a retired Central Intelligence Agency personnel director. Margaret was in her mid-sixties, five foot six, had red hair, and was well dressed. Her home was in a Palm Springs gated golf course community, just off Country Club Drive.

Margaret had begun her black ops business after getting what she called a "piss-poor pension and god-awful HMO" to look after her medical needs. Before receiving a cheap TIMEX watch and a small farewell party at an Olive Garden restaurant, she had developed a plan. After thirty years of running personnel and putting "assets" in place to do missions, Margaret knew which assets had enough of an attitude problem to work for real money—assets like Cordele and Parsons, who had been in the military and had been somewhat less than exemplary in their duties, yet extremely able to help her with her needs.

Margaret had also recruited two IT boys, whom she called Frodo and Freddy. Both of them were capable of more adventurous tasks than they had been given at the bureau—their aptitude tests had screamed it, but the Agency had never picked up on it. Margaret had.

She had moved her two bright young lads to Boulder, Colorado, put them in a condo with the latest computer and spy equipment (all paid for by the last of her pension funds), and they were in business. The boys found businesses that required a little extra assistance in getting contracts basically by tapping into their emails. Margaret then utilized a voice-altering device that provided her with a man's commanding voice. Her calls were also rerouted to her in Palm Spring from a phone in Seattle.

Margaret's business did extremely well. She was doing what the CIA had done but was getting paid for it. Instead of altering other nations' paths by killing key government officials or agents, Margaret merely helped businesses in the international field get what they wanted through bribery or elimination of competition. Margaret was impressed by how good business was. She provided a niche service—a concierge service of killers to businesses.

Margaret's black operations had made millions per year in the past five years she had been in business, and she had found a ruthless side she had not known she possessed. She was able to order any elimination her clients requested, and she ordered the same for any field agent who became unruly or too hard to handle. The years of frustration she had experienced in having to treat people with kid gloves due to human rights issues she now dealt with in an instant—a bullet to the head and a shredded file.

The situation she was now dealing with in Alaska and Canada was a problem. Targets were being killed to clean up mistakes, not to advance business. Margaret hated mistakes and hated misjudging people. The clients at Ironstone Investments were turning out to be a poor choice.

She looked at her watch; it was 3:45 p.m. She headed towards her garage, opened the door, and got into her golf cart. She had a bridge game with the girls at 4:00 p.m. and then dinner with some friends at six. She would be monitoring the kill of the professor in the early morning, and so she made a mental note to have only one martini with dinner.

CHAPTER ELEVEN

DETECTIVE MUELLER WATCHED FROM THE window as the plane descended towards the runway at the Deadhorse airport. The time was just past 11:00 a.m. and the plane was late—something the captain did not apologize for. A low, gray light broke to the south and the expanse of the Arctic came into view.

Flat was the word Mueller thought of—flat and white with pipelines everywhere. *Welcome to the Arctic,* Mueller thought. He had never dreamed of coming to the Arctic in all the years he had lived in Anchorage. The barren lands, as the Arctic was often called, had no appeal to him and now here he was, sixty-two years old, a drying-out detective in rehab in one of the earth's coldest places. *Lucky me.*

The plane dropped on the runway with a sudden bang, as if the pilot had missed the part about soft landings in flight school, the reverse thrusters came on, and moments later they were taxiing on the snow-covered runway past a mass of snow banks to the terminal.

Mueller peered out his frost-covered window to see a Quonset-hut-style building that said "DEADHORSE TERMINAL." Beneath the lettering was a smaller "Prudhoe Bay, Alaska" sign. Large buses pulled up alongside the plane, and the passengers got ready to leave. After pulling on their heavy parkas and mitts, they made for the door. The pilot had already announced a temperature of minus forty-five Fahrenheit with a ten-mile-an-hour wind.

Mueller followed Franklin down the steep metal stairs that had been brought up to the plane door. Everyone walked carefully down the stairs—cold temperatures turn steel into ice, the slipperiest damn thing anyone could ever walk on.

As Mueller came to the bottom of the stairs, he could feel his chest tighten; his breathing became shallower from the frigid air. Cold grabbed his lungs and wouldn't let go. It was like someone was sitting on his chest. He followed the rest of the men and women as they made their way to either the buses or the terminal.

Inside the terminal, he could breathe again. He inhaled warm air like it was a luxury. His lungs exhaled the cold, and he quickly took another breath to warm them up. He blinked a few times to let his eyes warm up and focus.

Walking towards Mueller with a grin was someone vaguely familiar, someone out of his past, from his days before multiple rehabs. He realized it was the grown-up Troy Mercury in an Arctic Oil Company Security parka.

When Mueller was sure he wasn't seeing a ghost, he finally said, "Well, I'll be damned. Of all the punk kids I busted back in Anchorage, look who grew up." Mueller almost embraced him but grabbed his hand in a firm handshake instead.

Troy flashed a smile. "Hell yeah, Detective Mueller, I decided to straighten up and fly right after all those shit kicking's you gave me in Anchorage."

Franklin was standing beside Mueller looking faintly amused. "You gentlemen want to clue me in?"

Mueller looked over at Franklin, and with a blushing smile, he said, "Sorry Joanne, this is Troy Mercury. He was a street punk in Anchorage some fifteen years ago, and I busted his ass numerous times. Not sure about the shit kicking's, but I did tell him just before he turned eighteen that the next time I busted him, he would do adult time. So what happened, Troy? You actually listened to me."

Troy smiled over at Franklin. "Hey, the talk he gave me was just enough to scare the shit out of me, and I moved down to Seattle with my aunt, finished high school, and then took criminal justice in university."

"Criminal justice—did you graduate?" Mueller blurted out in surprise.

"Hell yeah, graduated with honors at Washington State," Troy replied. He guided Mueller and Franklin out of the sea of workers and over towards the baggage pickup area, which was a set of rollers that received luggage from a small door to the outside.

"And you never joined the force. Why is that?" Mueller asked. Muller grabbed his duffel and then helped Franklin with her large CSI bag.

"Attitude, Detective, they all said I had the aptitude but not the attitude. I couldn't do enough 'Yes, Sirs' at the end of every sentence, so ten years ago I signed on up here. The pay is double what I'd get on the force, and I got a wife and kids I get to hang with every two weeks for a week. I kinda got to like this . . . know what I mean?" Troy smiled again at Mueller and Franklin, took one of the bags from Franklin, and ushered them towards the terminal exit.

Mueller placed his hand on Troy's shoulder as they walked. "You know, that does sound about your style, but I'm glad you turned out all right." Mueller really meant it, as too many didn't make it off the streets.

They walked past the two coke machines that were the terminal's refreshment center and past the forming line of oil workers shuffling their duffel bags to check in for the return flight to Anchorage. Mueller could see in their faces their exhaustion and their longing to get home.

A set of double doors lead them to the outside and the small parking lot that was full of pickup trucks belching exhaust fumes mixed with the freezing air. Clouds of ice fog rose into the air as Troy lead them to his crew cab truck that read ARCTIC OIL SECURTY. The truck was a black 4x4 with lights, a winch, and a front crash bar. Franklin threw her bag into the back seat and jumped in after it, and Mueller, who would have let Franklin take the front, threw his bag in the back seat as well and got in the front.

Troy drove the truck slowly out of the parking lot, peering through the ice fog made by the trucks in front of him, and then followed tail lights down the road. "Detective Mueller, is this your first time up here?" Troy asked as he glanced over at Mueller.

Mueller unzipped his parka, settled back in his seat, and replied, "Yeah, never been further than Fairbanks for some hunting until now."

"Well," Troy laughed, "let me give you the quick tour; right now we're passing the Prudhoe Bay Hotel, one of the two hotels up here. I've never stayed there, but a room with a bed is about $175.00 a night and I think that comes with some meals—so not bad," he said with a smirk. Troy pointed in the direction of some Atco trailers stuck together and raised on stilts. Snow was piled to just below the small windows, and pickup trucks lined the front of the trailers.

"Now over to our right, we'll be passing one of the largest oil field service camps in North America. You've got Halliburton, Schlumberger, and all the big guys up here to do service, and they all have their own camps." Troy motioned to the expanse as they slowly passed by. The camps appeared and disappeared in the ice fog as they moved slowly down the road. Snow banks lined both sides of the road, and tall posts with reflector lights shone back to indicate where the road was. Troy kept watching the reflector lights to see where he was.

Franklin, who was not interested in sightseeing, mostly because she'd, been there before, spoke up from the back. "Troy, what's the status of the crime scene?" She was leaning forward, her chin almost touching the front seat between Mueller and Troy.

"Well, it's partially intact," Troy said as he took his eyes only slightly off the road to answer.

"Partially…what's partial about it?" Joanne inched further forward in her seat, straining against the confines of her seat belt.

"Well, the female is intact; however, we had to move the male, and—"

"Moved! You moved one of the bodies!" Joanne's words exploded out of her, and had the seat belt not held her in place, she might have launched forward into the front seat.

Troy spoke slowly; he knew he was in deep shit. "Ms. Franklin, it was minus forty-five below this morning with a major wind chill. We also had a polar bear with an active interest in the body, and if we hadn't moved it, it would have frozen stiff, and so would've the men guarding it. We made a decision at 0800 hours to move the body to the medical room; however, the safety officer at Arctic Oil took a complete set of pictures." Troy turned his head only slightly to address Joanne as a large oil rig service truck pulled into the road ahead of them. The twenty-ton, five-axle truck with double smoke stacks belched enough ice fog to obliterate the road. Troy slowed the truck to a crawl.

Mueller looked over at Troy, sensing his discomfort. "What's your take on these deaths? The word I got is a murder-suicide. Did the scene look like that?" Mueller wanted to get a perspective before he saw the scene. Everyone saw different things when they viewed a crime, and he was interested in Troy's perspective.

Troy could not take his eyes off the Arctic road, which was just starting to reappear out of the fog. "You know, Detective, I would have bought that original argument myself, until I saw the blood on the door frame Marc Lafontaine supposedly went out of. Now perhaps the crime scene investigator will find different, but both the chief of security and I think he got help out the door."

"So, you have a killer still in your camp," Mueller said. He shifted again in his seat. The truck's heater was making him too warm.

"Yeah, that about sums it up, and we had a CCTV outage during the time of the killings, which makes one of our security staff a possible accomplice."

"You have someone in mind to interview on that?"

"Oh, yeah. We have two suspects who had access to the CCTV, but the one I particularly would like to get in a room would be Security Officer Cummings, and I would welcome the opportunity to assist you in the interview." Troy grinned over at Mueller.

Mueller smiled. "You know, Troy, nothing would make me happier than to do an interview with you in the room. It would be like old times, except we'd be on the same side of the table."

They both broke into laughter, and Mueller added, "I understand the camp is also in lockdown, and no one leaves until this investigation is finished, is that right?"

"Hmm, yeah that's right, and we have a meeting with the base manager as soon as we arrive. He has some instructions for you, but I can gave you a condensed version if you like," Troy said, turning to Mueller. The road had cleared and they could make better progress, although they still had another forty-five minutes to the Arctic Oil Camp.

"What would that be?"

"Get in, solve the damn case, and let him get back to pumping oil."

CHAPTER TWELVE

DETECTIVE MUELLER'S FIRST IMPRESSION OF the Arctic Oil Camp was that it looked like a Motel 6 on stilts. It was three stories high and had small windows and a low building that served as the entryway. Once inside, he determined that Motel 6 was a luxury compared to the camp. The room he had been assigned was a narrow bed with drawers underneath, a bookshelf overhead, and a telephone three feet away, a desk and chair, and a set of cupboards beside a narrow doorway that led into the room. The entryway had a door into a shared bathroom, and there were instructions posted on the door to lock the neighbor's door before use.

Mueller had been in fishing and hunting camps with more luxuries than this. Troy had led Mueller and Franklin to their rooms, with the "luxurious" shared bathroom, and they had gotten out of their outerwear, dropped their duffel bags, and prepared to meet the base manager.

Troy had given Mueller a briefing on the base manager, a man in his mid-forties named Patrick Kearns. Kearns was considered somewhat of a tyrant at Arctic Oil Camp. He yelled, he ranted, but he met production quotas, and everyone made a lot of money. He was an asshole, but an asshole that made money.

Mueller followed Troy down the corridors of the camp towards the administration offices. He could hear Patrick Kearns long before he saw him. A sound like a bullhorn bellowing from deep in a well reached him almost as soon as they reached the administration floor.

"I—don't—give—a shit—what—the media—wants—you don't—give 'em—fuck—all." Each syllable was pronounced, and set to a staccato rhythm. The air still rang after the speaker had finished.

Mueller rounded the corner following Troy, with Franklin behind him, and they found the source of the voice. Behind a large desk sat the owner of the name plate that read PATRICK KEARNS, BASE MANAGER. Kearns was a big man with big hands, big shoulders, a big chest, and one of the biggest heads with the smallest ears Mueller had ever seen. He thought for a moment that the reason Kearns bellowed so much was because he couldn't hear anything with those small ears.

His desk was piled with papers that showed graphs of drilling rig reports, and the wall behind was a mass of maps showing the Arctic oil field and drilling rig locations and pipelines. Two large-screen computers sat on his desk, and a television screen ran Bloomberg news on the credenza behind him.

Troy made the introductions, and Kearns jumped up from his desk and threw out his hand. "Patrick Kearns, base manager. How soon will you have this mess cleaned up?" He didn't offer a chair to either Mueller or Franklin, and Mueller got the message that this meeting would be brief.

"Well, we have to review the evidence, interview witnesses, and of course examine the victims," Mueller said, almost stammering. Kearns's large head had put him off.

"So, what are we talking about? Late today, tomorrow tops, you'll have this wrapped up?" Kearns said, his eyes bouncing back and forth between Mueller and Franklin, as if the two were going to compete to reply first.

"Well, as I said, this is a crime scene, and we must take care to catalog all the evidence. We may have to call up further personnel," Mueller said. He was not happy that he had won Kearns's competition.

"Crime scene? Crime scene? I thought we had a domestic dispute between a brother and a sister. The brother offs the sister in a fit of who-the-hell-knows what and then jumps out the side door and happens to meet with a polar bear and bam he's done!" Kearns was spitting the words as if he couldn't get them out fast enough.

"We don't know if those are the facts right now," Franklin said. She immediately wished she had said it with her inner voice.

"But, I'm telling you the facts." Kearns was smiling now. Big teeth sprung up in his big head. It was more a grimace than a smile.

"We'll start our investigation and let you know what we find." Franklin reached out her hand, hoping for a quick handshake and a sign that their conversation was over. She wanted to be out of there, and to see what the dead bodies had to tell her. As far as she was concerned, the living were talking nonsense.

Kearns was not letting them go that easily. He ignored Franklin's offered handshake and began waving his big hands, making circles and gestures as if he were painting a picture.

"Look," he said, his hands forming a bracket for the words, "this is simple." He pointed to the desk, hoping they would see the evidence. "We have an argument, a family spat, two people died, and we get back to work." He placed his hands on his desk as if he had made the final platform for his argument.

"I also want to remind you that we are losing seventy-five thousand barrels a day in oil production. My people are in stand down and lockdown. Do you know how much money we're losing?" He looked back and forth between Mueller and Franklin for the answer. It was obvious neither of them had a clue—and didn't know it was a test.

"We are losing over seven million dollars a day!" Kearns yelled the words, as if the very thought of the loss would be unfathomable to them. And, well, it was.

Franklin had long realized that when dealing with people of supposed authority, whom she oft times considered the village idiots, it was best to smile, agree, and walk away and then do what she wanted to do. She smiled at Kearns. "Absolutely, we will have this wrapped up in no time."

Kearns's face broke into a happy smile. "Wonderful, that's what I wanted to hear." He pumped all of their hands in crushing handshakes and dismissed them from his office by getting back on his phone. Troy led Franklin and Mueller out of the office, and they couldn't get out of there fast enough.

"Nice shine job," Muller muttered to Franklin when he caught up to her in the hall.

"Sometime you have to blow a little smoke up their asses," Franklin said.

"Well, that was one major asshole," Mueller said.

"Unfortunately I have seen bigger," Franklin sighed in reply.

They ended the conversation as they caught up to Troy. After a few minutes' walk down several hallways, they ended up at the first victim. Constance Lafontaine's body lay in her room, where Troy and Chuck had found her that morning. Franklin opened her crime scene bag, put on her gloves, and began investigating the body.

She could see that Constance Lafontaine had been an attractive and physically active lady in her mid-twenties. She was about five feet, ten inches tall, with broad shoulders and nicely muscled biceps and triceps. This girl had been to the gym. She lifted her hands and found no cracked nails, no bruises or scratches that would show a struggle. Franklin found it odd that a physically capable person like this would submit to strangulation. The marks from the cord or belt around her throat were still there, large welts turning black.

Franklin always found death by strangulation messy because it took time to cut off the victim's air supply. Victims would usually exhibit signs of resistance—bloodied hands or cracked fingernails. Here there was nothing. It was as if Constance had lain there, quietly, while someone had cut off her air supply and her brain shut down, followed by her heart and lungs.

The answer to the puzzle was on the victim's head—two large bruises, one on each side of her head, just above her ears. Someone had given her a two-fisted knockout blow. The brain would have gone into shock, and the victim would have been unconscious while the life was strangled out of her.

Franklin had seen these types of blows before, but usually in kung fu or karate tournaments. If her brother had in fact killed her, then he had done it quickly. She looked over Constance's face. It was calm, and the iPod music plugs were still in her ears. She might have been sleeping. No argument, no struggle, just eliminated quickly off the planet.

She examined Constance's hands again and found the fingertips odd. They were covered in a plastic—a rubbery plastic that moved as she touched it. *Odd as hell,* she thought as she bagged the hands in plastic bags, wrapped them in rubber bands, and made a note in her journal. Taking her flashlight and magnifying glass out of her CSI case, she checked the contusions on the victim's temples.

"Well gentlemen, someone likes their coffee," she said as she turned to Mueller and Troy.

"Why's that?" Mueller asked, staring over Franklin's shoulder at the body.

"There are circular marks on the victim's temples," she said as she pointed them out, "and I can see the faint trademark of a coffee tamper used by commercial espresso makers."

"Are you sure?" Mueller asked.

"I put myself through university in Portland working as a barista for three different coffee houses. I know coffee tampers well," Franklin said as she made notes in her book.

"How'd the killer use it?" Troy asked, peering over Mueller's shoulder.

"Someone approached our victim, who was obviously enjoying some tunes or sleeping, and quickly rapped both sides of the head with the tampers. The espresso tampers can weigh from a half pound up to two pounds each. A rap on the head with those things would be like having your head in a vice—boom—unconscious." Franklin made a quick motion of her hands coming together.

"And then our victim doesn't struggle during strangulation?" Troy asked.

"That's right, the killer was good, and he or she knew how to put someone down. I say we bag and tag, and after we've collected some evidence in this room, we ship this girl to the coroner's office in the south," Franklin said, packing her CSI bag and getting ready for the next victim.

They walked out of the room and headed down the corridor. There were workers in the hall, some staring from rooms, some in pockets of conversation. Conversations would be loud as they rounded a corner and drop to almost a whisper or silence as they approached. The camp knew through texts and Tweets that the detective and crime scene investigator had arrived. Rumors were flying. Workers were eager to find some information to ease the boredom, and rumors would do—for now.

Mark's Lafontaine's body was in the medical room, still slightly blue from the cold and slightly chewed by the polar bear, with a number of bruises to the head. Franklin looked the body over: the shirt was undone, and there were obvious signs that the bear had started to feed. What struck her immediately was the fact that the body showed no head bites or defensive wounds from trying to fend off the bear. She knew that when a bear attacks a human, it usually goes for the face or head. The bear wants to neutralize anything that could possibly injure it, including human teeth. In the wild, teeth are teeth, regardless of the creature.

Franklin had seen numerous bear victims in Fairbanks. Hands and arms were always involved. No one lets a bear stroll up and start a buffet on his belly. Not if he is conscious. Franklin's magnifying glass and flashlight found the same bruised temples.

"Yep, we got the same M.O.—a rap on the head with the tampers—but there is also a major contusion on the forehead. Looks like someone used this guy's head for a battering ram," Franklin said as she turned off her flashlight.

"Yeah, there was a blood spatter on the inside of the door leading to the exit. That's what led my chief to think this wasn't an accident," Troy replied.

"Well, your chief was right; this massive contusion was enough to kill our victim here. The killer probably performed the knockout blow with the espresso tampers and then used our victim's head as a door opener. He would've been dead by the time he hit the bottom of the stairs."

"So, the polar bear is in the clear," Troy said with a wry smile.

"Yeah, but the bear's probably pissed that someone took away his breakfast. Had someone not looked out the window, our bear would have consumed the evidence. You might have had to identify this guy's DNA from bear shit." Franklin smiled up at the two men.

"So where does this put us?" Mueller asked, looking at Franklin. He thought the talk of the polar bear was getting a little silly.

"Our brother and sister were both killed by an unknown suspect. This was no murder-suicide. We have two murders." Franklin placed the cover back over Mark's body.

Mueller turned to Troy. "This looks like a full investigation. We have to look at shift logs, find out whom they worked with and when, and start to interview everyone they came in contact with.

"I have those logs coming from personnel, as well as a list of everyone who flew in and out with our victims from the time of contract," Troy said.

"So, who's going to give the exciting news to melon head—oops, I mean Mr. Patrick Kearns?" Franklin asked. "I'd love to, but I have some bagging and shipping to do."

Mueller and Franklin both turned to Troy, who broke into a smile. "Hell yeah, you know I'd love to break the good news to him."

Troy's radio came to life. "Officer Mercury."

"Mercury here," Troy answered Braddock as he walked away from Muller and Franklin.

"Do you have the detective and the CSI with you?" Braddock asked. His voice sounded hesitant on the radio speaker.

"Affirmative, I do." Troy looked back and forth between Mueller and Franklin.

"Bring them to the C wing men's room—C145."

"What's up?" Troy asked.

"You'll see when you get here." Braddock's speech was now clipped, irritated.

"You know I hate surprises," Troy answered. Braddock's tone felt ominous to Troy. He felt like a small opening had been made in his gut and reality was seeping out.

"We found Cummings."

"Found him how?" Troy replied. He turned away from the detective and the CSI and moved the radio mike to his ear.

"You'll see when you get here." The radio went silent.

Troy looked up at his two companions and said, "Aw shit, this doesn't sound good. It looks like we've got another party to go to."

They arrived at corridor C, and Braddock was waiting outside the men's room. He opened the door and directed them to the first stall. Jason's body was sitting on the toilet, coveralls pulled down, head rolled to one side.

"The janitors found him here, just as you see him now. The stall door was locked from the inside. We unlocked the door using gloves and haven't touched anything," Braddock said, looking at Franklin.

Franklin could see that Jason's head had dropped far over to the right side and his right hand touched the floor. That was what had alerted the janitors—the odd posture on the toilet. She got out her magnifying glass and flashlight and this time went directly to the dead man's head to look for similar abrasions. They were there: two circular bruises, with the same slight markings of an espresso barista tamper applied with great force.

"Damn, this guy is good to the last drop," Franklin muttered under her breath.

"What's that?" Mueller asked, again standing over her shoulder.

"I said, looks like our killer got the drop on the guy," Franklin said out loud.

"Oh. Same M.O.?"

"Yeah, this killer doesn't deviate. A quick rap to the head for each victim, but this time he snapped the kid's neck for insurance," Franklin said as she motioned to the victim's head. The broken neck was obvious.

"So, you're sure it's the same killer?" Mueller asked.

"Well, exact same instrument applied with tremendous force to the temples, and then our barista killer had the strength to break the kid's neck."

"You know," Mueller said, "I wish you wouldn't call this unnamed suspect the barista killer."

"Why's that?"

"You'll put me off lattes forever."

"Sorry."

"Okay, same implements, strong suspect who can snap a person's neck. You have any idea of what we're looking for?" Mueller asked.

"Well, there is something," Franklin said as she looked again at the victim's head with her flashlight and magnifying glass. "Our killer made a more pronounced blow at the bottom of the tampers than at the top."

"Which means?"

"That the killer is shorter than the victim."

"How do you determine that?" asked Troy from behind Mueller.

"Our victim here is about six feet tall, and the other male victim was similar in height. Our killer strikes harder at the bottom than at the top, which would put our killer at . . . about five foot seven to five foot eight. He has more leverage at the bottom of the strike."

"So, anything else?" Troy asked.

"Yeah, our killer is one stocky little son of a bitch. There are few men who can twist the neck of a victim this size without some meat on their bones."

———

Troy's mind searched through a catalog of faces he had seen at the camp in the last few days, and more importantly, those he had scanned at breakfast that morning. He had already picked out a few possible candidates.

Braddock came up to Troy. "I guess we know who shut off the CCTV feed."

"Yeah, I guess Cummings wins the prize."

Mueller looked up from where Franklin was investigating the corpse. "I assume this was the man you suspected of turning off the closed circuit television camera?"

"Yes," Troy answered. He was pissed that one of his men had been involved.

"Looks like the suspect is tying up loose ends," Braddock added.

"Yeah, and the way he's clocking people with these coffee tamping instruments is getting damn right methodical," Troy said.

The three men stood back while Franklin examined the body further. There was a heavy silence. They all knew the investigation to come. There would be leads, interviews, and reports that would hopefully reveal the killer.

At the moment when the silence began creating a visible tension in the room, Troy asked, "Does anyone feel like a coffee?"

"Hell yeah," Mueller said. He looked at the others in the room. "Anywhere to get a latte?"

Troy replied, "Detective, we have one of those new-fangled coffeemakers that make lattes, cappuccinos, cafe Americano. And the best thing—no tampers required."

Mueller followed Troy down the hallway towards the camp cafeteria. He needed some caffeine and time to think. Murders always resonated with passion, money, or greed, and he was trying to connect the dots on this one. Two people, both working for the same company, murdered by someone, and then a third murder to cover up the accomplice who cut the CCTV transmission. He could feel there was something big behind these murders, a sense that forces had arrived in the Arctic to do something—but what? How would he explain his sense of foreboding to his chief of detectives back in Anchorage, who had sent him to look at a simple murder-suicide? How would he make his chief understand that he wasn't having detox flashbacks when he explained? Mueller sighed as he thought about it. He didn't like his chances.

CHAPTER THIRTEEN

PARSONS WAS LINGERING OVER THE Google Maps page of his target when the phone in his hotel room rang to signal that his cab had arrived. He shut down his computer, grabbed his bag, and headed downstairs.

Almost immediately after the driver pulled away from the hotel, the cab got stuck behind two snowplows and had to dodge heavy oil-rig-truck and semi traffic as it crawled its way to the airport. The driver pulled up in front of the small Fort McMurray Airport terminal at 6:45 p.m.

Parsons wasn't too worried about making the flight. He had only a small bag, and he would be through security in minutes. He saw Fuentes walk into the airport just ahead of him. He paid the cab driver, grabbed his bag, and followed him. Just minutes later, Parsons saw RCMP cruisers pull up in front of the terminal. No sirens, no lights. The cruisers came to a sliding halt in the snow and four officers charged into the terminal.

A big RCMP officer brushed by Parsons, and he could see Fuentes just ahead of him, inching his way into the security screening line.

Parsons froze in place. If they had found the bodies of the two that Fuentes had killed, then they were certainly after Fuentes. *Did they know about his connection to Fuentes? Should he run?* These thoughts raced through Parsons as he watched the scene unfold.

The officers came up behind Fuentes and grabbed the young man in front of him. A woman in jeans, a sweater, and leather jacket came out of the crowd and put handcuffs on the man, who resisted—bad idea. The woman kicked his legs out from under him, and, in the quickest takedown Parsons had ever seen, the man was rubbing his nose on the floor.

The woman hauled him to his feet with no assistance from the officers around her, and they marched the man out of the terminal. Parsons watched her walk by. She didn't look at him—her eyes were focused in the steely determination of one who has made a capture.

Parsons heard one officer say in a low tone as they went by, "Good takedown, Detective Callahan."

The commotion was over; Parsons and Fuentes made the flight. Both breathed a sigh of relief as they sat down in their seats, but neither of them dared to make eye contact or show that they knew each other.

Parsons glanced at Fuentes. He was sitting in the seat ahead of him watching reruns of *Two and Half Men* and giggling. He knew he could trust Fuentes to shoot any target or defend himself. *But will he watch my back?* Parsons wondered. He highly doubted it.

Parsons saw Fuentes as the ultimate asshole and was sure that his asshole switch had been turned on when he was a small child. He figured the asshole switch was left in the "on" position and never turned off. It was just the way Fuentes was wired. Somewhere in Mexico, there was a mother who loved Fuentes, and loved him just the way he was.

Parsons needed to take care of himself. He had ordered a wetsuit from Cordele. He did not care if the others wanted them—too many beach landings had left him soaked or with sand up the crack of his ass that would abrade his butt down two sizes by time the mission was over.

This time, he had ordered the equipment he would need, and he would be sure to maintain the rearguard on the mission. He hated getting shot by his own men. And these would not be his men, just men for hire with guns, the worst possible kind.

The airplane arrived in Vancouver on time at 11:45 p.m. There was a drizzle of rain, and the temperature was just above freezing. Both men were met individually by young Asian women, who led them from the main terminal to the parking garage. They kept the two men separate as CCTV cameras were everywhere.

They were led to a white van with tinted windows parked behind a pillar in the parking garage, out of sight of the cameras. The Asian contacts were young, and Parsons was unimpressed. The three young men were in their early twenties, slim, had long black hair, and were dressed in black Nike track suits. *If Nike ever wants to sponsor some gang bangers, these are perfect candidates,* Parsons thought. *These kids probably live with their mothers by day and run drugs and kill other gangs at night.* He wondered how the mothers got the blood out of their clothes. He did not like Cordele's pick.

They piled into the van and headed south from the airport to the harbor where they would board their boat. *At least they picked a plain white van,* Parsons thought. Had they used some Lincoln Navigator or Cadillac Escalade, there was a good possibility of getting pulled over by the local police. Parsons was only mildly impressed by their vehicle choice.

A half hour later, they arrived at a dock near Steveston Harbour, a small tourist and fishing harbor. The boat was a dark blue Sea Ray 60. Parsons' mouth began watering the moment he saw it. It was sixty feet long, a good eighteen feet wide, twin diesel, and had a fully covered cabin with a beige leather interior. His dream boat. He had always said that when he retired from the business, this would be his boat. He had never been on one. *I can't even afford to look at a boat this beautiful,* he thought, *and here are a group of Asian gang bangers with this beauty.*

Parsons and Fuentes jumped on board, and Parsons put his mind to going over the inventory he had ordered. There was one wet suit, his size. Cordele had not bothered getting them for anyone else, and Parsons did not care. He went below and changed into his.

There was an inflatable zodiac raft with paddles sitting on the deck, ready to be set up when they got across the straight. The Sea Ray had a draft of almost five feet, and they would anchor it offshore, and use the zodiac to paddle to the beach.

The Asians had given him and Fuentes Steyr TMP 9mm submachine guns fitted with sound suppressors and straps. There were also two Ti-Rant 9mm handguns with sound suppressors, extra clips for each weapon, and combat knives with web belts. Parsons was impressed with the choice of weapons. The Ti-Rants had been featured in a past issue of *Combat Handgun* in the USA, and he had not had a chance to get his hands on one yet.

The Sea Ray's engines growled to life, and the boat pulled away from the dock and into the channel. They had no running lights. The boat made its way slowly out of the channel until it came to the open water of the Georgia Straight. The captain hit full throttle and the big diesels launched the boat up on its prow as they sped across the water.

The Coast Guard and RCMP would be out tonight, but the chances of getting caught with all the commercial traffic in the straight would be slim. Steady ocean freighter traffic would be vying for berth space outside of the Vancouver harbor, and running amongst them would be a fleet of small boats, just such as theirs. Some would be carrying the famed BC Bud south, the highly potent marijuana grown in British Columbia and sought after by both Canadians and Americans. Others would be hauling cocaine and methamphetamines north. This was not what the politicians had in mind when they thought of free trade between Canada and America.

Parsons sat at the back of the boat, the cool air rushing by, feeling the saltiness of the sea on his skin. He was homesick for Newfoundland, where he had grown up. He had had an opportunity to go back to Newfoundland when he had returned from his tour in Afghanistan. He could have gone back to sea to fish with his father or run drugs to Maine from Nova Scotia with his old buddies. Instead, he had chosen his present work, or it had chosen him.

His old buddies had offered him a plan: buy BC Bud for fifteen hundred a pound and sell it to the Americans for four thousand a pound once it hit Maine. The guys in Maine would get the dope to New York, where it would sell for eight thousand a pound. It all sounded like a great plan, but Parsons thought there were too many amateurs involved, and too many guns.

He looked up at his three Asian contract killers and saw the same amateur equation with guns. Their names were probably Nguyyen, Pham, or Tran, but they went by Ben, Terry, and Vince. Vince, at the helm of the boat, was not a bad skipper, but Parsons could see he did not feel the boat. He drove it like a car, and had no respect for the sea. He would never have let him captain any boat he owned. He looked up at the sky; the moon was starting to show. He looked at his watch and saw it was 2:00 a.m. They were running late.

CHAPTER FOURTEEN

PARSONS AND HIS TEAM ROWED the zodiac inflatable through calm waves while Parsons gave his companions instructions for the attack on Professors McAllen's cabin

They reached the beach, pulled the inflatable up on the rocky surface, and quietly crept two hundred yards to the bottom of a cliff that sloped up to the house that was their objective. A small switchback trail led to the house at the top of the ridge about five hundred yards up. They stopped at the bottom of the trail, where Parsons instructed them to go up single file and to stop and cover for each other if necessary.

But the two young Asians didn't listen. Instead, they grabbed their submachine guns and charged up the pathway. Parsons had a feeling the two kids were high on something. He would never know. There was a loud sound. It was a sound like earth moving, like fragments going skyward. A scream in stereo came from the two men. Parsons knew that sound. In Afghanistan, it was the sound of an IED; an improvised explosive device.

The darkness rained earth, blood, and something sharp and shiny. Parsons bent down and picked up the shiny fragments—clam, mussel, and oyster shells.

"Son of a bitch, he made an IED out of shells," Parsons muttered to himself.

The next instant, he was hugging the earth. High velocity bullets whizzed by his ears. He could tell from the force of the bullets hitting the earth and from the trees exploding around him that someone up in the cabin above had a high-caliber sniper rifle. His mind went over the candidates for the rifle type and settled on the Barrett M82A1, the most commonly used and available sniper rifle in North America for recreation and the military. He was not pleased he had identified the weapon, because he knew that the presence of this weapon made his potential lifespan on earth very short.

To add to his dilemma, the distinct sound of two M16 machine guns made their familiar sound from the cabin above. Whoever was in the cabin had established a killing zone, and he and Fuentes were in it.

He rolled off the path and inched his way up to the bodies of the two young boys. They had been cut in half by the explosion. He made his way back to Fuentes, who was cowering in the bushes and firing off some rounds of his submachine gun up the path, but it was useless. The submachine gun had an effective range of seventy-five yards. The cabin was five hundred yards away. Fuentes was merely clipping tree leaves with his rounds.

Parsons could see that Fuentes was wild with fear. He was about to give him some instructions for a flanking maneuver—they could go up the cliff, one on the right and one on the left, to take out the attackers—but he never got the chance. Fuentes was on the run, heading for the inflatable raft on the beach. It was a suicide run of the desperate and scared.

Parsons yelled to him to run a zigzag pattern—to at least give the sniper a harder target—but Fuentes didn't listen. He ran straight. A bullet hit Fuentes in the right leg, and his leg spun up in the air as if he had been kicked by a mule. A .50 caliber round will do that. Parsons yelled out to Fuentes to stay still. There was no reasoning with him. Fuentes crawled inch by inch; he was determined to get to the inflatable raft.

The sniper proceeded to use Fuentes for target practice. The left leg, the right arm, and then the left arm. Fuentes stopped moving. The sniper was good. Finally, the kill shot. Fuentes's head exploded as the .50 caliber round found its mark.

Parsons now had a decision to make. His mission to eliminate Professor McAllen was over, as McAllen or whoever was up there in the cabin with the high-tech weaponry had him outgunned. He could wait here on the beach until they finished him off, or he could head for the boat offshore. The inflatable was out of the question, and swimming was his only option.

He wondered how long he could hold his breath underwater. He had practiced free diving in the Caribbean once. That was warm clear water in a relaxed atmosphere. There had been rum on the beach. Here there was a sniper up above, cold dark water and a jittery boat captain offshore. He did not like his chances, but at least he had some.

He peeled off his clothes and threw off his web belt and gun. He was again grateful he had asked for a wetsuit. He decided to leave on the black sneakers as he would need them to manage the rocky beach. Then he started calculating, something he always did in battle when shells were exploding over terrain. He had two-hundred yards of beach to cover, and a two-hundred-yard swim.

He was a fast runner, but he had to outsmart the sniper, as he could never outrun him. What Parsons knew about the sniper rifle was that the bullet traveled at twenty-eight-hundred feet per second, and his fastest run in the one-hundred-yard dash was just over ten seconds. There would be a shortfall—the shortfall would be him.

He scanned the beach and saw some natural cover points—a large rock seventy-five yards away and driftwood just near the water's edge. He needed to get to each without gaining some extra weight: the .50 caliber round. The rounds were a half inch in diameter and five inches long. He had seen the effectiveness of the bullets in Afghanistan. His body would explode into a pink mist if hit. He blocked the vision in his mind and started his run.

He ran a zigzag pattern, which is exactly what he had told Fuentes to do. The first shell exploded two yards behind him, and the beach rock showered him with shrapnel. He reached the rock as a second shell ricocheted off of it. His chest was heaving. He looked at the rock and saw it was a good five feet thick. The .50 caliber could pierce two feet of cinder block and inches of steel, and he had been lucky enough to hide behind a mass of rock large enough to stop the bullet.

His next goal was the large pile of driftwood by the beach. He had another seventy-five-yard run ahead of him. He looked at his watch. It was 3:00 a.m. He knew the full moonrise was at 3:43—he had to get off the beach before the additional moonlight gave the sniper an even better target. He started his calculations again, and this time he factored in the number of bullets left in the sniper rifle.

He was now positive the sniper was using a Barrett M82A1 sniper rifle as it had a ten-bullet magazine. He had counted two rounds in the woods, five rounds in Fuentes, and two had just missed him on the beach. The sniper had one more round before he had to change his magazine. That meant some precious seconds for him while the sniper made the change. Parsons could use all the seconds he could get. But he needed to get that tenth round fired. He took his black balaclava, attached it to a piece of driftwood, and extended it over the rock. He did not take time to feel the blast of air the shell made as it blasted through the balaclava—he was on the run.

By the time he hit the pile of driftwood on the shoreline, the sniper had reloaded. A shell exploded just inches from his heels as he vaulted himself over the wood and found shelter in a hollow of sand made by the sea. The sniper was now in rapid-fire mode. Shells punctured the large pieces of wood as if they were quarter-inch plywood. Parsons could only lie as low as his body would go in the depression in the sand and count the rounds. He forced his mind to count. The shell that almost took his foot off was one. There were six more in rapid succession, and then the sniper did a methodical firing of every three feet, looking for his poor, warm body behind the flimsy wood. There was number eight at the head of the wood, number nine just behind that, and number ten landed just inches from Parson's head. It was time to leave.

He rolled over and over until he hit the water, then made his best imitation of a seal and crawled on his belly in the water until he could submerge. He knew that to swim underwater, he needed to swim slow and relaxed. He took only a small breath in so as not to hyperventilate and create an imbalance of oxygen and carbon dioxide in his lungs. He had learned this in the Caribbean. The last thing he wanted to do was pass out, or have to come gasping to the surface for air.

He was hoping for some light wave action to hide his movements. The tide was starting to come in, which was creating some waves, and he thought the sniper would not find him too easily in the black water. He was wrong. Plumes of water erupted around him, and bullets shot past him underwater. He stopped swimming, knowing that snipers always tracked their targets and then set their sights on where they thought they were going to be. He was right. A bullet streamed through the water just inches ahead of him.

He came up, took a breath, and dived deeper. He knew he could not go deep enough to avoid a bullet, but he was hoping he would be harder to hit in the water due to the angle of deflection. He swam for some forty to fifty yards before surfacing again. He could see the boat; it was twenty yards away. Vincent was running back and forth on the back of it, shouting in Vietnamese. He had no idea who was in the water and was obviously hoping it was one of his gang members. He threw a long, trailing rope into the water.

With every last bit of energy Parsons had, he grabbed the rope. Vincent hit the throttle on the boat, and Parsons was body surfing in the wake. He knew that they had to get beyond the sniper's effective range, which was two thousand yards, and they were at only one thousand yards, in the kill range of any sniper. Plumes of water erupted around him as they sped out to sea, and several shots rang out as they hit the boat.

Parsons held on tightly, trying to keep his head above water, bouncing from wave to wave and trying not to suck in sea water; finally the boat slowed. They were some five miles out to sea. Parsons swam to the back of the boat and hauled his battered body onto the deck. Vincent stared down at him. It was not a welcoming look. Parsons looked at his watch; it was 3:30 a.m. The whole fuckup on the beach had lasted less than one hour.

The supposedly mild-mannered professor had hit them with improvised explosive devices, M16 machine guns, and surgical sniper fire. He had left three men dead on a beach. Parsons had never left a man behind in any operation. He needed to get on the phone with Cordele. Something had gone extremely wrong with their intelligence. He got up off the deck and made his way past the glowering Vincent to the cabin to change out of his wetsuit into his spare dry clothes and to find his cell phone.

In the cabin overlooking the beach, from which Parsons had just escaped with his life, stood Professor Alistair McAllen. He was dressed in battle fatigues and a bulletproof vest with an M16 strapped over his shoulder. He held a pair of night vision binoculars in his hands.

He looked the very image of a field commander. Had anyone done an extensive background check on this mild-mannered professor, he or she would have found that he had done a tour in Vietnam. The Canadian-born McAllen had fallen hard for a lovely American girl in the Marine Corp, and had joined the Marines to be close to her— unfortunately the love did not outlast the war. *Who knew love could lead to war,* he had thought at the time. From the Marines, he had moved to Special Forces.

Three men stood beside him. All similar in age, sixty-odd years old, they had all done tours with McAllen. There was Sebastian Germaine, a small, wiry senior who had manned the sniper rifle with precision. He had just turned sixty but looked a spry fifty. His long, braided hair made him look like a young Willy Nelson. There was Percy Stronach, the demolitions expert, a feisty, thickset man close to seventy who looked like a retired prize fighter, and Theo Martin, with the refined looks of retired banker in his late sixties, who had guarded the flank. He also held an M16. Sebastian was the youngest of the group.

They gazed down to the beach. The Barrett .50 caliber sniper rifle was still smoking. They looked at one another and smiled. It had been some thirty-six years since their last combat in Vietnam. They had all done tours on the Ho Chi Minh trail, raiding Viet Cong supply lines. And they had just now repelled invaders who had come to kill their friend McAllen.

They started to break down their weapons and stow their gear for travel. They would leave the cabin, the bodies, and head for a new location on another island. They knew they had at least a half hour before the RCMP would arrive. The sound of large caliber weapons and explosions would have any smart officer calling for backup. The backup, they knew, would have to come from the cities of Victoria or Vancouver by helicopter. They had time. They would be gone in the next five minutes.

They made their way down to the beach. Sebastian stopped and disarmed the other three IEDs he had made and left small flags so the RCMP demolition squads could finish the job. They checked the bodies of the two young men and then came upon the body of Fuentes on the beach.

"That is some good shot grouping," McAllen said, looking over at Sebastian.

"You know, I'd thought I'd lost my touch, but you know the old saying: just like riding a bicycle," Sebastian replied. He was standing beside McAllen. They looked over Fuentes like they were checking a target on the firing range.

"Hey Mac." Theo came up alongside the two men admiring Sebastian's kill. "This brought back the old feelings, you know, where your stomach goes from ice water to burning fire. I felt the old clarity of battle kick in."

"Yeah, no shit, there's nothing like a fire fight to hone ones instincts," McAllen said.

"Well, it was a little one sided, but it felt good," Theo said.

"Yeah, it always feels good when the other guy dies," McAllen said. He looked up and out to sea.

"Damn straight," Theo said. They moved away from the body and headed for the beach, where they found the inflatable left by their attackers. "Hey let's use this, saves us waiting for Grace to come ashore with her raft." Theo said as he began loading his weapon into the boat.

A twenty-eight foot Bayliner came into view. They blinked lights at each other, and the men dug their paddles in and made their way towards the boat. At the helm was the love of their lives, Grace Fairchild. Grace was in her mid-fifties, five foot five, and nice and round. Her long, once shiny black hair was streaked with gray, but her dark eyes shined as if there were a coal fire burning somewhere deep inside her.

The men had first met Grace when she was in her twenties, a young, Native hippie girl panhandling for change outside a bar in downtown Victoria. The men had washed up on the shores of Vancouver Island after finding America to be less than welcoming after their exploits in Vietnam. They had performed well in an unpopular war. They were spit on, yelled at, and involved in far too many fights. Although they got the best licks in, their police incident sheet grew. McAllen had suggested they chill out in Canada.

Chill they had. The amazing Grace Fairchild, who claimed that her tribe, the Nootka, had been the first to greet Captain Cook in 1778, had been the first one to really make the young ex-military boys feel welcome.

Grace had led the boys from the perils of downtown Victoria to a place called Salt Spring Island. There in a traditional teepee, she began a cleansing of their minds and spirits that would set them on a better path—the one they stayed on for many years.

She started their spiritual cleansing with sweat lodges, and then moved to chanting under the stars and magic mushrooms, lots of magic mushrooms. The young men hallucinated for days, and then Grace brought them back to reality with love. She brought three of her lovely young lady friends into the group and ensured that the young men got laid three to four times a day. To relieve the toxins and get rid of the anger in the Chakras, she told them.

The therapy worked. After a summer of magic mushrooms, good organic food, and getting good loving, the young men let go of their anger and were in love with the entire universe.

McAllen then went on to complete his degrees in chemistry, Theo set up a string of successful oyster farms, Percy became a renowned boat builder, and Sebastian began mixing music for rock stars. They had been saved from themselves, and Grace, was and always would be, their saving Grace.

The men came alongside Grace's boat in the inflatable raft, and one by one, they threw their gear in and jumped on board the Bayliner. They each gave Grace a long embrace and a kiss.

"Well, boys, I don't know what the hell you've been up to, but I do know we need to get out of here fast," Grace said as she looked around.

"What you have seen is the first strike of the S.F.O.S.B," said McAllen, looking around at his old companions.

"What's that?" asked Grace.

"SPECIAL FORCES OLD SONS O' BITCHES," McAllen said with a laugh.

Grace looked at her men, whom she once nurtured. She just smiled that beautiful smile of hers and hit the throttle on the Bayliner. Galiano Island started to disappear in the boat's wake. The four men stood together looking back over the stern. They had done the same in the Mekong Delta in Vietnam—now they were in action again. This time there would be no turning back, no politicians to pull the plug. The game was on.

The line was busy when Parsons first tried reaching Cordele on the phone. He changed out of his wet suit into dry clothes and started looked for his spare knife. It was missing.

His cell phone rang. "What happened?" Cordele asked when Parsons answered.

"How did you know something was up?" Parsons asked. He had a strange feeling about his situation.

"Your Captain Vincent called his boss, said the mission got fucked up and that you left his two friends on the beach. I just got off the phone with his very pissed boss—he wants your blood and one million bucks."

"Shit, this just gets better, doesn't it," Parsons said. He was walking around the cabin looking for anything he might use as a weapon. He could feel the boat slowing down.

"Well, I suggest that when that boat gets into harbor you're not on it, as I don't think you're going to get a good reception. What the hell happened out there?"

"Your professor had one hell of a welcoming party for us—IEDs, a .50 cal sniper rifle, and M16s. We walked into a kill zone. I think your intelligence gathering was about as good as George Bush's in Iraq, if you know what I mean."

"Yeah, I know, it wasn't worth shit. That was more information supplied by those intelligent Wall Street clients. Well, here's the deal, you'll have to be very careful to stay alive in the next short while…you hear me?"

"Hey, I always take the best care . . . when it comes to taking care of me. I'll call you soon, I gotta go." Parsons shut off his phone as he walked further back into the cabin. He needed a weapon, and the cabin had been picked clean to keep it light for drug cargo. In the galley kitchen, he found only one possible weapon: a Chinese wok. The proverbial mainstay of Asian cooking, it had heft, metal, and—*What the hell*, he thought, *it's better than nothing*, which is what he had.

The boat was slowing down more. He knew that Vincent had a plan. He had a plan of his own; it was to not get killed. He looked up the hatchway. Vincent had one hand on the wheel of the boat and one hand behind his back. His handgun would be cocked and ready. Parsons had only one chance to make a move.

He made it in one motion. He shot himself up the hatchway and threw the wok at Vincent in the same move. Vincent let go of the wheel to throw up his hands to fend off the projectile. Off balance, he fell back with the motion of the boat. Then Parsons fell on Vincent, one elbow finding his solar plexus and a fist pounding his forehead to the deck.

Before Vincent could recover, Parsons gripped him by his belt, removed his gun, and threw him overboard. He took the wheel, hit the throttle, and the Sea Ray 60 rose up, the twin diesels roaring to life. He looked over his shoulder to see if Vincent was treading water. He saw nothing in the black water and didn't care. They were five miles offshore, the water was below freezing, and Vincent could survive ten minutes if he had a life vest on. He did not.

Parsons grabbed his cell phone and called Cordele. "This is Captain Parsons calling," he yelled into the phone when Cordele answered. "I am now in possession of the sailing vessel and making waves, my son!" He yelled out a cry of joy, relief, and exhaustion.

"Well done," Cordele yelled into the phone. He then realized it was only three in the morning in his hotel room in Anchorage. "I suggest you get as early a flight out of there as possible, in case the Asians come looking for you," he continued more quietly.

"Aye, aye, Sir," Parsons yelled. He could barely hear Cordele over the roar of the big diesels. "I should be at the airport in about an hour, and I'll take the river channel that's five minutes from the airport, so I shouldn't run into our friends. Did I ever tell you how I hate Asian fucking gangsters?"

"Yes, I think you did mention that," Cordele replied. He could not stop smiling into the phone. He was genuinely happy that Parsons was alive.

"I'm glad we're clear on that. I'll call you before boarding the plane. I believe I'll be on the earlier flight at 0700 hours."

"Good, we need to get this mission back on track," Cordele said. He was rubbing his forehead in thought. He could not believe how screwed up it had become.

"Aye. I'll let you know when I have possession of the activation device and we can light the fire on this sucker and get going." Parsons did not wait for an answer from Cordele. He ended his call, placed both hands on the wheel, executed some masterful, slow turns, and felt the power of the beautiful boat. He felt the spray of the sea, looked up at the moon and stars, and felt alive for the first time in years.

Chapter Fifteen

N<small>O ONE EVER WANTS TO</small> call his boss to tell him he has failed.
Cordele was faced with that task. He knew his boss would be
awake—he always was during missions, no matter where Cordele was in
the world. He dialed the number and was not surprised when his boss
answered on the first ring.

"What happened?"

"Our target had teeth. Two of the Asian contractors and Fuentes
were taken out by IEDs and sniper fire," Cordele answered. He was
studying his hands; there was a slight tremor there. This screw-up could
cost him dearly—perhaps his life.

"Where is Parsons now?" the boss asked. There was excitement in
the voice.

"Headed back to Fort McMurray. He should be there by noon,
mountain time."

"Good, we will need to get control of the device for activation. This
event will increase our client's desire to move ahead." There was an extra
breath at the end of the sentence.

"I would assume so," Cordele said. He was listening hard to his boss's voice. This was the first time he had ever heard a crack in the voice, a chink in the armored smoothness.

"How is our man doing at the Arctic Oil Camp?" the voice asked after a pause.

"Well, he neutralized the security guard, he still has control of the activation device, but he's getting worried."

"How so?" The voice was even and smooth again.

"A police detective and a crime scene investigator are on the site. The camp is in lockdown, and sooner or later, with enough questioning and enough time, tracks will lead to him."

"Yes, we need to get him out of there, or tracks will lead to us. Once the device is active, that should be the diversion necessary to get him out of there. Do you have an idea how you can extract him?"

"Yeah, I was thinking of a low-flying helicopter from Fairbanks—should get me close enough to make an extraction. Is there any special message for our man when I pick him up?" Cordele knew what was coming next. His boss was consistent when it came to human failure.

"Yes, I believe you should do an exit interview," the voice replied in a firm tone.

"I understand," Cordele answered as he listened to the line go dead on the other end. He snapped his cell phone shut. Exit interview was code for a bullet to the back of the head. He had conducted three such exit interviews for his boss in the past. Failure was not an option on a mission, nor was poor attitude or non-compliance with orders.

He walked to his window, opened the drapes, and looked out into the Alaskan night sky. There would be no sunrise until 9:30 a.m. His watch showed 3:45 a.m. He had a lot of planning to do in the next few hours. Planning was his specialty.

He decided he would start his search for helicopter pilots. He always had a list of possible candidates, no matter where he went. There was always someone who would bend the rules for money—usually for a lot of money.

In Palm Desert, Margaret was staring out the window at the desert sky. It was 4:45 a.m., and light would start to break over the Santa Rosa Mountains at 6:00 a.m. She was considering her options. She had had missions go sideways on her before, where a target got spooked or an agent was discovered. This was different. The carnage of the past twenty-four hours was unacceptable. The mission had a very simple premise: install a device, activate device, everyone makes large amounts of money as stocks in oil surge, reverse the device.

Margaret had numerous repeat clients, and her credibility would now be on the line. Although her operation was secretive, there were others in the business as well. People talked. She would have a hard time living this down if she did not maintain control.

She got up from her desk and opened her patio doors. The desert was cool. Two desert doves cooed politely on her roof. She liked their company. She had to decide which plan of attack she would take—pursue Professor McAllen and eliminate him and whatever team he had put together to kill her people, or eliminate her greedy Wall Street boys, who had brought this fiasco on her.

She closed her balcony door. The doves flew off, their wings shattering the still desert night. Margaret decided to make herself some chamomile tea and review her options. She thought that at the moment, things could not get any worse.

CHAPTER SIXTEEN

SYNTHETIC OIL COMPANY HAD GIVEN Barbara Hoffman and Donna Semchuck, fourth year zoology students from the University of Alberta, in Edmonton, a grant to study the small wolf population that was known to roam the oil sands area.

Barbara and Donna were following the tracks of the wolf pack on Friday morning and had left camp at 9:30 a.m. The light was just coming over the horizon, and they were eager to see where the pack had traveled overnight. A radio transmitter had been placed on the pack leader.

The tracks led to a large oil tailings pond that was acres wide. At the far end, they could see the large Synthetic Oil plant, which mined sticky tar deep down in the ground and brought it to the surface. The oil was separated by steam, and the waste water and oil residue was dumped in the pond with a toxic cocktail of chemicals.

The noise of cannons boomed in the distance, an attempt to stop ducks from landing on the toxic ponds. Barbara stopped, undid her backpack, and started to take notes of the wolf tracks in the area. Then she saw them: human tracks. Snowshoes mixed with human footprints mixed with wolf tracks—and then she saw the blood.

"This is weird. You see this?" Barbara pointed to the dark stains in the snow. "There are snowshoe prints here, dark stains here, could be blood, and then look here—we got tracks of someone leaving. Only one track leaves."

"You're right . . . that is weird." Donna brought out her camera and started taking photos. She was adjusting her telephoto lens when she saw the hand: a tiny hand clenched in a fist with the middle finger pointed skyward. It was the middle finger of Alisha Sylvester. Alisha, in one last dying reflex, had made a fuck-you gesture at her killer, at the oil sands companies, and at the disgusting resting place of her small body.

What happened next would make waves around the world. Donna took out her cell phone, zoomed in on the hand, and took a video. She panned from left to right, showed the finger, and then videoing herself, said, "This is Donna Semchuck, at the scene of a crime. Was this done by wolves, or by man?" She uploaded the video to her YouTube and Facebook accounts and then called the RCMP.

The damage was done. Her friends back at the university were just finishing their first morning classes as their cell phones rang, buzzed, and chimed. The fuck you finger of Alisha Sylvester started to make it way around the world.

Alisha's "fuck-you finger" made its way around the university campus in seconds, around the city of Edmonton in minutes, and was the buzz of Canada in a half hour. The social network took over, and poor Alisha, still only known as the fuck-you finger from the tar ponds, had her finger proclaimed in Europe and Asia. It was the finger heard around the world.

Within a matter of hours, CNN, NBC, ABC, and Fox News had marshaled their fleets of airplanes with newscasters to the scene, and the small city of Fort McMurray was inundated with an army of reporters. Alisha was about to do for the tar ponds what many environmentalists could never have done. She was about to get noticed. Her death would cause all hell to break loose.

As the news was breaking, news writers were falling over themselves to determine what the one digit meant. Whose hand? How had the person died? What exactly was this saying to the world? They tried to come up with words that anchors on the nightly news could use to tell the Bible Belt of America the message that someone had left. The writers giggled, then broke into peals of laughter, and then sweated, as they tried to come up with the exact words.

Byron Jacks, a reporter with the *Anchorage Daily Mirror,* took special notice of Alicia's message. Byron was an efficient, hardworking reporter, aged twenty-seven, who loved being a journalist and envisioned that one day he would work his way onto the *LA Times.* He longed for California's beaches, sunshine, and crime beat.

Byron had come from Columbus, Ohio, fresh out of journalism school, with high hopes of going to the big papers. His credentials had landed him in Anchorage, and his stepping stone had become a landing area. Five years later, he was still working the crime beat in Anchorage and he wanted more.

Formerly Byron Jankowski, he had deep Polish roots in Ohio that he wanted to distance himself from. Byron wrote under the name Jacks as he saw himself becoming a famous crime novelist one day, on par with Michael Connelly.

As Byron scanned YouTube, where he found some of his best material, that day, he came upon the fateful finger in the tar pond. *Absolutely beautiful,* Byron thought. What made the video better was the shot of the wolf tracks around the pond. Good headlines sell papers, and when a reporter can link two events together, his or her name gets noticed. Byron had the two events: someone just that morning had sent him a grainy image of a polar bear just about to chow down on the body of an oil worker before being scared away. An informant had also texted him that a women had been killed, and a security guard at Arctic Oil camp.

He was already dreaming up his lead: WHEN ANIMALS FIGHT BACK AGAINST BIG OIL! *Perhaps a little harsh for Alaska,* he thought. *A republican state with roots in big oil. No use pissing off the republicans.* POLAR BEAR AT DAWN—GRAY WOLF AT NIGHT! This sounded better. He liked it. It was a little poetic, his editor might think it a bit too much, but he would float a few headlines past him to see what stuck. He had something to work on. He sat back, looked out his cubicle opening, and got a glimpse of the blue Alaska sky down the hall. He had some phone calls to make.

Byron's main sources of information in Alaskan oil companies were always the human resources directors. They were usually women, usually young, or young enough for Byron to be on their radar. Byron was handsome, in a Polish Brad Pitt kind of way—blue eyes, clear skin, a perfectly formed nose, and a shiny white smile that the best orthodontist in Cleveland could form. His hair was a mass of blond curls that the ladies went wild for.

The lady that Byron had set his sights on now was Della Charles. Human Resources, Arctic Oil Company. Della picked up the phone on the second ring. "Della Charles, Human Resources, how may I help you?"

"Della, its Byron Jacks, *Anchorage Daily Mirror.*" Byron could hear Della's chair creak as she leaned her large frame forward in her chair. The short hairs of his blond curls started to tingle.

"Why Byron Jacks, my lovely little boy. How y'all doing? It's been so long since I've heard your sweet voice."

Some of Byron's curls then started to straighten at the sound of her purr as he knew the cost of information from Della. It was always the same: a large steak dinner at Sullivan's Steak House in downtown Anchorage, and the girl could eat, and then sex at the Millennium Hotel close to the airport. Della was always good for information, but she would drain him of all bodily fluids before giving him the goods.

"So, Della," Byron began slowly, "I was wondering if you had identification on the recently deceased up there."

"Oh, my dear sweet boy, you know I can't give out that kind of information." She almost sounded sincere as she said the words. "I get off for rotation next week. Maybe we can get together then?"

Byron tightened his grip on his phone. He stared up at the ceiling. He needed the information now. By next week, the whole world would know the identity of the deceased as the Anchorage Police and Alaska State Police would be making a statement in the next twenty-four hours.

"Della, my sweet thing," Byron whispered the words, "you know I wouldn't ask you if it wasn't important, and you know what, I'll clear my entire evening for you when you come through Anchorage next week." Byron pounded his forehead as he said the words. He knew he was going to journalism hell, or at least purgatory, for his crimes of passion with Della. He could only repeat in the back of his mind *Los Angeles Times, Los Angeles Times.*

"Okay honey, since you're such a sweet thing . . . let me see . . . yes. I do have a Constance Lafontaine and a Marc Lafontaine. Both worked for Clear Water Technologies out of Vancouver, Canada, and it says here they were brother and sister. Now isn't that sad."

"What about the third murder, of the security guard?"

"Now, honey, that one I'll lose my job over, so you'll have to get that elsewhere. You know you're good, but not that good, honey."

Byron clenched his jaw. He had gotten much further than most other reporters. "So, is it a murder-suicide like the Tweets, or something else?"

"Well, honey, that Detective Mueller and a crime scene investigator are both up here, and what I am hearing from the hallways is murder," Della said. "Oh, by the way, I get in at 5:00 p.m. next Tuesday on the

Shared Services flight. Don't be late, my pretty." And with that, Della hung up.

Byron sat back in his chair. He had something. Two murders and possibly a third he needed to start digging into. He made a note of Della's flight and reminded himself to make an appointment with a chiropractor for the day after. Della was a big girl, with passion to match. He was hoping it would only take two adjustments to get his back into alignment.

CHAPTER SEVENTEEN

DETECTIVE BERNADETTE CALLAHAN OF THE Fort McMurray division of the Royal Canadian Mounted Police received the call regarding the body in the tar tailing pond.

The caller was RCMP Constable Tom Aulander, a sensible young man with five-years' experience on the force in Fort McMurray. "Bernie, we got two victims in a tar pond at Synthetic Oil." Tom was very familiar with Bernadette, and one of the few people who could call her Bernie instead of Detective Callahan.

"I thought we only had one," Bernadette said, speaking between gulps of coffee and bites of doughnut.

"We did a troll of the pond and came up with a second body," Tom said. He was standing near the tar pond and switching his cell phone from hand to hand to keep his hands warm.

"So, what do we have?" Bernadette asked as she wiped the excess doughnut off her mouth and reached for her pen.

"Male, Caucasian, about 6 feet 7 inches tall, maybe 185 pounds," Tom said. He gave the numbers in old school. For the report, he would enter 200 centimeters and 83 kilograms. He knew Bernadette hated metric.

"He was a real string bean. So… any connection to wolves?"

"Well, the wolves could only be connected if they learned to use sharp knives. There are knife wounds on both bodies," Tom said.

"Really? What do the tracks show?"

"Three enter, one leaves—you have to love winter murders and tracks in the snow," Tom replied. He was walking along the tracks as he spoke.

"You find any ID on the victims?"

"Yeah, from the name badges on the parkas, we have an Alisha Sylvester and a Kevin Buckner. They both have ID tags for Clearwater Technologies." Tom was holding the ID badges up to the light. They were covered in tar and oil.

"Okay, thanks Tom, I'll start my search on the victims and on Clearwater. How long will you be at the site?"

"Well," Tom replied, looking around at the several other RCMP officers and crime scene investigators, "I guess until we have the evidence wrapped. It doesn't look like there's much, so should be back after lunch."

"Great, we can have a conference by three or so and everyone can report where we are. Stay warm." Bernadette hung up and entered "Clearwater Technologies" into her computer. A website with some nice graphics came up—pure water flowing. *Imagine that,* she thought to herself. A Vancouver address and phone number was provided. Her first step was finding out who else the victims had been working with.

The oil sands mining operations were a mass of corporate infrastructure. Thousands of employees worked for the hundreds of companies in Fort McMurray, and thousands of subcontractors worked for the oil sands companies. All the companies maintained strict access points to their mine sites and maintained directories of who was on their sites at all times.

To get to the directory, Bernadette called her source at Synthetic Oil Company. Her name was Cynthia Ladoucer, a Fort Chipewyan First Nations single mother of one whom she had become good friends with in her three years in Fort McMurray. Cynthia was in charge of all contractors who came and went on the site. If you wanted a pass to get on the site, you saw Cynthia. If you wanted to keep getting access to the Synthetic Oil site, you never pissed off Cynthia. She was a round, low-to-the-ground, straight-dark-haired girl of thirty-one who was good natured until angered. A black bear and Cynthia would have been good companions.

"Hey Cynthia, how's the shit today?" Bernadette said.

"Hey Bernie, I knew you'd be calling. When the shit hits the fan, you're always upwind, girl," Cynthia answered.

"Hell yeah, you know there'll be blowback on this one." Bernadette was smiling into the phone.

"So, did the wolves do it?" Cynthia asked.

"Hell no, wolves are too smart to eat people. Too much cholesterol—bad for their hearts."

"Ha, Bernie, you know it. So what can I do for you?"

"Clearwater Technologies. I have Alisha Sylvester and Kevin Buckner who worked for them. Do you have anyone else listed as working for them at your site?" Bernadette doodled on her notepad as she waited for an answer—water drops over the Clearwater Technologies name.

"Let's see . . . Clearwater Technologies . . . yep, here we are. I have your Alisha, your Kevin, and . . . here we go . . . Emmanuel Fuentes; he is listed as their driver and supervisor."

"Do you have Mr. Fuentes on your site now?" Bernadette was leaning into her computer screen, entering the name of one Fuentes, Emmanuel into the system—the Violent Crime Linkage System; it linked every violent crime to every criminal in Canada and was the first choice for most RCMP. If Fuentes had done something in the past, he would show up.

Bernadette found it useful to enter any possible suspect into the system sooner rather than later, as she was always amazed at how many hits on felons she would get from the system. Bad guys seemed to do bad things in multiples.

Cynthia came back on the phone. "Our Mr. Fuentes left the site at approximately 1407 hours yesterday and has not come back since then. So, is he your suspect?

"Well, you could say he is a person of interest. Is he billeted at Synthetic Oil Camp or does he have digs in Fort Mac?"

"Ah, you know how I hate it when you go all official on me when the shit gets good. Now let's see . . . says here that Mr. Emmanuel Fuentes has been staying at the Best Western Nomad Hotel and Suites.

"Hey, you know it's the badge, not me. Thanks for the info. By the way, how is your little Ritchie doing?" Ritchie was Cynthia's four-year-old son, who was not doing well with leukemia.

"Ah, you know good days and bad. He just got back from the Cross Cancer Institute in Edmonton and man, I was happy to see the little bugger. Now he's making me crazy with the racket he's causing."

"Well, give the little guy a big hug from me," Bernadette said. "When I get some time I'll bring over some cheap wine, chocolate, and chips and we'll watch some trash TV."

"Hey, sounds good girlfriend. Call me if you need me, 'cause you know I'm always here," Cynthia said.

Bernadette ended the call. She wondered how long Ritchie had, and if he was responding to treatment. The incidents of cancer in the oil sands area appalled her. What really brought the situation home to her were the native murder victims she reviewed. The coroner's reports often showed high levels of heavy metal in their blood: mercury, arsenic, beryllium, copper, cadmium, thallium, nickel, zinc, and silver—all known carcinogens.

Her next call was to the airport manager at the Fort McMurray airport to get the passenger manifest for the past twenty-four hours. Mr. Fuentes was listed as boarding a Westjet flight to Vancouver that connected through Calgary. He had a return booked for that day, but the WestJet liaison informed her he had not boarded the flight in Vancouver. She called the Nomad Hotel, and found that Mr. Fuentes was still listed as a guest but that they had not seen him that day.

Bernadette leaned back in her chair, and her hand instinctively reached for the empty plate her doughnut had been on. She had eaten it. She made a mental note to stop eating crap and eat apples instead. She knew she would never read her note. Back on her computer, she entered the name Emmanuel Fuentes on the All Points Bulletin as a person of interest in the two murders. She also made a special note to the British Columbia RCMP to be on the lookout for him. She would send the picture ID that Cynthia had just sent her.

Her next stop would be the hotel where Fuentes was registered. She had a feeling he would not be coming back to Fort McMurray, so she would see what she could find in his room. She would pick up lunch first though. *Maybe something healthy this time?* She thought.

Parsons had caught the early flight from Vancouver that landed in Fort McMurray just before noon. The snow was just as deep, and the temperature was a balmy minus fifteen degrees Celsius—it had warmed up. He had to move fast. He knew that in time, the RCMP would identify Fuentes's body on the beach and link it with Clearwater. It was only a matter of time before someone went looking for the missing Alisha and Kevin from Clearwater as well.

Fuentes had been smart enough to drop his rental truck off at the airport. That would at least lead them away from Fort McMurray, but it was Parsons' job to make Fuentes disappear. He took a cab back to his hotel, dropped off his bag in his second-floor room, and made his way to Fuentes's room on the fourth floor. The "Do Not Disturb" sign had been left on the door, and Parsons breathed a sigh of relief. *At least the little asshole did something I told him to do.*

He waited until the cleaning ladies had entered other rooms and then slipped into the room using an old credit card in the doorframe as an entry key. *The key of all qualified thieves,* he thought. He never left home without it. The room was the usual Fuentes pigsty. Pizza boxes and beer cans. He grabbed what was left of Fuentes's clothes and shoved them in a duffel bag. The chrome case with the detonation device for the polywater was sitting prominently on the coffee table in the middle of the room. It was supposed to be in the closet or under the bed.

Parsons shook his head in disbelief at Fuentes's sloppiness. He snapped the case closed, left the room with the case and the duffel bag, and removed the "Do Not Disturb" sign. The maids were still in the other rooms. Just then the elevator chimed. The door was about to open on that floor.

He made a dash for the exit door, not wanting to be seen by anyone just outside Fuentes's door. He always had a "just-in-case" program running in his head. He made it inside the stairway door as Detective Callahan came out of the elevator with the hotel's front desk manager, who was telling Callahan what a good guest Mr. Fuentes had been as they walked to his room.

Parsons watched them from a slight opening in the exit door. There was no mistaking the woman. She was the same detective whom he saw take down the suspect the day before at the airport. Parsons felt lucky to have missed her. He realized his chances for luck were slimmer the longer he stayed in Fort McMurray. He padded softly down the stairs to his room, threw the duffel bag of what was left of Fuentes's clothes in his closet, and opened the chrome case. He stood over it, looking at the control dials.

According to his instructions, one click of the dials in the case and the polywater would be activated. The mission would be over. With the

RCMP closing in, his finger was twitching for the switch. He needed to speak with Cordele.

His cell phone rang, he could see from the area code it was Cordele in Alaska, "Hello Cordele," Parsons answered. "The shit is pretty thick down here."

"What's happening?"

"I just emptied Fuentes's room."

You have the case with the controls?"

"Yeah, and I just missed a meeting with a lovely detective lady who was on her way to Fuentes's room." Parsons still felt the fear of his brush with Detective Callahan. He had seen handcuffs on her belt—and they were definitely not sexy.

"Yeah, well, have you checked YouTube lately?" Cordele asked. "That may give you an idea of where we're at."

Parsons went to his laptop. It was still on the coffee table where he had left it. He turned it on and went to YouTube. There, prominent and pointing, was the fuck-you finger from the dead girl of the oil sands.

Parsons let out a slow whistle. "As they say back in my hometown in Newfoundland, we be fucked, me boys!"

"Yeah, the shit is going to hit the fan pretty quickly. Especially when they put Alisha and Kevin together with the deaths of Constance and Mark up here, as they were all registered with the same contractor. Do you have anything that ties you to Fuentes?"

"Not directly. We stayed apart for most of the mission; I made sure I was never seen with him." Parsons scrolled through YouTube as he spoke. The video of the fuck-you finger had over 10 million hits. The world loved it.

"You should be okay for a while," Cordele said, using his most reassuring voice.

"How long is a while?" There was a definite strain in Parsons's voice. He had heard bullshit before. His field commanders in Afghanistan would always say reassuring things when the Taliban had their asses pinned down with machine gun fire. "You should be okay" was always code for "we hope you live through the night."

"I'll speak with our boss in Seattle and see if we can activate the device and get you out of there."

"Soon would be very nice indeed. I dearly love the Royal Canadian Mounted Police, but I've never been their guest and have no need to try their hospitality." Parsons tried to put as much sincerity as possible into his words.

"I hear you. Stay close. I'll have an answer soon." Cordele hung up and walked over to his window. The sun was bright over Cook Inlet, bouncing a blinding light off the ice flows. He closed the drapes. He wanted this mission to end soon. There had been far too many fuckups. The client at Ironstone had given them terrible intelligence. He wondered about the decisions of his boss—he had worked for the disembodied voice on the phone for all these years, and rarely had miscalculations been this bad.

CHAPTER EIGHTEEN

RCMP CONSTABLE CHRISTOS CHRISTAKOS WAS the lone RCMP officer of the Galiano Island detachment. Now, in broad daylight, he surveyed the beach that Parsons had escaped from in the early morning.

Constable Chris, as he liked to be called, had heard the sound of gunfire and explosions in the early morning. All of Galiano Island had heard it. His phone had been flooded with calls, and he did what any level-headed RCMP officer would do in a one-person detachment: he called for backup—lots of backup.

Now on his once-quiet island roamed the Coast Guard, Drug Enforcement Squad, Bomb Squad, and the RCMP Emergency Response Team. Guns bristled. Helmets glistened in the sun. They picked up shell casings, investigated bodies, and performed line-of-fire calculations. Constable Chris felt like an outsider on his own turf.

The sergeant of the RCMP Emergency Response Team only wanted his statement of facts. What time did he hear the gunfire and explosions? What time did he call it in, and whom did he call? The one other item the sergeant wanted—who owned the house up on the ridge? They had determined from the impact wounds on the man on the beach that the majority of gunfire had come from the house.

Constable Chris gave the sergeant Professor Alistair McAllen's name, and the sergeant gave him a nod, slapped his notebook shut, and left him alone. The seagulls squealed overhead, crows and ravens circled in hopes that some of the body parts might be left for them. A single cloud advanced across the sky. Waves lapped rhythmically.

Constable Chris loved his island. He had grown up in Toronto, with deep roots in the Greek community. As he grew older, he tired of being a Greek Canadian. His mother yearned for him to have a Greek wife, raise good Greek children, and live nearby. His sister Lenya meddled in his life constantly. He wanted to just be a Canadian and blend in—watch hockey while drinking beer and catch salmon—simple things.

Galiano suited him well. The island was filled with good people who kept to themselves. A few stolen boats or salmon poachers to chase, but other than that, he had enjoyed good, clean living—Canadian style. The drug smugglers who now washed up on his shores were becoming a problem, however. He would be happier if they stuck to killing themselves out at sea.

He walked back to the lone body on the beach. The body looked Hispanic—dark skin, dark hair, or what was left of his hair. There was a massive bullet hole in his head. The arms, legs, and torso had similar large wounds. The RCMP crime scene investigator was by the body and asked Constable Chris to help turn him over. There very little recognizable in the face. A massive bullet had exited through the forehead and taken most of the face with it.

"What kind of shell does that?" Constable Chris asked the investigator.

"That looks like a .50 caliber," the investigator answered. The investigator was a thin, wiry, balding man in his mid-fifties. He looked like someone who tired of finding bodies to look at.

"Holy shit, that's some massive firepower. We usually get small arms fire—the 9 mm kind around here. Any ID on him?" Constable Chris asked.

"No, I've already checked his jean pockets—no wallet, no papers of any kind," the investigator said. He was starting to pack his examination case to get the body ready for bagging and shipping.

Constable Chris saw the small piece of white paper in the shirt pocket of the body. He pulled it out slowly—an airline boarding pass and seat assignment. Emmanuel Fuentes was the name on the boarding pass for Flight 144, which had left the previous day at 7:30 p.m. from Fort McMurray, and Flight 131 that had arrived at 11:28 p.m. in Vancouver. He showed the paper to the investigator.

"Looks like we have a tourist," the investigator said. He had developed a dry sense of humor from collecting bodies all day.

Constable Chris then did something he was not supposed to do. He opened his cell phone and checked his RCMP All Points Bulletin files for Fuentes, Emmanuel. He should have, by RCMP protocol, handed the information over to the officious sergeant of the Emergency Response Team. The sergeant's name was Tingly; Constable Chris thought it should be Tight Ass. The sergeant was barking out orders to the Bomb Squad, Coast Guard, and everyone else who was within range of his voice. Constable Chris thought Sergeant Tight Ass just liked to hear his own voice.

He walked over to a large pile of driftwood just by the shore as he scrolled through his All Points Bulletin file. There was a hit. The Fort McMurray branch of the Serious Persons Crime Unit was looking for Mr. Fuentes.

He first looked around the driftwood pile—the various teams had now moved up to the house, with the sergeant herding them as they went. He found the number of the Fort McMurray RCMP detachment and dialed the number. After a series of receptionists and other constables, he was put through to a Detective B. Callahan.

"How may I help you, Constable?" Bernadette answered. She was getting ready to head into the 3:00 p.m. conference with the other detectives and constables to discuss the tar pond murders. Her desk was a mess, and she was grabbing papers and her coffee as she spoke.

"Ah, Detective Callahan, I believe I may have found your person of interest, a Mr. Emmanuel Fu-e-n-tes," Constable Chris said. He was squinting at the boarding pass. He was good in Greek, but Spanish had never been one of his strengths.

"You have him in custody?" Bernadette asked. She stopped in her tracks, almost spilling her coffee.

"Well, yes and no. We have a dead body here on the beach at Galiano Island. I pulled a boarding pass from the body that states Emmanuel Fuentes, and from the description of the APB, the body height and weight might be a match.

"Do the facial features match?"

"Hard to tell—a large caliber shell pretty much took off his face." Constable Chris described the battle that had ensued on the beach. "I have what could be your Mr. Fuentes on the beach, and two young Asian males who look like they were impacted by explosives on a trail leading up to a house."

"Sounds like it was quite a party," Bernadette said. She was taking notes and listening intently. "Any idea of what they were involved in?"

"No, but the resident of the house, a Professor Alistair McAllen, is nowhere to be found. The investigators found a large number of M16 shell casings in the house, as well as some .50 caliber shell casings. I would say these boys were effectively repelled," Constable Chris said.

"Did you say Professor Alistair McAllen?" Bernadette asked. She had just been researching McAllen's role as the head of Clearwater Technologies.

"Yeah, the professor has lived here for years and commutes to the university, where he teaches chemistry. Quiet guy—until now, is he of interest to you as well?" Constable Chris said.

"I'm not sure. The professor came up as heading a company the dead guy on the beach worked for. Now it looks like we have more players and fewer answers. How soon until you get some DNA samples on your dead guy?" Bernadette asked. She was looking at her computer screen again, going back to the Clearwater Technologies website.

"I'll have the lead investigator on this scene forward this to you, as well as the rest of the identities as we get them," Constable Chris said.

"So, I take it you're not the lead on this case, Constable?" Bernadette asked.

"Nope, just happens to be my island, my detachment, but not my party," he said with a laugh. They both knew the shit he was going to get for making this call.

"Well Constable Chris Chris-tak-os," Bernadette said slowly in hopes she would get it right, "thank you for stepping up and getting this information so early. This really helps us with our case. If you are ever up here, I owe you a beer."

"I'll tell you what, where you are in Fort Mac it's damn cold, and your mosquitoes are hell in the summer. Drop down here, enjoy some island time, especially in the summer when the salmon are running. Salmon and beer is divine, Detective."

Bernadette flushed at the offer. It almost sounded like an offer for a date. She smiled into the phone and said, "Thank you for the offer, Constable. Your island is now high on my list of places to have salmon and beer. I'll let you know how this investigation goes down . . . unofficially. And thanks again for your help." She hung up and gathered her notes for her meeting.

The tar pond deaths had just developed another angle. Drugs could now be a part of it. She wondered if the chemistry professor and his company were the front for a meth lab—it wasn't that remote a possibility. Having two dead Asian's, who might be members of a west coast gang would add a new dimension to this investigation.

She had also just flirted with a Constable Christakos on the West Coast. She was going to check him out on Facebook later to see what he looked like, and if he was single. So far, the Greek guy sounded cute.

Bernadette surveyed the group of detectives and RCMP constables in the conference room. She never took the lead in the discussions but would relay information as necessary. The RCMP, and this she had learned early, was a male-dominated, testosterone-driven force of easily bruised male egos. To step on them would be at her peril.

She was excellent at her job—and her excellence extended to her navigation of the male RCMP psyche. Much of her intuition she had developed growing up on the reservation, where males dominated as well. Her grandmother had taught her that there was more intelligence in patience than in trying to attain the upper hand.

Bernadette waited for the chief of detectives, Riley Barnstead, to begin the meeting. Barnstead was a postcard Mountie: tall and athletic with chiseled good looks detailed with a trim moustache. He was in his mid-forties and spoke with a commanding voice. He was a good detective, but sometimes his reasoning and intuition were faulty. To make up for this, he often spoke in a resounding, almost radio-announcer-like voice, hoping the resonance would make him more believable.

To counteract his bullshit, Bernadette would drop easily findable facts in his way. Like a child picking up candy on the way to the gingerbread house, Barnstead would find his way to the doorstep of Bernadette's well-drawn conclusions.

This time, unexpectedly, Chief Detective Barnstead asked Bernadette if there were any new developments in the tar pond murders. She knew from him asking this that he had no ideas whatsoever.

She explained about the call from Constable Chris Christakos on Galiano Island and the correlation to their search for the person of interest Emmanuel Fuentes, who had worked with the victims. She provided a brief of the report that the constable in Galiano had given her—a gun battle and the house of a Professor Alistair McAllen.

"How is this Professor Alistair McAllen of Galiano Island of interest in this case?" The chief now had the luxury of lobbing questions at Bernadette's findings. This was his strength.

"My research shows Professor McAllen is the CEO of Clearwater Technologies, the very same company our victims from the tar pond worked for, and if the DNA matches, then Mr. Fuentes as well," Bernadette said. She replied in a nice, even tone, nothing too hurried. She never wanted to seem confrontational to the chief; playing nice always made her life so much easier.

"What do we know of Clearwater Technologies?" Chief Barnstead asked using his deep, commanding voice. He needed to keep the focus on himself as the leader of the meeting.

"I asked some officers at the Vancouver Police Department to do a check on Clearwater Technologies. They have a virtual office on Richards Street, where their telephones are answered and mail is delivered. The office was set up some six months ago, but no one from Clearwater ever showed up there, according to the people who ran the place," Bernadette said.

After reading further into her notes, Bernadette added, "Synthetic Oil, which Clearwater worked for, was given to them as a substitute contractor by another company that couldn't show . . . a Waterflow Technologies out of Houston."

"Has anyone checked with Waterflow in Houston, on how they know the Clearwater people?" Barnstead asked.

"Yeah, I did," Bernadette said. She was looking down over her notes. "Waterflow originally said they had contracts in both Alaska and Fort McMurray to solve water purity problems. They somehow got busy and had to subcontract, and Clearwater was recommended to them. They were vague about who recommended Clearwater."

"You think they got bought off? Like maybe given a big fee to let in Clearwater?" Constable Tom Aulander asked. Tom had a knack for putting things together.

"Well, with the number of bodies we have, there seems to be a lot more than water purification going on here. Contractors usually don't get murdered for doing a poor job. They usually get fired—at least up until now," Bernadette said.

Tom then gave a report of the condition of the two bodies found in the tar pond. The disappearance of the suspect Emmanuel Fuentes and the coroner's initial report that the cause of death was stab wounds to the thorax causing a mass of bleeding and suffocations.

Chief Barnstead took over the meeting again. "Okay, this is where we are. Callahan, get the Vancouver crime lab to process the DNA on our suspect in Galiano and see if we have a match. Let's find out more about where this Professor McAllen comes into the picture. We need to make a statement to the media in about a half hour on these murders, as two of the victims were American citizens. I think that about wraps it up." The chief stood up and scanned the room, and beamed "Good work," and walked out of the room.

Bernadette sat looking at her notes. The rest of the detectives and constables were getting up and leaving. She realized that the chief had missed the obvious once again. What were the Clearwater contractors doing at Synthetic Oil and all of the other sites that they had been to?

If this was about drugs, why had they not found traces in Fuentes's room or traces with the two young Americans in the tar pond? She needed to get a hold of Cynthia at Synthetic Oil and ask some more questions.

In Anchorage, Chief of Detectives Wilson was looking at his watch. It was 2:30 p.m. on a Friday, and he had wanted to be off early to watch his grandson's hockey game—he was not happy. He had not had a good bowel movement in three days or a good sleep in four nights. When he was a younger man, he could eat like a horse, shit like a steer, and sleep like a log.

Now, sixty-plus years had caught up to the chief. His stomach gurgled. He looked down at it in hopes that the gurgling might be the prelude to a good bowel movement. False alarm—he passed gas so hideous that it made his nose want to be elsewhere. He had heard rumors that his office had been nicknamed "the Gas Chamber." Deep inside, he knew that the rumors were real. So was the smell.

He coughed, shifted in his seat, and went back to reading the report from Detective Mueller that he had just received. The report pissed him off. He had sent Detective Mueller to Prudhoe Bay to get him out of his hair and deal with a simple murder-suicide, just a couple Canadian kids bringing their quarrel to Prudhoe Bay. That would have been simple.

Instead, Detective Mueller had sent a report of multiple murders by a suspect still at large, with a murder of a security guard thrown in. This was not good. He now had to have a press conference. The good people of Anchorage had sons, daughters, husbands, and wives up in Prudhoe Bay. He needed everyone calm; a killer on the loose in Prudhoe Bay was bad for business—everyone's business.

As he thought about the press conference he had to give, he realized the angle he could use. The two murder victims were, after all, Canadian, not American, and of course not Alaskan. The security guard, well, he was a Californian. *Okay, well a Californian is an American, but not an Alaskan,* he thought. He would push that angle. *These foreign elements brought their troubles with them to Alaska, and alas, they have been extinguished.*

He wasn't sure how that would play out, but he would mention that three had been murdered and the investigation was pending. There were various suspects, and they would have more to report soon. He decided against mentioning any company names, as he wanted to protect the oil companies, and also decided he would make the statement, answer no questions, and head out the back door for his grandson's hockey game.

His stomach rumbled again, and he headed for the door. This time he was hoping he might have the real thing instead of a gas attack. As he walked down the hallway, all the detectives and police officers gave him room.

CHAPTER NINETEEN

BYRON WATCHED CHIEF WILSON WALK into the Anchorage Police Department media room flanked by police officers and several detectives. The media room was simple: the American and Alaska state flags behind the podium, a few pictures of past and present Alaska governors on the walls, and rows of the hardest seats the police could find for the reporters to sit on while they asked their questions. Someone had had the bright idea to make it as uncomfortable as possible in the room to keep the interviews shorter. Sometimes it worked.

Chief Wilson looked pissed off and couldn't hide it. He was 5 foot 7 and a hefty 260 pounds. His barrel chest led to a keg-sized waist, and somehow his pants held on for dear life. It seemed that every wrinkle in the world had come to rest on his face. His forehead was a mass of wrinkles that weighed down on his eyes and then draped down to two jowls that would have looked better on a bulldog.

The chief's various nicknames ranged from Bulldog to Wrinkles, and some journalists called him Stinky. But those names would be used in the safety of Fletchers Bar at the Captain Cook Hotel and never repeated in earshot of the chief or other police detectives—not if they wanted to be invited to media briefings ever again.

Byron sat in the front row, wedged in amongst the TV, radio, and other newspapers reporters. The room was packed. This was the big story for the weekend. Every TV station had their cameras rolling, and on his left a pushy little reporter from *Haines Valley News* was elbowing his recorder in Byron's face.

On Byron's right was the very pretty TV reporter from the leading Anchorage news station. She was a petite redhead with flashing blue eyes that could stare an interviewee down as a cobra would a mouse. People were mere putty in her hands when she thrust her mike in front of them. Byron hated her but continued to sleep with her. They used each other for ego support, and stole stories from each other without shame.

The chief of detectives brought his full frame to the microphone and raised his eyebrows above it. His forehead broke into a frown. One wrinkle followed another as they collided into his receding hairline. He adjusted the microphone and it let out a squeal of feedback. Then he tapped it hard a few times. Just to annoy everyone.

"Good afternoon," he finally said. His voice was just above a growl. "I will be brief. In the past twenty-four hours, we have had three homicides in Prudhoe Bay. We have identified the victims as a Miss Constance Lafontaine and a Mr. Marc Lafontaine, who were brother and sister, and from Canada. We also have identified a Jason Cummings,of Bakersfield, California."

The chief adjusted the microphone again, got it to let out another screech of feedback, smiled to himself, and continued his address. "At this time, the perpetrator of the crime is unknown; however, we have numerous detectives and officers on the scene following various leads. As we have more information, we will make it known. As of now, we have no further comments."

The chief closed his notebook, looked left and right, and made his hasty exit from the room. The pretty redhead rocketed out of her chair with a series of "What about . . . , just one statement . . . could you clarify . . . ," but to no avail. Her words bounced off a chief hell bent on getting out of the room.

The reporters sat in silence. They had nothing to fill air time or columns with. They would have to do commentary, no interviews, and their editors and production managers would hate it. They nervously stared at one another. This was going to be a black Friday for news reporters.

Byron could not be happier. "No comment" was what he was looking for. He had the story, he had the connections. He had an exclusive, a reporter's dream. He smiled in a knowing *what-an-asshole* kind of way at the exiting chief and excused his way past the pack of reporters. He gave a special smile to the redhead. She was seething like a redheaded cobra, her hair flaring out.

Byron had a phone call to make. He had watched a Canadian Broadcast Corporation news report just before coming to the press conference. The broadcast was from Fort McMurray, where Chief of Detectives Riley Barnstead, with the RCMP, had made a statement about the deaths in the tar ponds.

The Canadians were more factual. They had named the two victims: Alisha Sylvester and Kevin Buckner, both from Santa Fe, New Mexico, and American citizens. They had named the company they worked for, Clearwater Technologies, and had stated that it was owned by Professor Alastair McAllen, who was now a person of interest, whereabouts unknown.

Byron had had his *holy shit* moment when he heard the mention of Clearwater Technologies, the same name that Della had given him. Five murders linked to one company all in the space of twenty-four hours across the space of thousands of miles. In news, Byron had learned, there are no coincidences—only dots to be connected. His job was to draw lines from one dot to the next.

From the moment Byron had spoken with Della and until the press conference, he had been on his computer. What he had turned up on Clearwater Technologies was vague. He wondered how they could have received a contract based on the information available on the web. There had been no reference to any other work they had done, nor did they show an organizational chart. There had been only one name— Professor Alistair McAllen, CEO.

While researching Professor McAllen, he had come across the term polywater. From what he could tell, it was harmful to the oil industry. Delving deeper into McAllen's history, he had found the lawsuit that McAllen had brought against the oil companies down in Baytown, Texas, many years back. He and his wife had claimed their two sons died from leukemia, a cancer they had argued was caused by the refineries' oil by-products.

That's when Byron had had his second *holy shit* moment. The connection of the dots was McAllen—the deaths all lead back to him. Somehow, the people who had died were involved in sabotaging the oil fields. They had to be. He could feel it. The dots were linking up and snapping the story into place.

He hurried out of the police station to his car, a Toyota Solara two-door convertible that he hoped would be his ride in California; it was great in Alaska for about four months of the year. The rest of the time, he got stuck in snow or froze his ass off. But he looked good in it.

He slammed the door, looked around to check if any other reporters were coming out of the police headquarters, and made his phone call. It was 3:00 p.m. Anchorage time. He was not sure what time it was in Fort McMurray, but he was hoping Barnstead was still there.

He asked for Barnstead first, but the chief had left for the day. The polite receptionist asked if he would like to speak to one of the detectives on the case. Byron agreed. He needed a quote, a comment, anything to tie the murders in Alaska and Canada to Clearwater. He was greeted by a less-pleasant-sounding Detective Callahan.

"How may I help you?" she asked. She had been informed by the receptionist that a reporter from the *Anchorage Daily Mirror* was on the line. She was curious as to why a reporter from Alaska would be calling.

"Well, Detective Callahan," Byron began, "perhaps we can help each other." He loved saying lines like that to the police. He knew they would be put off by it, but it made him feel all warm inside.

"Did you know," he said "that we have had three murders in Prudhoe Bay at an oil company work camp in the past twenty-four hours, and two of those murdered were employed by Clearwater Technologies?"

There was silence on the phone. "Are you still there, Detective?" Byron asked.

"Yes . . . yes I am. You have confirmation of this?" Bernadette finally asked. "Does the Anchorage Police have anyone in custody?" She tapped her pen, waiting for the response.

"The suspect or suspects are still at large, but somehow, two Canadians and two Americans, who worked for the same company, died, under suspicious circumstances, and within hours of each other. Does that not seem odd to you, Detective?" Byron was now fishing in big waters and going for the kill.

Bernadette didn't answer Byron's last question, so he decided to drop his little bomb of information. "Did you know that Professor Alistair McAllen, who is the CEO of Clearwater Technologies, has invented a product called polywater and has gone on record as saying this invention would be detrimental to oil companies?

"In fact, there is every reason to believe that Professor McAllen is a terrorist. He is also on record for suing oil companies for the deaths of his children—who, he claims, died of leukemia!" Byron made the last statement in the most emphatic voice he could, and then let the phone crackle with the tension.

Bernadette was stunned by the information. She had only just begun to look into McAllen, and she had missed Cynthia at Synthetic Oil to find out what the young Americans had been up to. Their work logs would show their movements at each site, and someone would know what systems they had been putting in place. She needed to get this reporter off the phone and get to work on her own investigation. The links were starting to form. This was no longer a drug-related crime.

"I have no knowledge of that information, and our investigation is ongoing," Bernadette said, using standard RCMP text. The unofficial term for this was *mushrooming*—keep them in the dark and feed them shit.

"Would you have any comment to make to the *Anchorage Daily Mirror* about the links between these four deaths and Clearwater Technologies, a company owned by Professor Alistair McAllen?" Byron asked. He had finally sprung his trap. This was the print that would hit the streets of Anchorage the next day.

"No, no comment . . . as I said . . . this investigation is ongoing and we have no comment at all," Bernadette blurted out. She hung up the phone. Part of her wished she had never taken the call. She knew the reporter would quote her, and he would use his preamble and her "no comment" to his advantage. But the information about the deaths in Alaska was invaluable. She knew Chief Barnstead would see that, but only after he hit the roof a few times.

In the parking lot, Byron stared into his phone. His digital recorder was by his side. He couldn't get the smile off his face. He placed a call to his editor and told him he was coming in with one hell of story—one probably in need of a front-page header. He had warm thoughts of LA.

Bernadette sat at her desk, reviewing her options. The information concerning Professor McAllen being a possible terrorist was a major concern. Where to take the information was another matter. She knew it should go straight to her commanding officer.

It was 5:30 p.m., and her boss would be at his usual Friday night place. He started with an early dinner at either a pizza or Chinese restaurant and then headed home to his big screen TV to watch NBA basketball. Barnstead was a diehard Toronto Raptors fan. He had mentioned twice that day that they were playing the Boston Celtics that night. Barnstead did not like to be contacted at home unless they had solved a major case, or had started a new one.

If she contacted him, and this turned out to be a dead lead, there would be a major shit storm. If this crime turned out to be a possible terrorist plot, and she did not contact him, her ass would be grass, and Barnstead would be the lawnmower.

Threats of terrorism or possible attacks on the oil industry were handled by the Canadian Security and Intelligence Service (CSIS), the American equivalent of the Federal Bureau of Investigation. There was a CSIS branch in Edmonton, but getting them involved would take time. She wondered how much time they had.

Bernadette had a more home-grown solution in mind, one that was her trademark in her work—she would reach out to her local help. Pierre Beaumont, the director of security for Synthetic Oil, was the person she had in mind. Pierre and Bernadette had a little bit of history together. There was a quick "hook up," some 6 months ago. A mutual attraction, a weekend in Vegas, then work got in the way. Neither of them were sure how to end…they just let their relationship slip away.

Pierre answered her call. "Well, the illustrious Bernadette Callahan, to what do I owe this honor? I've been grilled by one of your detectives regarding Synthetic Oil Company and the tar pond murders, but I would welcome a grilling from you."

Bernadette cringed at the greeting and wished caller ID had never been invented. "Hello, Pierre, no I won't be giving you a grilling, but if ever you should need one . . ." she let the last words hang for a moment. "So, on a more serious note, I received a call from a newspaper reporter in Alaska. He claims he has confirmation that two murders up in Prudhoe Bay are linked to Clearwater Technologies."

"Linked how?" Pierre had lost his flippant tone.

"He claimed that both the victims were employees of Clearwater Technologies, and he also claimed that Professor McAllen, who owns Clearwater, has developed a way to make water heavy—as in making it into polyester. The reporter went so far as to infer this McAllen is a terrorist. How am I doing so far?" Bernadette paused.

"You have my attention," Pierre said. "So what else did he have on this McAllen?"

"Well, according to the reporter, McAllen was involved in a lawsuit against oil companies for the deaths of his children."

"Shit, how did we miss this?" Pierre asked.

"Clearwater was a subcontractor for another company from Houston that was hired for the job but claimed it couldn't take it on due to time constraints. They were contracted up in Alaska as well. We'll probably report this coincidence to the FBI in Houston, but right now I think we need to address our own backyard." Bernadette was typing "Professor Alistair McAllen" into her computer as she spoke; she needed to find out more about him.

"Bernadette, thanks for the heads up. I'll get operations on this right away. We'll have to shut down all of Synthetic Oil and any other oil sands operation that these people were involved in. If they've tampered with anything, we don't want the plant operating in case it goes live." Pierre was scrolling through his phone contacts as he spoke. He was about to unleash a shutdown that would cause a panic in North American oil, but it was his prerogative—his ass was on the line if Synthetic Oil was compromised. Explanations to a bunch of suits in a boardroom in Calgary would come later—he hoped he was right.

"Hey, you're welcome. I hope this turns out to be nothing, but you know my motto—cover your ass."

"You're right, CYA is always a good policy," Pierre said.

"You got it," Bernadette replied and hung up. She had more digging to do, and calling the police in Alaska was now on her list. Her stomach growling told her she had missed dinner. Her doughnuts were long gone, and she had a few hours of work to go. She reached in her drawer, pulled out her stash of gummy bears, and then picked up her phone again to start dialing.

Pierre stared out his office window after hanging up the phone. His office was in downtown Fort McMurray, and from the sixth floor, he could see the lights of traffic returning from the oil sands mining operations back into town.

Pierre looked older than his forty-two years. Wrinkles of worry had shown themselves around his eyes five years back, and his dark black hair was turning prematurely gray and thinning both at the hairline and center of his head. The early ageing had coincided with the year he became director of security with Synthetic Oil Company and moved to Fort McMurray.

He had started in the security industry as a consultant, fresh off a ten-year stint with the Canadian Military Intelligence Corps. The pay had been great, the accommodations good—no Quonset huts or canvas tents in Bosnia or Yemen or dealing with armed factions shooting at him.

The oil sands were different. Pierre had to deal with Greenpeace, and any other organization that saw fit to launch a protest at one of the oil sands sites. Greenpeace protestors had breached security at other plants and chained themselves to trucks. They had showed up to protest a tailing pond pipeline. They made themselves into a security and public relations nightmare. Pierre often longed for his days back in the heat of Yemen. He knew who the bad boys were, and if protesters ever showed up anywhere, the protesting never lasted for very long. Lawyers were few in the sand dunes.

Pierre picked up his phone and called Lance Gregory, the vice president of operations. Lance was a real prick—obstinate, opinionated, and officious, but in a crisis, there was no one better. Pierre called

Lance's cell phone. He knew he would get hold of him. In the oil industry, people did not answer their cell phones only when dead. They slept with them.

Lance picked up on the first ring. "Lance Gregory, operations." He said it as a statement, not a greeting.

"Lance, Beaumont here. I'll be quick. The tar pond murders look like the prelude to a terrorist attack on our plants. I need your engineers to shut down the plants and examine everything that a company called Clearwater Technologies installed in the past three months." Pierre waited for the reply he knew was coming.

"Fuck! Who let the pricks in there?" Lance yelled into his phone.

"That's for another time. Right now, I need the technicians and engineers going over every inch of the plants looking at what these people installed. If they've put anything in place to damage our plants, we need to get at it."

"Okay, I'll have the plant engineers on it yesterday. I just hope the fuck you're right—know what I mean?"

Pierre knew exactly what Lance meant. The costs to the oil sands were going to be enormous. Just their plant alone shipped six hundred thousand barrels a day south. At a price of one hundred dollars per barrel, it was a sixty-million-dollar-a-day loss for every day the oil stayed where it was. Five more plants could be in danger. He was either going to get another raise for saving their collective asses or have his ass handed to him.

CHAPTER TWENTY

THE STOCK TRADERS AT IRONSTONE Investments had one eye on their screens and the other on the breaking news on CNN. Another screen was tuned to Bloomberg Investment News. The room was dark; the multiple screens provided the only light they needed.

The finger from the tar ponds broke onto the news at noon. The traders who traded oil commodities knew instantly what to do—they started shorting shares in Synthetic Oil stock, basically betting that the stock would drop. And they had little grins on their faces when the stock did just that. They didn't care about someone's death—they were making money.

Other traders in the room were betting that demand for West Texas sweet crude would rise over Alberta crude. There were always sentimentalists in trading, but a good trader took feelings out of trades. "Trade with your balls, not your heart," some said.

Duncan and Randall watched the traders from behind a one-way window in Duncan's office. They felt like bystanders at the scene of an accident. An accident they had caused. Duncan's phone rang; he could see by the number it was the black ops contact from Seattle. He gave Randall a look of sheer disgust as he punched the intercom button.

"Gentlemen," the voice on the speaker began, "I will get right to the point. We need to detonate the devices immediately. My people are in a compromised situation."

Duncan hovered over the phone. His forehead turned a bright red as a gauge of his anger. "I would say compromised is putting it mildly. The whole fucking world knows something has happened. What happened to Professor McAllen? Has he been dealt with?"

A slight pause on the phone was the only indication that Duncan's words had any effect on the speaker. "Your professor has escaped," the speaker said, and then, in a more commanding tone, continued, "I wish to report that your Professor McAllen mounted a sophisticated attack on my men. I do not know where you received intelligence about this man, but we found anything but an unarmed professor."

Duncan turned his glare from the phone to Randall. Randall needed to deflect Duncan's wrath.

Randall leaned forward into the speaker phone. "So where is McAllen now?"

"That is of no concern at present. You need to activate the devices and my team needs to leave the area. We will deal with McAllen after the primary mission is accomplished."

Duncan hit the mute button on the speaker phone, and his eyes narrowed as he focused on Randall. "You dumb ass. You brought Professor McAllen and this bullshit project to my door!"

He hit the mute button on the phone again. "Can you give us until the end of the trading day Monday? We're not in position yet with some of the contracts and stocks we need to purchase." He glared at the phone while giving Randall side glances. He did not know where to place his anger the most.

"Gentlemen," the voice continued in an even tone, "you will not have any time if my team is discovered with the activation devices."

Duncan now placed his gaze firmly on Randall. He now knew whom to hate the most. Through clenched teeth, he barely articulated, "Very well then. Activate."

"Thank you, gentlemen. It has been a pleasure doing business with you. I will monitor the events and let you know when the team will be traveling back to the area to set the second set of devices." The voice hung up.

The silence in the room was deafening. Randall stared at the speaker phone, hoping it had a portal that would transport him from the room and the wrath of Duncan Stewart.

Duncan's forehead was turning brilliant shades of red. If he were a thermometer, he would have popped. "Do you know this fuckup will potentially cost us millions of dollars?" He was holding both sides of the desk. His knuckles had turned white.

Randall's head snapped up from the phone. His eyes focused on Duncan, as if he had just seen him. "We will make it back when we reverse the process. I assure you that this will work." He steadied his gaze.

"What about McAllen?" Duncan asked. He was starting to breathe heavily. The heavy breathing combined with the bright crimson forehead made him no longer look like a scary figure—just a figure who looked scared.

"McAllen escaped, sure, but he's on the run. There's no way he'll mess with these black ops guys. These guys are pros. He probably got off a lucky shot—the element of surprise. That shit happens. We got this thing. We have the device that controls the polywater." Randall was talking fast. He was trying to convince Duncan as much as he was trying to convince himself. He could feel his existence hanging in the balance of this project. He had never felt so exposed, so vulnerable.

Randall stared up at Duncan. He was looking at his fierce gaze, waiting for him to throw him out of his office, which would be an escape. The tension in the room pressed down on him like a vice.

Duncan finally broke the tension. "We have one hour of trading left today. See what positions you can get before today's close." Duncan turned his back and walked over to his computer screens; commodities, stocks, futures, bonds streamed across the screens. He was no longer in command of events; he no longer had the oil men by the balls. His balls were now in a vice, and he didn't like the feeling. He adjusted his pant leg.

Randall walked stiffly to the door, fumbling the knob with his clammy hands. He somehow made it to his office. Rivulets of sweat proceeded slowly inside his shirt, making their way past his waistband and down to his shorts. There was no mercy. The sweat was bathing him.

In his office, he closed his door, turned the lights low, and breathed in deeply; he closed his eyes and tried to relax. When he opened his eyes in the sanctity of his office, there on the television was the full-screen view of Alisha Sylvester's finger. The finger was pointing at him. He could hear it, and it had a voice. It was saying, "Fuck you, Randall Francis, you caused all this." And he knew he had.

Margaret considered the problem of Professor McAllen. She wanted him found. The decision of what to do with him would be hers. She made a list of assets that she would utilize in the hunt on a legal pad on her desk, including her two computer geeks in Boulder, Colorado.

In a very fashionable condo in Boulder, Frodo and Freddy had a mass of computers that they used to tap into the surveillance satellites of the NSA, CIA, FBI, and the US Customs and Border patrol. Margaret would get them to tap into the big Kennan "Keyhole-class" reconnaissance satellites and look at each one as it passed Galiano Island. McAllen's boat might be somewhere in the traffic of fishing boats and freighters. They knew what time Parsons had escaped from the beach. Now they would look for any boat that had left the area after that.

Margaret looked out her window. The Santa Anna winds were blowing the palm trees. A hummingbird came past her window for a final pass at the flowers—his nightcap, she liked to call it. She looked back to her notepad and added one last note: "Decide what to do with the clients at Ironstone." She put her notebook away; it was time to meet the girls at the clubhouse for martinis.

CHAPTER TWENTY-ONE

PROFESSOR ALISTAIR MCALLEN AND THE SFOSBs were sitting in a large room in a six-bedroom cedar log cabin perched on a secluded island some three hours by boat from Galiano. They had chosen this new site for their operations some three months ago—McAllen had forecasted that things might get *hot* in their mission—he had been right.

Their new home overlooked a channel from a sheer drop of granite cliffs. A winding pathway led down to the boathouse, which hid the thirty-eight-foot Bayliner that Grace had picked them up in the previous night. Computer terminals in the large living room were linked to satellite dishes hidden in the trees. A lazy spiral of smoke curled out the chimney, and an Irish wolfhound sprawled in front of the doorway outside.

Theo had found the cabin some months ago, Percy had built an addition to the boathouse that was big enough to conceal the Bayliner, and Sebastian had installed the technology they needed in the cabin: computers and software that tracked satellites, and decoders, analyzers, and tracking devices that gave them all eyes and ears all over the planet. Sebastian had been a techno geek before it became a catch phrase in the twentieth century.

Sebastian's other hobby besides mixing music (he had worked with the Grateful Dead, Janis Joplin, Stevie Wonder, and half of the other wonders of music that were now either dead or retired) was "spy stuff." He had started quite simply, when he suspected one of his wives, in his multitude of marriages, to be cheating on him. The more he implemented high-tech spy apparatus, the more obsessed he became with learning about it, until he had bugged his cars and every room in his house. He was finally left watching only himself to see if he could catch himself doing anything weird. All his wives had left him.

Sebastian had had McAllen plant a tracking and listening device into Randall Francis's cell phone the first time he visited Galiano. He had then listened in on Randall's every call and had traced all the calls. They soon had the black ops contact in Seattle, Cordele in Anchorage, and Parsons in Fort McMurray.

To ensure that they had eyes on the ground, they had enlisted two of Grace Fairchild's nephews. One was in Arctic Oil Camp, the other in Fort McMurray. They had not been able to stop the murders of Constance and Marc Lafontaine and Alicia and Kevin. The murders, they had learned, had been the result of the Lafontaine's' greed—they had never suspected the Lafontaine's would try to shake the oil company for a million. Sebastian called their deaths instant Karma—the result of a bad decision. McAllen called them stupid.

They wished they could have stopped the deaths of Alicia and Kevin. The two young Americans were adamant that they would never carry cell phones, contending that cell phone waves were bad for the brain and could cause cancer and eventually kill. Had they had a cell phone, McAllen could have warned them about Fuentes. Now they were dead. The only consolation—their deaths had galvanized the world against dirty oil. Nothing says it like a fuck-you finger from a tar pond.

The irony of their new home was that everything in it had been purchased using the five million dollars they received from Ironstone for the initial implementation of polywater. They were supposed to receive another five million when the process was reversed. McAllen had needed a company like Ironstone to get him close to the major oil fields. The company had done its job well, but McAllen had an alternate plan, which was playing out in the room around him.

Sebastian was at his many consoles with his earphones on. He watched voice traffic on a screen and listened in with his headphones. He adjusted his dials to listen to background noise or inflections in voices. He was a perfect listener as he was paranoid, always thinking that people were saying something more than they really were. McAllen loved Sebastian's paranoia—it had saved their skins when Sebastian had overheard the plan for the intended attack on his island.

Percy watched several computer screens that tracked satellites and alerted them the moment any satellite was in their area so they would know to stay inside. Percy was the firewall, the guard. He watched systems and kept watch over any possible leaks.

Theo watched stocks, commodities, and oil futures on his screens. His headphones blared the Stones, "Can't get no satisfaction." He had been given the two million left over after their purchase of the house, the boat for Grace, and the computer equipment. His job was to build the two million into twenty million then two hundred million. He knew exactly how. He hummed along with the music.

Grace was in the kitchen. Her chubby brown face was angel-like in a smiling concentration as she cooked a West Coast bouillabaisse that simmered with clams, mussels, halibut, salmon, and crab. She wore ear buds and swayed gently to an old Bruce Coburn tune, "Wondering Where the Lions Are."

Grace could not be happier. She had her boys back again. They looked good as they concentrated in their prospective areas, all in one room where she could see them. They looked like the young men she had comforted back in the seventies, with the same energy. Sure they had gray hair, and age spots on their hands, and some had little bellies that hung over their fatigues, but they were vibrant, full, their eyes were clear. She had never been as attracted to them as she was now. She would probably sleep with one of them tonight.

Sebastian called McAllen over to join him at his computer console, and as McAllen walked over, he admired the view. Percy had picked a perfect spot. They could watch ships pass out in the channel and see the pair of eagles that had made their home amongst the tall pines that surrounded the cabin.

"So, what've you got, Sebastian," McAllen said as he sat down beside him. He had put his Seattle Mariners hat back on and was wearing an old tee shirt and a pair of jeans. He was never comfortable in battle fatigues.

Sebastian looked up from his screen and took off his headphones. "You know, I've been listening to this head honcho who's been calling the stockbrokers in New York from Seattle, and he's never sounded right."

"Meaning . . . what?" McAllen asked. As he sat down beside Sebastian, he could not get over his resemblance to Willy Nelson. All Sebastian had to do was braid his long gray hair into pigtails and he would be a match. His shaving lotion was always something that smelled of patchouli from the hippie days.

"Well, I've run some diagnostics on the voice through my sound mixer, and the highs and lows don't match a man's voice," Sebastian said. He adjusted the many silver amulets and bands on his forearms, something he always did when something was bugging him.

"Again, I'm not getting what you mean," McAllen said. He loved his friend Sebastian deeply, but half the time he never understood him.

"Okay, here's the skinny on this. When I do a voice analysis on this caller, I keep getting a high pitch. The analysis is telling me that this voice is being masked. Now, a masked voice is nothing new, but this is a gender mask." Sebastian pointed to the oscillating screens on his computer as if this fact would be more than evident to anyone with a brain.

"So you're basically saying that our caller from Seattle is a not a man but a woman," McAllen said. He was happy he had finally gotten Sebastian's point because he hated going around and around with him in conversations.

"Correcto mundo, my friend. And the voice recognition put the voice into the older age group—somewhere around mid-sixties," Sebastian said. His eyes lit up, shifting from their usual soft gray to azure blue.

"Hmm, that's interesting. You got anything else?" McAllen was staring at the computer screen as if it were an oracle that could provide further revelations.

"Yeah, the caller isn't even in Seattle but in a little golf resort in Palm Springs." Sebastian fairly beamed as he presented the information. "I've been running a search software program since I got the Seattle number, and the calls are being covertly redirected."

"What the fuck, you mean we have a senior citizen running a *black op* from Palm Springs?" McAllen laughed as recognition dawned on him.

"If my software program is correct, then yeah," Sebastian said.

"Holy shit boys," McAllen called out to the rest of the men in the room. "We got ourselves one hell of an adversary. We need to get us some eyes down there. Hey Grace, you have any relatives down in the Palm Springs area?"

Grace poked her head up from behind the stove. She could just be seen over the steam of the bouillabaisse that was filling the cabin with an intoxicating aroma. "Hell Mac, you know I got relatives everywhere. Remember, my people were here first."

"Yeah, you always remind me of that—about every ten minutes or so. We need someone to get a visual of this person, and get the background. Damn this is getting good." McAllen was grinning; he loved the hunt just as much as everyone else in the room.

"Hey, I'm on it, just as soon as you eat this amazing dinner I made," Grace said. She brought the steaming pot of bouillabaisse to the large table. Percy and Theo busied themselves with filling wine glasses, putting out bowls and cutlery, and cutting up sourdough bread that had just come out of the oven. Sebastian turned away from his computers and put the Grateful Dead greatest hits album on the sound system. Jerry Garcia sang, "The friend of the devil is a friend of mine."

After they had taken their places at the table, they lifted their wine glasses. McAllen looked at each of them and smiled. "Here is to the world, as we know it, and how it needs to become."

They clinked glasses and dug into Grace's fabulous feast. The light was fading in the channel. A pod of killer whales swam slowly by, chasing a school of salmon that was swimming for its life. Two eagles circled overhead, hopeful the salmon would surface in their attempts to escape the whales.

CHAPTER TWENTY-TWO

DETECTIVE MUELLER WAS RESTING IN his room at Arctic Oil Camp. It was 6:00 p.m. He was tired. The bodies had been tagged and bagged and shipped to Anchorage for autopsies. All personnel who could have come in contact with the victims had been matched to flights and shift records. Three names had come up: James Rice, Frank Starko, and Jason Stubik. Troy had instantly suspected Frank Starko, as the man looked like a compact version of a wrestler. Starko had a thick neck, a well-muscled frame, and fit the type that could break a man's neck.

Mueller and Troy had tried to establish some connections between the dead security guard and the two dead Canadians. There were none. No leads. No one had ever seen them talk to each other. Detective Mueller's mind was clicking over motives. He usually determined them quickly when he got to a crime scene. This was different. Three deaths, all by the same supposed killer—and yet they seemed unrelated.

He could hear the shower running in the bathroom. He knew that Franklin was in the room next door. He imagined her square features, water dripping down her breasts and legs. He got an erection—he was not remotely interested in Franklin. Since he had been in rehab, and off the booze, and on a multitude of vitamins, his sixty-two-year-old penis had had a mind of its own.

His dreams had changed as well. He used to have nasty dreams when he did drugs and drank alcohol; there were snakes and alligators and all manner of creatures that consumed him at night. Now, there was a recurring dream. This dream was the worst of all. He was in a courtroom, and the judge was always one of his ex-mothers-in-law. The jury was made up of his three ex-wives, plus all the women he had pissed off in his life, and the prosecution was his ex-fathers-in-law. They did not need to speak. Their eyes accused him. When he looked left and right at his defense attorneys, they at first looked like Johnny Cochrane and Robert Shapiro, and he would think he had a chance. He was wrong; his defense attorneys were his ex-bartenders. The jury always wanted to hang him.

His cell phone rang by his bedside table. He grabbed it and answered, "Hello, Detective Frank Mueller."

"Hello, Detective, this is Detective Bernadette Callahan, with the Special Crimes Unit of the Royal Canadian Mounted Police in Fort McMurray, Canada, calling. I must say you were a hard man to track down. Your detective squad in Anchorage told me how to find you."

"Well, I understand the Mounties always get their man, and you found me, so how can I be of assistance, Detective Callahan?" Frank Mueller was glad to take his mind off his erection and his strange dreams—and of course, a female voice was always welcome.

"We seem to have some crimes in common," Bernadette continued after a short pause to assess Detective Mueller's tone. "I was informed by a newspaper reporter from Anchorage that you have two Canadian homicides who both worked for Clearwater Technologies. Is that correct?"

"Yes, that is correct—so what is your connection?" Frank asked. He was wondering how the reporter had gotten the information, as he had received a text message regarding what Chief Wilson had said in the news conference; there had been no mention of Clearwater in the text.

"Well, I have two dead Americans who turned up in a tar pond here in Fort McMurray this morning, and they both worked for Clearwater," Bernadette said. She waited while the information sunk in with Mueller.

He sat upright on his bunk and almost hit his head on the small bookshelf over his head. "Do you have anything else on Clearwater?" Mueller asked. He grabbed his notebook from beside his bed and started to jot down the information.

Bernadette filled Mueller in on how the bodies had been found, the link to the deaths on Galiano Island, and the link to Professor McAllen in Vancouver. She also told him about McAllen's polywater substance that was supposed to wreak havoc on world oil. The last bit of information caught Mueller's attention.

"So you think the reason behind the murders is that these Clearwater people were trying to inject this polywater substance into Canada's and Alaska's water systems?" Mueller finally asked. He had finally connected the dots.

"Well, that's what we're going with, as of now. I have the director of security down here informing our operations people to shut down anything the Clearwater people worked on, to see if they tampered with anything." Bernadette neglected to say that there had been no we—she had made the call to do the shutdown. At present, her butt was very much on the line, as she still had not informed her chief of detectives.

"Have you found anything yet?" Mueller's brain was starting to kick in. He was now seeing the picture of the crime in front of him. He had just remembered what Franklin had told him about Constance Lafontaine. Her hands had had a plastic substance on them. What had seemed odd now made sense, as the plastic could be related to the polywater.

"We've just started shutting down the plants, and the systems engineers are starting the search. They're taking it very seriously."

"Yeah, yeah, I guess you would. Listen, I would love to compare some more notes with you, but I need to get this information to the base manager here," Mueller said.

"Always happy to help our American friends," Bernadette said.

Mueller hung up and put his cell phone down. He now knew why the pieces hadn't fit together before. The murders had been committed by an outside force—not the usual drug deal gone bad, or one person pissed with another. This was a case where forces were aligned to do serious harm to the oil fields, and someone had not responded to commands correctly.

Mueller slipped on his shoes. His feet were aching from the endless corridors of the camp he had walked. The three levels and different wings still confused him. He needed to get in front of Kearns with the information he had just received to let him know the shit they might be in.

Mueller closed the door to his side of the room quietly. He could still hear Franklin in the shower. He blocked out her image. He did not need another woody as he walked down the hall. He tried to remember which way the administration offices were. He knew that Kearns would still be there.

Troy should have been asleep by now. The Lafontaine murders had happened at the end of his twelve-hour shift. At 7:00 p.m., he was still walking the halls of the oil camp. Fatigue was there, just on the edge of his consciousness, but he wanted to locate Frank Starko.

Of all the suspects who had come into contact with the Lafontaines, Starko fit the profile of the killer they were looking for. In his personnel file picture, Starko had no smile, and his eyes looked like those of a hunter. Troy had the same eyes—it was as if he were looking back at himself.

In the past two hours, he had been everywhere in the camp: the cafeteria, movie theater, library, gym, and back to Starko's room three times. There was no sign of him. Troy knew he would show up eventually—he had to. There was no place to go.

Bernadette put down her phone in her office in Fort McMurray. She looked at her watch—it was 8:00 p.m. on Friday night. She had just pulled a twelve-hour day, which was shorter than the fourteen to sixteen she was used to.

She was hungry. The gummy bears she had eaten from the big bag in her desk drawer had produced a sweet "whatever-in-the-hell-did-you-put-in-your-stomach" feeling. Her stomach now wanted real food: pizza, ribs, or steak washed down with red wine—the stuff that would chase her back into the gym before her ass attacked her.

She felt she had done enough for the day. She had spoken again with the sweet-talking Constable Chris back on Galiano Island, who had informed her that Professor McAllen had told his neighbors he was going to a Buddhist meditation retreat for three months. There would be no way to contact him, he had told them. The neighbors were not certain if the Buddhist retreat was in Thailand or New Mexico. The professor had been vague.

Bernadette thought that Professor McAllen's story was either the perfect cover or the perfect alibi. The neighbors had not seen anyone else at the cabin, and the crime scene investigators had found few other prints. Perhaps the professor really was a lonely guy.

Speaking of lonely, Bernadette thought. She had done a quick Facebook search on the affable Constable Chris Christakos. There he was, single, good looking, about thirty-eight—all of that very nice. There was a picture of him by a stream in his shorts, fishing for salmon. The guy had great legs, nice pecs. *Down girl!* She finally told herself.

She clicked further into his page and checked his friends. It was the detective in her. *Yes, he has some nice friends on the island.* But then she got to the mother and sister. *Oops!* The Greek mother and sister looked like they would judge her and spit her out in a heartbeat.

She thought perhaps that was why this nice Greek RCMP constable was hanging out on Galiano Island. She realized that she should make a mental note to have nothing more to do with the good-looking constable. To the mental note, she added a red flag and put some red traffic cones and police tape around it. She just hoped she would see this when her hormones kicked in.

She closed her computer, grabbed her cell phone, and headed out of her office. She glanced at the front reception—the officers were chatting, drinking coffee, and getting ready for the calls to start coming in. Fort McMurray on Friday night was fueled by young men with big bucks from their high-paying jobs in the oil sands. They would be hitting the bars by now. In a few hours, they would be drunk and stoned, and in another few hours, their testosterone would override all brain functions and the fights would break out. The RCMP officers were the referees. They joked that it was too bad they did not get paid as well as the NHL referees. Those guys did not have to deal with knives.

As she got to the parking lot, she dialed Cynthia's number. She knew she would be home. Cynthia answered right away. "Hey Bernie, I was hoping you'd call. I just ordered a large pizza—you want to come over?"

"Has the pizza got meat on it?"

"Hell yeah, it's a meat lover's pizza!"

"Great, I'll pick up one of those elegant wines by the box and be right over. Should I bring a movie?"

"Forget bringing a movie. It's a Matrix marathon tonight. We can watch that cute Keanu Reeves's ass until our eyes bleed."

Bernadette laughed as she brushed the snow off her Jeep. "Girl that is why I hang out with you... you're a deviant. I'll be there in a half hour."

She jumped into her Jeep and hit the radio as the vehicle warmed up. It had been sitting out in the cold all day and was a block of ice. She had not been able to afford electric seat warmers when she had bought the Jeep. She sat there shivering as the vents blew semi-warm air and her butt turned to ice.

The defrosters finally warmed the front and back windows enough for her to see out of them, and she put the vehicle in reverse. As she was about to step on the gas, she glanced for the first time at the paper she had bought that morning with her coffee. It was sitting on the passenger's seat. The front page read "The oil sands will spend 180 billion dollars in the next 10 years on new projects."

As she drove out of the parking lot and into the black night and snow-covered streets, she knew exactly what that would mean. More young people chasing the dream of big money, which would mean more crime and more headaches—and it would wear on her, and make her fat.

Detective Mueller finally found the administrative offices. For the last part of the walk, he had followed Kearns's booming voice. As he walked to the outside of his door, he could hear he was engaged with what sounded like a reporter.

Kearns was yelling into the phone. "I don't care what fucking rumors you've heard about some terrorist fucking plot. This is just a couple murders of some people with cabin fever—have you got that? If you print anything else I will come down to Anchorage and tear you a new asshole—have you got that?" When Kearns slammed the phone back into the cradle, his large head was different shades of purple.

This time, Mueller did not wait for an invitation to sit down. He sat in front of Kearns, looked him straight in the eye, and said, "We need to talk."

Kearns was breathing heavily. He suddenly focused on Mueller. "What is it?"

"I have no idea whom you were just talking to, but I just received confirmation from a source in Canada that the Clearwater people may be tampering with the oil fields. This could be a terrorist plot."

Kearns's breathing got heavier; he pounded both big hands flat on the desk. "Fuck!" was his only answer.

Mueller took Kearns's answer as agreement to his statement of fact. He continued. "The source said two Clearwater employees have been killed in Canada, and they are shutting down systems to look for any evidence of tampering.

Kearns closed his eyes for a brief second. When he opened them, he was focused. "I need to close all water intakes to all the fields until I find out where they've been." He picked up his phone and started dialing.

Mueller realized he did not need to be in the office anymore. Kearns would be calling every operations person and every technician. He would have the entire Alaskan oil field shut down in a matter of hours. Mueller knew he needed to contact his chief in Anchorage, who would contact the Alaska State Troopers. There would then be a call to the Bomb Squad, the FBI, and probably Homeland Security. This murder investigation had become an international incident.

CHAPTER TWENTY-THREE

BYRON STOOD STILL IN FRONT of the bright lights. The makeup artist was adding the last bit of color to his cheeks. "A little blush to fend off the Alaskan pallor," the artist said. The makeup artist was young; her own makeup looked heavy. It covered up her bad skin. Her breath smelled of coffee and bagels.

It was 7:00 a.m. The cameraman from Channel 3 News was checking the light readings in front of his face. The pretty red-haired news reporter was doing sound checks and listening to her ear piece, waiting for instructions from New York.

They were getting ready to go live with Samantha Savage from CBS New York as part of the breaking news story "Terrorism in the Oil Fields." They were in the Channel 3 studio, and the newsmen and production people were in a semicircle, waiting for the cue.

Byron knew exactly where this had gone so wrong. He was supposed to have broken the story in the *Anchorage Daily Mirror*—front page headlines, the media fighting to get his quotes. They would beat their way to his little cubicle at the newspaper.

But the pretty red-haired news reporter from Channel 3 had tracked him down. She had noticed his absence after the police media event and sensed he was on to something. Like a wolf tracking a wounded deer, she had trailed him to the *Anchorage Daily Mirror.* The moment he had walked out the main door, all smiles, gleaming, his very pores exuding the exclusive he had on the Prudhoe Bay murders, she knew it—she smelled it on him.

In a mere nanosecond, she had flashed him her smile and moved in for the kill. She got in close—her eyes, her lips, the sweet, minty fresh breath that flowed over the perfect teeth and little pink tongue. He was lost.

She invited him for drinks. Cocktails at the Crows Nest lounge at the top of the Captain Cook Hotel, where they toasted his success with several martinis. She offered to buy him dinner. What man can refuse a pretty redhead buying dinner? They feasted on Bering Sea king crab legs. Their lips were soaked in butter, and their fingers covered in moist crab. They left greasy prints on their champagne glasses.

Dinner turned into more drinks back in the lounge, and they closed the place down at 1:00 a.m. She took him back to her place. She turned down her sheets and laid him out like her very own prize. He spilled. He gave her the story: the background, the angle—everything. At one point he would have confessed to being on the grassy knoll when Kennedy was shot. She was that good.

At some point in the evening, as the moonlight poured through the window of her downtown apartment, he realized she was on her cell phone. She was talking to New York—and he was admiring her cute little ass.

She was organizing shooting schedules and arranging secondary interviews with McAllen's assistants, interviews with people who had scientific backgrounds, and interviews with people who had oil and security insights. He realized he had been had.

The pretty redhead news reporter had worked the phone for nearly two hours to finesse every detail and squeeze every ounce of coverage out of the story. Byron's input? He would get a thirty-second spot as the person who had broken the story—but she might give him one minute with a lead-in.

He had lain there, transfixed, in her bed with the satin sheets, watching her as she moved from the computer, back to her desk, back to her notes, her hips swaying in the moonlight. He had realized then what a perfect male slut he was. He had given up his story. He had been betrayed by his pecker.

He heard the cameraman call out, "On in 3, 2, 1, and live."

The next moment, the red-haired news reporter, Naomi Walters, formerly Nancy Wolnick of Greenfield, Ohio, turned to face the camera and flashed her brilliant smile.

She gave a quick lead-in about exposing a terrorist attack on oil and then shoved the microphone in Byron's face. Byron stammered out his story about the connection of four of the murdered to Clearwater Technologies, and Professor McAllen, and the Professor's background. He felt sweat run down his face in small cascades of drops that were probably playing hell with the makeup. The young makeup girl watched from the sidelines, her pimply face a mask of sympathy.

He realized his voice was cracking. He had never had a voice for radio or television. When excited or emotional, his voice went from a sulky, sexy, low Clint Eastwood to a high-pitched kazoo, not unlike a Pee-wee Herman. Before he could get himself under control, he heard Naomi say the dreaded words: "Back to you, Samantha."

Byron watched in horror as the television monitor showed Samantha Savage on a split screen with Naomi. They had cut him out of the camera shot completely.

Samantha Savage was a cross between a young Katie Couric and a young Diane Sawyer—blonde, blue eyed, and fierce in her focus, like a young great white shark circling the waters, looking for prey.

She and Naomi discussed the implications of the terrorist plot on North America's oil supply, the cost to the American public and their jobs, and the economic ramifications.

Byron started inching towards Naomi, and she inched away, keeping him out of the camera shot. She was still talking with Samantha. He was about to interject, throwing in a thoughtful point, but they cut away.

The monitor now showed only Samantha. Then there was a split screen again, and she was interviewing a scientist in Berkeley, California, named Professor Adler. He was introduced as an eminent research scientist with numerous credentials who had once worked with Professor McAllen.

Professor Adler looked every inch the competent professor of science and chemistry—the gray-flecked hair, the short, cropped beard. Black-framed glasses sat on his intelligent-looking face, and his gleaming white lab coat fit neatly over his tall frame. Byron wondered who at CBS wardrobe had gotten to this guy.

The other screen showed a very disheveled and frightened-looking research assistant from the University of Victoria. The young man looked like he had recently been dragged out of bed—and he had. His hair was a mix of black and tan—there seemed to be no consensus as to color. His pale skin was blotched by far too much pizza and beer.

Samantha asked Professor Adler if in fact the McAllen formula of polywater was real or a hoax. The professor almost spit the word "hoax" as he expounded on the very reasons why polywater had no basis in fact.

As Byron watched the monitor, he could see Samantha's eyes widen. She had something. She was going in for the kill shot: news as theater equals ratings. Samantha asked the professor if he would like to see the polywater demonstrated in his lab.

The professor was, of course, speechless. Byron could see that this was a new experience for him. He stammered out, "Sure, of course, but we have no samples in this lab." He added a reassuring smile as if that might disarm the pretty blond news anchor. He had no such luck.

Samantha responded that the news team in Professor Adler's lab had a sample of the polywater, the very same one provided by the research assistant with the very bad complexion at the University of Victoria. At this moment, the research assistant with the very bad complexion and lack of sleep waved weakly from his side of the screen.

Professor Adler could do nothing more than flash a smile at Samantha. Samantha smiled back—her smile was better. A CBS production person came out from behind the camera, and a vial was provided.

Byron was in awe of Naomi and Samantha and how they had managed to orchestrate all of this between three in the morning and now. They had somehow tracked down McAllen's assistant and Professor Adler as well as numerous other people for the segment all in the past five hours. They were incredible.

The professor, with his pasted-on smile, dutifully emptied the vial containing the supposed polywater into a small glass bowl of water. They had used good California tap water for the experiment. Nothing happened at first. The professor's eyes and face were now eclipsing into a "see-I-told-you-so" expression.

Then the professor shook the bowl. It jiggled. He shook it again. It jiggled again. He looked up at the camera as if there might be an answer somewhere in the lens. He started to move the bowl violently. The bowl of what was once water now jiggled violently. It looked like clear, firm jelly.

The smile on the research assistant's face in Victoria was evident. Samantha Savage in New York was trying to hide hers.

"So, Professor Adler," Samantha asked, "an invention that has such obvious effects on the nature of water—how did the scientific community miss this?" Samantha had asked the classic interviewer bombshell question. Ask the big question and watch the person squirm. No television viewer could help but feel the professor's discomfort.

From Byron's viewpoint in Anchorage, he could feel himself sweating the professor's answer.

The professor was speechless, probably for the first time in his life, as he muttered a series of words that had no meaning or were incomprehensible. And all the while he kept jiggling the bowl of water that was now polywater. He was muttering to it as if it would answer him back.

"Thank you, Professor Adler," Samantha said. The screen then shifted to an international security analyst and a consultant for the oil and gas industry. They had been on the sidelines somewhere watching the scientific show in Berkeley. They were in a split screen below Samantha, as if she were a puppet master.

She directed the questions, the tone, and where the story was going. The security analyst confirmed that this polywater he had just seen demonstrated was one of the greatest threats to mankind. He could not name the exact threats offhand, but his furrowed brow showed that he was thinking about them at that very moment. Byron knew that the moment the analyst finished the interview; he would call his clients to inform them of the new terror that was now evident and would raise his fees accordingly.

The oil industry consultant immediately saw the threat. He stated simply that if the polywater reacted the same way it did in the experiment in nature, then oil would not be pushed to the surface. "It would be a bad day for oil," he said with a pained look on his face.

Samantha cut back to Naomi, who had quotes from the RCMP in Fort McMurray and from Chief Wilson in Anchorage. Both forces claimed their investigations were ongoing, and both had "no comment." Naomi Walters wore a lovely smile as she signed off for Channel 3 Anchorage.

Samantha did a quick wrap-up of events, and ended with, "Where is the elusive Professor McAllen? Is a terrorist attack on American and Canadian oil imminent?" The screen faded to "Terrorist Attack on Oil."

The television monitor in the newsroom at Channel 3 Anchorage went back to sports. The course at Torrey Pines, La Jolla, California, came on. The sportscasters were discussing the prowess and changes of Tiger Woods. He was not doing well; they were trying to keep the ratings up by discussing him anyway.

Byron turned to Naomi. Some black roots were showing in her beautiful red hair. She smiled at him, kissed him on the cheek, and with a wink and a "catch you later," she was back on her cell phone. She was talking to Samantha, who was congratulating her on the amazing job. Byron heard Naomi say, "A chance for San Diego? Really? Oh Ms. Savage, that would be wonderful."

Byron put on his jacket, his hat, and his gloves and walked out the door of Channel 3 News Anchorage. The whole episode had taken an hour. As he left the building, he saw the *Anchorage Daily Mirror* in a paper dispenser. TERRORIST PLOT UNCOVERED IN PRUDHOE BAY. His name was there, Byron Jacks, but the thunder was gone. Naomi Walters would be the story leader, and he was now the source.

He sat in his car, warming up the interior. At 8 AM, it was still dark and cold, his breath formed clouds in his car. He looked at his cell phone. He had several text messages. One was from his editor, a simple, "Why?" There was one from his dad in Cleveland saying how proud he was to see his son on TV.

There was one from Della, who had helped him break the story—for favors of course. Three hundred pounds of southern love had left a simple message: "Hey lover, looks like you were cozy with that pretty red-haired reporter down there, but when I get to Anchorage next week, your sweet little ass is mine."

Randall watched the CBS breaking news story from his Manhattan apartment. The apartment was one thousand square feet with two bedrooms and a breathtaking view of the Hudson River. He had purchased it for 1.5 million for it plus the cost of a designer to do up the place in style. He had a mortgage of 1 million dollars on it, with large payments. He was counting on the polywater project to make the upcoming payments.

He watched the news story on his new sixty-inch plasma television as he lay in his red calf-leather chaise lounge chair. His bathrobe was open; his stomach was a large mound of flesh and hair. He had to prop himself up on pillows to see over it. He was balancing a plate of two chocolate croissants on this belly. The news story caused him to start choking on his croissant; he spewed crumbs across his chest and onto the chair and beige alpaca rug.

His phone rang, and as he was choking he picked it up. His eyes were watering from the exertion—he could not see the phone number. He coughed out a hello and heard the voice of Duncan on the other line. Duncan sputtered as he yelled, "Fuck, fuck, fuck, fuck . . ."

Margaret watched the CBS news report in Palm Springs—it was 9:00 a.m. She was on the treadmill in her country club gym. *There's no need to panic*, she thought. They had agreed to activate the devices at 11:00 a.m. Alaska time.

Some of the devices were well hidden, some might be more visible. It did not matter. There were enough devices that if the engineers found a few, it would not make any difference. She headed back to her villa. She would need to be close in case Cordele needed to reach her.

Professor McAllen was standing over Sebastian's shoulder watching the news report. Theo and Percy were beside him. Grace was in the kitchen. She was making some high-fiber muffins to get her boys back on track. Grace thought a clean colon was next to godliness. The men were definitely feeling lighter in their bowels—not exactly in their spirits.

As the news special finished, McAllen looked at his three friends. "Well, so now they are on to us."

Sebastian looked up at McAllen from his large leather chair. He had gotten one with an added headrest, like the ones he saw lawyers on television using. He had always admired those chairs. "You mean they think they are on to us. Don't you think it's time for a little surprise for our Wall Street friends?

McAllen looked down at Sebastian. "You know, why not? Can you input an alternate program?

"I had the alternate program ready from the time you met those pricks. You know I've never trusted anyone born after 1955," Sebastian said without looking up. His fingers flew on his computer keyboard.

Bernadette watched the newscast from her fitness club in Fort McMurray. She was pounding the treadmill doing sprint and hill intervals trying to sweat out last night's feast. She had had her ass chewed out by her chief earlier that morning. She secretly wished the chewing would affect her weight—she would not have to go to the gym as much.

She had left him a voicemail the night before stating what she had spoken to the director of security about, but of course, the chief had had to weigh in about the lack of protocol and how she should have reached him for such a major threat.

Bernadette knew he was just spouting off so others in the detachment could hear him. He really had not wanted to be bothered last night. She had done the right thing in calling Synthetic Oil Security, as the CSIS agents were now on their way to Fort McMurray but would do nothing more than ask for reports. The real work was being done right now—Synthetic Oil technicians would be going over every inch of the plant looking for something left by Clearwater that could possibly do damage. What damage they were not sure. They only knew the idea of polywater in the system scared the hell out of everyone.

Bernadette was sweating. Every pore of her body was secreting pizza and red wine. She asked herself if she would ever learn. She knew the answer. A cute little twenty-something-year-old got on the treadmill beside her. There was not an inch of fat on her perfectly proportioned body. Bernadette tried not to secretly hate her—she hit the incline on the treadmill and tried to concentrate as her lungs exploded with the effort.

Detective Mueller only briefly saw the newscast. He had been on the phone all morning with his chief in Anchorage. He was to turn the case over to the FBI and Homeland Security when they arrived that afternoon. He was packing his bags to catch the late afternoon flight.

CHAPTER TWENTY-FOUR

CORDELE WATCHED THE NEWSCAST AT 8:00 a.m. on his cell phone as he boarded the helicopter he had hired from Fairbanks to take him to the Arctic Oil Camp. There was little he could do about the news—it was bad—but he would have to extract his man, Frank Starko, once he had activated the polywater devices, get him back somewhere private, and dispose of him.

They would be at the Arctic Oil Camp in three hours, arriving around 11:00 am, on the older Bell 430 he had hired. The sun would provide gray light over the Arctic horizon.

The helicopter pilot he had hired was definitely post–Vietnam War era, but luckily pre–Korean War. He was a tall, grizzled specimen with no discernible fat cells. His skin was so tight on his face that Cordele thought the man's skeleton would show if you shone a light behind him.

The pilot had accepted the twenty-five thousand dollars Cordele had given him with only the barest raise of one bushy eyebrow. The man seemed to grow hair in place of fat. His face was a mass of fur that led from his bushy hair down to a neck that seemed to disappear into a no man's land of gray chest hair.

The old pilot had only winked when Cordele had told him his mission was to pick up a friend in Prudhoe Bay and that there was no need to file a flight plan. He would get a quick flight to pick up Starko, no questions asked

Starko had sent Cordele a text message telling him which direction to approach the Arctic Oil Camp from and where to pick him up. There were maintenance sheds far enough away from the camp they could land near without causing too much attention.

Cordele sat in the copilot's seat as they sped over the dark landscape below. Moonlight flashed shadows of their progress. He felt the pressure of the Glock handgun holstered to his chest—the gun he would use to kill Starko. But where would be the question.

Starko sat in his room, knowing he was being hunted. He had avoided Detective Mueller and Troy Mercury for the past twenty-four hours. Soon, they would find him—there were few places to hide in the camp. He would have to submit to hours of questioning and work hard to keep his story straight, his breathing soft, and his expressions ones of interest but not too interested.

He had had interrogation training in the military—they had used every technique in the book, plus some of those in the margins. Water boarding was one. He still had nightmares about the feeling of drowning. Police interrogation was subtle—the calm questioning and waiting for you to slip. He preferred the water torture.

The gray light of Arctic dawn was starting to show outside his window. His watch said 10:59 a.m. He opened his metal briefcase. Encased in foam inside the case was a simple ten-inch laptop with a USB cable that ran to a small switch box.

He powered up the laptop, and the ten lights on the small switch box began to glow. There was supposed to be one light for each device that was active, which meant that none of the devices had been found.

Then he took a piece of paper from his pocket. Written on the paper was the password that the Wall Street boys from Ironstone Investments had sent him. The activation codes ensured that no one but Ironstone could release the polywater into the water systems of Prudhoe Bay.

The screen now flashed and asked for the password. Starko placed the piece of paper in front of him. With two fingers, he began to punch in the code: 1-19-19-8-15-12-5.

As he punched in each number, the number turned into a letter on the screen. The 1 became an A, the 19 was an S, the second 19 another S, and the 8 became an H. Starko had a bad feeling about this password but knew he had to continue. Once he had activated the system he could leave—not before. When he finished entering the final number, the password spelled ASSHOLE.

His bad feeling turned to mild panic. Panic was something Starko never felt, but it rose as he watched the laptop start to smolder. The smoldering grew. Suddenly, a flame burst out of the keyboard. He threw the laptop on his bed and tried to smother it with his pillow, but it was no use—the smoke turned thick and black, and the smoke alarm went off in his room. He could hear the doors in the corridor start to close— the main fire alarm for his sector had been activated. He grabbed his parka and boots and ran out the door.

Parsons opened his case in the airport parking lot in Fort McMurray. He had already checked into his flight to Calgary with a connection in Toronto. His final destination: St. John's Newfoundland. It would be a long day of travel—he didn't care.

He wanted nothing more of Fort McMurray. He longed for salt air and some good cod and chips washed down with enough beer and rum to make him forget this place ever existed. He vowed to himself that from now on, he would only take assignments in warm countries, but he knew he would falter on that vow the first time someone put a large amount of cash under his nose.

He had decided to activate the devices at the airport just a half hour before heading through security for his flight. He did not trust anything to do with professor McAllen after his escape from the beach, and almost getting killed by him. The brief case in front of him was supplied by McAllen; he opened it with care and trepidation.

He opened the case on the hood of a brand new F-150 truck at the farthest end of the parking lot and entered the password into his laptop. As the word ASSHOLE appeared on the screen, he could only mutter "Aw shit."

The laptop smoked and burst into flames. Parsons grabbed the case, threw it under the truck, and looked around. No one had seen him. He walked away slowly enough to not attract attention, fast enough to get away from the fire. As he reached the inner doors of the terminal, there was a large explosion in the parking lot. The truck had blown up. He whirled around in time to see the hood of the truck leap into the air.

People started to run to the front of the terminal, and two security guards and an RCMP officer ran towards the truck that was now billowing black smoke. One of the security guards had a fire extinguisher in his hands. The RCMP officer was calling on his radio as he ran.

A man who had come outside to smoke his cigarette asked Parsons, "What happened?"

"Damned if I know. Looks like someone got a recall on their truck," Parsons answered. He smiled at the man. He heard his flight being called and headed for security screening. Sirens were blaring, and a large fire truck was rolling into the parking lot. It was time for him to leave.

When he got through security, he took out his cell phone and sent a quick text to Cordele in Alaska, letting him know that McAllen had screwed them yet again.

Troy was in the main security office when the fire alarm sounded. The room where the fire alarm had originated was B220—Frank Starko's room. Troy had been there several times trying to locate Starko.

The fire crews ran towards the room. All oil field personnel were trained in fire prevention. The most feared event at the camp outside of a whiteout from a snow storm was a fire. Oil camp fires could leave a camp without power, which meant no heat and exposure to the cold.

Troy had the security officer on the closed circuit television console play back the tape in Starko's corridor. There he was, Starko, running from the room with his parka and boots just seconds after the fire alarm sounded. Men in oil camps run to fires with extinguishers. To Troy it was obvious—Starko was their man.

Troy called Detective Mueller's cell phone. When Mueller answered, Troy simply said, "I think we found our rabbit."

"What've you got," Muller asked. He was packing his gun into his duffel bag.

"We have a fire alarm that just came from Starko's room. The CCTV shows him running from the room with his boots and parka—looks like he's making for the outside."

"Well, well, that does look guilty as hell. Here we are looking for the guy all day and he sets off a fire alarm to let us know where he is. I love it when criminals do stupid things—it makes them look like criminals."

"Absolutely," Troy said. He was now staring at all the CCTV monitors. "I don't see him now, but it looked on the last monitor like he was heading in the direction of the gym or the laundry room. The outside monitors show no signs of him."

"Good, I'll head for the gym. Do you see anyone there at present?"

"Negative, the place is empty. That's why this camp is fat."

"Thanks for the fitness update. I'll meet you there." Mueller grabbed his gun, shoved in a magazine, and chambered a round.

"Roger that," Troy said. He put down this cell phone and took out his gun. He chambered a round but left the safety on. Then he turned to the three security officers in the room—all young men in their twenties. *They're all good with firearms, but will they be good under stress?* Troy wondered. Targets never fired back on the range.

"Okay, Starko is our prime suspect. Pull his ID up on the console and get a good look at this guy. We don't know if he's armed, but you should treat him as extremely dangerous. He is the suspect in three murders, so don't give him any breaks." Troy looked at each of the young security officers—they looked scared.

Troy headed out the door, and the three security officers followed. He sent one officer to alert the two state troopers in the administration interview rooms. He did not have their radio frequencies or cell numbers.

When they reached the corridor of the room that Starko had fled, they found that a group of men had already extinguished the fire. A man was walking out of the room with a melted laptop. Troy instructed the two officers to check the laundry room. He knew the room was huge. There were usually ten to fifteen workers in there dealing with the mass of laundry. Starko would be obvious if he had gone there, but they had to check it out. Troy continued on to the gym. He hoped that Mueller was as slow as he looked—he did not want him tangling with Starko before he got there.

Mueller reached the gym by a stroke of luck. He had grabbed his gun, made a left out of his room, and somehow arrived at the gym. It was empty. He scanned the high ceiling and rows of treadmills, elliptical machines, and exercise bikes along one wall. A television was blaring CNN news to an empty room.

Then Mueller noticed three darkened rooms at the back of the gym. Each had a large window. He advanced towards the rooms, his gun drawn. Common sense was telling him to wait for backup from Troy and the state troopers. He was not in a common sense mood.

Mueller reached the first darkened room and could see shapes inside. Large inflated exercise balls of various sizes were stacked on top of one another. Ropes and pulleys hung from the walls. Peering hard into the room to see if any shapes were human, he wished his eyesight was better.

He opened the door slowly, his gun in his right hand, extending his left hand to turn on the light switch. Suddenly, the door closed hard on his hand, and the pain in his wrist sent a blinding light to his brain. Then the door flew open, and Starko was charging at him. He hit him low.

Mueller could only register a shiny object in Starko's hand. He knew instinctively it was a heavy object—his brain was sending duck-and-evade signals to his body. He could see the end of his life coming and all his brain could manage was an "oh shit." His stomach was ice. Two shots rang out. The sound in the small gym echoed in Mueller's ears, and Starko stopped his attack. He rolled to his right, and leapt into a crouching run.

Troy was standing at the front of the gym in a wide shooter's stance, trying to train his gun on Starko. He could not get another shot off before Starko ran behind the exercise machines, hit the back exit door of the gym, and was gone.

Troy ran to Mueller. "Are you okay? You should've waited for me."

"Yeah, that makes a lot of sense now." Mueller said lying on the floor.

"Are you hurt?" Troy asked as he bent over and gave Mueller a hand up.

"Yeah, the little prick broke my wrist. Thanks for coming. I thought I was about to become another one of his espresso victims with that damn tamper he uses."

"Are you okay to move?"

"He broke my left wrist—I shoot with my right." Mueller felt his ribs ache. They were bruised from the frontal assault. Now he knew what a cowboy felt when a steer ran into him. He picked up his gun and looked at Troy. "Let's get that bastard."

They headed out the back exit door into a corridor with windows that looked outside. Troy could see Starko heading for the maintenance buildings. He could also see a helicopter starting to descend some five hundred yards at the back of the buildings.

Troy radioed his security team to meet them at the maintenance buildings, and they headed down the stairs and outside. The cold air hit them like a vice. Troy remembered the temperature was minus fifteen degree Fahrenheit with no wind. He only had on his security guard coveralls and a fleece vest, but the cold did not bother him—he was on the hunt. He could see Starko some two hundred yards ahead. His Glock sidearm was effective at two hundred yards but not very accurate. He needed to close the distance if he wanted to stop Starko before he got to the helicopter.

Starko was slowing down in the deep snow. With each step, he sank deeper in the snowdrifts that had piled up behind the maintenance sheds. Then he rounded the corner of the shed and was out of sight.

The polar bear had woken up from his nap beside the maintenance shed at the sound of the helicopter. Normally he would have run away in fear, but hunger was overriding fear. The man he saw struggling slowly in the snow was prey, and he acted in an instant. His large paws had no problem with the deep snow. The bear advanced on the man and hit him quickly from behind. He struck hard. His massive jaws bit into the man's neck, and he threw the man from side to side in his jaws. The man stopped all movement.

Cordele watched the polar bear charge Starko from the helicopter. There was nothing he could do. They were just about to land. The pilot had intended to do a quick hover landing, and Cordele had been about to open the back door for Starko. He watched in fascination as the polar bear did his work for him. A small smile spread over his face as he saw the bear throw Starko like a limp doll. He knew the bear had broken his neck. He turned to the pilot and motioned for him to takeoff

Troy rounded the maintenance shed first and was momentarily blinded by the snow from the prop wash of the helicopter taking off. He thought Starko was gone. As the snow from the helicopter dissipated, he saw the bear. It was jumping up and down on something in the snow, its front paws doing a dance on a dark object

As he approached, he could see it was Starko underneath the bear. He didn't know if Starko was dead or alive, but his instinct was to save him. He advanced on the bear, his feet sinking into the snow, his breath making clouds of steam as he labored to get to Starko. He had only a sidearm to deal with the bear and would rather have had a high-powered hunting rifle. They say a pistol just makes a bear mad, but he had no choice.

He moved up beside the bear, which was busy with the body on the snow. As the bear put his head down to start feasting on Starko, Troy placed his gun inside the bear's shoulder and fired three quick rounds. The bear shuddered. Troy knew he had hit the heart.

With an expulsion of air, the bear fell to the side of Starko. Troy bent down and felt Starko for a pulse. There was none. Mueller came puffing up beside him, the security guards and state troopers just behind him. They stood in silence looking at the scene. The bear's wound seeped blood onto the snow, and Starko looked a ravaged mess. The bear had started to work on his face to ensure he would not be a threat.

"Is he dead?" Mueller asked when he finally caught his breath.

"Yeah, the bear got him, finished him off quick. Troy said. "You know, it's kind of a shame I killed this bear. I wish I'd have known this shithead was dead. I think I'd have let him eat on him a little bit and then scared him off."

"Uh . . . you know you couldn't have done that," Mueller said. He looked at Troy to see if he was actually serious.

"Yeah, I know, but sometimes Alaska justice is the best kind," Troy said. He was still looking at the bear, the body, and the blood. His own body started to shiver as he finally started to feel the cold. "We best get back inside and let the troopers deal with this mess."

"Did you happen to get any ID on the helicopter that Starko was trying to get into?" Mueller asked.

"Nah, I was too busy dealing with the bear. You might want to call in about the helicopter, but there are lots of helicopters up here, so they may have to go after all of them."

"Yeah," Mueller replied. He looked over at the state troopers, hoping they had heard the conversation and would act on it. His hand was now hurting badly. The adrenalin rush of the chase was over. He wanted warmth, his hand looked after, and some really strong coffee. Mueller realized he had almost been killed. They had found the suspect, now dead, and they may or may not have stopped the terrorist plot.

He decided he would retreat to the warmth of the camp and seek out the medics for his hand. He decided to contact the RCMP detective who had called him from Canada and give her an update on what had happened in Alaska.

C*HAPTER* T*WENTY-FIVE*

O*N* M*ONDAY*, B*ERNADETTE* *WAS* *IN* her office at RCMP headquarters, Fort McMurray. She had arrived early at the detachment, after her usual stop at the Tim Horton's drive-through. The drive-through was open twenty-four hours, and they knew her well. Her morning ritual was a large double cream double sugar coffee with a whole wheat bagel and strawberry cream cheese.

This morning she had added a honey cruller and a maple dip—for later. Later… arrived about a half hour after she finished the bagel. The honey cruller was history. The second doughnut she had pushed to the far side of her desk. She was ignoring it…for now.

The weekend had been long. The CSIS had arrived from Edmonton mid-afternoon on Saturday, and another team of intelligence officers were on their way from Ottawa and would be in Fort McMurray by noon. She would need inordinate amounts of sugar and intestinal fortitude to put up with all the meetings.

Bernadette had been in a closed-door meeting with two young intelligence officers for all of Saturday afternoon and most of Sunday. They had debriefed her on all of the calls she had had with the media in

Anchorage and her discussions with Detective Mueller in Prudhoe Bay, as well as her talks with Pierre Beaumont at Synthetic Oil.

The two young officers had both been bright, well dressed, and detailed to a point that made Bernadette want to scream. She was detailed herself in her investigations, but the two officers had taken things to degrees she had never experienced. They had wanted to know every nuance of every conversation, every small detail of what she thought the other person meant, and how exactly she had come to her conclusions.

The one intelligence officer was Antonello De Luca, and he went by Anton. He was a good-looking Italian Canadian in his mid-twenties with dark, curly black hair, dark chestnut eyes and smooth brown skin. He could have come off some Italian pizza commercial. The other intelligence officer she thought just as yummy. His name was Alexio Alexandrou, and he went by Alex. He was an athletic and handsome Greek Canadian. The CSIS was churning out good-looking men. If they hadn't been so damn detailed, she would have found them even more attractive; however, she thought she might have a cougar complex, and had decided to keep her hormones in check.

She had given them the details of her phone call with Detective Mueller regarding the death of Frank Starko in Prudhoe. The death by polar bear had only mildly amused the pair. They had been more interested in Starko's background.

Alex was a computer science graduate. He had gotten a bead on Starko in seconds and found that Frank Gregory Starko was an ex-marine with an exemplary record. He had risen to the rank of sergeant and did tours in Iran and Afghanistan, and then he had been hired by several private security firms, where he was well paid. Banks recorded hundreds of thousands of dollars deposited into his account. His money usually left quickly to pay his credit card bills, which he racked up in Thailand during holidays.

Alex had then done a search on the hotels that Starko had visited. The websites all came up with images of young girls in various states of undress. It was easy to see Starko's vacation interests.

Both Alex and Anton had smiled at Bernadette. The man's hobby was obvious—pervert. What was also obvious was that Starko was some kind of plant. He had been put there in the role of shuttle driver for the Arctic Oil Company. His reasons for murdering the two Canadian technicians were still a mystery, but the murder of the security guard at the camp was obviously a cover-up.

Bernadette had explained to the young intelligence officers how Starko had committed the murders with the espresso tampers, and they had had to explain the tampers to her when she asked what they were for. She liked her coffee two sugars two creams. The caramel macchiato fancy stuff got in the way of good doughnuts.

They had had trouble finding any background information on Emmanuel Fuentes. He was what they called a shadow. He had no record other than one that had been created for him: a Mexican national born in Guadalajara in 1973 who had been employed by Clearwater Technologies as a supervisor and who had a degree in natural science from the University of Guadalajara.

Alex had then done a facial recognition search of Fuentes, and with a soft "Bingo," had turned to Anton and Bernadette with a smile. "We have a winner."

Bernadette and Anton had stood over Alex as he pulled up the true identity of Fuentes: the screen showed one Augusto Fernando Moreno. He had in fact been born in 1973 in Guadalajara, and that was the end of the similarities. His list of prior convictions dated back to 1983, when at the young age of ten, he was involved in gang activities. His crimes ranged from drug running to arms smuggling to suspected murders of several competing gang members.

"Looks like things got too hot for Augusto and he decided to cool his heels in Canada," Anton had said as he scanned the list.

"So why were two really bad guys hanging out with four nice kids doing supposed environmental work?" Bernadette had asked.

They had all agreed after an exhaustive weekend of searching records and looking into the backgrounds of the four dead Clearwater Technologies people that there was no reason for them all to be together other than to plant the polywater. Therefore, they reasoned that the Clearwater employees were all in on the crime.

Bernadette had gone to sleep on Sunday night thinking about the officers who would have to inform the parents of the young victims that they had been part of a crime against industrial Canada and America. The media would not be gentle.

Now, at 8:30 a.m. with little rest from the weekend, Bernadette walked into the conference room, her notes and large coffee mug in one hand and cell phone in the other. Anton and Alex were already there, seated on one side of the table. Beside them sat Pierre Beaumont, Chief Barnstead, and the lead of the Edmonton Security and Intelligence Agency, Jeffery Patterson.

Patterson looked every bit the poster boy for the CSIS. He was tall, with perfectly styled hair and mustache. His jaw line showed a slight wrinkle line, indicating he might be in his late forties.

Bernadette had not seen Patterson all weekend. He had been locked in meetings with Chief Barnstead and Pierre. They only acknowledged her with their eyes as she entered and then went back to their muted discussion.

Bernadette sat with Anton and Alex. They gave her a knowing wink and went back to the laptops in front of them. Large Starbucks coffees were at their sides, and they were typing furiously. Chief Barnstead looked at his watch and signaled to Bernadette to close the conference room door. She only mildly disliked him for that.

"Well, thank you for coming in this morning, as I know many of you also put in many hours on this case over the weekend," Barnstead began. He looked over at Bernadette, giving her a brief bit of recognition for her part in the case.

"It seems that according to the report from Mr. Pierre Beaumont, all the devices that could inject this polywater into the tar sands have been located—is that correct?" Chief Barnstead looked to Pierre on his left.

"Our engineers reported that all the sites that the Clearwater Technologies people entered have been checked, and ten devices with vials attached were located." Pierre looked quickly at Bernadette and flashed a smile. He wanted to add his thanks to her for the information on the devices, but he knew she had walked a fine line by informing him before her chief.

The chief smiled at the group at the conference table. "Then it looks like we have saved the world from an oil shortage crisis."

"There is something that I think should be noted, and this was brought up by Anton." Pierre said. "The vials were attached to a radio transmitter, not a timer. We assume someone would have needed to be in range to activate them," He passed around a photo of the devices that they had found in the plants.

Bernadette looked at the photo. The device had six vials attached in a ring to a small black box, which was obviously the transmitter. "So what was the transmitter supposed to do?" she asked Anton.

Anton looked up from his computer screen. "From what I have determined, the device had a simple release mechanism—nothing too complicated. A radio wave would open three of the vials, which were supposed to activate the polywater, and there were another three vials that were supposed to reverse the process. We took the vials and confirmed this."

"So, we have a terrorist who wants to limit North American oil and then reverse the process?" Bernadette said. "I've never heard of a benevolent terrorist."

Anton gave Bernadette an amused look. "I see your thinking, but perhaps this was not so much terrorism as manipulation of oil. If these people could cause a stoppage and then turn it back on again, they would stand to gain in the markets."

"Interesting . . ." Bernadette said. She was leafing through her notes. "Here is a very interesting note from my conversation on Saturday with Detective Mueller in Alaska. He claimed that just before Frank Starko fled from the Arctic Oil Camp, a laptop in his room had caught on fire. He said it had some kind of radio device attached to it. We also have a report that came in late Saturday from Fort McMurray Airport. Someone left a laptop under a truck and it exploded—a radio control device survived the fire."

"What do you think that means?" Chief Barnstead asked. He knew he should let Bernadette go with her intuition, as her instincts were usually right.

"It seems to me like someone has been sabotaging their own project. If the devices were radio controlled, then they should've been activated just after the four Clearwater employees were murdered. Wouldn't that make sense?" Bernadette looked around the room at the other officers. She was amazed these men could not see clearly what had become clear to her.

"Well perhaps you could clarify your thoughts for us," Barnstead said. Bernadette took this as code: *It is not remotely clear to him.*

"Okay, here is how I see this from the timeline of events." Bernadette sat up in her chair, arranged her notes, and squared her shoulders. She felt as if she was getting ready to launch. "We have two murders of Clearwater Technologies employees in Prudhoe Bay last week on Wednesday, followed by two more here on Thursday morning." Bernadette paused to ensure they were following.

When they all looked up from their notes and laptops, she began again. She loved an audience. "Then we have the killings of a Clearwater employee and two Asian lads linked to Vancouver gangs on Galiano

Island, and this is followed by the death of a person trying to escape capture by American authorities after a laptop with a radio device catches fire. Is everyone with me so far?"

They all nodded in agreement. Patterson was now looking only faintly interested. He seemed to be one who wanted to be leading the team, not being led by Bernadette.

"So, what I see is that these people who were trying to manipulate oil were either not on the same page or else someone decided to take over the project. I don't see why else you'd have dead people on Professor McAllen's doorstep on Galiano Island. If they had all been content with doing their jobs, we would've been no wiser as to their actions."

"You think they all double-crossed each other," Chief Barnstead ventured. *He is always wonderful at stating the obvious,* Bernadette thought.

"Absolutely, and I think the threat is still valid until we have Professor McAllen in custody."

"What makes you think that?" Patterson asked. He was now giving her his full attention.

Bernadette went back to her notes. "Here is something that I found on Professor McAllen. His war record shows he was with the Americans in Vietnam. He was trained in Fort Bragg, North Carolina, and attached to the Special Operations Command. His records show two tours and that he excelled in Operation Commando Hunt, which was on the Ho Chi Minh Trail. His specialties were search and destroy missions—I'm still trying to reach his commanding officer to verify some of his records, but this guy sounds far too wild to be a mild-mannered professor."

"What do you suggest his motives are? "Patterson said.

"I think you have a bona fide nut job on your hands, and he is not done with messing with world oil. He is on record for suing large oil companies for the deaths of his children." Bernadette looked Patterson in the eye and held his gaze.

Chief Barnstead broke the tension with a slight cough. "Detective Callahan, I thank you for your insights into this case; however, all files will now be handed over to these officers from the CSIS as they'll be taking it from here."

The shock that Bernadette felt went right to her gut. She instantly felt the extra doughnut she had inhaled that morning and wanted to throw up. They were taking the case away from her—one of the biggest cases she had ever worked on was being yanked, and there was nothing she could do about it. She tried her damndest to show no emotion. She merely looked over at Barnstead and made an attempt at a grim smile, saying politely, "I'm sure they'll do a fine job from here on in."

Pierre looked at her, there was something he attempted to say, and then stopped. Bernadette closed her notepad and picked up her coffee mug. There was nothing more for her to do. "Gentlemen, if you'll excuse me, I've a large quantity of notes to get ready for you."

"There is one more thing," Patterson added. He raised his hand as Bernadette was about to leave. "We have been in contact with the FBI in both Alaska and Washington. We will be providing a report to the press stating that we haven't found any bomb threats or devices of any sort, as yet."

"Why is that?" Bernadette blurted out the question before she had time to think.

"We've decided to watch the international oil exchanges in London and New York to see if anyone is making large oil plays. We think someone will be betting the devices have been activated and will try to profit from it. Hopefully they'll make large enough moves that they'll show themselves."

Patterson suppressed a smile as he looked at Bernadette. He had known all along they were taking over the case. He had let her rattle on about her instincts, which he would note in a margin somewhere and hand off to a junior officer to check out. If they were correct, he would take credit for them and move up in the ranks.

He'll probably move up in Ottawa, Bernadette thought, *where the other ass kissers live.*

She maintained her smile until she got out of the room and closed the door. On the way back to her office, the frown that descended on her face announced to all other officers that they should steer clear. She was given a wide path.

When she got to her office, she closed her door, found the one doughnut she had left for later, which was now, and attacked it with a vengeance. Sticky sugar and coffee were a momentary solace.

The phone flashed with a message waiting. She picked it up and listened. She had called Professor McAllen's former commanding officer from Fort Bragg at his address in Boca Raton, Florida, and had left a message the day before. He had not been at home.

A very nice, southern female voice had left a long message. The caller was the daughter of Colonel James Brigham, and she was awfully sorry the retired colonel could not reply to the questions of the RCMP detective from Canada as he was on a cruise in the Caribbean and would be back in Boca Raton in a week. She would let him know to call the detective then, as "Daddy," the colonel, did not like email and would not use the expensive cruise ship phone.

Bernadette put the phone down. She knew, and everything in her knew, that she should turn this information over to the nice young lads from CSIS. She just did not feel like it. Perhaps later—she knew she was playing like a dog not giving up a bone, but that was how she felt. It was her bone.

Her cell phone buzzed. It was Pierre. He was still in the meeting and sending her a text.

"Can I buy you dinner tonight?"

What the hell, she thought. *No flame like an old flame.* She texted back, "Sounds great, how about the Keg Steakhouse downtown?"

"7:00 p.m., meet you there."

Bernadette went back to her notes. She needed to get them in order for the CSIS team and then supposedly let them go. She decided to make a copy of them and then see where things went from there. They were taking her off the case, but she was not even close to letting it go.

CHAPTER TWENTY-SIX

MARGARET HAD BEEN AWAKE SINCE 5:30 a.m. She had had another restless night. In her dreams earlier that week, the finger of Alisha Sylvester pointed out of the tar sands—not at her, but at the sky, as if there were an answer there. Then a vision of a polar bear dancing on Starko's body took over the vision of Alicia's skyward finger. Cordele had called her on Saturday night with the news and the details about Starko's death. The dreams were too much. Being awake was easier.

She made tea and sat at the window of her Palm Desert villa to wait for the sun to rise over the Santa Rosa Mountains. On mornings like these, she wondered how a nice girl from a God-fearing, Presbyterian-Church-going family could carry out her life. She had grown up in Annapolis, Maryland, where her father was a naval officer and her mother a navy office administrator.

Her college life had been simple. She had attended the Presbyterian College in Clinton, South Carolina, excelling in business administration, economics, and political science. But it lacked intrigue—she had always wanted to know what was behind the closed doors. The tedium of life had pushed her to work in the Central Intelligence Agency and deal with other people's lives as they danced with death.

Now, she was behind those doors, creating the intrigue, and she wondered if she had gone too far. She caught a glimpse of herself in her dining room mirror. She thought she was looking old—well, older. She was dressed in a purple velour track suit, something she had sworn she would never wear as it was for old people. She realized she was there— old. *Get used to it,* she thought. She got up from her chair to open the balcony door; cool desert air with a slight smell of sage wafted in.

She had some serious thinking to do. Starko had sent Cordele a text before he died to tell him that his laptop had exploded in flames. Parsons confirmed the same information.

The obvious answer was that McAllen was sabotaging the mission. She understood sabotage. That was her main business—that and eliminating people. What she could not understand was why McAllen would scuttle his own mission. They had been so close to activation— was it revenge against both the Wall Street boys and her team?

Margaret understood revenge. They had killed four of McAllen's team. She had thought that McAllen was more mission driven than people oriented. Perhaps she had been wrong. There was something more she had seen in his profile that nagged at her intuition. She had been in human resources for years with the Agency. She had had to read men, especially those put into battle. She always knew who would cut and run and who would stand and fight no matter the odds. McAllen seemed like the latter.

This was the same man who had destroyed the assault on the beach on Galiano Island. The report was of .50 caliber sniper fire, M16s, and improvised explosive devices. This man was capable of anything.

Freddy and Frodo had been running searches for McAllen and had come up with thin air—he had vanished somewhere off of Canada's West Coast, somewhere in the hundreds of islands there. He could be anywhere. Spending time and resources on him was no longer a priority.

Margaret made up her mind to eliminate Randall Francis and Duncan Stewart as she watched the sun rise and the hummingbirds sipping from her feeder for their morning breakfast. The project they had brought to her was ill conceived and carried out with poor intelligence on their parts. She briefly thought that perhaps she shared some of the blame for the intelligence part, but she put that out of her mind. Clients were responsible for the work they brought to her.

They had paid 5 million and owed her another 5 million; she would cut her losses. The mission had cost 2 million since it started, in November of the previous year—that did not matter now. There was 3 million left over, tax free of course, and that would have to suffice.

The elimination of Randall and Duncan would be a matter of honor for her company and would show her competitors in the black operations industry that her company was not to be trifled with. It would be a reminder to others, like the medieval practice of heads on pikes at the castle gate.

It would also be good for morale. She poured herself more tea and went to her desk. She did not doubt that Cordele and Parsons felt somewhat abused by events. This would provide some closure. The one thing that Margaret had learned in years at the CIA was the importance of keeping employee morale high.

She closed the blinds as the desert sun streamed in. To set the plan in motion, she needed to tell a lie. She normally tried to keep lies to a minimum as they were hard to control once they were out there. CNN had reported that no devices had been found. Perhaps that was true, but McAllen had destroyed the radio control devices. Ironstone did not know that. She stirred her tea, replaced her spoon, and picked up her phone.

After flipping on the voice synthesizer device on her phone, she dialed Randall in New York. He answered immediately. "The package has been delivered" was all she said before ending the call.

She needed some time to get Cordele and Parsons in place—the lie would keep the Wall Street boys busy. Busy until her men got there. She dialed Cordele's number. She looked at her watch. It was now 8:30 a.m., and she wondered where the time had gone.

Cordele picked up, his voice coming out of sleep. "Hello?"

"Cordele, I have a job for you, one I think you will like," Margaret began. She spoke slowly, the voice synthesizer making her voice sound deep, masculine, and commanding.

"Will it be in a cold place?" Cordele sat up in bed and rubbed his eyes, realizing it was his boss on the line. He had just returned to his apartment in Portland. He had had plans to head to the big island of Hawaii that afternoon, but his boss always took precedence. His boss still instilled fear in him.

"Somewhat cold—the job is in New York. But I want to fly Parsons and you to Miami first. We will put you up at the Four Seasons in downtown Miami until it's time for your mission." Margaret paused and waited for Cordele's reply.

"What's the job?" Cordele let out a soft sigh.

"Eliminate Stewart and Francis at Ironstone," Margaret said.

Cordele ran his hands through his hair and looked at his clock. "That actually sounds like rodent extermination."

"Do you know how to reach Parsons?"

"Yeah, he's in St. John's on the East Coast of Canada, probably deep into a barrel of rum by now. I'll call him right away and get him moving."

"Sounds good. Look, you boys have been through a tough ride. The fee is double, and we throw in one week at a five-star, all-inclusive resort in the Caribbean." Margaret purred softly. It was all about reeling him in now.

"Can you make it two weeks? It was really cold up there."

Margaret almost spilled her tea at Cordele's request. She covered a laugh. *Never let them know you have a sense humor,* she thought. *Not these guys.* "Sure, you got it."

She ended the call and made notes at her desk. By Tuesday afternoon, the men would be in Miami. They could rest for a few days. The flight from Miami to New York was two-and-a-half hours. They would take care of Francis and Stewart and then fly back the same day. Margaret would put them up at a five-star resort and would probably have to pay a few hooker tabs, but it would be worth it. She would have two relaxed and happy employees for her next mission.

She promised herself a ten-day cruise when this was over. *On Celebrity or Holland America out of Fort Lauderdale would be nice,* she thought. She could afford Silver Seas or Oceania cruise lines, the ones where you got your own personal butler, but she made it a point to never show her money—living modestly was her best cover.

The large antique hall clock chimed 9:00 a.m. There was a breakfast date with her friend Myrna at Sherman's Deli on Country Club Drive to get to. All of the morning's plans had made her hungry. She backed her gray, five-year-old Toyota Camry out of the driveway and decided that this morning, she would have waffles.

Randall stood in front of Duncan's large desk. Duncan had his back to him as he watched his row of monitors. Six monitors streamed stocks and commodity prices. One monitor was tuned to CNN.

The large wall clock showed 9:45 a.m., Monday. The last monitor was tuned to the New York Mercantile Exchange. The crude oil trading pit and a small clock below it counted down the minutes until trading opened. Crude oil traded from 10 a.m. until 2:30 p.m. Eastern Standard Time.

Randall cleared his throat. "I just got word from our contact. He said the package has been delivered." His voice came out in a squeak, his nerves now frayed by the fine line he walked between Duncan's anger and acceptance. He had been raked over the coals since Saturday— Duncan had called this venture a colossal fuckup.

He now hoped the 5 million paid to McAllen to install the polywater and the 5 million to the black ops company to activate the polywater had actually worked. They were betting millions more on the outcome.

Duncan slightly turned his head to reply to Randall. "So why aren't CNN reporting problems with Alaska and Canada? The vials were supposed to be instantaneous. They should have shut everything down by now—wasn't that the scenario we bought?" The back of Duncan's neck was turning bright red, the first sign of his anger. Randall could see the bright glow of his red forehead in the window.

"Sure . . . sure . . . instantaneous. . . but the professor said it could take up to a week before it reached critical mass and propagated through the geological strata, thereby trapping the oil." Randall was speaking as slowly as he could, trying to squeeze the squeak out of his vocal chords. It worked.

"Ah yes… your wonderful professor. Too bad he isn't here to answer questions." Duncan turned to face Randall. "You're saying that if in fact the vials have been injected, that by this Friday at the latest, the oil in Alaska and Canada will slow to a trickle, and all hell will break loose, and we will profit like mad pirates?" He added the last words with a smile.

"Basically yes," Randall replied as he felt the tension in his body release. For some reason, his butt cheeks had been clenched ever so tightly in the anticipation of an ass kicking. He relaxed.

"Okay then." Duncan's color went back to excited red instead of angry red. Randall was the only one who could read the difference. "We bet long on oil. Do our call options in the pit in the 140- to 150-a-barrel range. We start picking options for Friday's close. Damn this could be good."

"I'll let the traders know we are going long and aggressive," Randall said as he turned and made his way out of the room. He started to breathe again when he shut the door to Duncan's office.

Randall was doing mental calculations, something he did to calm himself as money was better than yoga breathing. With Duncan now on side, they would bet very aggressively on oil. They would buy 100 million in options, and the cost would be 10 million in insurance on the bid. If they were right, they would make ten times their bid. If wrong, well, if they were wrong, they lost 10 million, and Randall knew he had better be on a plane out of New York. There would be no second chance from Duncan.

Professor McAllen watched the boats go by in the channel below. From the high perch of the cabin, the boats looked small. They appeared and disappeared in the early morning mist. The two resident eagles circled overhead, slowly wheeling from mist to sunlight. They were in search of breakfast—anything small that moved was on their menu.

He turned to look back into the great room of the cabin. His third cup of coffee was going cold in his hand as he surveyed his companions in the room. They were at their individual desks, and soft music played overhead. Another Grateful Dead album—Sebastian's favorite band. Strains of "I Know You Rider" sounded mournfully from the speakers: "Gonna miss me when I'm gone . . . the sun's gonna shine in my back door." Sebastian's musical interests seemed to be locked in 1970.

A low fire popped and wheezed in the stone fireplace; the dog slept in front of the hearth. The large dog only moved occasionally—its muzzle, then a paw, to prove it was alive.

Percy was glued to his monitors that tracked satellites overhead, watching for any activity on his firewalls. Theo, who had been awake since 3:00 a.m. to watch the Tokyo Stock Exchange, had multiple screens tracking stocks and oil options. Sebastian was at his desk with his headphones on. His head, with its long, gray, braided hair now in a blue headband, was tilted to one side.

Sebastian was wearing a Navajo shirt that Grace had given to him and a large, ornate silver necklace with blue turquoise stones that he claimed came from a New Mexico medicine man. The necklace was supposed to ward off evil spirits and keep the breath of death from his door. McAllen thought Sebastian was now adding bizarre to paranoid and surfing the edges of his own reason. McAllen hoped Sebastian did not take to wearing war paint.

Grace was in the kitchen again. Whole grain breads and muffins emerged from the oven and stews of mussels, clams, and fish bubbled on the stove. The men had never dined so well or felt so good.

McAllen saw Sebastian rock his head back. His whole body went stiff—he had heard something on the headphones. He had been listening in to the cell phone conversations of the Wall Street boys and the black ops people for days.

McAllen walked over slowly, placed a hand on Sebastian's shoulder, and asked, "What's up?"

Sebastian took the headphones off one ear and looked up. "Well I'll be damned. The black ops senior citizen in Palm Springs just sold out the Wall Street Boys." His silver and turquoise necklace jangled in his excitement.

"How? What did you hear?"

"She just told them the devices had been activated, and based on all the other cell phone conversations we've heard, her people know the opposite."

"What do you think she's up to?" McAllen waited for Sebastian's reply as he knew his paranoid scenario would be something they could work from.

"I think she's had enough of them. Probably pissed about the bad intelligence they had on you; hold on, she's back on the phone with

Cordele . . .” Sebastian put the headset back on and raised a hand to all those present—as if the people he was listening to could hear him.

“Shit.” Sebastian dropped the phones around his neck. “That little lady is putting a hit on the Wall Street boys.”

“What?” Percy jumped up from his screens of stock quotes. The New York Stock Exchange would not open for a few more minutes. He came up behind Sebastian.

Sebastian turned slowly to his companions, who now all stood around him. “So . . . these people do eat their young.” His grin flashed one predominate gold tooth.

“Did she say when?” Theo asked as he gulped down one of Grace’s super fiber muffins. He was spraying crumbs with his question.

“Yeah, she wants Cordele and Parsons to fly to Miami and then to New York to whack the little fuckers on Friday,” Sebastian said as he flicked muffin crumbs off his desk. He followed the movement with a scowl at Theo.

“Cool,” Theo said. He gulped hard before he said the word to reduce offensive muffin spray. He understood Sebastian’s scowl.

McAllen paced back and forth and then stopped in front of the other men. “Gentlemen, this bit of information could be an opportunity for us. Any ideas?”

The men looked at each other, and then Percy, Theo, and McAllen looked at Sebastian. He was the one to come up with the weirdest ideas; it was just his nature. Being paranoid made him think more than just outside the box—more like outside the universe.

“Hell yeah,” Sebastian screamed. The other men jumped back. Sebastian wheeled back to his computer and began pounding his keys and bringing up screens. “See this,” he said, pointing to the screen in the center. “These little pricks have millions of dollars in their accounts. I estimate it’s somewhere in the 100-million-dollar range, and all I need is a password.” Sebastian wheeled back around to them. He looked like someone who had received the best Christmas present in the world.

"How'd you find that out?"

"Simple. The bug I had you put on that creep Randall Francis's cell phone when he was at your place led me to all his email and Internet accounts. The little shit liked to be Mr. Big and trade from his cell phone. One account led to another, and bada bing bada boom, I got every account."

"So we're going to steal it?" Theo asked.

"Hell no... not if these guys are going to get whacked. Their money goes to their estates, and then the US government steps in with a whole bunch of lawyers and accountants who pad their pockets first, and then a whole shitload of money ends up in estate taxes. You know the government will just spend the money on devices to spy on their own people," Sebastian said in a pained voice with a look that said he would be doing the people of America a service by taking the Wall Street boys' money.

"Okay, we just need to get to New York, get in the room before these guys get killed, convince them to give us their pass codes before they die, which I'm sure they will, and get away unseen. Am I missing anything?" Theo said.

McAllen put one of his long arms around Theo's shoulder. "You, unfortunately, do not know of my well-thought-out master plan."

"Which is?" Theo asked dryly.

"We'll make it up as we go. The best ones work out that way. Sebastian, we're going south, off to America. Grace you want to come along?" McAllen shouted to Grace.

"Sure, I just made enough muffins to last a week. We should be good." Grace wandered in from the kitchen, wiping her hands on a tea towel.

"Good, Percy, you keep working the stock portfolio, and Theo, keep an eye on the listening post and keep us informed as to what's going on with our little Palm Springs lady and the Wall Street boys. I'm going to pack a bag." McAllen turned and headed for his room. He felt a plan developing. He would need a partner, and he knew exactly where to find the one he needed.

"Just one more thing," Sebastian called out. "If the Wall Street boys think the polywater has been activated, they are going to bet heavily on oil prices rising—they could lose a good portion of the 100 million before we get there."

McAllen stopped in his tracks and wheeled to look at Sebastian. "You know, you're right. We need to get the message out. I think I know someone who could do it for us. We'll talk more on the way." He turned and left the room.

CHAPTER TWENTY-SEVEN

B ERNADETTE WAS RUNNING LATE. SHE had spent hours putting together the briefing notes on the Clearwater employee murders for the CSIS and then reviewing the numerous cases of Fort McMurray mayhem that had washed up on the shores of the RCMP detachment that weekend.

The RCMP detachment was an outpost of law and order overseeing a demographic of predominately eighteen- to thirty-year-old males employed by Big Oil. Their penchant for stupid was fueled by alcohol and drugs. Young people claimed they could get crack cocaine faster than pizza on the streets of Fort Mac. Some called it Fort Crack.

There were the usual stabbings, but only one shooting (RCMP officers were always happy that Canadians did not have better access to guns) and only one bar brawl with numerous casualties. Many an oil company personnel officer would be visiting the hospital or receiving sick calls the next morning. Broken arms and gashed foreheads were the norm. None of them would lose their jobs; they were needed to run the plants.

Bernadette only had one death to review for the weekend. Another detective would handle it until Tuesday, but she would have to read the file so she could be active on it the next day. From a quick glance, it looked to be the usual: drugs that someone wanted, stole, or did not pay for, and a young man lay dead. The gangs had now moved into Fort McMurray. The profits from drugs were too good to keep them out. An RCMP gang unit had been formed last spring—they were busy.

When 7:00 p.m. rolled around, she realized she was supposed to be at the restaurant to meet Pierre. She had suggested the restaurant, agreed to the time, and yes, she would be late. She threw her files into her desk, cursed the day paperwork became a part of police work, and grabbed her coat.

Outside, the cold made her eyes squint, and she could just make out the outline of her Jeep under a foot of new snow. She fired up the Jeep's engine first, and then began working the snow brush. Snow fell down the back of her neck, down her sleeves, and she cursed the cold, the snow, and the fact that she never took vacations to Mexico.

When she arrived at the restaurant, Pierre was already there. She knew he would be. He had a habit for punctuality that made her habit for lateness even more pronounced.

Pierre was reviewing text messages as he looked up and smiled at her entrance. The restaurant was packed on a Monday night. This steakhouse was the best one in town. It was the place to make deals—where contracts got signed for oil services, transport, and workers. In the crazy days of multiple oil plant expansion, oil men had come here to strategize over stealing other companies' employees. Bodies had been needed to build the plants—anything with a heartbeat.

Bernadette walked in, put her gloves in her jacket, and unbuttoned her coat. The place was warm. Grilling steaks wafted their aroma, glasses clinked, and voices rose as alcohol loosened restaurant patrons' tongues.

Bernadette collapsed in her chair. "Sorry to keep you waiting."

Pierre smiled. "The bad boys being bad again?"

"Always," Bernadette said as she threw her leather jacket over the back of the chair.

A waiter arrived and placed an order of crab cakes and tempura snap peas and asparagus on the table. Another waiter followed with a bottle of wine and two glasses.

"I ordered some starters and wine—I thought you might be hungry." Pierre smiled again. His French Canadian charm was the thing that Bernadette had found attractive. She had stayed only briefly for the sex.

"Starving." Bernadette picked up a fork and speared a crab cake the moment it hit the table.

"Still have Tim Horton's doughnuts and coffee daily?"

"Hey, I now have a Subway sandwich—I'm a changed woman. And I started to drink that iced green tea," she said through mouthfuls of crab.

Pierre tasted the wine; he had chosen a Merlot from Nk'Mip wineries in Canada's Okanagan region. He thought the wine was okay. He was a California wine snob, but he knew Bernadette would like it.

Bernadette stopped shoveling mouthfuls of crab cake to sip the wine. "Nice. Nk'Mip wineries." She smiled at Pierre. "You know I like this winery, it's a great Native story. Native band in southern British Columbia puts together a winery with a five-star resort and golf course. And I hear they're hiring a few white guys now." She beamed at Pierre.

Pierre swirled the wine in his glass. He had heard the story several times as Bernadette never tired of telling it. "Yes, they make a passable merlot."

"Passable. Hell, they've won awards."

"Yes, yes. They've done very well. Listen I'll grant you all the accolades for the Native winery. It's wonderful." Pierre paused as Bernadette visibly settled down. He was never sure when she got excited if it was the Cree side or the Irish side. They both flashed with fire.

He began slowly, keeping his voice low. "Bernadette, I wanted to thank you for the work you did on uncovering the Clearwater affair. The Synthetic Oil people are extremely grateful. So grateful in fact, they wanted to know if you would like to come over to private security—their private security team. There would of course be the usual perks, twice your present pay, a nice car, and vacations to exotic places that you might have the time to go to." He paused and waited, watching her, seeing if an emotion would tell her thoughts.

Bernadette stabbed some tempura asparagus and munched on it. "You mean give up my pain-in-the-ass captain of detectives to come work for Synthetic Oil, where you would be my boss?"

"Yeah, kind of like that. You might find me nicer to work with than you think. My whole team loves me." He threw that charming grin again.

Bernadette took another sip of her wine and patted her lips with her napkin. "You know, Pierre, that is a sweet offer, and you're a sweet guy, but the RCMP would never survive without me. The very future of Canada would be at stake if I left the force." She smiled over her wine glass.

Pierre let out a low chuckle. "Mon Dieu. What am I to do in the face of such patriotism? Okay, okay, the country of Canada needs you. The company also wanted to offer you some kind of reward—perhaps a nice cruise or two weeks in an all-inclusive resort. I hear good things about Cancun."

"Which you know, of course, I cannot accept."

"Merde, shit, of course. The honorable RCMP. So I will buy dinner, and you'll have dessert, yes?" Pierre raised his wine glass in a toast.

"Of course. We're talking business," Bernadette said, raising her wine glass.

Pierre sighed and lowered his wine glass. "What business?"

Bernadette was about to launch into her conversation when the waiter came back to take their order for dinner. Pierre ordered the eight-ounce sirloin well done with a side salad. Bernadette ordered the baseball steak medium rare and sautéed mushrooms. She did not say no to the baked potato.

When the waiter left, she resumed. "Do you think the FBI or the CSIS has a chance of finding the guys who are behind this oil manipulation?"

Pierre poured more wine in their glasses and leaned forward. "I don't think the CSIS or the FBI have the slightest chance of catching these guys."

"Why's that?" Bernadette leaned closer. The tables were close together in the steakhouse. They did not want to be overhead. Fort McMurray was a small town. The ears were everywhere.

"Look." Pierre lowered his voice, providing a sense of conspiracy in his actions. "They can only catch these guys if they trade large volumes on NYMEX, the New York Mercantile Exchange—it has a watchdog. But if they trade on the International Oil Exchange, called ICE Futures, they'll be virtually unseen."

"How come?" Bernadette was leaning so close to Pierre she could smell his cologne. It brought back memories.

"Thanks to the past president, Bush, who allowed it, and the guys like Enron, who proposed it—just before they took themselves and a few billion with them."

"How'd they get it through?" Bernadette had to lean closer, as the restaurant was getting loud. Two young oil workers were enjoying themselves at full volume at the table beside them. She stared at them, just enough for them to feel it. They lowered their voices.

Pierre smiled and waited for her attention to drift back from the table of rowdies to him. "Some congressmen howled like crazy, but the Commodity Futures Modernization Act of 2000 was passed. The Act brought in a new way of trading oil called a futures 'look-alike' contract—a whole new way of speculating on oil that couldn't be monitored."

"And the government allowed that? My dear Grandmother would say that's like the fox asking the farmers to feed the chickens." Bernadette leaned back in her chair and then leaned in again. "So, you think these guys trade on this new . . . ICE exchange?"

"Yeah, I would bet on it. And they somehow convinced McAllen to come in to move the price of oil for them. There is a theory that 60 percent of the price of oil is caused by speculation. The war in Iraq caused a price spike because it's so close to Saudi Arabia. Afghanistan caused a blip in the price of oil because there's nothing there other than rocks, mud, and some opium plants. Did nothing to oil. Now the dustup in Libya—we had a 20 percent price hike back then."

"So, what will this cause? The threat of terrorism to Alaskan and Canadian oil—what kind of price spike do you see?"

"I see a 40 to 50 percent, and maybe more."

"That much?"

"Oh yeah, up until now, the main draw of North American oil has been safety. Sure, the eco-friendly Americans and Canadians hate the dirty Canadian oil. But without Canada's oil sands, they're hooped. Americans consume 20 million barrels of oil a day. Canada supplies 20 percent of that and 47 percent comes from the oil sands. Alaska provides another 5 percent of the oil delivered to the USA. If both of these oil fields were compromised, you would see gasoline at over three dollars a liter in Canada and on the upside of six dollars a gallon in America." Pierre sat back in his chair. The waiter arrived with the steaks, poured more wine, smiled at them, and left.

Bernadette cut into her steak. It oozed blood, and she smiled her satisfaction. "So the people trying to manipulate oil knew what they were doing when they hit these two oil fields."

"And so did McAllen. They hit the two places in North America that are vulnerable to a single-source water supply. If the polywater had done what McAllen claimed it would do, you might be looking for a new posting. Say, you would look great in the ceremonial scarlet RCMP uniform. I hear the tourists like to take pictures of RCMP in Banff. You're pretty photogenic." Pierre smiled and looked for the rise out of Bernadette that was sure to follow.

"Asshole," Bernadette scowled between mouthfuls of steak. "The last place you will ever find me will be in Banff, and other than at a ceremony, I do not wear the scarlet. Not that there is a problem with the scarlet uniform." She realized Pierre had successfully boxed her into one of his little conversation corners. She remembered this was one of the reasons she had broken up with him. The verbal jousting was a pain in the ass.

"So, why the interest in the case? The chief said you were off it." Pierre reached his hand across the table and put his hand on hers. "Not like that would stop you, of course."

Bernadette glanced at Pierre's hand on hers. She let it rest. She felt the old feeling—was this flirtation, or just concern?

"Well, you know me; I've always had this thing about the chase. Never stop until the other guy drops." She moved her hand from under Pierre's and patted her lips with her napkin. "Let's put it this way, I got two murders here in Fort McMurray, three on Galiano Island, and three more in Alaska all caused by McAllen and supposedly someone trying to manipulate oil. The natural tracker in me doesn't want to let go."

"But you're off the case." Pierre knew he was stating the obvious.

"Well, I believe the case has been reorganized, and I will look in on it as a casual observer."

"The RCMP does that?"

"No. I do."

Pierre put his wine glass down. "Ah, the unstoppable Detective Bernadette Callahan." He looked straight into her eyes and held her gaze.

There was a moment, when Pierre stared into her eyes—the little spark rekindled, the interest, the old excitement was there. She felt flushed and hoped it didn't show. She blamed it on the wine, the heat of the restaurant, and the cold outside. A thought entered the back of her mind and then took center stage. Did Pierre want to be involved again? Were they about to go from here to his place or hers? Was a quick hookup her style? Could she handle it? A message flashed to her brain: *Bernadette, you need your libido serviced. Time to light the fires, girl.*

Pierre looked at his watch. "I hate to cut our evening short, but I need to catch a flight to Calgary tonight. Some accountants at Synthetic Oil want a face-to-face. Risk assessment analysis and stuff. I never knew these guys would be up so late for something so boring, but that's the job."

Bernadette snapped out of the conversation going on in her head. "But there're no flights this late at night . . . Oh yeah, the Synthetic Oil private fleet." She let the words out slowly. Just as slowly, she let go of the vision of Pierre and her romping naked. *Yes, I'll be in the gym early tomorrow, to work off the sexual frustration*, she told herself

"We have the new Gulfstream G150 on the tarmac. I hear they can max at around eight hundred kilometers an hour. I should be in Calgary fifty minutes after wheels up."

"And wheels up are when?" Bernadette now had her composure back. She was no longer going to let her brain send her images she could not act on.

"Supposedly at 8:30, but I can push to 9:00. How about desert? I know you like your sugar." Pierre patted her hand again. This time it felt friendly. He smiled.

Bernadette returned the friendly smile. "You know me. Normally I would, but I hit my sugar max with a doughnut or two today. How about we call it a night? You go do your risk assessment, and I could use some downtime."

"You sure? They have that amazing chocolate cake you like." Pierre smiled again. It was obvious he wanted to leave as well.

"Absolutely. Matter of fact, I hate to eat and run . . . have some errands to do." Bernadette stood and extended her hand. She did not want the standard French Canadian hug in the restaurant.

Pierre stood. He got the message. "It was a pleasure; perhaps we can do this again."

"Absolutely." Bernadette squeezed away from Pierre, put on her coat and gloves, and walked out of the restaurant and into the street. Three young men looked at her with interest, making movements as if to approach. She glared back at them. They stopped in their tracks.

CHAPTER TWENTY-EIGHT

MARGARET ALWAYS ATE LUNCH AT Armando's Grill on Wednesdays at 2:00 p.m. Most of the tourists had moved on by that time and only a few locals would be there.

Armando's was the happening place for locals and tourists. Locals loved it for the famous Cadillac margaritas, served in large bowl-shaped glasses with loads of tequila and a splash of Grand Marnier. The food was Mexican, the atmosphere the same, but the real appeal was the location. Armando's was right on El Paseo Drive, Palm Desert's answer to Rodeo Drive in LA, where all of the glitz of Palm Desert went by on wheels or on foot.

Lexus's and BMWs with a few Bentleys roll down the street, and Palm Desert ladies hauling packages and poodles shopped the stores for fine clothing and art, or their next ex-husband. The place to see and be seen was El Paseo. Armando's had a promontory view with a street-level patio. The patrons on the patio got all the ogling they could absorb.

Margaret went there for the quiet, and the nacho chips and salsa. She was only slightly addicted to them, certain they were the reason for the weight she had gained in Palm Desert. With her other favorite, the fish taco (grilled not fried), and an ice tea, her lunch was complete. Her companions for lunch were *The Economist* and the *Wall Street Journal*.

Some found these a dry read. Margaret found them fascinating. *The Economist* provided snapshots of the capital output of countries and government sentiments. She used it like a gambler would use a racing sheet to bet on horses. She found countries suitable for her operations. The *Wall Street Journal* let her know what the boys of industry were up to and who could use her special assistance next.

She always sat on the patio, reserving one of the small tables just inside the entrance. The Palm Desert sun beamed down, providing light for her reading and warmth. Her table was waiting as she entered the restaurant. She smiled her satisfaction to the waiter, and with her magazine and paper in hand, she went to her table.

She noticed that only one other table on the patio was occupied. Three people sat over on the far corner—a tall, gray-haired, grey bearded man wearing a loud, red print Hawaiian shirt and gray cargo shorts, a round-faced Native-looking lady, and a small man with gray braids and a bandana. She thought he looked a lot like Willy Nelson. *Tourists,* she thought, and went about reading her magazine.

The waiter placed a margarita on her table. She looked up from her reading. She never ordered margaritas at lunch. The waiter knew he was doing something unwanted. "Senora Ashley, this is from the other table . . ." He let the words trail away and hurried off.

Margaret looked over. The tall man in the loud shirt and gray cargo shorts stood up and started ambling towards her. It took her brain a mere nanosecond to realize this was Professor Alistair McAllen. He had grown a beard and his hair was longer, but it was him. She recognized him from the TV broadcasts and profiles. It was him, here, in Palm Desert.

He moved slowly to the chair opposite hers. She tried to relax her breathing. She needed air to get to her brain. She placed her hands on the table. A Beratta Tomcat .32 caliber, loaded, with the safety on, was in her purse on the floor. The options did not look good. McAllen's other hand rested in his pocket. She assumed he had a gun. The strange-looking little man at the other table was eyeing her. She breathed deeply, waited for their moves.

"Mind if I join you?" McAllen stood in the bright Palm Desert sunshine. He was taller than he looked on television. The long hair and beard couldn't hide the keen sharp eyes that stared at her.

"Please do," Margaret offered. She instinctively wanted to withdraw her hands from the table. She stopped herself.

"Margaret Ashley my name is Professor Alistair McAllen, but you already know that. What you don't know is we . . ." he turned his head to motion in the direction of his companions, ". . . know quite a bit about you."

Margaret processed the information. Here was McAllen. He had found her and knew her name. She had lived so many years in the safety of the shadows. Now here, on her doorstep and threatening her life, was one of her pawns. Someone she had manipulated for money. She breathed deeply, and let it out slowly. "Well, Professor, you are far more clever than I gave you credit for. And to what do I owe the honor of this visit…revenge?"

McAllen took his hand out of his pocket and placed them both on the table. Margaret saw large, tanned wrinkled hands with age spots. "Revenge, no, but I guess you'd think that. I was pretty steamed when I heard about the deaths of the Lafontaine's and then Alisha and Kevin. But I saw how it transpired. The Lafontaine's got greedy, tried to get some extra money. You know . . . when you think you know someone . . ." He paused. The waiter came by. He ordered a Cadillac margarita.

"I hear the margaritas are pretty good here." He motioned to her glass. "You should try that. I ordered you the same, the Cadillac. They lace the top with Grand Marnier." He smiled at her, showing excellent teeth.

Margaret looked at her glass. Beads of condensation dripped slowly down. One bead then another dropped onto the tablecloth. A small wet stain appeared underneath. She took both hands and raised the glass to her lips. She was conscious that this could be her last moment in life. She would enjoy the sunshine and the tequila as it paddled its way to her brain, and she would go out with a smile.

When she placed the drink down, she fixed her gaze on McAllen. "So, you were saying . . ."

"Oh yeah. I guess I should have been upset with you for taking out my people. But I realized why—you were cleaning up a bad situation, trying to save the mission. I respect you for that." McAllen waved his large hands, as if there was absolution in the movement.

"You do?"

"Absolutely, I would have done the same. You know, I did spend some time in the military."

"Yes, I did see that." Margaret put her hands back on her glass; she felt the coolness on her hands. The tequila was ebbing its way into her brain—she was fascinated by McAllen.

"Well, we would go out on these patrols. We were mission oriented. Losing guys was secondary. Sure you didn't want it to happen, but it happened. So I understand what you did. Now, I did take out a few of your people, and I wasn't proud of that."

The waiter came back. He placed a margarita in front of McAllen, smiled at them, and moved on.

"Why do you say that? You defended yourself." Margaret took a second sip of the margarita. The conversation needed alcohol to make sense.

McAllen leaned forward. His eyes narrowed, his voice lowered. "But I didn't have to. I knew your people were coming. I could have easily disappeared, gone into thin air. You'd have never found me. But my guys, well, they wanted a little retribution, a little action. I gave it to them."

"I see. Something for morale."

"Exactly, just like you are about to do with the Wall Street boys in New York." McAllen leaned further over the table; his eyes wide open to heighten the surprise.

"You know about that?" Margaret took her hands off the table. They dropped to her lap.

"Margaret." McAllen's voice became very stern—commanding. "I'm going to ask you to put your hands back on the table; the little guy behind me has orders to shoot you if you drop your hands to your lap."

"Yes, yes of course." Margaret put her hands back on the table. She locked her fingers around the margarita glass for safe measure. She looked over McAllen's shoulder. The strange little man had been about to get out of his chair. He sat down again.

"I hate accidents," McAllen smiled. "Let's drink to better understanding and morale, shall we?" He raised his glass to hers, clinked, and took a large swallow.

Margaret instinctively followed suit. She raised the glass again to her lips and let the tequila and Grand Marnier blend work its way to numbing her brain. The fact that McAllen knew of her intention to terminate Randall and Duncan was too much to handle.

McAllen hunched low, bringing his height down to Margaret's eye level. "Margaret, I'll get down to business, as I know you are a business woman. I am proposing a partnership."

"A partnership—you and me?"

"Exactly."

"But we've been killing each other's people."

"Well, again, I understand why. You know, the Arabs have this saying: 'The enemy of my enemy is my friend.' I know it's odd, but you and I, we're a lot alike. We get the job done." McAllen picked up his glass, took a sip, and gave Margaret a wink.

"And what do you suppose we do in this partnership?"

"For one thing, we will make a lot more money than you have been making." McAllen flashed that knowing wink again.

"You know how much money I make?" Margaret sat straight up in her chair. She almost took her hands off the table again. One look at the little man at the other table made her stop.

McAllen motioned over his shoulder. "That little guy back there has this amazing computer program. He can get inside just about any computer—all he needs is email then bingo, he gets in. His program sends him back all this good stuff. Now, you're doing well, Margaret, about 3 to 4 million a year—nice income. But we could do better for you."

Margaret was not sure if her ears were buzzing from the tequila or from what McAllen had just said. "How exactly would you do that?" She really did want to know. McAllen was now either the craziest or most fascinating man she had ever met. Her fear was melting away from either the alcohol or the conversation.

"Glad I have your interest. For starters, when you whack the Wall Street boys—"

"—whack?"

"Sorry, eliminate Francis and Stewart; we know they have 100 million in accounts and that all we need is a password and we can electronically transfer this money into multiple offshore accounts."

"You assume that they'll just give you the passwords to millions of dollars before we kill them? Or 'whack,' as you put it?"

McAllen motioned over his shoulder again and then leaned forward. "The little guy back there—"

"—the one who looks like Willy Nelson?" Margaret interrupted.

"That's him. Back in Vietnam, he was the best interrogator we had. The Viet Cong would be singing show tunes by the time he finished with them." McAllen smiled in appreciation.

"You propose my people take him on the mission?" Margaret looked hard over McAllen's shoulder at Sebastian. The tequila had made her vision somewhat hazy. His long, gray hair with pigtails circled with a bandana made him look mystical. "How do you suppose we get him into the building looking like that?"

"Like what? Oh yeah . . . Look, he cleans up really well. There's a Brooks Brothers just down the street. We put him in a nice blue suit, white shirt, pinstripe tie, his hair goes under a hat—that's all the rage now—and bingo, he looks like a Wall Street analyst. All Wall Street analysts look a little weird, don't you think?"

Margaret had a decision to make: accept his proposal and possibly gain great wealth, or reject the offer and deal with the funny-looking little guy with the gun at the other table. She decided to explore the offer. "So what's in it for me, for taking your person in and getting the money transferred? Assuming that will happen." She was skeptical that the Wall Street boys would hand over money, even on pain of death. She knew she never would.

"Twenty million dollars." McAllen threw down the offer like he was dropping something on the table. The amount sat there, large enough to get her attention.

"That's an eighty-twenty split, and I'm doing all the work." Margaret could not believe she was saying the words, but her business instincts would not let go.

"Well, we did find the 100 million—your guys were going to take these guys out and leave the money," McAllen countered. He loved negotiations. She could have asked for half.

"True, but still, I dislike eighty-twenty splits. You have to think of the morale of my people if they found out. I prefer seventy-thirty," Margaret replied with just a tinge of implied indignation. She was hoping it was enough to get her the other 10 million.

"Ha, I love that." McAllen's face lit up with the words. "Okay, you got a nice 30 million for taking Sebastian in. We don't want to mess with morale."

"I can drink to that." Margaret raised her glass and took another sip. "Now tell me, other than this job, why should we be partners?"

"Margaret, I like you more and more. You ask questions. Too many people don't ask enough questions." McAllen leaned in closer. Margaret could smell his cologne, somewhat pungent with a little earthiness. "I have this vision. A vision that my polywater could knock the hell out of oil, coal, and nuclear power production."

He paused and looked around to ensure they would not be overheard. "Now, I'm not totally crazy like some of these eco-terrorists freaks who wants to destroy everything and lay waste to industry—I just want to nudge them in the right direction."

"A nudge. How do you nudge?" Margaret leaned in across the table.

"Again, I love your inquisitive mind. I plan to remove just enough oil, coal, and nuclear power to get the world to solar and wind power faster than we're moving now. Now, I know there's this big deal about renewable energy in the world, but from where I sit, these guys are dragging their feet. Look at Ford and GM; they still produce those big-ass fuel guzzling trucks because oil is too cheap. I intend to limit oil supply—and to profit by it."

"How will you profit?" Margaret was not sure if she was listening to the craziest man on the planet or the Warren Buffet of eco-terrorism.

"Because I'll know which commodity will be affected, just like the Wall Street boys did, only on a larger scale. Margaret, we will not only hand you 30 million for taking us in when we eliminate those guys—we can triple your money in the commodities markets in the next few months." McAllen leaned back, his hand on the table. He watched her reaction.

"But the devices...you sabotaged your own devices. How will you affect anything now?"

McAllen reached into his shirt pocket. With two fingers, he pulled out a small, blue package and pushed it towards her on the table. The package was a condom with the tiny words "Her Pleasure" written underneath the Trojan name.

The last time Margaret had seen a condom in a restaurant was in her senior year in college. Her date, in a drunken stupor, had flipped one onto their table in a pizza joint and had added the romantic line, "Let's get naked, Maggie."

"I don't see . . . ." Margaret stammered. Her face flushed as her eyes fixed on the shiny, blue condom.

McAllen let out a low chuckle that emanated from deep within his throat. "Yeah, looks a bit strange. This is the actually the delivery device for polywater in Alaska and Canada. Those other radio-controlled devices were to please the Wall Street boys. We knew they liked gadgets. I have ten of these in both Alaska and Canada—and not one of them has been found yet."

"How do you know that?" Margaret asked, visibly relaxing. The condom was now no longer an offer of romance but an item of commerce. The waiter walked by, looked at Margaret and McAllen, saw the condom, and moved away quickly. The waiter was Mexican by birth—he always thought the mating rituals of Gringos were confusing.

"Easy. My Native friend sitting back there has cousins in Alaska and Canada—all in place and giving us intelligence. She has them here to . . . ah . . . by the way, you might want to close your drapes early in the morning," McAllen said as he motioned over his shoulder at Grace.

The information was coming too fast for Margaret; she needed to slow it down, break it into parts she could comprehend. "You mean there is polywater in these condoms in place in the water systems of Alaska and Canada oilfields?"

"Exactly," McAllen said, his finger tapping the condom. "And they are ready to pop in about five days by my calculations. Each one full to the brim…well, to six inches by whatever width."

"How can you be so sure?"

McAllen shrugged as if the answer were obvious. "I'm a chemist. I studied the thickness of the condoms and then forecasted the agitation that would occur once they were in the water. Also, you have to factor in the fact that there is some oil contamination in the water, and latex hates oil. I then worked out the ejection or ejaculation if you will, pardon the pun, and there you have it: a simple delivery device."

"Did you plan this double-cross all along?" Margaret needed to know. She needed to know what kind of man she was dealing with. She executed enough sideways ventures of her own.

McAllen sighed, looked down at the melting ice in his glass, and then looked back up at Margaret. "You know, when I first met the Wall Street boys, I thought we might be a good fit. Then I realized they had no ideal greater than money—nothing greater than themselves. But they did lead me to you. You want money, but only for your personal security—I get that."

"How do you know that?"

"Margaret, you have 20 million dollars in the bank and you drive a Toyota Camry. You didn't even buy the deluxe model."

Since McAllen knew everything about her, or so it seemed, she had a question of her own. The day was cooling, and a slight chill was in the air. Margaret leaned forward. "And you, Professor McAllen, what do you want this money for?"

"That is a reasonable question to ask, Margaret." McAllen looked down at his hands and back up at her. "Money does little for me. I have simple needs. I do like a few fine things, like a good glass of wine, scotch, or a Cuban cigar, but I'd like to do some good with the money that comes out of the polywater capers, perhaps spread it around."

"You want to be a Robin Hood?" The words popped out of Margaret's mouth before she had a chance to reason with them.

McAllen just smiled. "Robin Hood? No, not really, just someone with a conscious mind who would like to see the world with less poison. Perhaps my boys and I can fund some alternative energy projects in

Africa or Latin America. I would like to see a world without contamination. As a chemist, I helped develop a lot of shit that got put into the world. Now I would like to take a little out—sound fair?"

Margaret did not know if it was due to the earnest sound of McAllen's voice or the tequila that was making a home in her brain, but his offer of partnership sounded good to her. She only made money to feel secure, as he had said. The idea of doing something more appealed to her. She looked at him and took her leap. "Professor McAllen, I think we'll make a great team. I'll put my people at your disposal."

McAllen picked up his glass in a toast. "Margaret, I think you and I will have a wonderful time together."

The waiter approached. McAllen ordered another round of margaritas, and Margaret did not object.

CHAPTER TWENTY-NINE

YRON SLUMPED IN HIS CHAIR at the *Anchorage Daily Mirror* office on Thursday morning. His cubicle was depressing. Gray fabric walls constricted a small desk and chair. A digital clock ticked over to 8:08 a.m. It was February 3. Byron had driven to work in the dark, and he would go home in the dark. Sunrise was at 9:17 a.m., and sunset would be at 5:10 p.m., and Byron hated that. His coffee was cold. He stared at a computer screen, at his Word document with three words written, his mind suspended in self-pity.

He was trying to get the sequence right: who shot whom first down in Homer, Alaska. Someone was dead, someone clinging to life. His brain was not aligning the words; his fingers sat motionless on the keyboard. The curser blinked on the screen. In the back of his mind was the story he had let slip. Terrorists in Alaska—it was his. He had given it away to the cute redhead.

He sighed deeply, realizing he was addicted to stupid. If there were rehab for people like him, who were addicted to stupid, he would be the first to sign up. *Perhaps the rehab place might be on a warm South Pacific island with sunshine.* He tried to focus his mind on the article.

His phone rang, and he picked it up without enthusiasm. He noticed the phone number was blocked. "Byron Jacks speaking, Crime News Desk."

"Mr. Byron Jacks, I'm happy I got a hold of you." The voice sounded happy.

"Who's calling?" He wasn't in the mood for happy callers. The other reporters had taken to calling and leaving rude messages about his screw-up on the terrorism story. He wanted to find out who was on the phone, tell him to fuck off, and get back to his dour mood.

"This is Professor Alistair McAllen calling. Do you have minute to talk?"

Byron stood up. He did a periscope maneuver, a complete 360, looking around at the other cubicles to see if someone was looking in his direction and on the phone with a sick idea for a practical joke. "Now why, if you are the Professor McAllen, would you be talking to me?"

"Tell you what, Mr. Jacks, I know you reporters need all kinds of proof—do you use Skype?"

"Yes, I do."

"Good, give me your Skype account number and we can communicate, face-to-face, and you can record it. Would that be acceptable?"

Byron gave the caller his Skype address and slowly sat in his chair, still looking at the other cubicles to see if anyone was watching him. He wondered how far the other reporters would go to play out this practical joke.

Moments later, a Skype call buzzed on his laptop. He punched the connect key. McAllen appeared on the screen. It was him—Byron couldn't deny it. He leaned forward into his screen.

"As promised, Mr. Jacks, it is I, Professor Alistair McAllen." McAllen was calmly sitting somewhere in the world in front of his laptop with a blank wall behind him.

Byron cleared his throat, once then twice, and swallowed hard. "I'm happy to see you, Professor . . ."

"Look, I don't have a lot of time. And I'm not doing an interview for you. I'm here to set something straight about polywater—are you recording this?" McAllen leaned into his laptop camera.

"Ah, yes, yes, of course I'm recording." Byron quickly hit the record feature. The newspaper IT guys had only recently added Skylook, which allowed all Skype calls to be recorded. He was glad McAllen had reminded him.

McAllen focused himself as if addressing the world. "Here it is. The polywater devices are inactive—I deactivated them. There is no threat of polywater in either Alaska or Canada. Did you get that?"

"Yes, yes, I did. And who removed the threat?"

"I removed it," McAllen said with a wave of his hand, not unlike a magician ending an act. He leaned forward into the computer screen for effect.

"You did? You removed it?"

"Yes I did. Now as for the oil companies saying there is a continued threat to the oil fields, that is a lie. That lie is costing the American and Canadian people millions of dollars a day at the gas pumps.

"Why would the oil companies be lying?" Byron knew the obvious answer; he was reaching for sound bites and good newspaper copy.

McAllen's eyes narrowed as his words became projectiles at his target. "Why would they lie? As the speculators raise the price of oil, the oil companies add millions to their billions. Oil hit 140 dollars a barrel yesterday and they are making another 40 a barrel profit—nice business, don't you think?"

"Well, that would be true if they knew the threat had passed and they were saying it still existed . . . but . . ."

"There is no but," McAllen jumped in, his speech now rapid. "I deactivated the devices remotely on Saturday. I have solid intelligence that all the devices were located. The oil companies are feeding you bullshit to steal your money. Now, I got to go, so go do what you do—because I am done here." The screen went blank.

Byron was vibrating. He'd recorded the call of his career. He was back on top. He did a fist pump, grabbed his laptop, and ran out of his office and down the hall to his editor's office. He repeated the words to himself as he raced down the hall: "Don't fuck this up, don't fuck this up, don't fuck this up."

McAllen logged off Skype and closed his laptop. He turned to Sebastian. "Do you think he bought that?"

Sebastian stood beside him, just out of sight of the webcam. "I think he was buying what you were selling."

Sebastian was now hardly recognizable. Instead of his previous Willy Nelson and Navajo shaman attire, he wore a blue Irish linen sport shirt, tan gabardine dress trousers with a black leather belt, and new black penny loafers. A black blazer rested on the chair in the room. He had also purchased a navy blue suit, white shirt, and striped tie, which were neatly packed in his garment bag along with a pair of dress shoes.

Sebastian's long gray braids had been the problem. They had dealt with them with a series of plastic pins that would not set off the detectors at airport security. Once the braids had been neatly compacted, they placed a dark blue Ivy hat on his head. He looked the height of old-guy fashion.

They had also purchased a raincoat, silk scarf, and leather briefcase. Everything had been purchased at Brooks Brothers on El Paseo, with the exception of the briefcase. The briefcases at Brooks Brothers were $350 and up. Sebastian had railed at the cost, and he and McAllen had ended up getting a simple black case at Office Max for $49.95. Some things were not worth fighting Sebastian over, and McAllen knew when to stop getting him agitated.

They were at the Embassy Suites in La Quinta, twenty minutes from Palm Desert. McAllen and Sebastian had shared one suite with two double beds the night before, and Grace was in her own room next door. They had worked quickly after the meeting with Margaret Ashley the previous day.

Sebastian was cleaned up, dressed, and booked on a flight to New York that left Palm Springs at 12:58 p.m. After a short stop in Los Angeles, Sebastian would arrive in New York just after midnight and would meet up with Parsons and Cordele at the Ritz Carlton in downtown Manhattan. The Ritz was a large business and convention hotel, where the three men dressed in business attire would easily blend in.

McAllen had placed the call to Byron to stop Duncan and Randall from transferring their money from their main account to their stock trading accounts. If they transferred money into their commodities trading account on Friday morning, Sebastian wouldn't be able to access it. He had decided to use the *Anchorage Daily Mirror* reporter as Byron had looked overwhelmed in the previous week's newscast with the pretty redhead. McAllen had seen the pain on Byron's face. He also was aware of the time; Alaska was one hour behind the rest of America. They would have more time to develop the story.

Sebastian hit some keys on his laptop and looked at McAllen. "So far, so good. The main amounts are still in their accounts waiting to be traded."

"You can still get at it, most of the 100 million?"

"You bet, I just need a seat at the table, so to speak," Sebastian said with a smile.

"Is Grace still sleeping?" McAllen motioned to the other room.

"Last I checked. That Ashley woman near talked her head off last night after we all got together. I've never seen someone light up from tequila like that. Didn't know it was a truth serum," Sebastian said. He

closed his newly purchased fashionable garment bag, which he insisted
he would include with his checked luggage on the flight.

"Yeah, that was special last night. You think this will go all right?
This hookup with Ashley's guys in New York?" McAllen looked at
Sebastian. He had put him in danger before back in Vietnam, but he was
almost always by his side—his backup. This time he would not be there.

"No worries, as the Aussie's say. But do I need to purchase
something for my meeting with the Wall Street guys?"

"You need a gun. You'll get one in New York. I ordered you a 9
mm with a silencer—compact, nice and light. Parsons and Cordele will
have it waiting for you."

"Hell no, guns just kill people. I need something special. I saw a
kitchen implements store when we were shopping at Brooks Brothers.
We can stop there on the way to the airport."

"You need something at a kitchen store?" McAllen said. He had no
idea what Sebastian needed there, but it was getting late in the morning,
and they needed to go. He picked up Sebastian's bag and they headed
out the door.

Margaret woke to a massive hangover. After her conversation with
McAllen and halfway through her second margarita, she had been
introduced to Grace and Sebastian. Sebastian had no longer seemed
scary, and Grace, well, Grace had given her the warmest hug she had
ever had. The hug from Grace was not just warm, it was comforting and
not just comforting…it was soothing. Grace was this large force of a
woman who smelled of herbal concoctions and warm bread. Margaret
had never trusted someone so completely.

They had talked for several hours over dinner, which included
another margarita, and somehow they had driven her back to her place.
Now here, this very morning, she felt she was either at the lowest point

in her life or at the start of a new beginning. Perhaps the tequila had cleansed her.

Margaret drank several glasses of water with an herbal concoction that Grace had left her. She instantly felt better. She composed herself, looked in the mirror, and saw an aging lady too old for the work she was involved in. With resolve, Margaret went to her desk, switched on her voice synthesizer, and called Cordele in Miami.

Cordele was happy, *and why shouldn't he be,* Margaret thought. *He's using my money.* The seafood was great, the wines and the hotel were excellent, and Parsons was enjoying himself. Cordele thanked his boss several times.

Margaret took the compliments, let them subside, and launched into a brief description of the new associate they would be taking into the hit on Francis and Stewart and why they were involving him. Cordele needed to know they would be aligned with McAllen.

Cordele was wary at first. McAllen was a worthy adversary, and he knew that in high-stakes espionage and sabotage, allegiances could change quickly. When his boss offered an extra half million for the job though, he jumped onside. Cordele loved money and feared death. The right amount of money always calmed his fears of death.

Margaret could have given them an extra million each, but it was the law of diminishing returns. Give them too much, they disappear. Give them just enough, they spend it and come back for more.

Cordele loved the plan. Actually, he loved the money—the plan was secondary. He agreed to leave a day early, which would be that night. A flight out of Miami would get them to New York at 11:40 p.m. They would go to the hotel and meet Sebastian when he arrived—there was no need to be seen meeting each other at the airport, where there were too many CCTV cameras.

Margaret ended the call, turned off the voice synthesizer, and ran her hands through her hair. The only people in her organization who knew her identity were her IT boys, Frodo and Freddy. Now McAllen and his people knew about her. She was exposed. *How much can I trust McAllen,* she thought? She had only trusted herself up until now, had done everything on her own. This was new. She felt uneasy for the first time in years.

McAllen dropped Sebastian off at the Palm Springs Airport for his flight to New York. McAllen had insisted he fly business class so he could sleep. Sebastian had accepted the upgrade.

Sebastian got out of the car, dressed in his Brooks Brothers travel clothes. McAllen thought he cut the image of an elderly businessman on his way to do a big deal. And actually, he was. Sebastian took the item he purchased from the kitchen store and placed it in his checked luggage, then handed the luggage to the skycap. His briefcase was empty; he had told McAllen he would fill it with magazines and some sundry items at the small gift shop before security screening, as an empty briefcase would be suspicious.

McAllen nodded to Sebastian and threw him a small phone. "Here, this is a throwaway phone that we activated on a bogus address. Use it to let me know how things go."

Sebastian grabbed the phone and put it in his jacket." Yep, I'll give you updates on our big score. By the way, that Skype call you made to Alaska—you need to move locations soon."

"Why?"

"I used some software to mask your laptop's IP address, but a sophisticated tracer will find you in time. They take about forty-eight hours, and the kids they're hiring at the FBI are getting good," Sebastian said, concern edging his voice.

McAllen put his hand on Sebastian's shoulder. "God, I love your paranoia. It's what keeps us safe. No worries, Grace and I will check out from the hotel this afternoon. I know just the place for our next location. So, see you back in Canada."

CHAPTER THIRTY

SEBASTIAN'S FLIGHT ARRIVED A FEW minutes early. It was Friday, 12:32 a.m. He had slept most of the way from Los Angeles to New York, waking briefly for the in-flight dinner before nodding off again. For Sebastian, sleeping before a mission was never a problem. In Vietnam, they would wake him just before battle.

He collected his luggage at baggage claim and stopped only to put his kitchen-store purchase back into his briefcase. He liked to keep his implements of persuasion close.

The line outside for cabs was not long. He joined the line, gave the cabbie his garment bag, and got into the back of the cab. A light snow was falling. The airport smelled of jet fuel and too many bodies. The cab smelled of mild curry with a hint of rose water. Sebastian preferred the smell to cologne. The cab driver, an East Asian, played soft Indian music on the radio. Sebastian closed his eyes and relaxed as the cab made its way to the hotel.

The taxi deposited him outside the Ritz Carlton a half hour later. The doorman greeted him. He was smiling high-end hotel charm—not effusive, just efficient and welcoming. Sebastian walked upon a sea of marble floors to check in and within minutes was whisked to a junior suite.

It was 2:00 a.m. Sebastian hung up his suit in the closet, ensuring his dress shirt would not get wrinkled. Then he called Cordele's room.

"Hello, Cordele speaking." He voice was very alert, very awake.

"I'm here," Sebastian said.

Sebastian went to their room, just down the hall from his. He left his hat on and still wore his blazer. He felt formal but did not care. The door opened, and a tall, blond-haired, blue-eyed man smiled at him as he entered. "Hi, I'm Matthew Cordele."

Cordele motioned for Sebastian to enter. He pointed to a large hulking man on the couch. "This is John Parsons." Parsons did not get up but gave a nod of acknowledgment.

Sebastian sat down in an armchair opposite Parsons and surveyed the room. Two small suitcases and two briefcases were in the hallway. They traveled light. He knew Parsons had previously been with the Canadian Special Forces in Afghanistan and Cordele with some kind of supply squadron with the US Forces. He wasn't sure what they knew about him.

Parsons stared at Sebastian. Sebastian stared back. Cordele finally broke the silence as he cleared his throat. "From my talk with my boss, we understand that there is some information you need to get from the gentlemen we intend to take care of today—is that correct?"

"Yes, that is correct, "Sebastian answered. He was still locked in a staring match with Parsons.

"You're trying to get a password—is that right?" Cordele ventured.

"Yes, a password."

"And, you expect them to just give this to us before we kill them?"

"Yes, I do expect them to give us the password, and as for killing them, I always kill the angry one first," Sebastian answered.

"The angry one? Why's that?" Cordele asked. He sat down in the other armchair. He was looking at Sebastian, who was still in the staring match with Parsons.

"Angry people never give you much—you need to take them out of the equation."

Cordele liked the answer. He poured himself some coffee they had ordered from room service. "Sounds like you've done this before."

"Yeah, a few times," Sebastian answered. He looked briefly in Cordele's direction, and then back at Parsons. Sebastian was enjoying the staring contest.

"So, you're one of McAllen's people," Parsons finally said.

"That's right. I'm with team McAllen," Sebastian fired back.

"Did you happen to man that .50 caliber sniper rifle back on Galiano Island?" Parsons asked his gaze level with Sebastian's.

"That was me," Sebastian answered with just the hint of a smile.

"You're a pretty good shot," Parsons admitted. He was not smiling.

"Obviously not good enough. You're still alive."

Parsons laughed and looked over at Cordele. "You know, I like this little guy—he's got balls of steel."

"Okay, now that we've made the proper introductions, let's get down to work," Cordele said.

Sebastian sat forward. "Do you have a layout of the building?"

Cordele placed a notebook computer on the coffee table and swiveled it so they could all see. "This is an old building, with a reception desk just for the financial company on the east side. The west side of the building, which houses Ironstone, has no CCTV cameras in the elevators or the hallways.

"What's the reason for the lax security?" Sebastian asked.

"I think Ironstone didn't want any of the potential clients or themselves on tape. They have cameras inside their offices. We'll have to find the controls when we get inside."

"So we go in with disguises?" asked Sebastian.

Parsons picked up a bag from beside the couch. "Here, take your pick." He presented three masks: presidents Bush, Clinton, and Obama.

Sebastian rolled his eyes. "I'll take anyone but the Republican. Now, how do we neutralize the rest of the people inside? I understand we have some stock traders and a security guard."

Cordele turned to Parsons. "Show our new friend our latest toy."

Parsons went into the bedroom of the suite and came back with a small canister and two chemical-warfare-style breathing masks. The canister bore what looked like Russian writing.

"This is Kolokol-1, the same kind of knockout gas that the Russians used back in 2002 to neutralize the Chechens who took hostages in the Moscow theater siege." Parsons tapped the bottle. "There's enough in here to knock these guys out for up to six hours."

Parsons held the bottle up to the light. "Now, my rudimentary Russian tells me that it may cause nausea, diarrhea, dizziness, etcetera— you know – the usual stuff."

Sebastian looked at the canister. "Didn't some of the hostages die from the effects of this stuff?"

Parsons stared at the canister for a second and then said with a grin, "This is the new-and-improved version. The guy who sold it to me promised they had made a better batch."

Sebastian raised his hand. "Okay fine, but let's keep our killing to the targets."

"Absolutely," Cordele said. "This is a surgical strike with minimal harm to non-combatants. Isn't that what they say in the military?"

"Perhaps now they do," Sebastian replied. "Back in my day, we would kill them all and let God sort out the innocent."

Cordele suppressed a chuckle. "Yeah, Nam was pretty bad. So, Gentlemen, it is now 0300 hours. We hit the streets at 0830 hours. Get some rest and be ready to roll.

CHAPTER THIRTY-ONE

DARREN, THE SECURITY GUARD AT Ironstone Investments, looked tough, a mountain of a black man who had stuffed his large features into a poor-fitting sports coats and gray dress pants and who wore a look that said "piss off." A shaved head, sunglasses, a ring in one ear, and a large caliber gun protruding from his jacket made his statement.

Three men wearing president masks and carrying briefcases and handguns with silencers walked into the reception area of Ironstone Investments and over to him. Darren raised his hands in the air. His momma never raised no fool.

The short man, wearing the Clinton mask, asked if everyone had entered the office for the day. Darren nodded yes. The man then removed Darren's large weapon from his jacket and put a set of plastic cable tie handcuffs on him.

The Obama mask locked the door, and the Bush mask asked Darren which door led to the trading room and which one led to the offices of Randall Francis and Duncan Stewart. Darren nodded to the trading room and then to the offices.

The Obama and Bush-masked men left in the direction of the offices. The short, Clinton-masked man remained with Darren and motioned for him to sit. Darren did not have a problem with that.

Darren started to sweat. A large drop started on his brow and formed the first of several rivulets making a river into his eyes. He blinked several times. He did not move. After what seemed like forever, only the man in the Bush mask returned.

Then the Clinton and Bush-masked men motioned for Darren to lead them into the trading room. He walked ahead of them and pushed the door open with his shoulder. None of the traders noticed them as they entered. They were intent on their screens. The stock market was about to open.

The Clinton-masked man spoke up, his voice muffled by the mask. "Gentlemen, your attention please. Put your hands in the air while my associate collects your cell phones. Failure to do so will result in the last trade of your lifetime." He punctuated his statement by firing a shot into the TV screen showing the Bloomberg channel.

The screen went blank and twelve traders stood in unison with their hands in the air. The Bush-masked man walked among them, picking cell phones out of their pockets and off their desks. After he dropped the phones into a shopping bag he had pulled from his briefcase, he handcuffed each trader.

Not one trader said a word. They stared ahead in silence. They knew Ironstone's trading methods were illegal and had expected the Securities Commission with police to come barging in at any time. They would have preferred the police to these men.

"Now," the Clinton mask announced, "you will all walk single file into the lunch room."

The stock traders, in their uniform black pants, white shirts, and multi-patterned ties, marched into the lunch room.

The Bush mask looked at Darren. "Where is the CCTV control room?"

Darren couldn't give the information fast enough. "Sure, it's in Mr. Stewart's office, on the left side of the room, behind his liquor cabinet."

"Excellent," the Bush mask replied. "Now, if you would join your companions in the lunch room please, it would be appreciated."

Darren walked into the lunch room with the other Ironstone traders. Some of them were shaking, some breathing heavily. One had a dark stain on his pants that produced a puddle on the floor—the others gave him room.

The masked men closed the door to the lunch room, removed the canister from a briefcase, and put on their chemical-warfare masks. Then they put the nozzle of the canister under the door and opened the valve.

Thumping sounds came from the lunch room—traders dropping to the floor. Then a hard thump, like a tree falling, signaled that Darren had dropped. They nodded their heads in their masks and headed for the offices of Randall and Duncan.

Randall and Duncan were on their knees, their hands on their heads in Duncan's office, with Cordele in the Obama mask holding his gun with the silencer at their heads.

Parsons removed his chemical mask as he walked in the office. "The CCTV controls are in the bar." He walked over, pulled a few bottles of expensive Scotch aside, removed the tapes, and turned the recorder off.

"I guess I can remove this now," Cordele said as he pulled his Obama mask off. He watched Sebastian as he removed his chemical mask, put his hat back on his head, and placed his briefcase on Duncan's desk.

Sebastian looked down at the two men. "Gentlemen, there is really no need to introduce ourselves. So dispensing with formalities, we have a proposition to make."

"I don't want to hear any of your fucking propositions. Get the fuck out of my office immediately." Duncan sputtered the words. His face was a mass of blotchy red.

Sebastian cocked his head to one side. "Ah, the angry man. I love the angry man." His words came out smooth and quiet. "But you haven't heard my proposal yet."

Duncan looked up at Sebastian. "Sure, tell us what you want—and we'll tell you to fuck off."

Sebastian brushed some lint off his Brooks Brothers suit and checked the shine of his dress shoes. He seemed ready to do an interview. "So, our proposal is simple—give us the passwords to your five main accounts. I've written them for you on this piece of paper." He took a piece of paper from his coat pocket and presented it to Duncan.

"Fuck you. Neither of us will do that," Duncan yelled. He turned to Randall. "Don't give these bastards anything! You hear me? Nothing!"

Sebastian looked over at Cordele and winked. "We have our angry candidate. Shoot him."

Cordele raised his gun and placed a round into Duncan's head. Duncan rocked back and fell to the floor. His blood formed a pool around him. Cordele walked closer and then fired two more shots into him.

Randall looked at Duncan on the floor. Just moments before the man in the Obama mask had walked in the door; Duncan had told Randall he was fired. Duncan had had enough of his screw-ups – the polywater caper had been blown by Professor McAllen on television the day before, and the stock traders were running for the exits on oil. Oil prices were dropping.

Now this. Duncan lay on the floor. Randall could see the redness leave his face. Red blood drained onto the carpet, like he was leaking his anger.

"Now we have contestant number two," Sebastian said with a grin. "Gentlemen, stand our next contestant up. I would like the passwords to the accounts."

Randall was in a daze. The shots of the silencer rang in his ears. He knew he'd brought all of this here, right to his door, to this moment in time. The first time he had seen the fuck-you finger of the dead girl from the tar sands, he knew he was a marked man. The finger pointed at him. He could see his death now—it was calling him.

Randall looked at Sebastian. "If I give you the passwords, you're going to kill me. Why should I do that?"

Sebastian opened his briefcase. He revealed a shiny set of kitchen shears and showed them with admiration to Randall. "German steel. You have to love German steel—just a cut above anything else on the market."

Sebastian took a Montblanc pen off the desk, and in one motion, cut through the pen with the kitchen shears. There was no resistance—a quick "thwack" sound and the pen was in two, ink oozing on the desk.

"Now you, my friend, we're not going to kill." Sebastian looked Randall squarely in the eye. "From you, we do extractions. Dare I say a finger or two, maybe an ear, but we will start with your penis. I find all men are quite attached to their penises. Don't you?" Sebastian looked down at Randall's crotch.

"Now, my friends here will hold you while I remove your body parts until you provide us with the passwords. The body parts will be taken from here and dumped in the dog park at Central Park, or, you provide us the passwords." Sebastian nodded to Parsons and Cordele, who grabbed Randall and pulled down his pants. He stood in his shirt and tie, with his pants and briefs at his ankles.

Randall squirmed against the two men holding him. "Fuck you."

"Well, when I finish with you, you won't be fucking anything. I plan to perform a ritual called a brit milah. The Jewish people call it a Bris—know what that is?"

Randall didn't answer. He was shaking in fear, his eyes on the kitchen shears.

Sebastian began again. "Well, a Bris is the Jewish rite of circumcision, and, oh my . . . I see you were never circumcised. Quite unsanitary, some claim. Never mind, we'll take care of that."

Sebastian advanced on Randall as Parsons and Cordele held him in their iron grip. The kitchen shears lowered towards their target. Before Sebastian could perform the amputation, Randall was screaming passwords. They streamed from him like chants. He spit the numbers out as the only defense between the shears and his penis. Sebastian smiled, put the shears on the desk, and wrote down the numbers.

Sebastian moved around to the computer on the desk, careful to avoid the blood seeping from Duncan, and entered the passwords. He whistled softly as he looked at the screen. There was 102 million US dollars in the account.

He sent the money in groups of 10 million dollars to overseas accounts in Barbados, Bermuda, and Aruba. The money would only be there for minutes. He had already set up transfers that would rocket the money to three other countries and multiple accounts before finally settling in Panama.

He made a separate transfer for Margaret Ashley, sending 30 million to the account number she had given him. Her money would be untraceable as well after bouncing through four separate countries and multiple banks.

When Sebastian had finished, he stretched out his hands like a pianist completing a masterpiece. He turned to Cordele. "You may shoot contestant number two now."

Randall looked wild eyed. "But you said I'd live if I gave you the password."

Sebastian looked at Randall with all the kindness and compassion he could muster. "Young man, the world lies, governments lie, Wall Street lies, and you have been told the ultimate lie—the lie about your life. You're lucky that you've found this out at your young age. You will no longer live in darkness. May we have the gunshot please?" Sebastian turned to Cordele.

Cordele raised his gun and fired two quick shots into Randall's head. Randall fell onto Duncan. Their blood mingled on the expensive Persian carpet.

The three men stared down at the two dead men. "Should I pull his pants up?" Parsons asked.

"Yeah, it's the least we can do. He was a great contestant," Sebastian said, dropping the kitchen shears into his briefcase.

They made their way out of the offices and down to the street, where they hailed a cab and went back to their hotel. The time was 10:00 a.m. There was some cleanup to do before they left. At the hotel, Parsons and Cordele changed into jeans and sport shirts—they were heading to Miami and then Jamaica. Sebastian changed into his travel slacks and blazer. He wasn't ready to go back to his Navajo-shaman look—not just yet.

In Cordele's room, they placed their weapons in a padded courier bag along with the kitchen shears and dropped the bag off at the concierge desk on their way out of the hotel. The package was addressed to Strategic Financial. The guns and shears would be destroyed by a company already paid to do so.

They took separate cabs to JFK airport. Parsons and Cordele went first, and then Sebastian. When Sebastian reached the airport, he checked in for his 3:59 p.m. flight to Seattle and went to the men's room to make a phone call. He went into a stall and ensured there were no CCTV cameras around.

First he dialed McAllen. "It's done—transfer complete."

He then dialed 911. When the operator answered and asked what the emergency was, Sebastian gave her Ironstone's address and said immediate assistance was needed, providing the name of the gas they had used. He asked the operator to repeat the name to ensure she had it right. Then he turned off his phone, took out the SIM card, and wrapped it in toilet paper.

He flushed it down the toilet and watched it swirl. He did the same with the disposable telephone. It did two laps before disappearing.

Sebastian grabbed his briefcase and walked out of the stall. A large man in a suit and raincoat was shifting nervously from side to side. It was obvious he needed the toilet in the worst way. Sebastian looked at him, smiled, and thought the man should get some of Grace Fairchild's high-fiber muffins.

Parsons had never shot a man at close range before. The sound of the bullets entering the two stock traders' heads had put him on edge. In the military, the targets were across a field or in a mountain range. You fired at them with everything you had and checked the body count.

Cordele had calmly put rounds in Duncan's and Randall's heads as one would an animal being put down. Parsons found himself shaken by the sight. In that frame of mind, as he and Cordele shuffled through the check-in line, Parsons saw a police officer approaching. He had a piece of paper in his hand and was looking at Parsons and Cordele.

Parsons grabbed Cordele by the arm and yelled, "Run!" Cordele was a lighter, smaller man than Parsons, and suddenly he was being dragged through the airport terminal past a sea of terrified passengers.

Cordele would have reasoned with the police officer. He probably would have looked over the piece of paper the officer had produced and come up with numerous reasons why they were not suspects. But that possibility was gone. Parsons had made them look guilty, and all they could do was run like hell. The police officer yelled, "Stop or I'll shoot," which both men knew was not going to happen in a crowded terminal.

They ran down the escalator, taking the stairs two at a time until they reached baggage claim. The taxi stand was just outside. Between them was a sea of black-shrouded Arabic women in full chador. Their men pushed baggage carts piled high with suitcases and were surrounded by young children holding hands.

The sea of black parted, and Cordele and Parsons pushed on down the center. A lone police officer stood in front of them and then dropped into a crouching position, his gun aimed at their chests. He yelled, "Halt or I'll shoot."

Cordele pushed Parsons from behind, like a quarterback attempting to rush a tackle and using his blocker as a shield. A shot rang out. Parsons dropped. A second shot and Cordele spun to the ground.

The sea of black-shrouded women disappeared with their entourage of men, children, and baggage. They had just arrived from Iraq, and killing was nothing new to them. They had thought America might be different.

Parsons felt his breath leaving through the hole in his chest. Cordele on his left made no sounds— he was gone. Parsons knew enough of battle wounds to know he wasn't far behind. He heard some words, almost from a tunnel. "You son of a bitch, Santos, these aren't even close to the men you're after."

McAllen and Grace sat on the patio of Margaret's home in Palm Desert. The late-morning sun was warm, golfers were teeing off, and a plane flew overhead, leaving a vapor trail in the clear blue desert sky.

McAllen closed his cell phone and turned to Margaret. "Margaret, you're 30 million dollars richer than you were yesterday. What do you think of our partnership so far?"

Margaret was sitting in a lounge chair beside Grace, who was giving her a shiatsu massage on her hand and arm. Margaret had never had one. Grace pressed and released on her hands with her fingers, where her chi was supposedly out of balance. It felt good—perhaps she was right. She smiled back at McAllen. Yes, everything felt good so far.

CHAPTER THIRTY-TWO

BERNADETTE WALKED INTO HER APARTMENT, took off her heavy, down parka, and flipped off her Sorel boots in the hallway. Two papers, the *National Post* and the *Edmonton Journal*, were wedged under her arm with a large protein shake she had purchased at the health club. Today was the day for a new health regime, starting with two hours at the gym to release the effects of the doughnuts—she knew she was fighting a losing battle.

She surveyed her apartment. Today, Saturday, was clean-up day, laundry day, and shopping-for-food day. The apartment was adequate in size—715 square feet with one bedroom and one bath. The rent was $2,200 per month, which would be fine if it were in New York or Chicago, or even Vancouver looking over the water. This was in a quiet neighborhood in Fort McMurray.

Bernadette could purchase a one-bedroom condominium in Fort McMurray for a little over $325,000. It didn't seem right to her. If she were going to buy something, it would be a house. A decent house in Fort McMurray was in the $650,000 range. A mobile home went for just over $300,000. She also thought that Fort McMurray was only temporary. Although temporary had become three years, each year, she had felt only a little more connected to the place. Maybe next year she would buy something.

Dropping the papers on the kitchen table, she opened the refrigerator to get some water. The refrigerator revealed a few slices of leftover pizza, three eggs, one apple, and milk with a questionable expiry date. The emptiness screamed "shopping trip needed!" She got the water and slammed the fridge door shut, ignoring the emptiness.

To make room, she moved dirty dishes from the kitchen table to a pile that was resting above the dishwasher. The dirty dishes waited patiently to be placed in the dishwasher. They needed to wait their turn. The clean ones had to come out first—a fact that was obvious to everyone but Bernadette.

She scanned the newspaper headlines and read McAllen's recent announcement. The same newspaper reporter from Alaska she had spoken to, Byron Jacks, was quoted as breaking the story.

Bernadette had watched McAllen on her laptop on Thursday and Friday night. Something was wrong. Something did not feel right. She had watched McAllen's face and eyes, even his hairline, as he spoke. She was watching for a tell, like in poker. He was lying, she could see it, but about what?

Her cell phone rang. The screen displayed the name Anton De Luca.

"Well, Officer Anton, to what do I owe this call?" Bernadette was delighted to hear from the young officer. He was not only cute as hell but one of the cleverest intelligence officers she'd met in some time.

"Detective Callahan, I hope I'm not disturbing you on your day off?" Anton asked.

"No, not at all, I'm just doing a little housecleaning. You know, Saturdays," Bernadette replied as she wiped a rag over a spill on her kitchen table. She threw the rag, which arced wide, missed the sink, and landed on the dishes lined up by the dishwasher.

"I came on to some information. Now I know you're off the Clearwater murder case, but I thought you might want to hear this."

"Absolutely, I'm all ears. What's up?" Bernadette said.

"Remember how Patterson said that the CSIS and FBI would be on the lookout for any big investors in oil stocks?"

"Yeah, did something come up?" Bernadette picked up a pen off her kitchen counter and poised her hand over her newspaper to make notes.

"Sort of. You see, the CSIS and FBI put out an All Points Bulletin about this, and some NYPD detective thought we might be interested in a strange homicide in New York on Wall Street."

"I thought all homicides were strange, so what's so strange about this one?"

"Okay, the thing about this one is that three guys in presidential masks entered a company called Ironstone Investments. They moved the security guard and stock traders into the lunch room and hit them with knockout gas."

"Knockout gas? Like laughing gas? What kind?"

"No, really sophisticated stuff. Some Russian stuff that could've killed them had a warning call not been made about it."

"A warning call? One of the perpetrators made a warning call?" Bernadette scribbled knockout gas and warning call with numerous question marks at the top of her newspaper.

"Yeah, the 911 operator gets this call, and this guy gives the address of Ironstone and the name of the gas and then asks the operator to repeat the name of the gas back to him to make sure she has it right."

"Okay, that gets into strange territory. So who was killed?"

"They found Duncan Stewart, the owner of the company, and his assistant, Randall Francis, both shot execution style."

"And how does this fit into the oil stock manipulation that you're investigating?" Bernadette wrote the names Duncan Stewart and Randall Francis beside the question marks.

"Well, okay, here it is. The FBI decides to run IDs on the victims. Turns out Randall Francis has a passport, and they check it."

"And . . . they found what?" Bernadette was starting to wonder if this conversation was worth delaying the laundry that was calling to her over the dishes.

"They have a hit. Randall Francis entered Canada last year in August. A smart junior clerk did a run on flight records. The late Mr. Francis took a flight to Toronto, then Vancouver, and then—"

"Yes, and then?" Bernadette was beginning to find the conversation excruciating.

"Galiano Island," Anton said with satisfaction, knowing his information would be the punch line that would rock Bernadette's world.

"Holy Mother of God, these are McAllen's connections. So McAllen must be cleaning up, or doing a revenge hit." Bernadette wrote "McAllen" with arrows back to Stewart and Francis.

"It could be either. A team of FBI agents is combing the place. They'll have a computer expert doing a forensic sweep of all the computers—they might find some answers there."

"Did anyone see these guys with their masks off, or get a description?"

"Two big guys, one short guy, with Bush, Clinton, and Obama masks on. They took the CCTV tapes from the room. The building had no main cameras."

"These guys knew what they were doing." Bernadette wrote "Professional" and circled it.

"Yes, definitely professional. Now, I have to get back to my other cases . . . so . . . you didn't hear this from me. And have a great day."

"Hey, Anton, you're great, thanks for the info." Bernadette hung up and stared out her window. Light snow fell; a breeze blew the wind chimes on the balcony. The thought of what McAllen was up to circled in her brain. It swam slowly like a fish looking at a hook.

Bernadette took a long slurp of her protein shake, reviewing the notes on the newspaper. Her cell phone rang again. It was the RCMP headquarters' main phone number.

"Detective Callahan, it's Tammy calling from reception." Her voice dropped to a whisper. "I know I'm probably not supposed to do this . . . but I just had a caller looking for you, Colonel James Brigham from Naples, Florida. He said he was returning your call about Alistair McAllen. Do you want me to pass this on to the CSIS contact I have on file?"

Bernadette chuckled. "You're sweet, Tammy. I have the colonel's number. I'll pass it on to CSIS. Thanks for calling." Bernadette couldn't believe how well she could lie.

She scrolled down the numbers on her cell phone. The colonel's was one she had copied from the case file, along with a few others. As a good Catholic, she'd have to go to confession on Sunday. Her confessions were getting longer these days.

The voice of the colonel was dry and cracked when he answered. "Colonel James Brigham speaking."

Bernadette thought it amusing the colonel still announced his rank. "Colonel, this is Detective Bernadette Callahan of the Royal Canadian Mounted Police Serious Persons Crime Unit calling from Fort McMurray, Alberta, Canada."

"Well, how may I be of assistance to the Royal Canadian Mounted Police?" The colonel drew the words out as if he had just won a prize.

"We need to get some background information on Alistair McAllen. I believe he was under your command back in Vietnam."

"Oh, Mac. McAllen . . . goodness, yes he was." The colonel launched into a dry laugh that ended in a coughing spell. He finally came back on the phone. "What's he done? Is he in some kind of trouble up there?"

Bernadette treaded carefully with her words. "Well, no trouble that we know of, but he is a person of interest who could give us information about some homicides and threats to the Canadian and Alaskan oil fields."

"Well, I'll be. Mac was a fine officer, with a bit of a hellfire streak in him, but I don't see how he could be mixed up in something illegal."

"I agree, however, we don't know if he is directly involved," Bernadette replied. She realized the colonel must not have read any newspapers on his cruise—no need to go into details. "We need to get any background information you could provide."

"Sure, anything I can do to help," the colonel replied.

"We need some background on his military record; did he perform well? Any citations or problems with . . . well, with attitude?"

"Oh no, no attitude problems. Mac and his platoon were extremely effective. They did patrols on the Ho Chi Min Trail, and the booby traps they set were amazing."

"Booby traps? What kind of booby traps?"

"Well, we called it the six-foot Mac attack. He would set these little mines, you know, the anti-personnel kind." The colonel was chuckling as he spoke. "Well, Mac would make sure they could find the first one easily. Then Mac would place another mine in the trees with a trip wire. The mine would be six feet up, and the poor little Viet Cong were short you see, and BAM, they'd trip that second mine." The colonel broke into loud fits of coughing brought on by his laughing. "My god the boy was good."

Bernadette felt a chill run up of her spine. The reason that McAllen had called the newspaper in Anchorage was now obvious. His first trap had been sprung.

"Colonel, thank you, you've been most helpful," Bernadette said. She needed to get off the phone and deal with this information.

"Oh, I have? The colonel paused and then asked, "Is it snowing up there?"

Bernadette sensed the colonel wanted to chat and she felt for him, but she needed to get off the line. "Colonel, yes it is snowing hard and it's extremely cold, and if you'll forgive me, I must go out and feed my team of sled dogs." She winced as she told the lie.

"Ha, I knew it, you RCMP officers—a rugged breed, just like in the movies. Well, I'm sure you'll get your man." The colonel broke into another dry cackle that precipitated another coughing fit as he hung up.

Bernadette put down her phone and picked up a pen. On the top of her newspaper she wrote, "Six-foot Mac attack." She remembered that one of the victims found in the tar pond was very tall and very slender. She had to find out if the victims in Alaska were the same. There was only one way to find out.

It was 10:00 a.m. She figured it was 8:00 in Alaska. She dialed Detective Mueller's cell phone number—another number she had copied before handing over the case—and hoped he was an early-Saturday-morning riser.

Mueller answered on the third ring after putting his coffee down first. His left hand was in a splint from his run-in with Starko. "Frank Mueller speaking."

"Detective Mueller, I hope I'm not getting you at a bad time. This is Detective Callahan calling."

"Detective Callahan, there's never a bad time for you to call," Frank Mueller replied smoothly. "You're a legend up here. Everyone in the Arctic wants to meet you, since you alerted them to the polywater devices."

Bernadette flushed at the detective's words. "Detective Mueller, that's very kind of you, however, I don't think we're done with Professor McAllen and his polywater. Do you remember how tall and slender your Clearwater victims were in Prudhoe?"

"Yeah I do. Marc Lafontaine was over six feet and pretty lean, and his sister Constance was the same. How does that affect the case?"

"I spoke with McAllen's old army commander. He said McAllen's specialty was setting anti-personnel mines that the Viet Cong would find easily and then other ones six feet higher— "

"You think he's set a trap? A second set? And just let us find the first ones?" Mueller cut in. He sat up in his chair. He had been home in his apartment in Anchorage since last week going stir crazy on medical leave.

"I believe we speak the same language, Detective Mueller. I kept wondering why McAllen would make that call to the Anchorage paper, and this is only reason I can see."

"So, you think there's another plant of this polywater stuff and McAllen's little talk with the reporter up here was to blow smoke up our asses?"

"It just plays that way in my head. I can see no other reason why McAllen would call. He must have a second device ready to blow, and that call on Thursday was his diversion. Most of the world bought it," Bernadette said.

"How do you want to do this?" Mueller asked.

"I'm calling the oil company security person I know—he'll check with the operations people. If the intake pipe is too small for a person to get into, then problem solved."

"And if the intake pipes are large enough?"

"We tell everyone the sky is falling," Bernadette said.

"Gotcha. Listen, I'm actually off the case, so without going through too many channels and getting too many people excited, I'll find out what you need and get back to you," Mueller said.

"I'm off the case as well. Looks like we detectives only get to chase the crack heads, and when the really good stuff comes along with some excitement, they take it upstairs."

Mueller chuckled. "Hey, obviously we work for the same outfits, just different countries. I'll talk to you soon." He closed his cell phone and started to dial again. He knew just the person to call. He was hoping Troy was still on his shift in Prudhoe Bay.

Bernadette put down her cell phone. She needed to locate Pierre and get him working with the operations people. If her theory was right,

McAllen was still a threat. If her theory was wrong, a few oil workers would get some overtime pay, and no harm done.

She looked at the pile of dishes, the dirty laundry, and she could sense the plight of the lonely ingredients in the refrigerator. They'd have to wait. She headed for the shower, stripped off her clammy gray sweats, and grabbed her semi-clean bath towel. Saturday's clean would have to wait—she had a case to solve.

CHAPTER THIRTY-THREE

B ERNADETTE SHOWERED AND THREW ON some reasonably clean clothes after doing a smell check. The clothes passed—barely. She'd stay downwind of people. Grabbing her parka and Sorel boots, she headed out the door and closed it quickly on the sorry state of her apartment. It would be waiting for her return.

Bernadette needed the computer at RCMP headquarters to access more files. She would have to do it quietly and hoped Detective Barnstead wouldn't see her. It was her day off. She had already logged too much overtime and needed to take days off in lieu of overtime pay so as not to overstretch their budget.

Traffic was heavy for a late Saturday morning in Fort McMurray. Lines of traffic moved slowly through the town filled with shoppers— mine workers with their families doing the Costco-Safeway-BestBuy shuffle. The oil mines paid well, and mine workers spent heavily.

When Bernadette reached RCMP headquarters, she greeted Tammy at reception with a knowing smile. "I forgot my gloves in my office."

Tammy responded with a wink. "Sure, no need to sign in."

Head down, shoulders hunched, she made it to the detective room. There was no one there. She sighed in relief. No explanations, no cover story, no lies to make up for her presence.

She turned on her computer and pulled up the Clearwater case files—the files that had been sent to the CSIS, and that she was not supposed to have anymore. The coroner's report on the two victims confirmed her observation. Kevin Buckner was 6 foot 7 and a slight 170 pounds. She wondered if that was thin enough to fit inside the intake pipe for the oil sands water supply.

She dialed Pierre but was directed to voice mail, so she dialed his corporate security office to find out where he might be.

An officious-sounding receptionist in the Synthetic Oil corporate security office would not give Bernadette anything until she reintroduced herself. "I'm with the RCMP Serious Crimes Unit." She emphasized the last three words.

The receptionist got the hint. "Security Director Pierre Beaumont is in a meeting in Houston. I have the number here in case of emergency." She read off the number to Bernadette.

Bernadette dialed the number, and after a few minutes, Pierre answered. "How did you find me?"

"Hey, Indians have been tracking Frenchmen in North America for centuries—ever since you landed here," Bernadette replied. She was glad that Pierre did not sound angry, only puzzled.

"Very funny. Thanks for the history lesson—so why are you calling?" Pierre had just stepped away from a meeting with the Houston FBI. They were trying to find out how Clearwater Technologies had gotten the contract that was supposed to go to Waterflow Technologies of Houston. So far, no one at Waterflow wanted to talk. The silence would be cleared up as soon as charges for accessory to terrorism were handed out.

"I think you need to shut down all the oil sands plants again to look for another threat left by McAllen," Bernadette said. She knew how to get Pierre's attention.

"Holy Christ! You've got be to kidding me—how do you figure there's another threat?" The FBI looked up from their discussions in the other room.

"Okay," Bernadette began, "let me walk you through this so you'll see how I came to this conclusion."

Pierre lowered his voice and moved away from the conference room door and the FBI. "Yes, please do."

"There were two things; the first is McAllen's speech to the Anchorage newspaper reporter—you remember that?"

"Couldn't forget it. So what's new with it?"

"He leaned into the screen when he spoke to the reporter, just when he said he had deactivated the devices—he leaned in. Did you see that?"

"Well, maybe I did. I was more intent on what he was saying," Pierre replied. He looked back at the FBI agents. They were getting annoyed—this was supposed to be a no-calls-taken meeting.

"Okay, in poker games, we call it a tell. Anytime someone throws chips in to raise the stakes or call a hand, if they move forward, I know that 90 percent of the time they're lying about what's in their hand," Bernadette said.

"You do? How do you know that?" Pierre was getting uneasy, wondering what poker hands had to do with terrorists.

"I just do. My brothers banned me from all poker games back home on the reservation. Now here is the second-most-important thing. I contacted McAllen's old army commander. He told me McAllen was an expert at setting booby traps because he always let the enemy find the first one. The second one was always set six feet away. Two of the Clearwater employee victims were over six feet tall. Am I making sense now?"

"Merde . . . shit. You think this bastard set a second set of polywater devices?" Pierre looked up at the ceiling.

"The only way to know for sure is to find out if the intake pipes for the water treatment plants are wide enough to fit a man. Then six feet in is where you have to check," Bernadette said, hoping that Pierre understood the urgency of her message.

"Okay, what the hell. Your intuition found the first set. If you're wrong about the second, well, fifty-fifty in the security industry is what we call even. I'll call the vice president of operations in Fort McMurray and get him to shut down the plants and run an inspection. I'll let you know what we find. Oh, and one more thing . . ."

"What's that?"

"Are you sure you don't want to work for private security? If the second threat turns out to be true, then Synthetic Oil will give you my job."

Bernadette laughed. "Pierre, you're such a charmer, but once again, Canada wouldn't be safe without me in the RCMP.

"Okay, I tried. I'll call as soon as I have something." Pierre hung up and walked back to the FBI agents in the room to explain why he was leaving the meeting. They were not pleased.

Detective Mueller got through to Troy in Prudhoe Bay within minutes of dialing. Troy was not due to head back to Anchorage until Sunday.

"Hey, Detective Mueller, good to hear from you, how is that banged-up hand of yours?" Troy said when he answered the phone in the security guard office.

"Just fine, I should be back at my desk by next week. They'll have me type up reports one handed and shuffle papers for a while," Mueller said. What he didn't mention was that his hand hurt like hell. He had refused the pain killers the hospital had offered while being treated in Anchorage. Mueller's last rehabilitation had been about getting off

Ambien, Vicodin, and OxyContin. He had partied with them before—and did not want to continue.

"Hey, good to hear," Troy said.

"Listen Troy, I'm not really calling to catch up. That lady RCMP detective down in Canada thinks that McAllen has another set of polywater stuff ready to blow. I just got off the phone with her."

"Shit, that's bad news—how'd she figure that out?" Troy said. His boss, Chief Braddock, was standing by the console looking in his direction, wondering what the conversation was about. A security guard at the CCTV console looked back at his monitors.

"All I know is the detective got information from McAllen's old army commander. The commander said McAllen was an expert at setting secondary mines—and he always let the enemy find the first one," Mueller said. His hand was throbbing now. He put it back in the ice bucket at his side.

"So you think that RCMP lady detective has got a bead on McAllen?" Troy asked. He looked back in Braddock's direction. Braddock was frowning, waiting to hear the news.

"Yeah, I do. I'm convinced she's on to something. And if not, what the hell, at least we checked it out. Look, without stirring up too much fuss, how about just checking if the intake pipes are large enough for someone to crawl into. You could check with the big-headed guy, the base manager —"

"You mean Patrick Kearns. Hell yeah, I'll go and see him right now." Troy lowered his voice. "This shit will probably make that giant head explode...happy to do it."

"Sounds good, let me know what you find out. I told the RCMP detective I'd get back to her on this. Meanwhile, I'll be here sitting on my ass in Anchorage watching the snow fall."

"Hey, Detective Mueller, you take care of that ass of yours down there—you know all the girls think you're cute." Troy laughed. He hung up the phone and turned to Chief Braddock. "Chief, looks like we got some shit to check out. Could be another set of devices in the water intake pipes."

Braddock headed for the door, opened it for Troy to walk through, and said, "You can brief me on the way to Kearns's office."

Bernadette knew there was something that she had forgotten to ask Colonel Brigham. She needed to know if McAllen had any old war buddies he remained friends with. The firefight on Galiano Island was conducted with military precision, according to the reports she had read. The homicides in New York sounded professional as well. There was professional military written all over the case.

"Colonel, sorry to bother you again, but there is something I forgot to ask you when we spoke earlier," Bernadette said when the colonel picked up the phone.

"Sure, fire away, glad to be of service." The colonel was delighted to be back on the phone with Bernadette. He would repeat the story for days in his retirement community in Naples, Florida.

"Do you happen to know if Alistair McAllen stayed in touch with anyone from his old platoon?"

"Well, you know, let me think . . . he did send me a picture once . . . him and his buddies and some gal. Strange picture. They were all in Native getup, you know, war paint with some teepee in the back. I thought it was a gag, you know, him just having me on."

"Do you happen to have the picture?" Bernadette asked. She knew it was a stretch.

"Sure do, right here by my desk. Put it in a frame to show some of my buddies when they come by. Picture's kinda yellowed, but its right here."

"Could you scan the picture and send it to me if I give you an email address?"

"Oh sure, I'll have my grandson do it. He's here this weekend. Smart boy. Knows all about that computer stuff. Helped me with this Facebook stuff. He's got me downloading stuff and uploading stuff—"

Bernadette cut in. "Ah . . . that's great, Colonel. If you could send it to me at your earliest convenience that would be great."

"Oh sure," the colonel chuckled. "Sorry to carry on. I realize you've got to be getting your man. How are those sleds dogs of yours, by the way?"

"Fine, just fine, Colonel. I had to scare the polar bears away."

"Polar bears? I didn't know polar bears were that far south in Canada. You wouldn't be having an old man on now, would you?" the colonel said, chuckling.

"You're right, Colonel, I'm pulling your leg. We have no polar bears where I am—my apologies for my misinformation. I shouldn't have done that." Bernadette was embarrassed. She hoped she hadn't annoyed the colonel.

"Ha, no harm done, Detective—if you can't shit a neighbor, who can you shit?" The colonel broke into loud laughter. He would have fun reminiscing about this conversation and how he played with an RCMP detective for months.

Bernadette put down the phone. She was blushing from being had by the colonel. He was a smart old man, having fun with her. She'd walked right into it.

She decided to straighten up her desk and began by throwing out her stash of gummy bears and the other hidden snack demons that inhabited her desk. She filled half a trash can with junk and was about to leave the office when an email from the colonel with an attachment arrived.

The attachment was the picture of McAllen and three other young men. They sat; legs crossed, in a semi-circle, no shirts. Despite the yellowness of the photo, Bernadette could see they were tanned. They wore war paint on their bodies and bandanas on their heads. A young

Native girl stood over to the side. A teepee in the background swirled smoke from its top.

The men were smiling, happy, in the bright West Coast Canadian sunshine—young men free from the terrors of war. On the bottom of the picture was a message: *"Hello from West Coast Canada, our new paradise. Hello also from Theo Martin, Percy Stronach, and Sebastian Germaine. You would love our new friend, Grace Fairchild. We call her Saving Grace."*

Bernadette entered all the names into the central computer to search for previous convictions. None of the names had hits. They were all clean. Then she ran their names through the central database. The four men had landed immigrant status but still retained their American citizenship. Grace Fairchild had reservation status with a First Nations tribe on Vancouver Island.

The first name she researched was Theo Martin. He had been born in Winter Harbor, Maine, had gone to college, and then enlisted in the army and rose to corporal in the Army Special Forces—called the Green Berets in Vietnam. Theo was a martial arts and weapons expert and was listed in the who's who of Vancouver Island business. A business article claimed he had just sold his large oyster farm to an American firm. Theo was listed as living in the town of Duncan, Vancouver Island.

She checked Percy Stronach next. Born in Sarasota, Florida, no college—right out of high school into the army, where he rose to the rank of specialist, and his specialty was demolition. *Hmm, making things go boom,* Bernadette thought, *just like the night on Galiano Island.* Percy received an honorable discharge, and was listed as a retired boat builder. His present address was Nanaimo, on Vancouver Island.

The last name was Sebastian Germaine. Born in Seattle, Washington; Sebastian was a college dropout who had gotten caught up in the draft to Vietnam and had become a master sergeant in McAllen's platoon. He had won sniper competitions at his army base before going to Vietnam. His occupation after leaving the military was sound mixer, with his own company. Pictures of Sebastian and Janis Joplin and Jerry

Garcia, along with other long-dead musicians, were in his web photos. His website listed Victoria, British Columbia, as his address.

Bernadette sat back at her desk. All three men lived within a short distance of McAllen. Their weapons specialties from the military were the same ones used to fight off the people who attacked them on Galiano Island. She was certain that if she began checking their whereabouts, none of them would be home.

A check of Grace Fairchild turned up an environmental activist with no arrest records and no fixed address. She had had many close encounters with RCMP on Vancouver Island—protests over old growth logging, protests over Native rights, but she would never push it far enough to be put in jail. *One very smart Native girl,* Bernadette mused.

The people in the old photo with McAllen looked like a fraternity. She wondered if they had become a fraternity of terrorists. It was something she would have to pass on to the CSIS. She had gone as far as she could in her search, being off the case. She dropped the files into an Outlook folder and emailed them to Anton. He would want to see this.

She grabbed her jacket and took a pair of gloves out of her coat. She would flash them at Tammy at reception on the way out the door to prove she had come to get her gloves. Bernadette's conscience was starting to nag her somewhat for the many half-truths, somewhat-truths, and little cover-ups she been telling to keep involved with the Clearwater murders and McAllen. In time it would come back on her—when was the only question.

Sebastian arrived in Seattle late Friday night from New York. He took a cab from the SeaTac Airport and checked into a small boutique hotel in the historic district of Seattle. The hotel was chosen by McAllen for its proximity to the Fisherman's Terminal.

On Saturday morning, Sebastian made his transformation from business suit to jeans, denim shirt, fleece jacket, and an all-weather raincoat. He still wore his Ivy hat, which kept his long braids hidden. He made his way to the Fisherman's Terminal, and amongst the large fleet of fishing schooners, he found his way to the *Alaskan Seeker,* a forty-five-foot halibut boat that was some fifty years old and in good condition.

A young relative of Grace's welcomed him aboard and directed him below. In the small galley cabin he met McAllen and Grace. They hugged each other and sat down with mugs of coffee. The aroma of multigrain muffins filled the air. Sebastian knew Grace had been busy.

"Any problems?" McAllen asked.

"No, not really. We exterminated a couple of vermin and filled our pockets with cash; I would say it was a successful mission."

"Great job," McAllen said. He slapped Sebastian on the back. The engines of the fishing boat began to rumble, and they felt it slip its moorings as they headed out of the harbor.

The trip from Seattle to Vancouver Island was two-and-a-half hours on the passenger ferry. They would take a little longer. Grace had used her connections in what she termed the "Moccasin Highway" to get them back to Canada. No passports, no questions. In America, the three of them had used fake identification for flights.

Sebastian wanted some sea air and started to climb topside. At that moment, a door opened from the sleeping quarters, and a person he had not expected to see came out and smiled at him. Sebastian shot a questioning glance at McAllen.

McAllen only smiled. "Grace's project," he said.

CHAPTER THIRTY-FOUR

THE INFORMATION ABOUT A NEW threat to the oil fields scared the hell out of Patrick Kearns. He called each field's chief of operations, telling each of them to place men—tall and thin men—into the water intake pipes to check for any devices containing polywater.

The military wished they could act as quickly as oil men when executing orders. The difference was simple. Military were either offensive or defensive, and governments moved them. Oil men were about making money—money moved them.

Troy stood with Braddock on his left and Kearns on his right. Numerous engineers and plant operators stood in the back, staring at a large pipe. A tall, skinny man, dressed in a white polyester coverall zipped up to his neck with a hood that encased half his face, stood before the pipe. He put on a facemask with a breathing apparatus with a long line that attached to an air cylinder.

He wore a safety harness with a long line attached, which was held by another man behind him. The harness was standard practice in confined spaces in the oil industry. If Kearns's had had his way, one man would have held the skinny man's feet while he crawled into the pipe. The safety manager for Arctic Oil would never even consider that.

The skinny man crawled into the pipe with a large flashlight, and Troy watched as he disappeared. The room went quiet. They could hear the rustle of his polyester suit against the pipe as he wiggled his way down.

Troy hated confined spaces. His skin crawled to think of the closeness, of the smell of the oil and water in the pipe. After a few minutes, the line jerked in the handler's hand at the head of the pipe. He pulled slowly, hand over hand, and the man emerged from the pipe. He was covered in a thin film of oil and grime. The pipe was an intake for both oil and water. The water was separated and returned back to the field.

The skinny man held a fishing line in his hand. Standing in front of the pipe, he started to pull it slowly. He was delicate, like someone pulling a small fish to shore. At the end of the line, a six-inch condom appeared, full of an opaque liquid. He held it up high, like someone catching a fish—a prize at a fishing derby.

Some men in the room whistled, some laughed, and a few asked, "What the hell is that?"

Kearns asked, "Is that it?"

"Yeah," the man replied, his eyes still blinking as he adjusted from the darkness of the pipe. "There was only one line anchored by a washer secured by crazy glue and the line stretched down the pipe."

Troy called all the other teams at the other water intake plants to tell them what to look for. One team replied back, "Yeah, we found the fishing line, but the condom thing at the end was broken. Looks like it shot its load."

Kearns heard the report and grabbed the radio mic out of Troy's hand. "Any drop in flow pressure yet?" Kearns yelled into the mic. It rang in Troy's ears.

"Yeah," the voice on the radio said. "The plant operator has noticed a drop in pressure since yesterday. There seems to be nothing coming from the drill sites back to the manifold building. The guys out at the drill site say they should be wide open but nothing is coming through."

Troy watched Kearns's large head turn several shades of purple. He wondered if he was breathing at all. Troy knew that the news from the other site meant that the polywater had expanded into the oil field site.

His knowledge of polywater was rudimentary, but he understood that if it turned water into a polyester-like substance and expanded, it had probably encased the oil down below, trapping it in a gelatinous mass and stopping the oil from coming to the surface.

The only good thing about the report was that the field the polywater had hit was the smallest. A mere five thousand barrels a day came from that field. Troy did the quick calculation. Five thousand barrels a day equaled one hundred and eighty million dollars a year. There might not be bonuses this year from Arctic Oil.

There was nothing more that Troy could do. His two-week shift was over, and he was due to head back to Anchorage on the afternoon flight. Braddock would handle the reports. Troy walked out the door of the water treatment building and headed for his truck. It was 10:00 a.m. on Sunday. A gray, feeble light was showing on the horizon. Light snow fell. The snow crunched under his feet as he walked to his truck.

One hundred yards away, a white shape moved. White on white. A large polar bear stood, staring Troy down. They regarded each other, man and bear, and the bear moved on.

Troy sat in his truck and watched the bear disappear. Then he took out his cell phone and sent a text to Detective Mueller. He would call him when he got to the airport and give him a full report—he owed him that, both Mueller and the Canadian RCMP detective. They had saved a major part of the Alaska oil field.

Troy thought he might do something for Mueller when he returned to Anchorage. He couldn't buy him a beer. Mueller was in rehab. Maybe a home-cooked meal with his wife and kids. Mueller looked like he could use a friend.

———

On Sunday morning, Bernadette returned to her apartment after Sunday Mass. She was a semi- devout Catholic. Her Catholicism was half belief, half guilt. Her mother, who had passed away when Bernadette was a teenager, had made sure she was confirmed as a child, as she was convinced Bernadette needed God's intervention to save her from eternal damnation due to her hell-raising tendencies.

Bernadette still attended Mass and went to confession—as often as she could. Confession was to get clean of the venial sins, usually described as fault finding, impatience, or small lies. In Latin, *venialis* means "easily pardonable." Bernadette could rack venial sins up by the dozens in a day, and she still felt that the small or venial sins might build up into one big mortal sin.

Her brothers back on the reservation had put the notion into her head. They had said it was like Monopoly, where four houses turned into one hotel on the board. For years, Bernadette had believed them, until a kind priest set her straight. She got even with her brothers for their lies —and then went to confession for it.

She felt refreshed. She had confessed her little lies to her superiors—she felt better. The apartment was clean after a late-night frenzy of cleaning, laundry, dishes. She had also taken a trip to the market to fill up the refrigerator. The food in the fridge now was even wholesome: vegetables and meats that needed cooking, not thawing and microwaving.

Her thoughts were still on the polywater case, on whether her intuition was correct about McAllen and his second set of devices. Bernadette turned on her laptop and found a message from Detective Mueller in Anchorage. His email claimed that nine devices had been found intact—one had burst. Mueller went on to explain how McAllen had used condoms to deliver the polywater. Bernadette had to hand it to McAllen; the man had ingenuity.

Her cell phone rang—it was Pierre. "Pierre, how's everything? Did you find any devices? I just got an email from Alaska. They found nine devices, one broken, and get this, they used a condom." Bernadette was breathless.

"Bernadette, thanks for the update. Yes, we did find devices, and my god, yes, they were condoms. Two were broken. Those two plants have been experiencing problems with their steam-assisted gravity drainage system for the past few days."

"Their what?"

"I take it you don't know about the assisted gravity drainage, or SAGD."

"Well, I'm not a mechanical girl, so perhaps you can fill me in." Bernadette had been in Fort McMurray for several years but was more concerned with crime than oil.

"Well, simply put, the water is heated into steam, which makes the heavy oil into a slurry that moves up a column to the surface."

"So how much has the polywater affected these two plants?"

"Not as much as you might think. The polywater substance ruined one chamber in each plant, so the plants have to move their operations to a new area. It may take a few months, but they'll be back in operation."

"Back to making oil."

"Yes, back to making oil. Now, if McAllen's strange devices had hit all the plants at once, he would have had a major affect on North American oil. However, since we were able to confine it to two plants and keep the other ones operating—well, what can I say, you were right again."

"Ah, yeah, on that note Pierre, is there a way you can keep me anonymous on this?" Bernadette shifted uncomfortably in her chair as she spoke.

"How do you mean—you don't want the credit for discovering the second set of devices and saving North America from a major world oil shortage? You're joking, right?"

"Remember, I was off the case. Detective Barnstead is real stickler for protocol and will likely blow a fuse if he finds out how I went out of prescribed channels to alert Alaska and you."

"Ah yes, the prescribed channels. Yes, I can see how you might ruffle some Mountie tail feathers, especially the brass's, but in this case, the case of the national security of oil, you think they might make an exception."

Bernadette sighed in her reply. "Pierre, let's just say I don't want to tempt fate in going for the exception."

"You're saying you have a bunch of hard asses you're dealing with and you want to keep out of the limelight."

"Pierre, I believe you've nailed it. Now can you keep me out of it?" Bernadette crossed her fingers, hoping not to rack up more venial sins she would have to confess.

"Mademoiselle Callahan, your secret is safe with me. You can rest assured that as an honorable French Canadian, I will not breathe a word of your amazing feat to save Canada and the world from the ravages of McAllen and his gang of terrorists. Now, what about the Alaskans? Will they keep your name a secret as the whistle blower on this affair?"

"I hope so; I asked Detective Muller the same thing. He thought it was an odd thing to ask but said he will say the lead came from an unconfirmed source."

"And you think your chief will buy this and not suspect that this was you cracking this case once again? You do have a reputation for solving things."

"Barnstead will think it's me, but as long as no one confirms, he won't admit it. He has the ostrich syndrome. Keeps his head down, ass up, and is always happy."

"Okay, well good luck with Barnstead, and from all of us at Synthetic Oil, a heartfelt thanks. I owe you dinner, you know. Last time was rushed, and you never had time for desert."

Bernadette felt the same mixed feelings for Pierre, somewhere between desire and friendship—she was never sure where they were. "Sure," she finally said. "When we've wrapped everything up."

Bernadette ended the call. Suddenly she had the urge for a big slice of stuffed crust pizza with extra cheese, extra pepperoni, extra peppers, and extra everything. Her fridge was full of good, healthy food. She needed to go out. She grabbed her jacket and boots and headed out the door. The day was bright sunshine, a mild minus ten Celsius, and light wind. She would walk the ten blocks to the pizza place—burn a few calories.

Sebastian looked up from his computer in the cabin. The email he was reading was short and to the point—there were reports from their operatives in Alaska and Fort McMurray. He turned around to McAllen and the rest in the room. "Gentlemen, they found the devices."

There was a chorus of "shit" from those in the room. McAllen walked to the window and stared out into the channel.

CHAPTER THIRTY-FIVE

ON MONDAY MORNING, BYRON KNEW something had happened in Prudhoe Bay. His two paid informants who worked for Arctic Oil had sent him text messages. Both of them he had recruited from the same bar, the Fancy Moose Lounge in the Millennium Hotel near the Anchorage Airport. Byron had plied them with beer and promises of cash for stories, desperate to get leads on what McAllen was doing with the polywater attacks on Arctic Oil.

The first text was from Brandon, a young kid with peach fuzz and pimples who thought he actually worked for the newspaper. He called Byron "Mister." He sent his text in a reporter-like fashion: "9 devices found and deactivated but one breached, and damage to an oil field. The field is no longer producing."

The second text came from Travis. Travis was different—he did the reporting for Byron because he really didn't like a lot of people, including the people who worked for Arctic Oil. The more crap he dug up on the company, the more people he could piss off. Travis liked that.

The text from Travis said, "One oil field totally fucked! Polywater rules!"

Byron leaned back in his office chair and looked out his office window, compliments of his handling of the McAllen Skype interview. For anyone working in cubicles, a cubicle with a window was the ultimate status. Byron even had job offers from other newspapers. Nothing from the *Los Angeles Times* yet—his dream job hadn't called. This new story could get him there.

He needed more information, and his main resource, Della, was on days off back in Louisiana. Della's alternate for the shift was Julia Cortez, and she was the sweetest thing Byron had ever seen.

Byron knew he would have no problem romancing her. Julia was a petite, dark-haired Latino beauty in her twenties with a sweet sexiness that Byron wanted to plunder. He had met her only once when dropping Della off at the Anchorage Airport. Julia was just coming in from her home in San Bernardino. He heard Latino music as her hips swayed down the walkway. He was instantly in lust.

He knew she would take his call. And maybe, just maybe, she'd give him the added information to fill in his story. He dialed the number for Human Resources Arctic Oil Prudhoe Bay. He was breathing heavily with thoughts of Julia—he needed to calm down.

The phone rang three times and was answered in a silky southern accent. "Human Resources Arctic Oil, Della Charles speaking."

Byron stuttered. "Della . . . what a surprise. I thought . . . you were back . . . in Louisiana."

"Why sugar," Della purred, "I know that Julia was supposed to be here, but her momma took sick in Fresno, so I just hustled my little self back up here to look after the store. Here I am and here you are a-callin…what a nice surprise. Now what can I do for you my sweet little biscuit?"

Byron's skin went cold. The hot flush for Julia was replaced by the cold fear of Della. Della Charles, the big southern girl with the never-ending appetite for both food and sex. Their last meeting in Anchorage had ended with Byron in need of three chiropractor treatments. She'd brought a six-pack of Viagra with her, telling him it was "insurance that he would meet her needs."

Now, here she was again, the possible break in the story of the new polywater attacks—and he knew the price. The potential for the story was too great; he had to make the deal. Cold sweat ringed his shirt collar. He felt his penis retract, like a turtle's head shrinking back in fear.

"Well, Della," Byron began, "I just heard rumors that this polywater stuff got activated at one of the sites and I wondered if you knew anything." He held his breath waiting for her reply.

"Ah sugar, you know Della has her finger on the pulse of everything that goes on up here. Now just this morning over coffee, one of the security boys told me that Kearns, the base manager, was all excited after he got a phone call."

"Any idea who phoned with the information?"

"Well now," Della's voice grew soft as a whisper. She moved forward in her chair. Byron could hear her chair screech in protest with the weight shift—to him it was like fingernails on a chalkboard. "I heard from the nice security boy, all hush hush, you know. But he says it was this Canadian gal, you know, the RCMP detective. This Detective Mueller says he got the notion from the RCMP gal, and he calls to Mercury. And just like that, the whole base is in a panic and running to all the oil fields to find this new threat."

"So they did find some of this stuff—the new threat?" Bryon was on the edge of his seat, his pen poised over paper. His fear of Della was replaced by his need for the story.

"Oh yeah, they found the stuff all right, but you'll never guess what it was," Della said in a coy tone. She was delighted to have Byron on the phone.

"Ah, no, I probably couldn't guess." Byron was peeved about the games Della was playing. He was trying not to show it in his voice.

"Ha, if it weren't a big condom filled with this liquid, this polywater stuff, and attached to a regular fishing line. A guy, you don't know him,

Fred Harris from operations, well, he took pictures when no one was looking, and he sent them to me. I think he's a little sweet on me. Maybe wants a little Della time—know what I mean?"

"A picture? You have a picture?" Byron bolted from his chair. He looked into the phone as if the receiver had produced magic words.

"Ah sweetie, I sure do. Right here on my little computer. And you know Della could send that to you. Now what would my sugar do for Della?"

There it was: the question. It rang in Byron's ears. *What would I do for Della?* The words were like a freight train coming down the track—there was no escape. Byron summoned his most convincing voice. "Well, whatever my sweet Della wants. I'm sure we can arrange another night in Anchorage when you pass through next."

"Honey, I think something like this calls for more than a night. Something this good, I mean, with pictures and everything, calls for a weekend. I mean look, I helped you with the Clearwater employee murders and all I got was a little romp in Anchorage. This calls for a weekend." Della's voice had lost the southern silkiness—the tone was all business.

Byron heard the words. They ricocheted around his brain. He could hardly survive one night with her—she was demanding a weekend. "A weekend," Bryon responded weakly.

"Hmm hmm, that's right sugar. A weekend in San Diego at one of those fine hotels on the harbor. And honey—"

"Yes?"

"Just you and me and room service." Della moved back in her chair, which let out another screech of protest.

Byron weighed his options. Say no, and the story of his career and chance of *Los Angeles Times* would be gone. Say yes, and he would get the story of his career, plus a possible move to Los Angeles, and maybe he could be out of Alaska before he had to make good on his promise to Della.

He could see himself in front of cameras, quoted by CNN, CBS, and NBC. Reporters from the *New York Times* would call for his in-depth reports. He heard himself say, "Now Della, that sounds fine. You just let me know when you want me to set that up."

"You know I will sugar, my little Byron Jacks, the big newspaper reporter. I just can't wait to get my hands on you."

"Ah yeah, likewise . . . and the picture?" Byron asked.

"Coming right now, sweetie. Now I gotta go. Bye." Della hung up and with a punch of her keys sent the file to Byron. She looked around her office. Her assistants were away from their desks, and her outer door was slightly closed. She was sure no one had heard her. She had just scored a weekend in San Diego with her sugar and she felt great.

What Della hadn't noticed was Fred Harris standing behind the door. The Fred that she had mentioned to Byron, the Fred that she had said might be sweet on her. Fred was very sweet on Della. She was in his dreams. Visions of Della had visited Fred every night from the moment he had met her.

Fred had given Della a picture of the polywater to please her. Like someone giving a flower, Fred had given Della a picture of a condom gorged with a pale liquid. She had laughed and her eyes had sparkled at him—she had touched him on the arm.

He had been about to knock on the door and announce his love for her when he heard her conversation with Byron. Fred was crushed. Not knowing what to do, he had pulled out his cell phone, put the phone in the door opening, and hit record for video and audio.

When Della had finished her conversation with Byron, Fred put his phone back in his pocket and walked slowly away. He walked the slow steps of a broken man, a rejected lover. He did not know what he would do with the recording yet. It might come to him later.

Byron sat holding his head in his hands. He was a male whore. He knew it—he accepted it. He had once again given himself for a story. A weekend with Della in San Diego: she would want first-class airfare, an expensive hotel, and steak and lobster every night. And worst of all, he, Byron Jacks, would be servicing her sexual needs every night. His back ached in imaginary sympathy for his fate.

His email pinged with the email and attachment from Della. The picture showed a condom filled with an opaque liquid resting in a jar. A hand held the top of the jar. Polywater.

He forgot everything about his fate with Della. Grabbing his phone, he dialed Arctic Oil and asked for Steve Zeeman in the public relations department. He knew they would have to call a press conference soon. Steve was a wily adversary for all media types. He could smooth a large oil spill into a meaningless drop of oil and a pipeline crack into a mere blip on the landscape, and Byron was sure Steve would have some quick thinking for the polywater attacks.

When Byron reached Steve, he responded with his usual and artful enthusiasm. "Byron, good to hear from you. Hey, I see you've been doing a great job cracking stories. The paper must be so proud of you."

"Steve, I'll get right to the point, as I know how valuable your time is," Byron said. Byron was just as good at throwing bullshit. He had been raised on it. "I need to confirm the latest attack on your oil field, assess your total damage, and get a quote from you on how serious you consider this situation to be for your future." Byron sat back. He had done a comment lob, the newsman's throw down to public relations.

"Whoa, Byron sounds like some heavy questions. I admit we had a slight disruption in the Prudhoe Bay area today." Steve Zeeman was leafing through his notes and wondering just how much Byron knew.

"Steve, I'll make it simple for you, so you can go easy on the soft-peddling PR stuff. I have pictures; I have confirmations from people on the ground up there. You've been attacked, you've lost an oil field. Now you can give me a quote from your department or I go with my bare basics story and the world comes running to your door tomorrow looking for your side of the story. What's it going to be?"

"You have a picture of what?" Steve asked. He was staring at a picture on his own computer. He hoped Byron did not have the same one—the condom. This was a public relations nightmare.

"Looks to me like a condom with some kind of opaque liquid. So what's my headline? POLYWATER SCREWS ARCTIC OIL! I like the ring to it." Byron couldn't get rid of the chortle in his throat as he said it.

Steve sighed. Of all the things to attack his oil company, it had to be something encased in a condom. He would have preferred an actual terrorist. Some terrorist asshole would have been more photogenic than this condom.

"Okay, I'll give you what you need if you'll guarantee you'll report that the damage is limited to one small field with Arctic Oil and that we'll be coming out with a full report in a few days. Also—no picture. If you do that, we go on record and give you the exclusive." Steve had the devil he knew on the phone—he would sell this to his superiors later. With a newspaper, he had one more day to get the reports back from the engineers, and they would draft a memo in the morning that would marginalize the effects of the polywater.

"You can count on me to recite you chapter and verse. And I'll bury the picture," Byron said. He knew he was lying the moment he said it. He would burn bridges that would get him out of Anchorage and into a southern newspaper. He felt the *LA Times* in his blood.

"Okay, I have your email address on file, Byron; I'll fire you a quick press release in advance, and I expect to see good copy tomorrow," Steve said.

"Hey, that's what I'm here for, to build relationships." Byron put the phone down. He had one last comment he needed for the story. The RCMP detective in Fort McMurray had supposedly called Mueller, and Mueller had called Prudhoe Bay. He knew Mueller would give him nothing—that was his style, but he wondered if the RCMP, being polite Canadians, might be open to giving him a comment.

He dialed the number for the Fort McMurray RCMP detachment and asked for Detective Bernadette Callahan. The receptionist told him the detective was out on a case and asked if he wanted to leave a message. Byron hesitated. His clock was ticking. He needed a quote, a comment, and at this point, a "no comment" would do.

"I wonder if there is someone who would like to comment on the recent information your Detective Callahan provided Alaskan officials? The information that saved part of the oil field this morning?" Byron threw another comment lob. He would get either a "no comment" or someone to come to the phone. He waited.

The receptionist listened, said nothing, then gave a polite "one moment please."

The voice that came on the line announced himself as Chief of Detectives Barnstead. "How may I help you?" The voice was filled with icy antagonism.

Byron could not be more pleased. "Detective Barnstead —"

"Chief of Detectives Barnstead."

"Ah, yes, Chief of Detectives Barnstead, I have a report here in Anchorage that a Detective Callahan from your department was instrumental in alerting oil companies to another threat of polywater here in Alaska."

The phone on the other end went quiet. "And you say this happened when?"

"This morning. Numerous new devices were located; however, one was confirmed to have erupted, which is quite comical as the device was a condom. However, the information from your detective saved a good part of the Alaskan oil field."

Another pause on the phone signaled to Byron that Barnstead knew nothing of what the detective had done. "I take it you have no knowledge of Detective Callahan's actions, Chief of Detectives Barnstead?" Byron finally asked. He knew the obvious; he wanted Barnstead to admit it.

"I cannot comment on the actions of one of my detectives at this time. This is an ongoing investigation that involves various members of our detective teams and specialized forces. Now, I have numerous cases to attend to." Barnstead escaped off the phone.

Byron knew crap when he heard it. The chief had just given him a bunch of words that meant nothing. Like an octopus releases a cloud of ink to get away, Barnstead had thrown a cloud of words to get off the phone.

The story was solid. He knew it. Callahan had somehow figured out the second threat, but there was no time to figure that out now. The paper needed to get the story of the threat out as soon as possible. Byron would complete the story and get it ready for the morning news. He would send out multiple tweets to dangle the advance of the story beforehand, and post an advance on his weblog. By tomorrow morning, the world would be waiting in expectation for Byron Jacks and his exposé: NEW ATTACKS ON ALASKAN OIL FIELDS. And then he would wait for the phones to ring.

Barnstead sat in his office in a state of shock. A slow anger was growing. Bernadette Callahan had gone over his head and outside of channels to alert the Alaskans to a possible threat. Being in the vanguard and protecting assets and the public was commendable—going outside of channels and not contacting superiors was incomprehensible.

He'd felt like…something he'd never felt before…like he had no idea what was going on…and he knew Detective Bernadette Callahan was to blame. The phone call from the journalist had confirmed it. Barnstead let his shock turn to anger, and let the anger smolder.

Byron was leaving his office to head to his editor with his exclusive but got sidetracked by Addison Thorncliff, the business news reporter. She was standing outside a cubicle as he walked by. Addison motioned for Byron to look at something. Addison was in her late twenties, a well-dressed and well-manicured brunette who would have nothing to do with Byron's many advances.

He was intrigued by her calling him. As he walked into the cubicle, Addison motioned for him to look at the laptop playing on the desk. A program called *CTV News* was showing a newscast, and the reporter was claiming that two polywater devices had been released in Fort McMurray. The reporter did not say what the devices were—only that eight others had been found that had not been released. In a cool and calm Canadian manner, the CTV newscaster claimed that the oil companies believed the threat had been contained.

Byron couldn't be more thrilled. He had a picture of the polywater that he would be unleashing to the world on Tuesday morning. He winked at Addison, got the usual "piss off" look, and headed down the hall to his editor. The world was his.

CHAPTER THIRTY-SIX

BYRON WAS AWAKE WHEN HIS cell phone rang at 3:30 a.m. on Tuesday. He had hardly slept. The story on the polywater attacks and his picture were going to be front-page news in the Alaska Daily Mirror newspaper that day. He had spent most of the night sending electronic copies to all the major newspapers and news stations in the lower forty-eight states.

Newspapers from the lower forty-eight states called in rapid succession, wanting Byron's quote with the story. Byron was in his element: he gave quotes and spoke of how close he was to the story, of how he had developed it using his keen investigative journalism. He made no mention of Della Charles at Arctic Oil.

He had fought hard with his editor over the headline. He had wanted POLYWATER WREAKS 6 INCHES OF DESTRUCTION ON ALASKAN OIL FIELDS and the picture of the six-inch condom gorged with opaque polywater front and center. They settled on POLYWATER WREAKS HAVOC ON OIL FIELDS IN NEW DEVICE. The editor liked the picture—it was "6 Inches of Destruction" he didn't agree with. Somehow he didn't think it would meet Republican sensibilities. Democrats, the editor knew, would accept anything as a threat.

The calls came one after another, and somehow in the morning, he managed four bites of stale pizza from the night before and three pots of coffee. He took bathroom breaks while on the phone by sitting on the toilet to pee so he wouldn't make unnecessary background noise.

His cell phone would ring the moment he ended a call, and by 10:00 a.m., Byron had spoken to a dozen newspapers and television stations. He had calls waiting, texts coming in. The world wanted his opinion and more of his story.

Back at Arctic Oil, Steve Zeeman looked over the newspaper article and mumbled several times about how Byron had screwed him over. He needed to call a press conference. Byron Jacks, *the son of a backstabbing bitch*, would not be invited, would not be allowed in the room much less the Arctic Oil building. Zeeman hated being lied to by reporters.

Byron was exhausted by the afternoon. California media wanted interviews from him as they were the most vulnerable to disruptions in the Alaskan oil supply. Several text messages from the *LA Times* came in. They not only wanted interviews, the editor wanted to speak to him about a job. He was a newsmaker. He was a game changer. He decided to let them wait a while longer before getting back to them—let them sweat a little.

Detective Mueller sat on his couch in his apartment, his left hand wrapped in an ice pack—it still hurt like hell—and his right hand holding the TV remote. He flipped between news channels—from CBS to NBC then back to CNN headlines news. All the channels carried the picture of the condom full of polywater. News anchors threw out technical questions at supposed professionals. Mueller could see that the anchors really wanted to ask, "Just how fucked are we really?" *No one has the balls to ask the question,* Mueller thought.

There were numerous mentions of the Canadian RCMP detective who had alerted the Alaskan and the Canadian oil fields to the polywater threat, and one news station had dug up a photo of the detective, a graduation photo from Bernadette's younger years as an RCMP constable. She was dressed in the RCMP red tunic with the brown Stetson and riding boots, standing ramrod straight in front of the Canadian flag. There was a smile on her face, but it was almost a smirk. Mueller could see all of Bernadette in that look—one of determination and attitude.

She was a damn fine looking women, Mueller admitted. *Probably still is.* He felt bad he had not been able to keep her name a secret. His telephone call to Troy must have been overheard by someone in the security guard office. Mueller knew there were few secrets in what was called the "oil patch." Rumors became gossip and gossip became fact in a matter of hours with oil workers. If someone had overheard something about Bernadette Callahan being the source, there was no way of keeping it quiet.

Mueller had sent a "sorry your secret got out" text to Bernadette just after he had watched the news in the morning. *She'll have to deal with it,* he thought. *Sometimes you have to reap the wind of your good intentions.* Police and detectives walked a fine line between doing what was right and doing what was proper through channels of the force. He'd crossed the line many times himself and knew what the consequences were—he felt sorry for Bernadette.

———

Fred Harris wrestled with his dilemma of what to do with the video he had made of Della and her conversation with Byron Jacks. He turned it over in his mind. If he published the video, he gave up his precious Della. As the day wore on, however, and more coverage of Byron came on the television and radio, Fred's longing for Della was replaced by his hatred for Byron.

Fred was a proud man. He would fight this interloper for Della's affections. With a quick keystroke on his cell phone, Fred uploaded the offending video of his Della and Byron to YouTube.

By 3:30 p.m., Byron was exhausted from talking on his cell phone to numerous media outlets about his story. There had also been two television interviews at news stations over lunch hour, and one radio station interview. This time, he had controlled the interviews. The lead was his. His day could not have gone better. *Well, maybe it could be better,* he thought. What he needed were some accolades from his peers. To truly breathe the heady air of his fame, he wanted to surround himself with his fellow reporters back at the newspaper.

Byron walked through the doors of the *Anchorage Daily Mirror* office with his chest puffed like the prize-winning journalist he knew he was. He readied himself for the praise, hearty slaps on the back, and invitations for beer at their local hangout. Entering the press room, he was instantly recognized by the other reporters. They looked up, they stared, they smiled, and they started to laugh. Laughter was not something he had expected. His polywater story was serious journalism; okay, the condom on the front page, that may have been a little much, but he hadn't expected laughter.

He walked to his cubicle, the coveted one by the window, and Addison Thorncliff was standing by his doorway. She looked into his eyes as he approached. He looked her up and down like a lion taking inventory of a gazelle on the African plains. His day was getting better.

"Hey, sweet biscuit," Addison said in a southern drawl, "y'all have a caller from the *LA Times* on line two." She gave him a wink and walked back to her cubicle.

Sweet biscuit? Byron thought, confused. She had called him asshole and shithead but never sweet biscuit. *And the southern accent—what's up with that?* Byron had some serious apprehensions as he sunk into his office chair and picked up the phone.

"Byron Jacks, this is Marty Krieger with the *LA Times*. I'm following up on the YouTube video of a conversation between you and a Miss Della Charles, who demanded sexual favors in return for your story. You agreed to the said favors. Would you like to comment on that?"

Byron slammed the phone down and turned on his laptop. He brought up YouTube and entered "Della Charles." There it was—the conversation from yesterday: Della telling him about the polywater, the condoms, the Canadian detective, and then bargaining for a weekend in San Diego. And the worst part: she had clearly said his name at the end. The video had half a million hits already and the number was rising. Most people had "disliked" it.

Addison came back to his door, her eyes a wide glare of satisfaction at his destruction. "Hey sugar, the editor said to get your sweet little biscuits down to his office when you come in." She blew him a kiss and walked away.

Della didn't know anything was wrong until two security guards appeared with Patrick Kearns at her door. There was a simple rule at Arctic Oil: you could gossip amongst others at the camp—you never talk to media. It was a simple rule, and Della had violated it. Her firing took seconds, and she was escorted out the door with her belongings minutes later.

There were no flights back to Anchorage and then Louisiana until the next day. Arctic Oil had booked Della on the next morning's flight and had reserved a room for her at the Prudhoe Bay Hotel for the night. They were that pissed. Kearns didn't want Della Charles on Arctic Oil property for one more minute.

Chuck drove Della to the hotel. He drove up to the door and motioned for her to get her suitcase out of the back of the truck. Chuck was ex-marine and didn't like any of what Della had done to Arctic Oil. As Della got of the truck, he called to her, "Hey, Ms. Charles, your flight is at 0900 hours tomorrow. Now, most of the workers will be gone to work, so it may be hard to get a ride to the airport, which is only about a quarter mile."

Della looked up at Chuck. Her face, which had been about to break into tears, broke into a sweet southern smile. She was expecting Chuck to say that he would be back to give her a ride. "Well, that'd be nice of you," she said.

"Ah, no, I got duties tomorrow at 0700. I just wanted to make sure that if you have walk to the airport, keep a lookout over your shoulder—there's been a polar bear alert here, so don't tarry on your journey." Chuck slammed the truck door shut and headed back to the camp.

He could see Della standing there in the rearview mirror. Ice fog from the truck exhaust was lifting into the dark Arctic sky.

Byron walked out of the Anchorage newspaper office with a box of his belongings and a copy of his newspaper article. His dreams were done. Byron Jacks was an anecdote on YouTube, a name linked to sweet biscuits and sugar and Della Charles, not to professional journalism. Polywater had been his, and now—well, now it wasn't. He scrolled through his cell phone—the only message was from his dad. He wanted him to come home, back to Cleveland.

CHAPTER THIRTY-SEVEN

BERNADETTE WAS TWO HOURS NORTH of Fort McMurray at an oil sands camp investigating what looked like an attempted murder. Monday night someone had not paid someone for drugs, or had delivered the wrong drugs, and after going around and around on the case, the police had nothing—a big goose egg for three days of investigation. The victim wasn't talking. And so, on Friday morning, she headed back to Fort McMurray with Detective Symons, her partner on the case.

Bernadette knew something was brewing back at RCMP headquarters. Detectives had sent her texts letting her know that Barnstead was furious over the media attention. She was the darling. The media wanted her story. News anchors wanted her for interviews. *The Tonight Show* called from New York, Jay Leno's people called from Los Angeles. Could they send a plane for her?

She and Detective Symons drove the two hours back to Fort McMurray in silence. Light snow fell, the snow swirled over the pavement like waves blown by the wind. Detective Symons drove under the speed limit. He was in no hurry to get Bernadette to Fort McMurray.

The impending showdown with Chief of Detectives Barnstead was obvious.

Bernadette's hunch about the second threat of polywater had been right. But, she had been off the case—and should have used the channels. And thus, the shit storm of Tsunami-sized proportions was bearing down on her.

They arrived at the RCMP detachment; two media trucks were parked outside. They lay in wait. Symons drove around back. Bernadette grabbed her overnight bag and slipped in the back entrance. The other RCMP detectives and officers nodded in her direction and parted the way as she moved through the office. They were not being cowardly in avoiding her—it was self-preservation in the RCMP. Bernadette understood and accepted it.

She walked to her desk, removed her gun and holster, and placed it in the desk. She noticed Chief Barnstead get up from his desk. He opened his door and spoke her name. "Callahan." It was loud—not shouted, but loud.

She walked into Barnstead's office. Her head was not cowed, and her eyes flashed a mild defiance as she stood in front of Barnstead's desk.

"Take a seat," Barnstead commanded.

"I'd rather stand, sir."

"Very well, Detective Callahan." Barnstead's voice was quivering with anger. His eyes narrowed as he gazed at her. "I understand you're quite the hero. The phones have been ringing while you were away. People think you're some kind of savior. Know what I think, Detective?"

"No, I don't, Sir." Bernadette said evenly. She knew what was coming.

"I think you are a loner who doesn't belong in the RCMP. You have no idea how to work with a team or through channels or with your superior officers, and that makes you an inferior Detective, and a weak link in this detachment."

Bernadette stood, her face blazing red with anger. She knew the deeper shit she would be in if she said what she wanted to say to Barnstead. Her only words were, "Yes, Sir."

"I have been on the phone with my superiors in Ottawa and Edmonton. Oh, they wanted to commend you; however, I reminded them of your lack of discipline, your lack of working through channels, of how you were off this case—and they saw my view."

Bernadette thought about how much Barnstead must have ranted and raved to get the commanding officers in Edmonton and Ottawa on side. Barnstead was a rock steady RCMP officer. His father had been in the RCMP, and so had his grandfather. As far as Bernadette knew, a Barnstead relative was part of the first arrival of the North West Mounted Police in 1874. Barnstead had clout, and he used it to his advantage.

"I, of course, asked that you be reprimanded," Barnstead continued. "And although that would be the case in most circumstances," he cleared his throat, "as the circumstances in this case warrant it, you will be transferred to another detachment—effective immediately."

"Another detachment," Bernadette said. She wondered what lonely outpost Barnstead had succeeded in having her relegated to. Would she be demoted back to a constable?

"Yes, you will be attached to the detective squad in Red Deer." Barnstead said. He tried to make it sound like a demotion. But even he knew it wasn't. It was not even close.

"Red Deer," Bernadette said, more for affirmation than surprise.

"Yes, Red Deer. Now that is all. Pack your desk and turn over all pertinent casework to the other detectives. Hopefully you will work through proper channels in your next detachment.

Bernadette was slightly amused as she turned and walked back to her desk. Red Deer was a nice-sized city between Calgary and Edmonton and some 7 hours south by car. Nice lakes nearby, close to the Rocky Mountains, with a much warmer winter than Fort McMurray. Barnstead had only succeeded in getting Bernadette out of Fort McMurray. She was not only landing on her feet, she was going up a notch. Not bad at all—she felt good.

Several hours later, she turned over her case files to the other detectives. They all wished her well in her new city and promised to keep in touch. Grabbing her jacket and making an exit out the back door, she took back roads to avoid the media. She gave thanks when she reached her place and saw that no media had staked it out.

Her cell phone rang as she walked into her apartment. She wasn't going to answer it, but the caller ID showed Pierre Beaumont. "Hey Pierre, can no one keep a secret in the oil business?" Bernadette said as she took her coat off and dropped it on her kitchen chair.

"Yeah, sorry about that. I told the vice president of operations at Synthetic Oil that it was you who had provided the information on the threat of polywater so he would take it seriously. Unfortunately, he did not keep the information to himself."

Bernadette just sighed. "Oh yeah, not too good on keeping secrets. Worse than old women—or should I say old men?" She opened her fridge to start foraging for anything that might be edible.

"I want to make it up to you, Bernadette."

"Um . . . I'm listening." She opened a Tupperware container. The smell that wafted up made her eyes water.

"I wanted to invite you for dinner tonight," Pierre said.

"Ah, I'll have to pass on that. There're more media types crawling around here than flies on a Moose carcass, and I've been told to be in Red Deer on Monday. Bernadette picked up a container of leftover Chinese food. This time she approached it more carefully, sniffing before opening it fully. It wasn't too bad. *I may not have to order in.*

"Yeah, again, sorry about that . . . Red Deer, nice spot. But I'm not talking about dinner in Fort McMurray. I'm talking about dinner in Vancouver."

"Vancouver? Just when do you think I'll be in Vancouver?" Bernadette asked. She was searching through her cutlery draw looking for a fork—there were none. She hadn't emptied the dishwasher.

"Tonight."

"Ha. Pierre Beaumont, you crack me up. I like you because you're a dreamer. And of course we did have fun in Vegas that one time—"

"Bernadette," Pierre quickly cut in, "there's someone else here on the line I wanted you to speak with."

Shit. Her face a hot red, she squeaked out a "hello."

"Hello Detective Callahan, this is Agent Anton De Luca."

"Hello, Anton." Bernadette recovered her composure. "What're you doing with the private security hack? Slumming?"

Anton laughed. "Yeah, the private security guys bring the neighborhood down. Listen, I wanted to invite you to a little party we're having in Vancouver, and Synthetic Oil graciously offered to fly you here for the festivities tomorrow morning."

"Festivities? What kind of festivities are being planned by the CSIS?" Bernadette stopped searching for a fork and closed the drawer.

"Tomorrow morning we plan to apprehend Professor Alistair McAllen and his band of merry men."

"You've found McAllen?"

"Yes," Anton said. "And we couldn't have done it without you."

"How did I figure into this?" Bernadette asked. She sat down in her kitchen chair and rested her hand on her cheek.

"You sent me the information about the other men, and the woman, McAllen was associated with. Your hunch was right. You said he was probably still with them, and we tracked them through real estate."

"You found them through real estate?" Bernadette's hand came off her cheek, and she sat up in her chair.

"Yeah, the CSIS Forensic Accounting guys did a search of all real estate transactions on the West Coast. Turns out that one of McAllen's friends, Percy Stronach, had a bunch of numbered companies. He used one of the companies to buy a private island with a large house about two months ago. You know what they say about trying to hide from the government—you can run, but you can't hide.

"We've had a spy drone flying over their area for the past few days, compliments of the Canadian Air Force, and we have a complete joint task force of navy, army, and air forces with the RCMP ready for a takedown tomorrow. You've been cleared for the mission—from the highest levels, I might add."

"Highest levels . . . how high?"

"The clearance came from the prime minister's office. You've impressed a lot of people in a lot of high places with your intuition. Look, I know you got in some hot water with Barnstead, and unfortunately there is nothing anyone can do. The RCMP and their chain of command," he muttered. "But your actions in putting the alert out on polywater—that was priceless. You've got a lot of friends in Ottawa now."

"Well, if I've been cleared by the prime minister—"

"Bernadette," Pierre came back on the line. "The Synthetic Oil jet is at a private hanger just east of the main terminal at Fort McMurray. Do you know where that is?"

"Yeah, I know it, what time does it leave?"

"When you get there. You're its only passenger. Dinner here can be at 8:00, 8:30, or whenever you get here."

Bernadette felt a tingling sensation down her spine. She had just been shit on by her chief of detectives and cast out of Fort McMurray, her home of three years. Now here was an invite to Vancouver to be in on the takedown of Professor McAllen—an invite from the prime minister. *Well, what's a girl to do,* she thought. *Might as well go to the party.*

"So, where's dinner? Do I need a dress?" She instantly regretted saying that. She had been at an oil camp for the past three days. Shaving her legs and the impending bloodletting that she was capable of was not high on her list.

"There's a nice restaurant in the Fairmont Waterfront Hotel, where you're staying, called the Heron. Nice place, good seafood—and steaks," Pierre hastily added, as he knew Bernadette was a major carnivore. "They're what you call smart casual, which I believe is a step above jeans and a T-shirt. So we leave it to you."

"Okay, I'll throw some stuff in a bag and head for the airport. It's 6:30 my time. Should be at the airport in a half hour.

"Sounds great, see you at the airport in Vancouver. We look forward to a fun day tomorrow," Anton said.

Bernadette headed for the bedroom, grabbed a small suitcase, and threw in a toiletries bag, a bag of makeup, which she hoped had what she needed, a pair of black slacks, and a white silk top she had purchased in Edmonton for her nephew's graduation.

Just then her intercom sounded. She looked out her apartment window and saw a media truck. They had found her. Bernadette grabbed her cell phone and punched in the number of Constable Tom Aulander. Tom was her best go-to guy on the force, and she hoped he would do her a favor. When Tom answered, she quickly detailed what she needed and went back to finish packing.

When Bernadette looked down to the street again, two RCMP cruisers had boxed in the media truck. Bernadette smiled that her RCMP detachment still had her back.

A light snow was falling as Bernadette pulled her Jeep onto the highway and headed south to the airport. The traffic was heavy on Friday night as many oil workers commuted back to Edmonton on weekends. Her jeep was dwarfed by the big half-ton trucks and crew buses that lined the freeway.

She turned onto airport road; the traffic was jammed in the parking lot. She felt lucky to be at a private terminal, beyond all the chaos of the main terminal. A Synthetic Oil employee at the entrance directed her to a private parking spot hidden from view.

The Synthetic Oil private jet was close to the hanger. An employee escorted Bernadette to the plane, and a flight attendant in a navy blue uniform welcomed her aboard. She got a brief look at the young pilots, who smiled in her direction, and then she took a seat in the center of the cabin. She only had a moment to look around before the lights dimmed and the jet rolled forward. Twin engines roared in takeoff, and they leveled off in the northern night sky in what seemed like minutes.

Bernadette had never been on a private jet. She'd been in a bush plane, hunkered down with hunters who smelled of mosquito repellent and beer. And she had been on numerous commercial flights in cattle class with the screaming kids, the frazzled mothers, and always the big guy who crowded the armrest.

This was nice. Bernadette put her large leather seat back and kicked off her boots. Toes touched plush carpet. Soft leather seats, mahogany wood panels, warm wall sconces throwing soft light—where had this been all her life?

The flight attendant came forward and asked what refreshment she would prefer. Bernadette was about to say "just water," but thought, *well, maybe a beer,* and the words "scotch please" came out.

The flight attendant with the most perfectly aligned teeth and the bluest eyes asked, "Do you prefer a Highland, Lowland, or Islay?"

"Just something smooth would be fine," Bernadette replied as if in a dream.

A crystal tumbler with a large pour of scotch was placed on a Synthetic Oil linen napkin, accompanied by a bowl of cashew nuts. The flight attendant announced the scotch was a Highland Dalwhinnie 15 year old. Bernadette sipped, rolled it around her tongue, and let the warmth spill down her throat.

Outside, the darkness of the trees and the snow of the northern landscape gave way to clouds, then stars, then moonlight. The flight was smooth. So was the scotch.

A light mist was falling as the jet landed in Vancouver. It was just past 7:00 p.m. The jet taxied past the main terminal and arrived at a private hanger. Pierre and Anton waited outside, their raincoats buttoned up, their faces turned away from the light wind.

Only brief words were exchanged as they took Bernadette between them, walked through the hanger, and got into a Lincoln Navigator SUV in the parking lot.

Vancouver is always in mist, Bernadette thought. She remembered it only once in bright sunshine, but perhaps it had been a dream—she wasn't sure. She preferred it like this. Dark, misty, lights twinkling on Grouse Mountain in the background. It brought something mystic to bear. A port city with secrets, a city that was hiding something, that was hiding McAllen.

Anton was driving; Pierre was in the front seat. Bernadette threw her question at them. "So, where is McAllen holed up?"

Pierre looked back at her. He smiled and said, "We'll give you the entire layout over dinner. You're going to like it. Relax, enjoy the scenery."

Bernadette was not satisfied with the answer. She wanted details, plans, execution points, and the amount of manpower involved. Her mind had been spinning with questions the entire flight. She resigned herself to settling back and watching the Friday night traffic wend its way down Granville Street.

Pedestrians with umbrellas dashed across streets and into shops. Restaurants were filling with evening customers. Small shops displayed fruit and flowers on their sidewalks. Green cedar trees formed hedges along the street, and green grass glistened on the boulevard. *How unlike anywhere else in Canada*, Bernadette thought. She had left the frozen north only a few short hours ago.

The Navigator pulled up to the entrance of the Fairmont Waterfront Hotel. They had already checked Bernadette into her room, and in minutes, she was in a suite overlooking the harbor. The inner harbor lights, the view, the large bathroom with soaker tub and warm terry cloth bathrobe would've been hard to leave, but the discussion of McAllen, and his capture, was the dinner topic. Bernadette performed the quickest change and makeup fix of her life and was in the restaurant to join Pierre and Anton in minutes.

The restaurant was nice—white tablecloths, nice view, soft music—and Bernadette could care less. The topic of conversation was McAllen. She sat opposite Pierre and Anton and sipped on a glass of red wine they had poured for her.

The waiter came by, and after a brief glance at the menu, she ordered the seafood chowder with mussels, clams, and chorizo, and the beef tenderloin medium rare, and then returned her attention to the men. "So, what's the layout? How close are we to where he's hiding? How many officers are involved?" The questions came in rapid fire. They had been inside her head for too long.

Pierre laughed over his wine glass. He wiped his lips with his napkin and placed his glass on the table after swilling the wine to give it more air. "My dear Detective Callahan, you do have a lot of questions. Well, first of all, McAllen isn't here in Vancouver—he's off the coast of Vancouver Island."

Bernadette had to stop herself from blurting out her response. She chose to use a soft, but explosive whisper instead. "Vancouver Island? Then what the hell are we doing here?"

Pierre chuckled. "Well, better accommodations, better wine . . . no, just kidding. The truth is, we didn't want the Synthetic Oil private jet seen anywhere on Vancouver Island."

Anton leaned forward. "Bernadette, we've found in our search of Grace Fairchild, one of McAllen's connections, that many of her relatives and contacts are in both Fort McMurray and Alaska, as well as all over Vancouver Island. We think they've been their eyes and ears. "

"So what's the plan for the takedown tomorrow? Where is the command center?" Bernadette asked.

"Oh, you'll love this," Anton said. He pulled out his iPad and placed it on the table in front of Bernadette. The screen showed a navel destroyer. "This is the Canadian Naval Destroyer *Algonquin*." He hit the screen again. "And these are Kingston Class coastal ships that will accompany her."

"You have Canadian Navy in this?" Bernadette said.

"Oh yes, and a Griffin helicopter that ten Canadian Army Special Forces officers will rappel to the island from."

"Isn't this a little overkill?" Bernadette said, looking at the pictures as Anton scrolled down the list of armaments each ship carried. Bernadette's eyes glassed over when she saw the *Algonquin* had a Vulcan cannon that could fire six thousand rounds a minute. She thought of bodies being shredded.

"Look, I know, I know, it sounds a little much." Pierre raised his hand in defense of the plan. "But, you have to understand, the world is scared shitless of McAllen. If this polywater would have actually worked, we would have had to peddle our way from the airport to the hotel."

"So, where am I going to be watching this from?"

"You, my fine Detective Callahan," Anton said, as he flashed a wink at Pierre, "have been given a seat at the table."

"Which means?"

"Which means you'll be taking a helicopter from the helipad just minutes from here at 0430 hours tomorrow over to Canadian Forces Base Comox, and then a Sea King helicopter will land you on this destroyer, where you will be at the command center for the capture of McAllen. How does that sound?" Anton looked at Bernadette from across the table. His smile widened.

Bernadette was silent as she took in the information. Helicopters. She had never liked helicopters. Something about the whirling thing, called a blade, being on the top never seemed right. Now, two helicopter trips, both over water, and one to land on a ship bobbing on the ocean? She took a long sip of her wine, smiled, and said, "Sounds great."

CHAPTER THIRTY-EIGHT

THE MOOD ON MCALLEN'S ISLAND on Friday was somber, quiet, and reflective. Light rain fell on the windows, and a fire flickered in the hearth. They sat in overstuffed armchairs and sofas in a semi-circle around the fire. A dinner of venison stew and several bottles of red wine had disappeared at the long dining room table. They lingered by the fire with large snifters of cognac. Percy and Theo sat on a sofa in the center of the room, and McAllen and Sebastian sat to one side of the sofa in armchairs. There was little conversation.

Grace came into the room and lit several candles. A cathedral-like quality came over the room. The candlelight danced, and shadows formed and fled as the light breeze moved the flames. Grace sat down on the sofa beside Percy and Theo.

The door to Grace's bedroom opened, and Margaret stepped out. Sebastian looked up and watched her as she walked across the room and sat beside Grace, who placed her hand on Margaret's shoulder and smiled. They looked into each other's eyes. Sebastian saw a loving look. He didn't think it was sexual—it looked like one of two sisters, like two who had found each other.

Sebastian had been observing Margaret's transformation. Gone were the velour track suits and finely coiffed hair of Palm Springs. Margaret now wore blue jeans and sweatshirts and her hair tied back in a piece of deer hide with beads.

Sebastian noticed a change in her face too. Gone now were the steely, calculating eyes. They were soft now—there was a light behind them. She breathed differently too. The first time Sebastian met Margaret, she was breathing through her mouth, short, quick intakes that only fed the synapses of her brain. Now she breathed slowly, through her nose, and her belly rose and fell as her breath came deep from within her. Yoga breathing—the same technique Grace had taught him years ago. Grace had worked wonders with Margaret in a few short days. Why Margaret had chosen to join them Sebastian didn't know, but she was welcome.

Sebastian was about to say something when their large Irish wolfhound stalked into the room. The dog usually occupied a place by the fireplace, sleeping, or on the outside porch, with one eye open. The dog paced around the room, went to the windows, and let out a low, growling sound. Sebastian knew the dog sensed something was coming.

McAllen looked over at Sebastian. "How soon until they hit us?"

Sebastian looked at McAllen. "Percy saw the spy drone two days back. He estimates the tide and weather will be right for them sometime after 8:00 a.m. tomorrow.

McAllen stared down at his cognac glass. He tipped it to the side and watched the amber liquid shine in the firelight. "What do you think our chances are?"

Sebastian looked back into the fire. "Somewhere between slim and none. They'll come in by boat, probably a bunch of zodiacs—which is fine as we got that covered—but the air cover is what we need. Right now we got those two resident eagles—don't think they're up for the job." Sebastian looked over at McAllen and smiled.

Both men watched the fire burn, embers dying and wet wood crackling. McAllen lifted his head and looked over at Margaret. "Say, Margaret, how good are your boys in Boulder at hacking into computers?"

Margaret looked over at McAllen. "My boys are the best."

Could they get into the Canadian Forces computers?"

"They can get into anything." Margaret smiled.

McAllen looked over at Percy. "Percy, could you help Margaret with that, show her what it is you need access to?"

Percy sat up from his deep slump in the sofa. "Absolutely. I know the door they need to open; the boys just need to provide the key."

"Okay, let's get on it," McAllen said. He turned to Sebastian. "We might have changed our chances from slim to maybe."

CHAPTER THIRTY-NINE

B ERNADETTE WOKE TO THE RINGING of the telephone in her Vancouver hotel room at 3:30 a.m. The sound rang into her consciousness, and she swam over the multiple pillows and comforters of the king-sized bed to answer the phone. A cheery voice informed her of the time and the weather, three degrees Celsius and light rain. Bernadette swung out of bed in one motion. She headed for the bathroom in the blackness of her room. A nightlight shone in the bathroom, a beacon for the confused hotel guest.

The capture of McAllen was on her mind—the first thought that came to her. She had left the restaurant at 10:00 p.m. last night. No desert, only two glasses of wine. She had a Granville Island lager from the minibar and soaked in the luxurious marble tub for hours. Somewhere around 1:00 a.m. she fell asleep. Sleep had been short.

Lack of sleep didn't matter now. Her senses were alive, thinking about the capture of McAllen. She did not know why she wanted him apprehended so badly. She guessed it was because he was outside the law: she represented the law. Cut and dried, black and white, that's how she saw it.

The shower was cold as she got in. It jarred the last recesses of her brain awake. Now everything was on board, ready to fire.

Throwing her evening clothes and shoes and toiletries into her bag, she slipped back on her standard travel clothes. Jeans, tee shirt with a V-neck sweater over top, and lace-up boots. Anton had given her a GORE-TEX rain jacket to wear the night before. She stuffed her leather jacket into the bag. Leather, she had realized, did not do well on this wet coast.

A mere fifteen minutes later, she rode the elevator down to the hotel lobby. The lobby was quiet. The only occupants were maintenance and front desk staff. Anton was waiting beside the elevator with a large coffee in his hand.

He smiled as he offered the coffee to Bernadette. "Two sugars two creams?"

"You're a savior," Bernadette said as she took the coffee. The mere smell of the caffeine and sugar was heaven.

"Where's Pierre?" Bernadette asked as she took the first sip of coffee.

"Pierre's a civilian, won't be allowed on this trip, and actually, neither will I," Anton said as he ushered Bernadette to the Lincoln Navigator. He took the keys for the SUV from the doorman and placed Bernadette's bag in the back.

"Why not?" Bernadette asked as she climbed into the passenger's seat.

"Bernadette, I only have basic weapons training. I'm really an agent analyst. I'll be watching from CSIS headquarters here in Vancouver."

"You're going to miss the fun stuff."

Anton looked over at her as he started the SUV and pulled out of the driveway. "The Italians have a saying: *Quelle sono le interruzioni nella vita*, which basically means 'Those are the breaks in life.'" He smiled as he headed for the heliport.

Bernadette laughed in between gulps of her coffee. "So when will we meet again?"

"Hopefully soon. Pierre will pick you up at the Comox Airport in the Synthetic Oil corporate jet later today and fly you back to Fort McMurray tonight. I'll be heading back to Edmonton in a few days. How about we all meet in Edmonton at a great Italian restaurant I know once you get settled in your new place in Red Deer?"

"Sure," Bernadette said. She sat up in her seat as the heliport came in view. There on the landing pad was the Canadian Forces helicopter. It had just arrived. The helicopter was yellow and black with red rotor housing. In large letters on the side were the words CFB RESCUE. Neither the looks of the helicopter or the name on the side gave Bernadette any comfort. Rotors on top and on the tail seemed odd. She knew that if the back rotor stopped functioning, the thing had to come down in some kind of rotational maneuver that seemed unnatural.

Anton turned to Bernadette. "There's your ride. Now when you get to CFB Comox, Sublieutenant Prefontaine, a navy liaison, will meet you and take you to Naval Supply to get you fitted with the gear you need."

"Gear? What gear are you talking about?"

"Oh, yeah, that was the one thing Pierre and I forgot to mention last night. You're getting combat gear: bulletproof vest, gun, helmet— the works. You see, the people in Ottawa want pictures of you next to McAllen when the arrest is made. To show we always get our man." Anton smiled again and this time winked. "And, not to worry, you'll be taken care of during the arrest to ensure nothing happens to you."

"So, I'm in a photo opportunity to be used by our government?" Bernadette had just realized the position she'd been given.

"Detective Callahan." Anton looked hurt as he put a hand on Bernadette's arm. "We all play our part to ensure we present a good picture to the public of how we protect them."

Bernadette smiled back at Anton. She couldn't be mad at him. Government bullshit was government bullshit. They would capture McAllen and show him like a prize stag hanging on the wall. She would be arm candy. What the hell.

Bernadette climbed into the helicopter. The two navy pilots gave her a thumbs-up after she put on her life vest, buckled in and they lifted off. The chopper did a quick hover and headed out of Coal Harbor, and the lights of North Vancouver. They would be in Comox in less than a half hour.

Harbor lights gave way to the dark expanse of the Georgia Straight. Moonlight shone on the ocean, making a silver glow on the water. Small ships and freighters plied the waters between the islands. The helicopter climbed higher; fog obscured the ocean below.

Bernadette looked down to the sea below when they were halfway into the channel. The fog parted. A long Haida war canoe appeared below. The paddles flashed in the moonlight. The fog closed in again—was it a vision? A dream? She wasn't sure.

The chopper's altitude dropped, and land came into sight—the coast, then a golf course, and then a runway: on the left was a commercial terminal; on the right was the military. A small commercial commuter plane was being prepped for morning takeoff. The chopper landed in front of the naval base, and the blades came to a stop. Bernadette got out; thankful her first helicopter trip had been successful. She counted it a success that she hadn't died at sea in the thing.

A dark green truck pulled up to the chopper, and a young officer came towards Bernadette. He was dressed in dark navy and had gold bars on his lapel. His baseball cap had HMCS ALGONQUIN embroidered in gold on it. "Sublieutenant Marc Prefontaine. I'll be your guide to the *Algonquin*, Detective Callahan."

Bernadette climbed into the truck, and they sped off to the Naval Supply room. The supply clerk handed Bernadette naval combat gear and offered her a change room. As she donned the standard issue naval bulletproof vest, she wondered if it was any better at stopping a .50 caliber sniper round than an RCMP vest.

She had been thinking of McAllen and how he had killed Emmanuel Fuentes on Galiano Island using a .50 caliber sniper rifle and M16 machine guns. She wondered if McAllen still had them—would she face them that same morning?

From the Stores room, they made their way to another helicopter. A large gray machine was warming its blades up slowly on the pad. The officer informed Bernadette that this was a Sea King, her ride to the naval destroyer *Algonquin*.

Bernadette looked at the sub lieutenant with mild fear in her eyes. "This large thing is going to land on a ship?"

The officer looked at Bernadette with a knowing smile. "Not to worry, they'll be using a bear trap this morning."

"A bear trap?"

"Yeah, it's a line that the Sea King drops down, and then the helicopter is pulled to the landing pad. We do it all the time, nice and safe." The officer took her arm and guided her to a seat inside the helicopter. Seats with buckles and webbing lined the walls. Gear had been stowed that was being transferred to the destroyer, and a mean-looking machine gun was locked in position beside the door.

The helicopter took off long before Bernadette was mentally ready. The ground gave way, and this time, there was no window to look out of to see the relationship of the craft to the ground. Bernadette adopted her best nonchalant face and stared at the back of the pilots' heads.

She was told the flight to the destroyer was only thirty minutes. It seemed longer. Bernadette had gone from a corporate jet the day before to flying in something that sounded like a cement mixer. She inadvertently said a few Hail Mary's softly to herself.

The helicopter slowed and hovered. Bernadette felt a tugging motion, and the helicopter inched lower with the help of what she knew was the bear trap. Finally the chopper came to rest in a lurching motion, and Bernadette's tailbone met with her throat by way of her stomach. Not her best experience.

The cargo door opened, and Bernadette stepped onto the deck of the destroyer. Her view was gray: gray metal, gray surfaces with gray paint. The sea formed a backdrop of black waves tipped with foam set under cloud and fog. It was 6:00 a.m. The sun would not rise for another hour and a half.

Bernadette immediately felt the rise and fall of the ship, something she never experienced before. She had been on a rowboat and a motorboat on a lake, but never a ship, not even a ferry boat. The motion: her legs moved to fight it, to stay steady. Her stomach was wondering what to make of it. A square-set man introduced himself as Chief Petty Officer Keller, and Bernadette and Prefontaine followed him forward and, thankfully, below deck.

Bernadette tried to follow as quickly as she could as Keller shot down the stairs and walked the narrow corridors as if his feet had magnets attached to them. The motion of the ship and the narrow corridors reminded Bernadette of a maze she had been in once. She hadn't liked the maze—wasn't sure if she liked this.

They arrived at the mess hall, another narrow room with rows of tables. An opening at one end was the kitchen. The aroma of eggs, bacon, and sausage assaulted her nostrils, smells that normally would wake a craving in her stomach for salt, fat, and sugar. Now, strangely, her stomach found these smells confusing.

Bernadette found a seat at the mess table and sat down. Her legs no longer wanted to navigate the motion of the decks. Just as she was about to explore what the sensation of her stomach was all about, a hand rested on her shoulder. She turned and looked into the eyes of a tall RCMP constable. She thought about what she would tell Cynthia when she saw her next. *He has dark hair, olive skin, brown eyes, and the charming good looks of one of those great-looking men in travel commercials who say, "Come to this island and you'll meet someone just like this."*

"Detective Callahan, we finally meet. I'm Constable Chris Christakos."

Bernadette forgot her flip-flopping stomach, her fatigue and raw nerves. This was the Constable Chris Christakos of Galiano Island. The one she had spoken with numerous times on the phone, the one who had helped her ID the dead body of Emmanuel Fuentes on the beach.

Here he was, flesh and, well, *very good-looking flesh,* she thought. She was speechless. Of all the places to meet someone she had checked out on Facebook and had had a mini-fantasy over, here he was, on a naval destroyer. "What a pleasant surprise," Bernadette finally managed to squeak out.

Chris grinned and sat down beside Bernadette. "I know this is kind of a surprise. I was hoping our first meeting would be on my salmon boat off of Galiano Island. I heard from my commanding officer that you were joining us on this mission."

The sub lieutenant returned to the table with a coffee for Bernadette and said, "I see the RCMP is forming a posse. Would you like to fill the detective in on our plans while I check in with my commanding officer?"

"Sure, happy to," Chris said. He watched as the sub lieutenant walked away and then turned to Bernadette. "So this is a pretty big operation they've mounted—looks like they're serious about apprehending McAllen."

Bernadette took some exploratory sips of navy coffee, added some sugar, and asked, "So what's the master plan?"

Chris paused a moment, looking into Bernadette's eyes. "Well, this destroyer has four large zodiacs on board, the new Hurricanes with 600-horsepower engines. They'll have nine personnel each on board. We launch for McAllen's island just after sunrise, which is 0730 hours, but there's some heavy fog out there so they may delay a half hour to an hour.

"The four zodiacs will hit the beach just in front of McAllen's island, which is just below a large house on a cliff. Army Special Forces officers will rappel from a Griffin helicopter to the back of the house, and the Sea King helicopter you just rode in on will provide covering fire from above with a large caliber machine gun. Plus there will be three navy Kingston Class coastal ships with capability of covering fire."

"Wow, sounds like quite the armada. Now do you think that McAllen will surrender without firing a shot from that .50 caliber sniper rifle or the M16 he used previously?"

"I guess there're chances of that. The joint command thinks this is a complete surprise. They've had a spy drone overhead for several days without an increase in activity from McAllen." Chris shrugged the shrug of an RCMP officer about to go into harm's way based on the decision of command. His shrug said it all—*it's what we do.*

"You know, back home, we always say that the angriest bear is a surprised bear. I really hope joint command is right," Bernadette said.

"Me to. I'd hate for our first date to go badly." Chris smiled.

Bernadette couldn't help herself—she smiled then blushed, and then her cheeks went another shade of red that gave her away. *Damn this is bad timing,* she thought.

———

Everyone in McAllen's cabin had been awake since 4:00 a.m. McAllen, Sebastian, and Theo moved a large tube, tripod, and base plate out of the shed, assembled it under the overhang of the front porch, and stacked a dozen shells beside it. It was a French long-range mortar, capable of lobbing shells a mile into the channel.

Theo made some final adjustments to the mortar and they covered it with a tarp. Sebastian looked anxiously into the sky to see if the spy drone was overhead. The wolfhound stood beside Sebastian, also staring up at the sky, as if he could help.

They all went inside, except for the dog, which now paced back and forth and growled into the dark morning. Grace brought a batch of her famous high fiber muffins out of the oven, and some Salt Spring Island Canopy Blend coffee was brewing.

Margaret and Percy were in deep conversation at Percy's computer. They looked up at the men as they walked in.

"Can we do it?" McAllen asked as he walked into the kitchen and helped himself to some coffee.

Percy looked at Margaret, then at McAllen, and then threw up his hands as if the air had the answer. "Maybe, if we hit the right database and the virus goes viral throughout their system and their firewalls don't block it. Yeah, if not . . ." He left the words hanging.

They looked at each other and wondered if they had ever been in a tougher situation than this and if there was a way out. They would find out soon. Dawn was two hours away.

***

Bernadette and Chris were lost in a bubble, the bubble that forms around two people attracted to each other. Thirty or so navy and RCMP officers provided a wave of conversation around them, and their bubble sailed amongst them.

They talked about RCMP basic training in Regina, drill sergeants they hated, commandants they admired, and why they both loved the RCMP. There was comparisons of good detachments, not so good, and the in-between.

Two officers, lost in attraction to each other, oblivious to their surroundings. Somewhere in that time, breakfast appeared for Bernadette. Her stomach had miraculously recovered from its queasiness—funny thing. She didn't give it another thought.

Then the loudspeaker sounded. "Task force to the zodiacs." The voice broke Bernadette and Chris out of their trance. They gathered their gear and followed the rest of the RCMP and navy personnel through the narrow corridors and up on deck.

On deck, the fog surrounded the ship like a soft cloak. The sea was now a dark blue, and only light waves rolled by the ship.. A group of officers stood in a ring of conversation. One was on a cell phone, the other on a radio. Bernadette heard one officer say to the other, "Ottawa wants to proceed anyway—air cover or no air cover, it's a go."

As they stood waiting for the climb down into the zodiacs, Bernadette could see the flight deck where the Sea King helicopter was. A group of technicians were scrambling over it. It did not look in ready-to-fly mode. It looked like in ready-to-sit mode.

A young sailor behind Bernadette said to his companion, Looks like we got a SNAFU." Bernadette knew that term. It meant "situation normal all fucked up."

Bernadette climbed down the ladder into the zodiac. She was dressed in her brown navy combat pants, jacket, bulletproof vest, and life vest. She felt like the Michelin Man: big, bulky, and slightly inflated. Chris sat down in the seat beside her. She was sandwiched between two large RCMP officers and sitting behind the command controls.

The coxswain of the zodiac looked around as they took their places. He smiled at everyone and said, "Okay, minor SNAFU. Air support is down as radar is out. We've been informed we're going in regardless, so check your weapons and stay sharp. We'll have cover from the three Kingston Class boats in the channel." He took the zodiac's controls and steered the boat away from the destroyer.

A ship appeared off to their left, one of the Kingston Class coastal boats. It dwarfed the zodiacs as it plowed through waves. They were called boats but were actually 180-feet long and 37-feet wide with 4 diesel engines. The coastal boats were to get there first, get close in, and then the zodiacs were to land. That was what Chris told Bernadette as they slowly made their way behind the big boats, rocking in their wake.

Bernadette looked over her shoulder to see the Sea King on the destroyer deck. It was going nowhere. Its large rotor blades hung limp. Bernadette wondered if McAllen had done that—sabotaged the aircraft radar. A strange feeling developed in the pit of her stomach. It wasn't sea sickness this time—it was a feeling that things were going wrong.

The coastal boats disappeared into the fog, and the zodiacs bobbed on the ocean, waiting for the command to advance on the island. A radio came to life, and the words, "Engage, engage, engage" came over the radio. The coxswain hit full throttle, and the zodiac rose up on its prow. Sea spray and cold air whipped Bernadette.

There was fog. Fog and dark blue waves. Somewhere ahead was the outline of an island, which only the coxswain could make out. They made a sharp right, and then Bernadette could see the outline of dark trees and waves crashing on a shore. It must be McAllen's island.

They came around in another sharp right. *This must be it; this must be the beachhead,* Bernadette thought. She looked over her shoulder to the left. The coastal boats were supposed to be close in. She could make out an outline of them, but they seemed far away. Large plumes of water were erupting around them. Like geysers or columns, water shot up into the sky.

The zodiac's engines roared, an officer at the helm yelled to "look sharp," and then he yelled, "Incoming."

Bernadette had never experienced artillery fire. It had never been part of RCMP training. Gunfire sure, but geysers of water erupting around her on the water from shells was a new experience.

The zodiacs went from high speed to slow and then stopped. The engines still whined. The motor blades sounded like they were churning something heavy, a heaviness that was not water, like something in the water had become solid. The engines stopped.

Bernadette immediately knew what had happened. McAllen had lobbed polywater at them. The sea around them had become a heavy gel. Their boats and motors couldn't move through it. Bernadette had been worried about the conventional weapons, and McAllen had used his own invention to defend himself.

The radios came to life. The three coastal boats were stuck a full mile out in the channel. They couldn't get in close enough. Fog was now enveloping the zodiacs. They could only barely see each other. The RCMP and navy personnel quietly talked amongst themselves.

Bernadette and Chris exchanged looks. There was nothing they could do. The fog deepened. There was quiet. No waves slapped on the shore in front of them. The sea was now a gelatinous mass under their boat. One navy man tried to get out of the boat. The polywater was like Jell-O. His leg punched into the mass, and his fellow officers had to pull him up before he sunk into it.

The sound was faint at first. Bernadette wasn't sure if her ears were playing tricks on her in the fog. There it was again. Paddles—paddles in unison, coming towards them.

Out of the fog, at first the prow was visible, then a figure at the prow. A large lady stood. She had a bowl, and from the bowl she shook a cedar branch. The prow moved. As it came into view, Bernadette could see it was a Haida war canoe. It was coming straight for them. They couldn't move. A chorus of machine guns and side arms were slung off shoulders and taken out of holsters in the zodiac. Gun safeties came off, filling the air with a metallic clatter.

The war canoe moved closer and closer and then moved off to the left and proceeded to plow its way between the zodiacs. The words "hold your fire" came from both zodiacs. The helmsman of the war canoe knew what he was doing. By coming between the zodiacs, the canoe put itself in the line of fire, but the RCMP and navy were in the line of fire as well.

Bernadette could only watch the war canoe slide past. The woman in the prow shook what was obviously the polywater antidote into the water and they moved forward. The war canoe was long, and at its paddles, Bernadette could make out, from what she knew from a picture from long ago, were Percy Stronach, Sebastian Germaine, and Theo Martin. There were several other paddlers, probably Haida, or Natives from Grace's band. There was a lady with red hair as well, but she was not very visible as she was on the far side of the canoe.

Bernadette knew it was Grace Fairchild at the prow. She was much larger than in the photo, but the face was the same, a face set in focus, almost serene. As the boat slipped by, she saw a tall figure at the helm with a large dog by his side.

It was McAllen. The boat moved slowly by, and McAllen looked over in Bernadette's direction. He smiled, took one hand off the tiller, and waved.

They disappeared into the fog.

EPILOGUE

BERNADETTE WAS ON THE LAST leg of her evening run along a Red Deer city pathway in late June, just after 8:00 p.m. A nice 7.5 kilometers suited her in the evenings, helped her unwind. Her two-year-old German Shepherd, Sprocket, was keeping pace, tongue hanging out, eying her and the road ahead.

The dog was from the RCMP canine training unit in Innisfail, Alberta, a town not more than a half hour south of Red Deer. He was a dropout from the RCMP training Program—he couldn't complete the seventeen-week basic training course and needed a home. Bernadette didn't need a dog for protection—she could protect the dog—but as a running companion, the dog was great. He was lop-eared and ran with a long, easy gait, never seeming to tire.

Bernadette thought of the past few months as she settled into an easy stride for the homeward stretch. The dog looked up at her and matched her pace. The disappointment of watching McAllen slip by her and all of the force that had been sent to capture him was finally starting to fade. Almost five months had passed since the incident.

The disappointment had been felt throughout the RCMP and the Canadian navy and air forces. They hadn't been prepared for McAllen to spread a virus and shut down the Canadian Forces radar, they hadn't been prepared for McAllen's polywater, and, well, when they faced it, they simply hadn't been prepared.

The blame was laid on the RCMP brass, naval generals, and Air Force commanders. Everyone forgot to mention the politicians who had wanted McAllen captured so badly that they neglected to allow the joint task force to prepare properly. The politicians created the sound bites on the news channels—they knew whom to blame.

The polywater was no longer a major threat to the world. Chemical engineers had found a concoction of what they called biocides, which were essentially biological detergents that destroyed the polywater and dissolved it. McAllen was no longer a threat to the world—but he was still at large—somewhere on the planet.

Bernadette could see her house come into view as she rounded the corner of the street. She had been able to purchase a comfortable half of a duplex with three bedrooms, two bathrooms, a garage, a backyard, and a deck. The backyard was for the dog. One day she might even learn to BBQ on the deck.

She thought about her relationship with Constable Chris. They had been spending considerable time together: a weekend in a houseboat just south of Vancouver had been followed by another weekend at a bed and breakfast on Vancouver Island and then a full-blown Easter week in Seattle. Things were heating up. They had mutual fondness for food and making love. Conversation was great, and the man could cook—an art that still escaped Bernadette. But she was scared as hell—commitment to one man was daunting.

Chris wanted to take things to the next level, with a visit to Toronto so Bernadette could meet his mother and sister, the very people Bernadette had found scary on Facebook. She was hesitant. Bernadette knew that Greeks called all non-Greeks *Xenos,* the word for "stranger."

She was part Dene, part Irish Catholic and wondered what the Greek word for that would be.

At the last block, she picked up her pace and started sprinting, her legs firing like pistons; the dog easily matched her speed. Her chest was almost exploding as she slowed down by her street-side mailbox to pick up her mail. There were the usual bills, flyers for pizza and carpet cleaning, and one white five-by-seven envelope. The stamp was from Mexico—no return address—and the letter was addressed to Detective Bernadette Mary Callahan. Very few people knew her middle name.

Bernadette walked into her house, gave her dog some water that he sloppily inhaled, and poured herself some water from the fridge. She opened the envelope. It was a picture made into a postcard with cute graphics and a border.

There was no mistaking the photo. Alistair McAllen, Sebastian Germaine, Percy Stronach, Theo Martin, and Grace Fairchild all looked happy. And there was another woman beside Grace—*who is she?* They were on a beach, tanned, happy, with their hands on drinks that sprouted those silly little umbrellas. Underneath was printed, "Wish you were here."

She turned the postcard around and read the handwritten note: *Detective Callahan, I understand you were in one of the boats we passed on our way off the island. Sorry we didn't get a chance to meet. Maybe next time.*

Alistair McAllen, PHD.

Bernadette took the photo and a magnet from her fridge and slammed the photo onto the refrigerator door. "You son of a bitch— you've just made it personal!"

ACKNOWLEDGMENTS

I WANT TO THANK MY faithful readers who have been with me on my journey on this, my first novel. This has been an amazing experience for me, and one that I've always wanted to have.

It was a real pleasure to have a group of readers give feedback along the way. I read all of your comments and was enlightened by some, chastened by others. You made me keep the story real—which was as real as my fantasy can abide.

Sometimes what kept me going was knowing that five readers were waiting to see what concoction I would come up with or wondering if I had lost my nerve and gone off to watch daytime television instead of writing.

So to my Tessa, who every Friday evening would read, and correct, and discuss—thank you. To Ada Loving, your enthusiasm and the love of my character Bernadette Callahan was always refreshing—you made me fall in love with her character as well. To Rhody Launders, I thank you for the time on the phone and for giving me insights about the Arctic I missed. To David Krygier, the time spent over coffee as you dissected my work was invaluable. And to John Robb, you were the teacher onboard. You provided insights in pace, character development, and story, which was like having an exam almost every two weeks.

Further acknowledgements include Steve Redmond, Bob Torstensen, Joe Nahman, Jacqueline Bourque, Geoff Bourque, Jane Nudo, Ian Nicholson, Murray Semchuck, Bill Loving, and Scott Morrison.

All of these people gave of their knowledge in their areas of expertise to help this book ride the edges of fact and fiction that a writer must tread in order to keep the reader from losing faith.

ABOUT THE AUTHOR

LYLE NICHOLSON

L YLE NICHOLSON WAS BORN IN British Columbia, Canada in 1952. He is the youngest of three sons born to a father who was a cook, and a mother who was a waitress.

His father, who died when Lyle was 15, was a storyteller and an avid reader, something that Lyle adopted at an early age and never forgot. His life would lead him to travels in Europe, then five years in a Monastery. He found out he was not a good Monk, as poverty was easy—it was the chastity and obedience that was a bit of a stumbling block.

He left the Monastery in 1979, and met and married his wife in 1982. There were several years where Lyle tried numerous businesses that either failed or he was fired. He hadn't found his calling.

Lyle spent two years working in the Security industry, providing Services and Systems for large oil companies in Calgary, Alberta, the nerve center for Canada's oil. And then in 1988 he started his own company to sell safety work wear to oil companies in Canada and Alaska.

His company was a success, and he retired in 2011, and began a career in writing. Writing was always one of his passions. He now lives in Kelowna, British Columbia with his wife of thirty plus years, where he indulges in his second career of writing, fine cooking and fine wines.

PIPELINE KILLERS
BY LYLE NICHOLSON

Book Two of the
DETECTIVE BERNADETTE CALLAHAN MYSTERY SERIES

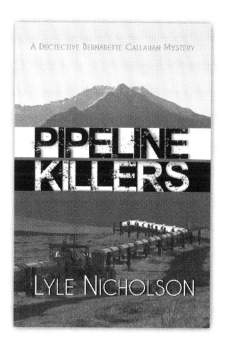

PIPELINE KILLERS (2014) - Detective Bernadette Callahan of the RCMP Serious Crimes Division is called to investigate the scene of a mysterious industrial accident. A man has died near a pipeline on the outskirts of a small city in Canada. The death will lead to what at first looks like an experiment by university students that went too far.

What the students thought was a prank, has become real. And their invention has the potential to wreak havoc on the world's pipelines. When terrorists steal the experiment to use as a weapon, Detective Callahan must find a way to stop it or find the only man who can.

Chapter One

ETECTIVE BERNADETTE CALLAHAN WAS SPEEDING. The single-lane asphalt highway shimmered in the August heat. Cresting a small hill, she felt the Jeep Cherokee's chassis rise. She let off the gas a little. Jeeps were built for rough terrain, not high speeds. She reminded herself of that, and slowed down to 120 kilometers per hour.

The investigation she was speeding toward had not yet been classified as either an accidental death or a homicide. The chief of detectives from the Royal Canadian Mounted Police Serious Crimes Division wanted her take on it. There was, "something strange about the body," according to Jerry Durham, RCMP Chief of Detectives. He needed her eyes on the scene.

A body had been found under a pipeline that crossed a stream just outside of Red Deer, Alberta. Bernadette did not think of what caused the death. She never thought of victims until she saw them. Usually the way a victim laid or looked would give a clue as to what happened moments or days before. They always told a story. Either Bernadette would figure it out or the Crime Scene Investigator would. The CSI would painstakingly plod around the scene in hot polyester coveralls, detailing mountains of evidence. Bernadette was glad she was a RCMP Detective and not a CSI. She hated polyester.

Bernadette was mid-thirties, 5-foot-8, with a mildly athletic build that showed constant efforts in the gym mostly nullified by a diet of junk food with a focus on donuts and double cream, double sugar coffee. She had short-cropped brunette hair with highlights of red showing that were not Miss Clairol, but real Irish roots blended with Dene First Nations. Her green eyes were set against her slightly beige complexion, where her Irish roots again battled for dominance, showing up in freckles that fought for space on her arms and face.

The asphalt highway turned west toward the Rocky Mountains, the hot, glaring sun causing Bernadette to don her dark aviator glasses. She took another swig of her now cold coffee, grimaced as the tepid sweet fluid drained down her throat, and reminded herself to bring her coffee thermos cup next time. She would forget the reminder.

A large German shepherd named Sprocket was sitting alert in the back seat, checking the clouds, the trees, and the cows as they shot by. He never barked. He knew better. He was obedient enough for that. Sprocket was a dropout from RCMP dog training school. Not attentive enough. No spunk, they said. No killer instinct.

Sprocket was the perfect dog for Bernadette. He was a good running companion, a good listener—for a male—and never judgmental when she consumed pizza and boxed red wine. She often wondered if she could find Sprocket's traits in a man.

A large oil service truck appeared in the distance. Bernadette's Jeep came up behind it, overtook and passed it. The road dipped, and then turned a bend. A black mass appeared ahead. Bernadette began to slow, glancing in her rearview mirror to locate the truck she had just passed. It was gaining on her.

The black mass started to fly. A flock of crows feasting on road kill. A sea of black wings took to the air, cawing their displeasure at being chased from their afternoon meal. One bird did not fly; it hopped and then started to flap. Too slow. The Jeep's grill made first contact. The bird bounced from the grill onto the hood, and did a cartwheel past the window.

Bernadette saw the bird was a hawk. "You son of a bitch, that serves you right for feasting with crows . . . you dumb ass." Bernadette fumed as she resumed speed, not wanting the large oil truck to rear-end her. She was shaken by the incident, and mad at the hawk. "Damn thing is supposed to be a hunter, not a scavenger," she muttered over her shoulder to Sprocket. She was pissed at killing the hawk.

Sprocket did not move from his seat. His tongue flicked out, did a long circuitous route around his nose before hanging out. One of his eyebrows twitched. The large bird hitting the windshield was a shock to him as well, but he dared not bark. Bernadette did not like barking in her Jeep. The dog went back to staring out the window.

The turn Bernadette wanted came up on the right. She braked hard, dropped the Jeep into four-wheel drive and followed a gravel road that turned into a dirt track. There were numerous fresh tracks. The other patrol cars would be there. And oil service trucks. Bernadette had been told this victim was in the middle of an oil spill. Oil spills were bad. In cattle and farming country near a river they were especially bad, and that's what Bernadette had been told this was.

The town of Red Deer, where Bernadette's RCMP Detachment was based, was home for hundreds of Canadian oil companies that sent their rigs and men hundreds of miles in all directions to drill and service oil wells. Red Deer was also rich farming and cattle country. The farmers and ranchers did not always get along with Big Oil, especially when the oilmen were careless.

The dirt track led through a field of tall wheat, their heads full and leaning with the weight of their grain. In a few more weeks, the threshing machines would be mowing these fields. Right now they bathed in the sun.

The road came to a stand of trees that lined a creek. A fleet of oil services trucks parked at different angles circled two RCMP cruisers. The oil trucks flashed yellow lights; the RCMP cruisers flashed red and blue lights. Like the circus dropped just beside the creek, and someone forgot to put out the announcement.

Bernadette parked, stepped out, and opened the back door for Sprocket to go for a run. She gave the dog strict instructions to stay close to the Jeep, and not chase gophers. The dog looked up, cocking one eye and one ear in her direction, and took off into the field. Bernadette shook her head and headed down to the creek bed.

The creek was deep; a winding path led down to the creek bed. Large poplar trees rattled their leaves in the light breeze. With each step downward in the rich dark earth, the temperature lowered from the scorching afternoon heat of the wheat field to the coolness of the creek below. The smell of oil assaulted Bernadette's nostrils and burned the back of her throat. Descending the path, she could see a small army of oil workers laying absorbent booms around the spill and mopping up any oil that escaped. They looked defeated by the large task at hand.

Black oil glistened on the rocks. It oozed down the creek, slowing the water into thick molasses. Low hanging branches dragged their leaves in the thick morass and became black paintbrushes hanging ever lower, sucking the acrid oil into their roots.

The pipeline was elevated on a trestle that carried it from one side of the creek to the other. Bernadette stopped halfway down the path and surveyed where the victim lay. The pipeline on the trestle was cut in two, and one end was bleeding oil through hundreds of porous openings. *Like the whole pipe had developed a bad case of Swiss cheese*, Bernadette thought. She was told the oil in the pipeline had been shut down, but the oil had gushed for hours before being discovered.

Two crime scene investigators wandered around a yellow tarp that lay half submerged in the creek, the legs in blue coveralls rested in the creek and the boots, with toes pointed upwards, glistening with oil. Bernadette ruled out drowning. She gazed up at the height of the pipe to the creek bed. It was perhaps 4 meters. A height usually good enough for broken bones, unless the person did a header—fell headfirst. She looked up and down the stream and continued her walk down the path.

She recognized the two CSIs as she approached. One was a short, round Filipino named Basilio, whom everyone called Bas. The other was a tall, wiry older guy nicknamed Angus for his habit of eating beef at almost every meal. He was from Hungary, not Scotland, and his real name was Antal, but his friends swore he consumed an Angus cow a month, so the nickname stuck.

Bas and Angus turned to Bernadette as she crunched on the streambed toward them. Angus raised a hand that held a clear bag of evidence he'd been collecting, "Hi, Detective, glad you could make it."

Bernadette walked up to Angus before responding. She didn't want the oil workers listening in on their conversation. "What's so important about this vic that I needed to drop out on this fine day? This kind of has industrial accident pasted all over it, if you know what I mean."

Angus smiled. His somewhat crooked teeth looked like weapons he used to consume his daily beef quota. "I called your chief because this vic looked way strange, as we say in the technical sense, and I wanted you to see it." He flashed another smile at his CSI humor, and motioned for Bernadette to view the body.

Bernadette crouched over, and Angus pulled back the tarp to reveal the victim. A skinny, sandy-haired kid, no more than mid-twenties, lay underneath. He wore blue coveralls, with an oil logo emblazoned on one side of the chest, and the name "Nathan Taylor" on the other.

"So, what do you figure for cause of death and time?" Bernadette asked, as she looked the body over.

"Well, that is the question. There are no outward signs of trauma or injury, other than a small gash on the right arm." Angus held up the victim's skinny arm to point out a small rip to the coveralls. "You see here, a 4-centimeter tear in the fabric, and a 3-centimeter tear in the epidermis. The depth of the cut to the arm is maybe .158 centimeters."

"So, we're talking about a cut maybe a one-sixteenth of an inch deep, that doesn't sound life threatening. What time did our victim die?" Bernadette asked. Bernadette still hated metric, and converted everything to the old school measurements when she could.

"Interesting question, and I could normally nail that for you with body temperature. Only the victim has been lying partially in the creek, and the cold water skews my estimate," Angus admitted while gazing at the slow-running creek. "Now, my other method would be liver temperature, and I got a problem with that . . ."

"So, what's the problem?"

"From what I can see of this body, we are light on some organs."

"Light on organs? What are you saying? How can this body be missing organs? I thought you said there was no external trauma other than the small cut on the arm." Bernadette knelt down to look more closely at the body.

"There isn't. Not another mark on him." Angus opened the victim's coveralls, and Bernadette saw that his abdomen was shrunken, exposing the telltale contours of the spine. "But see, this is where we should have the stomach, liver, kidneys, and I feel nothing. Gone . . . vacant . . . nada . . . as in not here."

"Is this kid an alien, or some kind of freak?" Bernadette pulled the tarp further back to examine the body more closely. The kid looked normal, very skinny but normal.

"No, I don't believe we have an alien, but we do have a strange victim," Angus said, and covered the body back up. The oil workers were edging closer. He didn't want them seeing the remains.

"Any idea how long this body was here or who discovered it?" Bernadette asked as she looked around the scene. The oil workers went back to mopping up the oil in the creek. They made like they weren't trying to eavesdrop on Bernadette's comments.

"The farmer up there on the ridge said he found the body this morning around 10 a.m., and the kid's boss standing next to the farmer said he sent him to this location at 8 a.m., so we have maybe a two-hour corpse tops. Bodies don't lose their organs that fast. Organs may shrivel inside a cadaver over time, but this feels like they're missing. I have a rush put on this with the coroner's office, but I wanted you to see this before we sent the vic there." Angus stood up and stretched, his tall frame blocking the afternoon sun, and throwing a shadow over the yellow tarp.

"What's in the evidence bag?" Bernadette asked, pointing her boot toward the plastic bag containing a small Plexiglas carrying case with several vials.

Angus pointed toward the top of the bank, "No idea, maybe the oil guy at the top of the bank knows what it is. We found several of these vials around our body; most of them were broken open."

Bernadette glanced up to the top of the bank. Two RCMP constables were in conversation with oil company personnel, and a very loud farmer. The words of the farmer rolled down to them. He was pissed his creek was defiled with oil. "This shit was never supposed to happen—god damn it— you said you had a shit load of checks and balances—and what I see is a shit load of oil in my water."

The farmer's words echoed into the deep creek. The black oil had silenced the rushing creek water, and only the anger of the farmer was giving voice to the disaster that was in the creek bed.

Bernadette walked up the bank and joined the group. Constable Stewart was on the edge of the crowd. Bernadette stood by his side and quietly asked, "So, what do we have here?"

Constable Stewart looked all of 19, blond, short-cropped hair, blue eyes set off by the still-pink hue on his cheeks. His body was that of a brawny weightlifter; his biceps bulged out of his shirtsleeves. No one dared call him youngster.

Stewart nodded at Bernadette. "Hi Detective." Stewart pulled out his notepad and read his notes quietly to her. "The victim worked for the pipeline company. His boss is the one the farmer is yelling at. What we have ascertained so far is the victim was here to do some routine inspection on the line. How this catastrophic failure in the pipeline began is unknown, nor do we know how the victim met his death." Constable Stewart snapped his notebook shut and placed it back in his breast pocket.

"Sounds like the usual bizarre case." Bernadette walked into the group and tapped the farmer on the shoulder. "Excuse me sir, Detective Bernadette Callahan of the RCMP Serious Crimes Division. Might I have a word with this gentleman for a moment?" She motioned to the oil company exec the farmer was berating.

The farmer took a breath, "Hell, I'm not done chewing out his ass yet."

"I completely understand your anger at the oil spill; however, we also have a death of this person's colleague to consider. I'll bring this gentleman back as soon as I'm done." Bernadette managed a small look of consolation towards the farmer. The man was more concerned about the death of his stream, than the body of the young man. The farmer scowled and backed away reluctantly. There was enough anger in him to fuel at least another hour of shouting at the oilman. Oil was smelling up his stream, destroying his water supply, his precious wheat in jeopardy. No, he wasn't even close to done venting his anger.

Bernadette walked the pipeline man away from the group. He introduced himself as Steve Sawatsky, Quality Health and Safety Manager for Tamarack Pipelines. "Thanks for getting me away from that guy; even a short reprieve is appreciated. How can I help you, Detective?"

"What exactly was this young man sent here to do?"

"He was doing what we call oil coupon inspection. Oil coupons are small pieces of metal that rest inside the pipeline, and are used to judge the thickness of the pipeline wall. We pull them out and check them for wear. The kid was sent here to do that."

"The vials that were found around his body, are they part of the testing?"

Sawatsky lowered his voice, looked around to see who was in earshot, "Look, I have no idea about the vials. He was here on company business to pull a piece of metal out of a hole, make a record and move on to the next one." He moved closer to Bernadette, "If this kid put anything in the pipeline that caused this mess . . ." He stopped in mid-sentence as if the air had leaked out of his voice. "We were just lucky the pipeline came apart in the creek, and whatever caused this didn't go further. I've never seen a pipe become so perforated like it is here." Sawatsky moved further away from the group, "Look, between you and me, the kid wasn't supposed to be on the trestle over the creek. It looks like he opened a valve and then fell. I'm in all kinds of shit on this. The kid shouldn't have been working on his own today, but I was short staffed . . ."

"Did Nathan Taylor know he'd be on his own today?" Bernadette asked.

"Yeah, sure he did, I told him two days ago I'd be sending him out for testing, and he'd be going solo. He seemed all happy about it. So was the rest of my crew."

Bernadette scribbled in the notebook in her illegible handwriting. She called her scratches on paper handwriting; her detachment chief called them hieroglyphics. Bernadette looked up, "You think this young man was responsible for the pipeline breach?"

Sawatsky hitched up his pants, pursed out his lips and looked up at the sky for a second. "Look, this kid was a smartass university summer student, always mouthing off about how oil was causing all these problems. A real shit disturber with the crew, and a slack-ass son of a bitch who couldn't pull his weight. We put him on monitoring detail to keep him away from the crew, so as he wouldn't get his ass kicked. There was no one within miles of him."

"You can account for every one of your crew?"

"Absolutely, we were running pigs an hour's drive from here, and all my crew was signed in and with me for the whole day. We started at 0730 hours this morning, and like I said, I sent the Taylor kid off by himself to do some testing over this creek. He left on his own in a company truck. I got here when called out by our emergency response spill people at 1000 hours."

"What are pigs?"

"A sensor we use to check the pipes for weakness. We don't have to shut the oil flow down to use them. We've been running these checks all week.

"No one followed him?"

"No, I can swear to that. I had 5 guys on my crew, and they were all there, and I was on my cell phone for most of the morning with my office, so check the GPS on my phone if you want to check my whereabouts." Sawatsky threw out the last statement like a dare.

Bernadette just scribbled, *boys working with pigs,* and looked up, "You have the contact information for the next of kin for the deceased and his last known address in town?"

"I gave it to your young constable there. There was supposedly some girl he was rooming with in town, kept bragging about how tired he was from screwing her all night," Sawatsky smiled at Bernadette to accentuate the word screwing. "Is that everything? Because after that farmer gets done chewing on my ass, corporate in Calgary is fixing to get on it." Sawatsky stopped and put his head down, "Look I'm sorry if I sound like a hard ass about the kid. He was a pain in the ass, but no one wanted to see this tragedy. Deaths and injury are part of our business, but we don't wish it on anyone."

Bernadette smiled at Sawatsky and watched as he walked back over to the farmer, who immediately resumed yelling at him. She shook her head in mild sympathy and found Constable Stewart, "How about if we take a ride into town and visit the address of our deceased?"

"Sure Detective, not much more going on here. The other constable can wrap it up as soon as the body is sent to the morgue," Stewart said as he walked toward the parked vehicles with Bernadette.

They came out of the shade of the trees and back into the heat of the sun. Bernadette put her sunglasses back on. "Did you get what university this kid was from?"

Constable Stewart turned back as he was about to get into his cruiser, "Yeah, they said the University of Victoria, supposedly a chemistry major."

"Shit." Bernadette stopped in her tracks.

"You look like you've seen a ghost. What's up?"

Bernadette composed herself and laughed. "You know it's probably just a coincidence, but the reason I'm in Red Deer is because of someone from the University of Victoria."

"Long story?"

"Hell yeah, really long story, probably a three beers and nachos story. It can wait." Bernadette smiled. She looked round, whistled for Sprocket, and moments later he came loping out of the high wheat covered in burrs. Bernadette cursed mildly, grabbed the pair of gloves she carried for this exact purpose and picked the burrs out. She poured a flask of water into a bowl, and watched Sprocket lap at the water with his large tongue, there seemed to be no apology for his misbehavior, there never was.

Constable Stewart pulled ahead, leaving a cloud of dust in the hot summer air. Bernadette followed in her Jeep. They reached the highway asphalt and sped off into town. Rounding a corner, Bernadette saw crows feasting on the dead hawk. She muttered to herself, "See what happens when you hang with the wrong crowd?"

CHAPTER TWO

NATHAN TAYLOR'S APARTMENT WAS JUST off of downtown in an older section of town, dominated by mostly apartment buildings. The Red Deer River, now running slow in the summer heat, meandered just a few blocks away from the four-plex that was the apartment.

The buildings had seen better days, and probably better landlords than the one that owned it now. The outside was peeling yellow paint, with two brown wooden balconies hanging on for dear life. One enterprising tenant had placed a piece of two by four against the sagging balcony to keep it from dropping off the side of the building. A lone kitchen chair bleached by the sun and cigarette butts sprouting from a coffee can were evidence that someone lived there.

Constable Stewart pulled up ahead of Bernadette, popped his trunk and put on his armored vest that made his massive weightlifter chest even more defined. Bernadette averted her eyes. The constable was way too young for her. But those pecks of his were eye candy, and she couldn't help but take a peek.

Constable Stewart looked up at Bernadette as he closed the trunk, "Not wearing your vest, Detective?"

Bernadette laughed, "Hell no, I intend on standing behind you—you know I always got your back."

Stewart shook his head in mock disapproval, "I think the apartment's the one on the right side." He led the way as they walked across the broken cement walkway that stretched over the parched brown lawn. A dog barked from the lower unit, a face appeared at a window next door and quickly disappeared. "*No one really likes to see the RCMP,*" Bernadette thought.

Constable Stewart pounded on the metal door of Unit 4, disregarding the doorbell that hung from a single wire, dangling in disrepair, but daring someone to use it anyway. His heavy fist made a thumping sound that echoed into the quiet neighborhood. The dog next door stopped barking.

Bernadette rested against the back of the peeling porch rail, hoping it would hold. "What do you think? We go get a search warrant and come back?"

Stewart held up his hand, "Wait, I think I hear some movement inside."

A shuffling sound was followed by a door lock being turned. The door came open a crack, and a sleepy female voice said, "What do you want?"

"RCMP, we need to speak to you about Nathan Taylor, please open up," Constable Stewart said to the door. He placed one hand on the doorknob.

The door opened fully to reveal a disheveled young blonde clad in tight-fitting t-shirt and panties. She was cheerleader pretty, full bosom, wide hips, and portioned like a beer ad for Coors or Miller Lite. The only blemishes were metal rings on her nose and above her eyes. The young lady shielded her eyes from the bright sun, "What'd you want with Nathan? He's still at work."

Bernadette stepped from behind the large frame of Constable Stewart, "Sorry to inform you Miss, but Nathan Taylor was found deceased out on a pipeline this morning."

The young lady stood back from the door, dropped her hands to her side. "Oh . . . that kinda sucks."

"Were you and Nathan Taylor not close then, Miss . . . ?" Bernadette asked. The answer to this was obvious but she thought she'd ask the question.

"The name's Chandra Rice . . . no, god no, we were just roomies . . . my girlfriend moved back to Toronto, and I needed help with the rent. Nathan Taylor answered the ad, he looked harmless, and so he took the other room. I work nights at Cowboys' Bar and Grill. I hardly saw him."

Bernadette took out her notebook. "Oh? I have a note here from his boss where he says you two were quite an item." She looked back from her notes, staring down the young blue eyes with her own steely green.

"Yeah, he wished," The young girl flipped her hair; the other hand massaged her tummy.

"So, there was nothing between you?"

Chandra pursed her lips, looked down at the floor while examining a pink toenail, "You know you . . . could say there was something. The little guy was some kind of a perv; he liked to watch me when I had guys over. I'd be doing it with my boyfriend, and the little jerk would be at the bedroom door with a camera."

"You knew this?" Bernadette asked. She noticed Constable Stewart's eyes widen.

Chandra bowed her head. Her long hair covered her eyes. "Yeah, I knew it got him off, and I figured what the hell . . ."

"Sounds like it got you off as well," Bernadette countered.

Chandra flipped up her hair; a knowing smile edged her lips. She forced it back. She shrugged her shoulders. "You can come in if you want . . . I've got nothing to hide."

"Obviously. How about if you put a shirt on Chandra. I need my constable's full attention," Bernadette nodded towards Constable Stewart as they walked into the dark apartment.

Chandra flashed her eyes and smiled at Stewart, and whirled to walk back to her bedroom. Stewart's eyes stayed glued to her ass as she walked out of view.

"Easy, Constable, they say you can go blind from watching that." Bernadette smiled in Stewart's direction.

"Yeah, but if I had that seared into my retinas, it might not be so bad," Stewart laughed.

Chandra returned wearing a shirt, her long legs still catching the constable's eye, and flicked the lights on to the main living room and kitchen. The place was a disaster of empty pizza boxes, beer cans, and fast food cartons. The smell that rose up as they closed the door was stale pizza and beer. Bernadette thought she smelled young hormones as well, but thought better than to comment on it.

"Nathan's room is down this hallway," Chandra motioned to them. "Look, I have to shower and get ready for my shift, so look around, ask me whatever, but I gotta be outta here in an hour . . . okay?"

"Sure," Bernadette said as she followed Constable Stewart down the hallway.

Nathan Taylor's room had the same design as the rest of apartment. Empty pizza boxes and beer cans, half-consumed cans of beans with a spoon stuck at half-mast, with clothes scattered about the room. A laptop computer sat in the center of the room on a small desk with a chair that looked like it had been rescued from a garbage bin. A Sony video camera was plugged in beside it, and one Post-it Note stuck to the side of the laptop. The Post-it Note said, "Today is the Day."

Bernadette turned to Constable Stewart, "How are your computer skills?"

Constable Stewart stood over the laptop, his large fingers hovering over the keyboard. "You know we can't access this unless we have a warrant or permission from his next of kin."

"Uh-huh, sure I know that, I'm up on my law. Did you by any chance reach the deceased's next of kin?"

Stewart shrugged, "Ah, no, I placed a call to the number I got from the pipeline company, but I got no answer . . . I left a message."

Bernadette squared her shoulders, as if about to make a speech, and turned to face Constable Stewart. "Constable, I believe that on this computer we will find evidence that will lead us to who killed one Nathan Taylor, therefore no warrant or permission is required."

Stewart lowered his large frame onto the desk chair, as he powered up the laptop, "Okay, that's a bit on the fringes of the law, but that works for me, Detective."

The laptop was still powered up, with no password protection required. Stewart got onto the videos and documents site, and the first thing that came on was Chandra. Chandra in low lighting straddling atop a male with his hands on her thighs . . . the volume was on high, and the loud sounds of Chandra's enjoyment were obvious. And then . . . Chandra turned her head toward the camera and winked.

Constable Stewart's head lurched back. "Damn, these two had one hell of a kinky relationship."

A voice behind them said, "Am I in trouble?"

Bernadette turned to see Chandra standing at the door, "No, videotaping sexual acts between consenting adults is not a crime . . . It would seem from your actions . . . the wink you gave to Nathan that you were aware of the taping. Whether this makes you as perverted as Nathan, well I leave that up to you."

Chandra looked away and left the doorway. Bernadette looked back at the computer. "Constable, can we look over another file, as I am quite sure our victim did not die of this . . . though he may have turned himself partially to stone . . ."

Stewart's face turned visibly red, "Sure, sure . . . I'll access some of his recent places on the Internet."

They viewed a few more sites, and then came to the PLK website. The site was populated with a graphic from Star Trek, and various planets bounced around. Then four young men came into view. "This looks like a video conference our victim saved," Bernadette said.

A tall blonde kid sitting at a table spoke first. "Nathan Taylor, your mission, should you accept it, is to strike a blow for all Humanity. To avenge the wrongs done to our former leader, Professor Alistair McAllen, and show the world that we . . . these gentle nerds here, and I . . . have more power than anyone in the world. By tomorrow, they will no longer fear Al Qaeda; they will fear us, the Pipeline Killers. I, your commander, Paul Goodman, command you to go forth and do battle. Our fellow warriors, Bill Hirschman, Martin Popowich, and Jason Campbell, will monitor your feats, and will go forth to do battle once your attack is successful. Live long and prosper."

The video ended with a Star Trek Voyager space vehicle streaking across the sky, and music playing in the background. Bernadette stood back from the laptop "Damn it, this is as bad as it gets."

"What's as bad as it gets?" Stewart looked up from the computer, "This looks like a bunch of university kids doing a spoof on Star Trek."

"Yeah, it would be if they hadn't mentioned Professor McAllen . . . look, grab the laptop, and meet me back at detachment headquarters. I need to meet with our chief and make a call to a guy I know at the Canadian Security and Intelligence Agency."

Bernadette headed outside. The strong light of the late afternoon hit her as she walked down the steps and got into her Jeep. Her mind was flashing through all the possibilities of what was about to hit the oil industry this time. The first time McAllen surfaced he almost put Alaskan Oil and Fort McMurray Oil Sands into mothballs. His lab creation called polywater could have suspended production for years if she hadn't figured it out. But what the hell was he up to this time?

CHAPTER THREE

B ERNADETTE WAS ABOUT TO DRIVE directly to the RCMP detachment, until she looked at Sprocket. In order to keep the dog cool, she'd left him in the Jeep with the a/c on and the windows rolled up. Someone had once tried to steal her Jeep with the big dog in it once, and found themselves on the pavement and looking at a set of snarling teeth. But she would never leave the big dog in the Jeep for any longer than she had to.

She was 10 minutes from her home and another 10 minutes back to the detachment. She could spare the time and drop off the dog. Her chief was a fan of dogs, but RCMP trained dogs, not untrained like Sprocket.

Traffic was light, and she drove up to her duplex a few minutes later. The dog bolted from the Jeep toward the house as soon as she opened the door.

"So that's the thanks I get for taking you on a road trip," Bernadette yelled to Sprocket. Sprocket raised one ear in response and scratched at the door.

The door opened in the adjoining duplex, and Harvey Mawer poked his head out, "Hey Bernie, you back already? I heard there was a big oil spill, and a dead body out west of here."

"Damn, news travel fast in this town," Bernadette said as she waved at Harvey.

"Hey, I'm still hooked in to the Oil Patch, you know old wives and oilmen, and we're about the same for good gossip. You got time for a coffee?" Harvey walked toward her door, standing there, waiting for her reply.

Harvey was a great next-door neighbor. Retired for the third time from different careers in what was called the "Oil Patch," which meant the oil business. Harvey was crowding his 70s with bad arthritis that kept him from a fourth run at the oil business. He looked out for Bernadette, watered her lawn and mowed it, shoveled her snow in the winter, and looked after Sprocket when she worked late, which was often.

"Sorry Harvey looks like I'm the one investigating the dead body, and I have to get back to work. You mind watching Sprocket a bit, maybe walk him a little?"

Harvey walked over, scratched Sprocket behind the ears, and let him lick his hand, "You know I never mind. I got some new dog treats he'll like. What time you expect you'll be back?"

Bernadette shrugged and blew out her breath. "Who knows? This latest one's got all kinds of things piled into it. I'm hoping by early evening. You can leave Sprocket inside my place after."

"Oh, heck no, I got the whole series of World War II CDs, and I'm making some firehouse chili. Sprocket and I can watch those till you get back."

Bernadette hugged Harvey, "Thanks Harvey. God, I'm glad you're too old for me, because I'd be hitting on you all the time."

Harvey stood back from Bernadette, "Hey, easy young lady, you'll make my new girl friend jealous."

Bernadette let Sprocket into the house, got him some water, and then headed back to the Jeep. She really would love to hang out with Harvey and Sprocket on the back porch, it was Friday night, but there was something there, something in the recent video from the so-called Pipeline Killers she needed to deal with. All of it made her feel unsettled, queasy inside, like right after she'd eaten a large Monte Cristo sandwich.

The RCMP Detachment was the usual beehive on Friday night. The late night bars in Red Deer would be busy as young people with too much money from the oil fields were ready for a good time. Their ability to have fun would be fueled by massive quantities of alcohol and drugs, and from midnight to 2 a.m. the officers would be busy sorting out the mess.

Bernadette found her Chief of Detectives, Jerry Durham, in his office. She liked Jerry. He was a fair guy who worked hard at his job, and hard at his relationship with his family. A straight up guy in his mid-40s with 20 years of marriage and two teenage kids and enough ambition to keep the higher-ups in Ottawa happy. Jerry tried to keep in shape, but the job showed the strain, a small paunch showed on his mid-weight frame, and his hairline was receding far beyond his ability to deal with it. He wasn't about to do the close shave or baldhead, not his style, not yet.

"Hey Detective Callahan, I got this laptop that Constable Stewart dropped off, which I made him fill out an evidence report for." Jerry called out. He added a small frown in Bernadette's direction. "Now I assume that you've cleared the viewing of this computer with the deceased's next of kin?"

"Yeah . . . about that, Chief," Bernadette dropped into the chair in front of him. "I was in pursuit of the possible suspect or suspects who may have been involved in the murder of our victim." She threw a weak smile with the words, and then watched to see if they worked.

The chief dropped his head in his hands. "You know Detective; I wonder why I have any hair left at all with some of your procedures."

"Chief, did you look over the video that Constable Stewart and I viewed today?"

"Yes, I did, and I saw what looks like a Star Trek spoof, just like the constable mentioned. How can this be something that could have put our victim in harm's way?"

"Because they mentioned Professor Alistair McAllen," Bernadette leaned forward placing her hands on the desk.

"Detective, I know you had some past history with this guy, but I doubt if he can cause more mayhem from wherever he's hiding. You think that maybe you're just a little paranoid where he's concerned?" the chief asked as he reached for his ringing phone.

"No, I don't think I'm paranoid at all, I'd like to be ready for him this time . . ." Bernadette's words trailed off as the chief raised his hand and put his ear to the phone.

Bernadette sat there in an uneasy silence. She could hear the chief talking with the coroner. The coroner had a loud Scot's Brogue. He'd been in Canada for 45 years and still sounded like he'd walked out of the Scottish Moors yesterday.

The chief dropped the phone in the cradle, his face looking a slightly whiter color. "The coroner says we've got to get to the morgue right away, there's something he wants to show us."

The morgue was quiet. At 6 p.m., most of the staff was gone. The security guard let them in. Their shoes squeaked on the linoleum tile as they walked down the long hallway. The smell of formaldehyde hung in the air. Someone once told Bernadette they thought it was the cologne of the dead. It was all always there. It would linger in your clothes after you left the place. It enveloped you like a glove when you walked in, assailing your nostrils first, then the back of your tongue, and then the stuff would slip down your throat until you were forced to swallow it. Gagging was optional.

They walked down the long hallway in silence, pushed through a set of double doors that sighed softly as air pressure was released, and found Dr. Keith Andrew. The Doctor was a mass of long grey hair, bushy eyebrows and four days of five o'clock shadow on his face.

Bernadette could never get over not seeing pants under his white smock. Dr. Andrew wore a kilt both summer and winter. If you asked, and if you knew him well, he would take you aside, and confide that it was, "So the boys could breathe." Bernadette realized he meant his balls.

"You made good time," Dr. Andrew yelled to them in his rich brogue. He drew the words out like a poem from Robert Burns. The cadence was there, it sounded the same to Bernadette. Dr. Andrew was an abnormality for a coroner who was actually a Doctor, and his fame for dropping his medical opinions into his reports was legendary in the small city.

"Doctor, what are you in such a hurry to show us?" Chief Durham asked.

"Oh, aye, the most recent body is quite the sight. I don't believe in my many years I've had the opportunity to view something as amazing as this." Dr. Andrew's eyebrows rose as if a conductor was motioning for the orchestra to begin.

Andrew motioned them towards the body, and drew back the sheet, "You'll notice there are no contusions on the body that suggest bruising or blunt force trauma."

Bernadette scanned the naked Nathan Taylor from the top of his head to the bottom of his feet. She had to agree, there was not a mark on the kid. "So what killed him?

Andrew's eyebrows rose in unison, "Ah, now that is the fascinating question. Here we have a corpse that we think is missing organs, but its not."

"The CSI told me he felt no organs in the abdominal cavity," Bernadette said, leaning closer to the body.

"Yes, it would appear that way, but look," Andrew said as he removed a small cover that was covering the intestines in a tray beside the body. "You can see they are here, but flattened and perforated. It looks like something ate into them."

Bernadette's head shot back at the sight. "What does that?"

"Interesting question," Andrew said. "Now, in my travels in South America, I came upon this in the Amazon. Corpses literally eaten alive from the inside, by something the Portuguese called the Candiru or vampire fish, which is a tiny parasitic fish. It had the locals so scared men would tie a string around their penises before they went swimming, they believed it protected them from the fish crawling up their . . . you know what I mean . . . " Dr. Andrew examined the faces of both Bernadette and Chief Durham to see if they were getting his explanation.

Chief Durham touched his crotch, as if warding away the evil of the vampire fish. He looked up, realized where his hand was and quickly moved it, "Really, you think this kid was eaten inside by a vampire fish?"

"Absolutely not, just pulling your leg, telling you bit of lore. No, Canada is far too cold for these fish; the streams freeze in winter. The things would die. Now then . . . I reasoned that something must have entered our victim's blood stream and this is where I found our culprit," Andrew said, his smile widening at his captive audience, and loving the joke he'd played.

Chief Durham relaxed visibly. The vision of a tiny vampire fish swimming up a man's penis was slowly vanishing from his brain, "So, what thing have you found?"

"Things, my good man. Things," Andrew said. "I realized that something attacked this man through his blood stream from the tear in his arm, and I needed to examine his blood. There was very little in him. The human body should have about 5 liters of blood. This body had a tenth of that."

"Now, what little blood he did have I had analyzed, and found something very significant." Andrew paused. Only the sound of the air conditioning could be heard in the room. "Our victim had an extreme case of Hemochromatosis."

"Hemo . . . what? Bernadette asked.

Dr. Andrew's eyes widened. "This essentially is a buildup of iron in the body. I won't bore you with the entire prognosis of this disease, but from my analysis, this victim had quite the advanced stages of the disease, which is exactly why he was attacked."

"Attacked by what?" Bernadette asked with exasperation in her voice. The merry-go-round of vampire fish to an iron disease in the blood was getting tiring. She wanted answers.

"That, I must show you," Dr. Andrew motioned for them to come over to his counter where a microscope was set up. "Look in here and tell me what you see."

Bernadette adjusted the powerful microscope to her eyes. The viewer came into focus and a mass of small moving shapes came into view. They were white in color and looked like little sausages. "What am I looking at?"

"From my tests, we are looking at a microbe that consumes iron. Industry has been working on this technology for years. I recently read a study from a company that wanted to engineer a process called *bioheap leaching* with microbes that would live on sulphur and iron the way we live on protein and carbohydrates," Dr. Andrew said. He swayed side to side as he spoke. His kilt made a gentle swishing sound.

Chief Durham looked into the microscope. "You think this is what killed our victim then?"

"Aye, I do, and from what I heard of your pipeline spill out west of here, I believe this young man, now a victim of his own means, tried to inject these microbes into the Pipeline, and they attacked him as well when he cut his arm. Let me show you my other experiment." Dr. Andrew motioned for them to follow him to another counter. The counter had a glass case with a small pipe inside.

"Now watch this," Dr. Andrew said as he drew a small eyedropper from the microscope glass, and dropped a bit of liquid on the metal pipe. He snapped the case shut, smiled and looked down in anticipation.

At first, there was nothing, just the pipe as Bernadette watched, her eyes staring hard, waiting for a change, something, or anything to prove the

Doctor's hypothesis. Then, there it was, parts of the pipe became lighter. Then holes appeared. "That is exactly what happened to the pipeline west of here." Bernadette turned to Chief Durham. "Now do you believe me when I tell you we need to be worried about the video on the laptop?"

Chief Durham's face changed color. His normal off-beige had morphed into a pasty white. "I think we need to get Canadian Security and Intelligence Service involved in this. This reaches beyond Red Deer."

Bernadette pulled her cell phone out of her pocket. "Chief, I know an agent with CSIS in Edmonton, whom I worked with on something like this before. He'll want to be in on this, and he knows just the people to call." Bernadette had Anton De Luca on speed dial. He picked up on the second ring.

"Hey, Detective Callahan, long time since I've heard from you, what is up in your little city," Anton asked.

Bernadette loved Anton like a younger brother. He was 26, a well-educated, good-looking Italian Canadian. They had worked hard together to try and capture Professor Alistair McAllen a year earlier when he'd invented a threat called polywater that made water too heavy to force oil to the surface in oil fields. His invention had threatened both Alaskan and Canadian oilfields. They stopped the threat of polywater, but never captured McAllen.

"Anton, great to talk to you, and I need to get to the point. We found a microbe that attacks pipelines; we think Professor McAllen is behind it. I'm going back to the detachment and send you a video of some University of Victoria students we think are involved."

"Bernadette . . . you said McAllen?" Anton asked after a pause.

"Yes I did, if what I just saw in this lab is real on a large scale, then someone has developed a microbe that can attack pipelines." Bernadette looked over at Dr. Andrew, who was nodding in agreement.

"Send me the file. I'll talk to you soon," Anton said.

Soon did not come until just before midnight. Bernadette returned to the detachment, sent the file, completed her reports and returned home. She rounded up Sprocket. Harvey's door was open. Both Harvey and the dog were snoring on the couch while the Allies stormed Normandy yet again, but this time in color on Harvey's big screen TV.

Bernadette walked the dog back to her place, and he lay on his dog bed and was back to sleep in seconds. She rummaged for food, found some recognizable leftovers in the fridge and some red wine, and curled up on the sofa for her usual Friday night . . . alone.

The cell phone rang. It was Anton, "Hi, Bernadette, sorry it took so long, but the guys in Ottawa can move slowly."

"How unusual," Bernadette said in her sarcastic tone.

"So, here it is . . . once they understood the threat, all kinds of higher ups and government officials got excited by this case. The defense of oil is one of their main agendas. We've already called CSIS in British Columbia. They contacted City of Victoria Police and three of the young men on the video tape have already been taken into custody."

"My god, that was quick," Bernadette said as she took a gulp of her red wine.

"Well, here's the other part. I need you in on this case. And we need to be in Victoria tomorrow morning for the interrogation."

"You want me in on this?" Bernadette almost inhaled her wine.

"Yes, I'll fly down to Calgary, and we'll catch the 11:25 direct to Victoria. I can brief you on what we have in the morning. Sleep fast, Detective. I'll buy breakfast tomorrow."

Bernadette looked at her watch; it was midnight. She needed to send an email to her chief telling him she was going to Victoria, pack a quick bag for who knew how long, and get up early for the hour and a half hour drive to Calgary to be there by 10:25 a.m. She drained the last bit of wine in her glass, washed it in the sink, and started on her preparation.

PIPELINE KILLERS – available for purchase
Paperback and eBook

Amazon.com

Kobo.com

Barnes and Noble.com

Smashwords.com

Visit Lyle Nicholson at his author site
to read excerpts of his novels.
www.lylenicholson.com